A Tender Soul

M.A. Nichols

Copyright © 2021 by M.A. Nichols

All rights reserved. No part of this publication may be reproduced or transmitted, in any form or by any means, electronic, mechanical, photocopying, recording, or otherwise, without the prior permission of the copyright owner.

The characters and events portrayed in this book are fictitious. Any similarity to real persons, living or dead, is coincidental and not intended by the author.

Books by M.A. Nichols

Generations of Love Series

The Kingsleys

Flame and Ember
Hearts Entwined
A Stolen Kiss

The Ashbrooks

A True Gentleman
The Shameless Flirt
A Twist of Fate
The Honorable Choice

The Finches

The Jack of All Trades
Tempest and Sunshine
The Christmas Wish

The Leighs

An Accidental Courtship
Love in Disguise
His Mystery Lady
A Debt of Honor

Christmas Courtships

A Holiday Engagement
Beneath the Mistletoe

Standalone Romances

Honor and Redemption
A Tender Soul
A Passing Fancy
To Have and to Hold

Fantasy Novels

The Villainy Consultant Series

Geoffrey P. Ward's Guide to Villainy
Geoffrey P. Ward's Guide to Questing
Magic Slippers: A Novella

The Shadow Army Trilogy

Smoke and Shadow
Blood Magic
A Dark Destiny

Table of Contents

Prologue 1
Chapter 1 6
Chapter 2 15
Chapter 3 24
Chapter 4 30
Chapter 5 37
Chapter 6 43
Chapter 7 49
Chapter 8 57
Chapter 9 65
Chapter 10 70
Chapter 11 76
Chapter 12 83
Chapter 13 93
Chapter 14 103
Chapter 15 108
Chapter 16 115
Chapter 17 123

Chapter 18	131
Chapter 19	141
Chapter 20	149
Chapter 21	157
Chapter 22	165
Chapter 23	172
Chapter 24	179
Chapter 25	187
Chapter 26	193
Chapter 27	200
Chapter 28	206
Chapter 29	213
Chapter 30	219
Chapter 31	225
Chapter 32	235
Chapter 33	241
Chapter 34	248
Chapter 35	255
Chapter 36	261
Chapter 37	269
Chapter 38	276
Chapter 39	283
Epilogue	290

Prologue

Summer 1819
Bristow, Essex

Avebury Park boasted some of the finest views in Bristow, and though the library's prospect was not among the best the estate had to offer, it featured a footpath that meandered between the great oak trees and across a swatch of green in a picturesque fashion. Lydia Hayward's gaze wound along that route, wondering what it would be like to set off without a backward glance. It did not lead to London (nor could she manage the journey on foot), but Lydia's imagination conjured images of setting off. Of escaping her present course.

Of finding him.

Tugging open her reticule, Lydia gazed upon the handkerchief resting inside. Shadows obscured much of the embroidery adorning the corner, but she knew the simple flourish that surrounded the initials. She hadn't thought to ask Mr. Owen Marks what his middle name was, and now, she spent far too much time pondering what the D signified. David? Daniel? Dennis?

Lydia supposed it did not matter, but contemplating that mystery was better than focusing on the man himself. What was he doing at that very minute? Perhaps with another student, walking his charge through the quadrille or la Boulangère? Lifting the bag to her nose, she breathed in the scent, though his cologne had long ago disappeared, leaving only the memory of the spices.

"Lydia."

The sound of Mary's voice made her jump before she closed the reticule and turned to greet her sister. But as she opened her mouth, Lydia froze at the sight of her. Mary's looks had never been deemed beautiful, though Lydia had always thought that due to the shortsightedness of men; her figure was more lanky than lithe, and her features bore far too much of a resemblance to their papa, but there was a grace and poise to Mary's bearing. Done up as she was for her wedding, Lydia thought the lady was fetching and certainly worth catching the eye of her husband-to-be.

Mary moved slowly across the library, careful not to disturb the babe asleep on her shoulder, and Lydia closed the distance to take Mary's hand in hers. With bright eyes, Lydia turned her gaze to the child.

"Is that her?"

Leaning her head close to the babe, Mary pressed a kiss to the dark curls. "Isn't she beautiful?"

Lydia touched a gentle hand to Dottie's back, though the child didn't stir. She could hardly believe today her sister would become a wife and mother; the young lady everyone believed would end her days as a spinster had found happiness, and Lydia's heart warmed like coals in a kitchen fire at the thought that Mary had found the love she deserved.

"You fixed your hair," said Lydia.

Mary gave a wry smile and brushed a hand across the shorn locks. "Unfortunately, there was no option but to take the lot of them."

"It looks lovely," she said with all the earnestness she felt. Though Lydia had never cared for short coiffures, it suited Mary. The lady's dark hair had gained some waves, which curled at the nape of her neck and softened her strong features. "I am so glad that my ineptitude did not ruin it completely."

Mary's gray eyes sparkled with a smile. "It was not the coiffure I'd anticipated, but I suppose that is to be expected when I allow someone who has never trimmed hair to make their first attempt on mine."

Her eyes drifted from her sister, and Mary glanced about the empty room with a furrowed brow.

"Did Mama and Papa come?" Mary's words stretched off into silence, and Lydia could not meet her sister's gaze.

"I am alone," she murmured. "I don't know if they shall ever forgive you for marrying against their wishes."

Lydia's ribs squeezed her heart as her sister's gaze dimmed. Mary brought her free hand up and rested it on the babe's back as she closed her eyes and gave Dottie another kiss. When she met Lydia's eyes once more, Mary motioned for her sister to follow her out of the library.

"Please, you must join us. It is nearly time to go to the church—"

Lydia stepped away, shaking her head. "Mama and Papa would be so very angry if they knew I had come, and they will miss me if I stay too long, but I had to sneak away to offer my apologies for how I spoke to you. It wasn't fair of me, and I am so very pleased you've found someone who loves you like your Mr. Ashbrook."

Shuddering at the memory, Lydia wished she could retract those hurtful words she'd uttered during their last conversation. Love may not have a place in her future, but there was nothing wrong with Mary grasping for it, even if it made Mama and Papa so very angry. Those terrible condemnations she'd spoken a sennight ago had been born of jealousy—the attack of a young lady wishing to destroy the happiness of others simply because her situation was so bleak. But that was not fair, and Lydia refused to allow those petty feelings to taint her.

"You needn't return to them, Lydia." Mary's voice dropped low as though afraid that their parents might overhear. "Ambrose would welcome you into our home." Mary paused and clarified, "We haven't a home at present, but that is only a detail. You have a place with us. You needn't marry that wretched Sir Duncan simply because Mama and Papa wish it."

Lydia stilled, her very heartbeat pausing as her sister voiced aloud the thought that had tantalized her since meeting Mr. Marks. Her stomach gave an unhappy turn (though she'd not been able to eat that morning), and her mind returned again to all those daydreams of what her life could be like if she chose him over Sir Duncan.

A life of unending bliss with her devoted husband. Joy compounded as their family grew. Children with their father's handsome smile and warm brown eyes. True, no life was perfect, but with Mr. Marks as her husband, none of it would matter. The cares of the world would mean nothing if her days were filled with his laughter. But the tightening of her throat reminded her of all the many reasons that was not possible, and Lydia gave Mary a bright smile and laughed, "Newly married people do not need nor want their family invading their home."

Her sister's expression tightened, her brows scrunching together. "I do not need nor want to see you married to satisfy our parents' ambitions."

Lydia's lips trembled, her grin growing brittle. "I will be the wife of a baronet. What lady wouldn't desire such an illustrious marriage?"

Mary's arm darted forward, taking her sister by the hand. "Do not pretend you care for such things, Lydia. Mama and Papa are forcing you into this unhappy alliance, but it will do no good. Whatever you give them, they will never be content. They will simply take more."

Lydia tried to swallow, but her throat closed tight, and she dropped her eyes to the floor. "I cannot go against them, Mary. I am not in my majority yet, and they have every legal and moral right to dictate what I must do."

"That is not true!" Mary blurted, but Dottie stirred, and her new mama paused, running a hand down the babe's back and crooning. When Dottie was settled once more, Mary spoke quietly. "They may have legal control of you, but even the law cannot force you to marry. And if you wish to stay with us, we will sort out the legalities of it. It may take time, but it would be well worth the fight if it meant you were free of their control. I have freed myself of their influence, and I will do everything I can to aid you in doing the same—"

"Mary, no!"

Dottie squawked at the sharp tone, and Lydia stepped away, shaking her head.

"I know you mean well, Mary, but I cannot do it. I owe them too much. They have done everything for me, and I cannot repay their generosity by betraying them in such a manner."

Lydia moved forward, taking her sister and Dottie in a quick embrace, and stepped away.

"I only came to give my apologies and to wish you every happiness with your Mr. Ashbrook," she said, hurrying towards the library door. "But I cannot stay another moment."

"Lydia, please!"

But the young lady fled down the corridor before she allowed those tempting words to sway her. Lydia clutched her reticule to her chest. She ought to burn the wretched handkerchief, for it only served to remind her of that which she had lost, but Lydia clung to that reminder of what she had given up and why. Sir Duncan was not who she wanted, but it would secure her parents' financial future and make them happy. Duty was not such a horrid thing. And soon, she would have a Dottie of her own to coo over and cuddle.

Surely that was enough.

Chapter 1

*Summer 1826
Hexford, Kent*

A widow ought to mourn her husband. At the very least, a woman ought to feel something poignant when the man to whom she was bound was no longer among the living. Yet Lady Lydia Whiting felt little except the odd flutter of relief. At some other time, she might've felt the twist of a guilty conscience at that terribly inappropriate sentiment, but little penetrated the numb haze wrapped around her heart. At least she wasn't gleeful. That was a blessing.

Mama clutched Lydia's hand, patting it and dabbing at her eyes with a handkerchief that was both well-used and bone dry; the lady muttered at intervals about the great sorrow to be found in a life cut short while Papa played the part of the stoic soldier holding firm to his dignity though faced by Sir Duncan's loss.

The Dowager Lady Whiting's commanding composure hid her emotions behind a stony facade, but no amount of decorum erased the redness in her eyes. The older lady sat with the regality of a queen bestowing the blessing of her presence on the unwashed masses, but having been acquainted with the Dowager for over seven years, Lydia knew how great a blow it was for her to have lost her dear son.

Lydia turned her gaze to the others scattered about the drawing room. The footmen had set up a row of chairs, arcing around where the solicitor stood; Mr. Pendergrass had insisted they bring in a particularly fine console table from the library to serve as his lectern. It was bad enough that all those who stood to benefit from Sir Duncan's estate were forced into this dramatic affair, but Mr. Pendergrass stood center stage to deliver with zeal every word of his former employer's last testament.

"Haven't they the decency to mourn dear Sir Duncan properly?" whispered Mama, and Lydia's eyes traveled to the pair who had earned the lady's ire. Ever since her arrival, Mama had taken every opportunity to chastise and berate the new baronet and his wife—though never within their hearing.

In truth, Lydia thought the new baronet was showing Sir Duncan as much deference as his late cousin deserved. Sir Jude may not be grim-faced, but he wasn't shouting for joy over the title that had landed in his lap.

"I overheard the pair of them scheming over all the changes they intend to make in *your* home." Mama squeezed Lydia's hands and added in hushed tones, "Your husband is hardly dead, and yet they are desperate to see you tossed out into the cold. The vultures."

Lydia blinked and wondered why she did not feel the same righteous indignation. Surely a widow ought to feel anger or resentment at the prospect of losing her home of seven years. But rather than anything natural, Lydia couldn't help but think of the hypocrisy rife in Mama's condemnation of people eager to benefit from Sir Duncan's untimely demise. Lydia's parents had been positively giddy when they'd arrived from Essex not two days ago. After all, the wife of a baronet's pin money was nowhere near as vast as the widow's jointure. While they'd only shared hints of their plans for Lydia's new wealth, it was clear Mama and Papa had done at least as much scheming as the new baronet and his wife.

Mr. Pendergrass read through his former employer's will with the dramatics of a stage actor, giving Sir Duncan one final moment to shine in this world before he was utterly forgotten. The solicitor listed off the various gifts and stipulations, which bestowed a morsel of beneficence to those Sir Duncan had deemed far below him when he had walked this planet.

"'To my dear friend Evangeline Sinclair, who has been a blessing and a solace to me for these many years,'" said Mr. Pendergrass, with all the deference due to someone of such distinction as to be deemed a "dear" friend to the great Sir Duncan, "'I give and bequeath Westwood Cottage along with the sum of five thousand pounds to maintain it; as it has been your home for these many years, there is no other who deserves ownership of it.'"

Though Mama's grip tightened, Lydia felt no twinge of jealousy or resentment for Mrs. Sinclair's good fortune. It was only proper that the woman who had given her a respite from Sir Duncan's attention receive proper compensation for it. Lydia had never stepped foot in Westwood Cottage, but she would forever adore that little house on the edge of town in which Sir Duncan had spent so much of his time. Mrs. Sinclair had earned her present good fortune.

The lady in question let out a stifled sob, burying her face in her handkerchief as Sir Duncan's mother gave a disapproving sniff over the outburst.

"'To my cousin and heir, I begrudgingly bestow my titles and lands,'" said Mr. Pendergrass with a haughty upturn of his nose, and Lydia felt a begrudging respect for the fellow's loyalty to his former employer; it seemed imprudent to antagonize the current baronet, yet Mr. Pendergrass was steadfast to the bitter end.

Sir Jude chuffed far louder than was seemly for such a dour event but seemingly with as much deference as the fellow felt for Sir Duncan's words. Mr. Pendergrass and the Dowager Lady Whiting shot narrowed looks at the fellow, but he met those with thinly veiled dismissal.

"He speaks as though he had a choice in the matter; the lands are entailed, and the title is hereditary," grumbled Sir Jude, just loudly enough for everyone to hear it.

Mr. Pendergrass straightened, glaring down his nose at the new baronet, and repeated the line, giving the words all the haughty disdain that Sir Duncan would've employed had he been around to speak them.

Mama and Papa straightened as the solicitor continued, moving on to the part that they'd awaited since Lydia had spoken her wedding vows.

"'To my wife, whose dereliction of her duty left me without a child worthy of the Whiting name, I give the sum of one-hundred and fifty pounds. It should cover travel costs to return you and your horrid parents to Essex when this business is concluded. The day I married you, I thought myself blessed to have found such a lovely young lady. My greatest regret is that I cannot go back to that foolish man and stop him from making such a grave mistake. Had I known your womb was poisoned, I would never have married you and made myself so wretchedly unhappy.'"

The hands of the clock stopped, and Lydia stared at Mr. Pendergrass, trapped in his disdainful gaze as the words hung in the air like glowing sparks of dust caught in a ray of light. They twisted and swirled about her for several long moments as time held her prisoner. Lydia had thought herself beyond feeling, but pain surged through her as her heart crumpled in on itself, leaving behind a gaping void in her chest.

There was nothing left for her to feel for she had nothing left inside her.

Time skipped forward, with everyone moving and speaking at once, the actions and sounds coming in rapid succession, blasting Lydia with a tempest of noise. Papa was on his feet, shouting at Mr. Pendergrass, while Mama wept in earnest. Others joined the fray, adding to the ruckus with their accusations or defenses. Their words swirled around Lydia, filling her ears yet having no impact on her mind as she remained in her seat with only the blinking of her eyelids signaling that she yet lived. The voices rose, blending into an angry cacophony.

Lydia stood, and no one gave her any notice as she skirted the battleground, slipping out of the drawing room. Her ears rang in the silent corridor, her slippered feet moving quickly as she wound her way through Elmhurst Court to the only place in this whole cold building in which she might feel anything.

Down the halls and up the stairs, Lydia knew that pathway well. As she pushed open the door, her eyes swept the nursery, not resting until she saw Isabella lying in the corner. The child's eyes were bright with tears, her lips trembling as she met her mother's gaze; with a watery cry, Isabella reached for her, and Lydia scooped her up, drawing her daughter close.

Letting out a shaky breath, Isabella rested her head against her mother's shoulder as Lydia slid to the ground, rocking the child and rubbing a hand along her back.

"You're not supposed to be here," said Nurse Jones from her chair by the fire.

"Mama," whimpered Isabella as she shifted in Lydia's hold. The braces on her legs poked her mother's side, and Lydia turned her daughter, cradling the child across her lap. Isabella kicked her feet, her hands reaching for the bits of leather and metal binding her legs as tears began anew. Lydia tugged at the nearest strap.

"Don't take that off," barked Nurse Jones. "The physician says she must stay in them at all times."

"But they are hurting her," murmured Lydia.

The nursemaid narrowed her eyes. "Sir Duncan and Lady Whiting ordered me to make certain the child remains properly harnessed."

"*I* am Lady Whiting." The words were weak, even to Lydia's ears, and Nurse Jones chuffed, turning her attention back to her knitting.

Her vision blurred, and Lydia turned her teary eyes to Isabella. Feathering kisses along her tender cheeks, she gave her child the only comfort she could. Isabella sighed and whimpered, and Lydia longed to rip the braces free; for all that the physician claimed they helped Isabella, the only thing they accomplished was her daughter's misery.

"You are more than worthy of the Whiting name," she whispered, stroking Isabella's cheek. "It is they who are not worthy of you."

Isabella's lips quivered, and Lydia took her hand, raising it to her lips as she hummed a tune. It was a nonsense ditty her sister had sung to her as a child, and the melody gave Lydia as much comfort as it brought Isabella. It was the sound of happiness and love. With a watery smile, Isabella opened her left hand (though the other clung to her mother's), her little fingers opening and closing.

Placing a finger in the center of Isabella's palm, Lydia swirled it around, her finger dancing along to the lyrics. Inching the finger up Isabella's forearm, Lydia tickled the little girl's stomach and arms, eliciting the beginnings of a laugh. Isabella squirmed to get away, though the minx continued to open and close her hand whenever Lydia stopped.

Rocking her daughter back and forth, Lydia lost herself in that stolen moment. Nurse Jones melted away into the shadows, joining Sir Duncan, her parents, and all the others plaguing her. Just mother and daughter.

The afternoon light filtered through the little window, catching Isabella's fine hair and setting the light blonde aglow. Lydia wondered if her own hair had been that bright a shade when she was a little girl.

"You're riling her up." Nurse Jones's words pierced the happy bubble, bringing Lydia back to the here and now.

Tightening her hold on Isabella, Lydia refused to look at the nursemaid as the woman stood and crossed the room. With hands adept at snatching unruly children, Nurse Jones took hold of Isabella, forcing Lydia to release her daughter or hurt her.

Nurse Jones loomed over Lydia as Isabella shrieked, and the nursemaid glared at Lydia as though the noise was solely her doing. Isabella reached for her, and Lydia rose to her feet, but even as the first signs of fire kindled in her heart, they sputtered and died. Any protest and Isabella would be made to pay the price; Lydia knew better than to look for support from her mother-in-law or any of the others.

Lydia's shoulders slackened, and her hands fell to her sides as she watched her daughter cry. Giving Isabella a tremulous smile, Lydia tried to comfort her from afar, but there was no good to be had in tormenting them both. Turning, she slipped out of the nursery, leaving the sounds of Isabella's distress muted behind the thick door. Lydia leaned against it, her head resting against the wood.

Perhaps Sir Duncan's final words to her had been true, and Lydia's womb was poisoned. Perhaps it was a punishment for all the times Lydia had longed to be a widow and dreamt of a life beyond Elmhurst Court. Though it seemed cruel to force Isabella to bear the scars for her mother's shortcomings.

Footsteps drew her attention, and a maid walked by with an armful of linens. Unperturbed by her mistress standing there, the young woman passed without so much as a look in Lydia's direction. No bob or acknowledgment. No turning aside to give Lydia privacy. Merely a dismissal as thorough as if Lady Whiting herself had given it. If Lydia had needed any further evidence of her low standing in the Whiting household, that one moment cemented it.

Lydia pushed off the door and wandered the halls of the home that had never been hers. It was filled with people who viewed her as an interloper and an irritant whose undeserving title meant nothing. Seven years in this prison. Days filled with disdainful looks and biting words. Nights marred by her husband's demands. All that suffering had been borne for a purpose that was nullified by a few lines in a will. Her marriage had been for naught, and Sir Duncan's revenge was acute.

The world pressed in on her, and Lydia placed a hand on her stomach to calm the roiling seas inside. A breath in and out as Mr. Pendergrass's voice replayed in her mind. Isabella had nothing, and Lydia had little more than that. They were cut off and set adrift.

What future did they have now? One where they were the unwanted poor relations forced to live upon the charity of a family who never wanted them? Lydia longed to return to the numb haze that had held sway for so long, but as thoughts of the coming years swirled around her, a weight settled inside her.

Reaching for her cuff, Lydia tugged the handkerchief free and stared at the worn piece of linen that bore those beloved initials: ODM. Her fingers ran over the stitches. She'd married into wealth for her parents' sake, but it had done no good. If Lydia had married as she'd wished, she may have been poor, but at least she'd have her dear Mr. Marks at her side.

Her thoughts drifted to the special place that calmed her wretched heart; it was a fanciful land outside the realm of regret, where she and Mr. Marks had chosen differently, and her life remained untainted by the Whitings. Lydia spent so much time escaping into these fantasies that she had accumulated quite a number of felicitous scenes from which to choose as she wandered away from the nursery. In quick succession, she imagined the little flat where that other Lydia cooked and cleaned, waiting for her husband to return from his dancing lessons, and evenings spent together before their cozy fire, its flicking light casting that world in a golden hue. This was a place where darkness and despair could not reside—not so long as Mr. and Mrs. Marks were together.

"There you are, my darling," said Mama in a strained tone.

Lydia jumped, shoving the handkerchief up her cuff, and she rushed down the hallway and into Mama's hold, seeking comfort there as readily as Isabella had moments ago.

"That horrid man." Mama fairly growled as she held Lydia close. "To have treated us in such a fashion!"

Lydia flinched at the mention of Sir Duncan, and Mama's touch brought a shiver down her spine. Memories of his pawing, grasping hands had her stomach twisting, and Lydia wrenched free of her mother's embrace.

"Yes, we ought not to cause a scene here," said Mama, guiding Lydia towards her parents' bedchamber. "Come, your father and I need to speak with you."

The storm inside her calmed, allowing her heart to settle beneath a layer of down, sheltering her from all the things that threatened to overtake her. None of her troubles mattered now, for Mama and Papa would sort things out. All would be well.

Chapter 2

With quick movements, Mama ushered Lydia into the bedchamber and shut the door. Taking a seat beside the fire, Lydia ignored Papa's frantic pacing and stared at the window to her left; the sun shone through the glass, and in the distance, the trees bent and bowed with the summer breeze. She rather liked the countryside around Elmhurst Court; it reminded her of her home in Bristow and a time when she'd been free to explore the fields with Mary before the onslaught of obligations had made such carefree moments impossible.

What was her sister doing at this very minute? Was she happy? Had she and her husband added to their brood? Had they a good home in Lancashire? Those questions bounced about Lydia's head, though she had no answers. Perhaps now that Sir Duncan was gone, she might be able to write Mary. Once she was at home in Bristow, it would be far easier to secret a letter into the mail with her parents none the wiser.

"Lady Whiting!" Mama fairly shouted, breaking Lydia free of her thoughts. Swinging her gaze from the window, she found her mother standing before her, watching her with raised brows.

"Pardon?"

"We were speaking of our plans," said Papa, pausing in his pacing to watch his daughter.

Blinking, Lydia nodded. "Of course. Please forgive me, Papa."

"No doubt it is difficult to concentrate after suffering such a blow," said Mama. "That wretched, horrid snake of a man! To have treated us in such a fashion. It is unforgivable."

"And the devil is likely giving Sir Duncan his reward for that selfishness as we speak," said Papa. Thoughts of eternal torment seemed to ease a bit of Mama's fractiousness, though Papa paid it no heed as he turned to the subject at hand. "Your mother and I discussed matters, and I will continue to pursue our legal options. There might be some avenue by which we can force his estate to give us our proper due."

Mama narrowed her eyes. "It ought to have been included in the marriage contract."

Papa swung his arms wide with a huff. "We had a gentlemen's agreement that he would provide for us, and a baronet ought to be a man of his word. If I had pushed him to include provisions in writing, he mightn't have married her in the first place."

"What little good that did us." Placing her fists on her hips, Mama turned her gaze to the window, staring out at the world beyond for several quiet moments. With a shake of her head, Mama turned away from the window to face Lydia. "We need to be pragmatic. Perhaps if we'd provided a dowry or if there was something in writing, we could force the estate to provide a widow's jointure for you. But as we did not and you failed to produce an heir, we shouldn't waste time pursuing legal options. Even if we are granted some recompense, it shan't be our fair due."

"Which is why the servants are packing our things," said Papa with a nod. "It is best if we return to Bristow."

Lydia's heart began beating a steady, languid rhythm,

shedding some of the darkness that had taken hold of it. Bristow was precisely where she and Isabella needed to be. Someplace familiar and welcoming. Where her family was pleased to see her and the servants treated them with respect. Without a nursemaid standing in the way, Lydia could be a true mother to her daughter. Though life had not turned out as expected, those years at home had been happy ones. Lydia couldn't think of anything better for the two of them.

"Sir Jude has generously offered us the use of his carriage," said Papa, though Mama scoffed at his kind description of Sir Jude. "And by the end of the week, the three of us will set off for home."

Enamored with thoughts of Bristow, Lydia nearly missed the most crucial detail. "Three of us? What about Isabella?"

Mama arched a brow at Lydia, cocking her head to one side. "She should remain where she belongs."

"She belongs with me."

With a wave of her hand, Mama wandered to the window. "She is far better off as the ward of the new baronet."

"And as Sir Duncan did not specify a testamentary guardian in his will, his heir would be the most likely candidate," added Papa.

Lydia's eyes widened. "But she is my daughter."

Coming to her own daughter's side, Mama took Lydia's hand in her own. "And I understand how difficult it may be to leave her behind, Lady Whiting, but it is for the best. She will be well cared for in Sir Jude's household, and I would hate to take her from the only home she's known. Besides, a child will only make matters more difficult. Men do not want wives who are saddled with children."

The air drained from the room, and the warmth of the summer sun evaporated as a chill swept over her skin. It felt as though she was submerged, her lungs fighting to breathe yet unable to reach the world above her watery grave. Though she hoped it was naught but a misunderstanding, dread skittered across her skin and settled into her heart.

"Mama?"

The lady squeezed Lydia's hand and patted her daughter on the cheek. "Do not fret. Your papa will make certain the gentleman signs a more binding contract next time. We can count it a blessing that we discovered Sir Duncan's duplicity before it was too late to try again. Seven and twenty is not very old for a widow with your beauty. I have no doubt you will make a splash in Bath society."

Lydia blinked, her mouth slackening as she tried to form words. "Bath?"

Papa strode past them, walking the length of the room. "London is no longer a possibility. Sir Duncan's passing is too recent, and the Season is too near to ending to be of use to us. And Bath is far more economical."

Mama nodded. "We will return to Bristow for a few weeks, but then we shall retire to Bath so you can take the waters and recuperate after the loss of your beloved husband. A baronet's widow will have many doors opened to her, and you can slip into society. It isn't as extensive as that which we'd find in London, but it has bachelors and widowers enough."

Lydia's muscles hardened, petrifying in place as she stared at her parents. Fighting to free her mouth, she managed a quiet, "You wish me to marry again?"

Straightening, Mama wrinkled her nose. "Of course. What other option do we have?"

Shaking her head back and forth, Lydia struggled to know what to address first, as the whole situation was ludicrous. "You wish me to abandon my child in order to secure another husband. You cannot be serious, Mama. Even if I wished to remarry, I could never leave Isabella behind. Do not ask that of me."

Brows rising, the lady stared at her daughter for a long, silent moment. "Would you prefer to remain a pauper? To sentence not only yourself but your parents to penury? After all we have done to further your prospects and give you a good life, you would turn your back on us as *she* did?"

Lydia's breath caught, her eyes slanting towards her mother. That was the first time in years Mama had deigned to mention her eldest daughter; to Lydia's knowledge, neither of their parents had spoken Mary's name in the past seven years.

"I didn't mean to cause you pain," said Lydia, her shoulders dropping low. Gaze falling to her lap, she twisted her fingers together.

Coming close, Mama laid a gentle hand on her daughter's head. "Of course you did not, my darling. You are not like your conniving and selfish sister who cared only about her own happiness. We always knew you were better than her, which is why we gave you so very much. You are far more deserving."

Light sparked in her heart, giving Lydia a moment of pleasure over Mama's words, but the sentiment died a quick death when she considered those words as a whole. Defenses sprang to her mind, begging Lydia to speak up on Mary's behalf, but she knew what would come of it. She could not bear the thought of Mama's tears. Her parents had done so very much for her, and it was not right for her to repay them so poorly.

And yet her hands shook at the thought of starting this all over again when she had only just freed herself of Sir Duncan. The future unfurled before her, telling her with all certainty what awaited her. No gentleman of younger years would risk marrying a widow unable to produce sons. It was those older, debauched gentlemen who would come calling—those who already had their heir secured and only wanted a pretty wife to cater to their needs.

"You are my good girl," said Mama, patting Lydia on the cheek once more. "You would never turn your back on us. We are only doing what is best for you, and you must do what's best for your daughter."

With one last smile and pat, Mama turned to Papa and began planning their journey and Lydia's future.

It had been so long since she'd felt anything of significance that the slightest flutter of emotion was like a buffeting wind, pounding against her. Lydia felt as though she was tumbling about, pushed along by those feelings that twisted and writhed within her. She couldn't breathe or move. Even her heart seemed to stop as it braced itself against the torrent.

Leave Isabella? Marry again? Either prospect was unbearable. Together, they were revolting.

Lydia's chest ached, and she sucked in a breath. A swirl of dizziness made her head ache as she focused on that tiny movement. In and out. When her breaths came too quickly, she forced them to slow and allow her head to clear. Her parents' voices drifted into the distance, and thoughts of her sister took their place.

Though she'd refused to foster resentment towards Mary, in Lydia's darkest moments it was hard not to feel a whisper of that dark sentiment for the sister who had snatched her own happiness despite the pain it caused others. In many ways, it made sense. Mama and Papa had never spent an unnecessary cent on Mary, so it was little wonder she felt no obligation towards them. Yet a part of Lydia's heart had always ached at how readily Mary had abandoned her family in favor of Ambrose Ashbrook.

Now, Lydia fully understood her sister's choice.

Surely her responsibility towards her parents' finances and standing had been fulfilled. True, it had not come to fruition as anticipated, but did that suppose that Lydia was required to sacrifice more of her life in service to their pocketbook and ambition? How much more could they take?

But even as she asked herself that question, ice swept through her veins as Lydia realized Mary had been right: her sacrifices would never be enough.

...

Stealing across the hallway, Lydia slipped through the darkness. With everyone still abed, the candles and fireplaces were not lit, and the curtains were drawn tight against the night, leaving Elmhurst Court shrouded in black. But Lydia had spent far too much of the past seven years skulking these halls for them to hold any mysteries for her. She stepped lightly along, stifling her shallow, shaky breaths that reverberated through the emptiness. Her hands trembled, but Lydia held fast to the portmanteau that bumped against her thigh as her slippered feet slid along the floor.

A tune echoed in the hall, and Lydia's heart thundered as she dodged to the side, ducking into the shadows. Holding her breath, she stilled, though she was certain the young maid could hear her thundering heartbeat. The girl hummed some jaunty tune as she strode into the library; she left the door ajar, and Lydia sent out a silent prayer, hoping for some divine wisdom to guide her actions. As much as she longed to wait, it was too great a risk. If the morning fires were being lit, the hour was far later than she'd thought.

Squeezing her eyes shut, Lydia gathered her courage and moved from her hiding place, sneaking past the library doorway and up the stairs.

"Hello?" called the maid.

Lydia's footsteps paused, her breath freezing in her lungs, but the question faded into silence, and the girl started humming once more. With steps more frantic than careful, Lydia hurried up the staircase and did not stop until she reached the nursery. Inching open the door, Lydia slipped inside, grateful that Nurse Jones's snores masked the sounds of her movement as she snuck into the alcove that housed a pair of beds. The nursemaid was placed to the farther side, giving Lydia space to sneak to Isabella's cot without disturbing the woman.

Setting down the portmanteau, Lydia pulled back the bedding. Isabella stirred as Lydia slipped her hands under the child, slowly lifting the darling to rest on her shoulder. Squawking, Isabella twisted, shifting in Lydia's hold as her mother bounced her a few times. Nurse Jones fell silent, and Lydia froze, squeezing her eyes tight against the fear that stole her breath.

For several long moments, she stood there as Isabella settled once more, fast asleep. When Nurse Jones's snoring returned, Lydia did not waste a moment. Bending carefully to snatch up her bag, Lydia hurried out of the nursery.

Dawn trickled through the window at the top of the staircase, warming the space with its golden hues, but the sight had Lydia moving faster, her pulse racing in time with her steps. Pausing just long enough to ascertain that the maid had left the library, Lydia ducked inside the room, rushing through it to the side door. The main entrances boasted fine locks and sturdy wood to protect the Whiting family from robbers and villains, but this overlooked doorway had never been secured to that same level. With a bit of wiggling and a firm shoulder, Lydia had it open.

Her portmanteau banged against her leg as she hurried across the lawn, her arms burning as she struggled to hold it and her daughter. The movement jostled Isabella, whose face crumpled, her plaintive cry ringing through the silent morning. Lydia sang to her, trying to hush her daughter, but the sight of a passing cart erased all other thoughts.

Lydia dared not shout at it as she rushed across the vast stretch of lawn that separated the house from the lane, but her heart rang with the sounds of her desperate prayers. The walk into town was too far with such burdens, and they would never make the morning coach. There would likely be another cart passing soon, but Lydia didn't dare risk the wait.

The cart lumbered forward, the horses plodding along as the driver guided the beasts along their path. With no free hand to wave the fellow down, Lydia moved as quickly as she could while weighed down, and Isabella began to cry in earnest. With their stealth abandoned, Lydia called out to the fellow, and the farmer pulled the cart to a stop.

"Good gracious," he said with raised brows. "What are you doing out this early?"

Her lungs heaved, but Lydia managed to ask, "Might I beg a ride into the village?"

The farmer's brows pulled tight together, and he glanced back the way she'd come, his eyes landing on Elmhurst Court.

"I can pay you," she said.

Now that they were stationary, Isabella calmed some, rubbing her eyes before collapsing back onto her mother's shoulder. Lydia dropped the portmanteau and shifted her hold to reach a hand into her reticule. In truth, the coins inside it were meager. As the funds her husband had promised her had yet to appear, Lydia was left with the remnants of her pin money. Yet it should be enough for the journey. She dug inside, but the fellow shook his head and waved the gesture off.

"It's no bother, ma'am," he said, nodding for her to come around the other side. "The village is where we're headed."

"My thanks," said Lydia, though those words could not contain a fraction of the gratitude she felt.

At a word from the farmer, the lad beside him relinquished his seat and helped Lydia up before climbing into the back of the cart, which was filled with milk canisters. The farmer said not a word as Lydia tore at the bindings of those wretched braces on Isabella's feet. She worked open the straps as the cart rumbled forward, and when she pulled the first one free, Isabella gave a sharp cry.

"I am so sorry," she whispered, rubbing her daughter's foot as it curled inwards. Then, with equal efficiency, Lydia removed the other, and Isabella's little foot twisted. Lydia cooed at her, rubbing at the misshapen appendages, her own throbbing in sympathy as Isabella whimpered. The farmer slanted looks in their direction but remained silent as Lydia launched the braces into the ditch. With gentle touches, she rubbed Isabella's feet, rocking and singing to her.

The cart bumped with each dip of the road, and Lydia's heart lightened like the sky above as the sun crawled up through the heavens. With every turn of the wheel, she and Isabella moved closer to Lancashire, her sister, and the freedom that awaited them there.

Chapter 3

One Month Later
Greater Edgerton, Lancashire

The sun shone brightly in the sky, spreading its glorious light across the world. The summer had already proven itself to be a dry, hot thing, and those who made their living from the soil were praying mightily for rain, but Robert Bradshaw was hard-pressed to worry about anything but the beauty that surrounded him especially with Nell's hand wrapped in his as the pair strolled along the streets of Greater Edgerton. Robert slanted a look at his daughter and reassessed the pleasantness of the morning. Not to say that her presence diminished the gloriousness of the day, but a heavy silence clung to the child.

"I am sorry we cannot go out on a drive today as we planned," he said, squeezing her hand.

Nell nodded, though her light gaze drifted from him with a look far too ponderous for someone who had only eight years to her name. Though he had business to attend to, Robert was in no hurry to relinquish his daughter, and he led them along a circuitous path to their destination.

Having spent sixteen years in the area, he'd witnessed the town's growth, and it was heartening to see more buildings and businesses sprout up along the roads. Greater Edgerton was by no means a booming city, but to his thinking, it was the perfect blend of town and country. A series of stalls had been erected along the thoroughfare, and the cries of the vendors were a siren's call. He glanced at the strawberries, but it was the lure of pork pies that pulled Robert to a stop.

"Would you like a treat?" he asked, nodding at the pie stand.

Nell's eyes brightened as she glanced from her father to the delectable pies all lined up. At her nod, Robert selected a couple and paid the fellow. He handed one to Nell, and they struck off again, their path meandering along River Dennick. Across the water, the mills and factories churned, setting about their business with the efficiency of industry. Robert took a bite and was surprised to find that the baker had stuffed a pickled cucumber in the middle of the chopped pork—a rather intriguing addition. But when his gaze drifted to Nell, he discovered she had only nibbled on the edge.

"Is your pie off?" he asked, offering his in exchange.

But Nell shook her head. "Mrs. Chad says eating on the street is gauche."

Sputtering, Robert tried to cover the laugh at his daughter's tone when speaking that final word. It held an echo of that domineering lady with a dash of curiosity that spoke of one repeating something she did not fully understand.

"You needn't worry. Gauche is a good thing," he said, taking a bite of his pie.

But Nell narrowed her eyes. "Not how Mrs. Chad said it. What does it mean?"

"It means Mrs. Chad is apt to find fault wherever she goes."

"Papa." Her tone was such a perfect blend of childish exasperation and impatience that Robert had to grin.

With an arched brow, he glanced in her direction. "It means unrefined and coarse."

Her lips turned downward. "That's what I thought."

Robert squeezed her hand and slanted her a smile. "But it doesn't matter if Mrs. Chad says eating on the street is gauche, for I am perfectly content with being unrefined and coarse."

He winked at her, but rather than eliciting the laugh he'd intended, his words caused Nell's expression to droop, leaving Robert at a loss.

"Does it matter if your foolish papa is gauche?"

Nell glanced towards the river, the pie dangling at her side. "I want to be a lady, and a lady is refined."

"Oh, my dear little girl. You are far too young to be worrying about such things," he said with a smile. But that did not achieve the desired response, so Robert continued, "I am certain you will be perfectly ladylike when you are older, but you needn't fret about such things now."

Nodding, Nell nibbled on her pie but did not eat with any gusto, and though Robert wanted to prod her further, he decided to leave it be. Whatever mood had taken hold of his daughter was certain to shift before long; as much as she may think herself a little lady, she was still too young to cling to ridiculous pretensions.

Before long, they turned down Marbury Lane and passed a row of townhouses all squished together like rolls in a pan. Though the buildings themselves were fairly uniform in their design and overall appearance, there were little details that set each apart from their neighbors. The doors were painted various shades of black, brown, red, and blue, and some had pots of flowers or other ornaments sitting on the front steps. Among them was the green door that belonged to the Humphreys.

As loath as he was to leave Nell, there was no avoiding his pressing legal matters that needed attending, and Robert had lingered long enough. Giving a quick rap of his knuckles, he waited as the maid opened the door and ushered them inside. Even if the Humphreys' home had been a large, imposing thing, it would've been easy to locate the family without her prompts, for there was enough noise coming from the parlor upstairs that the neighbors on either side of the townhouse would be well aware of the children's location. Nell ran ahead, and there was a clamor as her cousins rushed to greet her.

Robert followed after her and found his sister-in-law seated on the sofa with their newest addition cradled in her arms. Her head was leaned back, and her eyes closed despite the chaos, the babe fast asleep as well. Her two eldest ran circles around Nell while the youngest of the three mobile children toddled after them.

"Prudence?" asked Robert.

His sister-in-law's eyes snapped open, and she jerked, jostling little Hugo, who did not wake as easily as his mother.

"Robert," she said, rubbing her eyes with her free hand. "I am sorry I did not hear you come in."

He grinned and nodded at the trio. "I imagine you have your hands quite full with your horde, and I know I previously said I did not need your assistance today, but a matter has arisen that requires my attention. I'm afraid I must forgo my afternoon with Nell."

Rising to her feet, Prudence nodded and smiled at her niece. "Of course, Robert. Nell is a treat to have around."

"I owe you more than I can ever repay," he said, stepping towards the door, but as Robert glanced at Nell, he stopped. Motioning for Prudence to come closer, he lowered his voice. "Has Nell been out of sorts lately? She was acting quite strangely on the walk here, going on about being refined and ladylike."

Prudence shifted Hugo, lifting the baby to her shoulder, and nodded. "Not long ago, she mentioned something about wanting to be called Eleanor rather than Nell."

Robert's brows furrowed, and he glanced at his daughter. She had Sadie and Ernest by the hands and twirled about with all the carefree joy of childhood. Muriel struggled to keep up, but when she fell, Nell helped her to her feet and had the others make space for her in the circle.

"Why must she rush ahead? She is still a child and ought to remain so for some years," he said.

His sister-in-law gave a warm smile, though her gaze held a touch of wistfulness. "I suspect she wants a connection to her mother."

Slanting a glance towards Robert, Prudence pinched her lips together for a moment before she added in a cautious tone, "Perhaps it would do Nell good if you were to talk with her about Eleanor."

Robert cocked his head to the side and gave Nell an assessing glance. "I often tell her stories about her mother. I had thought I was quite free with sharing anything Nell wishes to know."

Prudence reached over with her free hand and squeezed his arm. "You do a wonderful job, Robert, and Eleanor would be proud of you. Nell is a good girl, and you will sort this out."

With a nod of thanks and a goodbye to his daughter, Robert strode back onto the street, moving far quicker than before. He'd lingered for far too long and needed to be on his way. The sooner this business was done, the sooner he could collect Nell and return home.

Robert felt like cursing Mr. Milton for procrastinating to this degree; the gentleman had struggled to decide upon the finer points of his contract, and now expected Robert to hurry and make up the lost time. Some part of him wished to ignore his client and spend the afternoon as he'd planned. Heaven knew Robert did not require the work, but Mr. Milton was too lucrative a client to slough off so carelessly. Perhaps it was time to take on a partner. Robert didn't care for that prospect, but if it allowed him the freedom to avoid such last-minute emergencies, perhaps it mightn't be such a terrible thing.

Robert moved along the streets, his feet finding the familiar path without prompting; he'd walked the distance between the Humphreys' home and his office more times than he could count, and it left his mind free to mull over the subject of his daughter.

No doubt Eleanor would know what to do for Nell. While Robert did not lack brains, she'd had a way with people. A preternatural sense of sorts. With only a few words, Eleanor saw into the heart of a person and knew just what to say or do.

But Prudence was right. Whatever was amiss with Nell would come to light eventually, and Robert doubted it was anything serious. Too many childhoods were tainted by deprivation and despair—his own included—but Nell's was blessed with comfort and a loving family. Despite her lack of a mother, Nell had an adoring aunt who stood in Eleanor's place. And though it was natural for her to long for a proper mother, Robert had done everything to help her know the one she'd had.

Surely, Nell's current troubles were minor things.

Puffing out his cheeks, Robert let out a breath as he realized he was bound for a lifetime of such worries: the more Nell grew, the larger and more complex such issues would become. To think he'd fretted so very much during her first years of life. Caring for an infant's demands was far simpler, and at least he'd had staff on hand to help him with those never-ending needs. While the Humphreys would do their part to aid him, Robert wondered if it would be enough.

Chapter 4

Robert turned a corner, and his heart lightened at the sight of his office. As brooding about Nell's future did little good, Robert was grateful to embrace the distractions that laws and contracts offered. The smell of ink and paper greeted him as he stepped through the door, and he sucked in a deep breath of that comforting scent.

"Good afternoon, Mr. Bradshaw."

"Mr. Osmet," he greeted, though the lad hardly looked up; his small desk was stacked high with various legal papers and books, and Mr. Osmet was buried behind them.

"Mr. Shirley left a few minutes ago to speak with Mr. Breadmore concerning the—"

But Robert waved the words off. His youngest clerk felt a need to report all their happenings, but he'd worked long enough with Mr. Shirley to know that if the fellow was not at his desk, then he was conducting important business elsewhere.

Similarly, Robert knew not to ask after Mr. Darby. The lad's family may have high hopes for his future as a solicitor, but Mr. Darby showed no genuine skill or interest in the legal profession. Once his articles were fulfilled and his time as a clerk was complete, Robert would be glad to see the back of him. It was his own blasted fault for taking the boy on; he'd felt uneasy from the first moment the Darbys had approached him about their son, and he ought to have listened to his instincts.

Mr. Osmet nodded and disappeared behind his tome once more, and Robert hid a smile. He was so very eager to learn everything all at once, and Robert knew that though there were still many years to go in his clerkship, Mr. Osmet would prove to be one of the few clerks to excel in the profession. One could not have such determination and zeal and not find success in some manner.

Robert shed his jacket, hat, and gloves and moved towards his office in the rear, but stopped when Mr. Osmet's book snapped shut.

"I forgot to mention that a Mr. Pendergrass called earlier," he said, holding out a business card.

The gentleman's name was written across the front in elegant script, though Robert could not recall ever having met him.

"He insisted that you call on him at The Royal Oak the moment you arrive," said Mr. Osmet.

Robert huffed and shook his head at the card. It said enough about the gentleman that he'd chosen the finest lodgings in town (a fact that was echoed in the pretentious name), but for the stranger to demand anything only ensured Robert would not do as Mr. Pendergrass wished. Tossing the card onto the desk, Robert shook his head and turned back to his office, ready to do battle with the day's work.

Mr. Milton's financial agreements always proved a bit of a megrim—nothing beyond Robert's ability, but the gentleman was exacting and overly cautious. While Robert commended Mr. Milton's care with his contracts, they required many edits and changes before they were accepted, and the gentleman had no understanding of timeliness. But then, some people preferred a life lived on the edge of chaos to planning things out properly. To Robert's thinking, it seemed a poor business tactic, but as Mr. Milton was quite solvent, Robert supposed there was no use in judging.

Delving into the paperwork, he made marks here and there, writing out instructions for his clerks, who would transcribe the finished product. Robert had lost himself in the minutiae, moving phrases here and there and adding the necessary addendums, when the sound of the front door drew his attention. While that was not a wholly unusual sound, the blustering demands that followed were notable.

Robert remained where he was, though he kept an ear turned towards the disruption. His desk faced the doorway, but as it was not aligned with the main entrance, Robert couldn't see the intruder. However, the entire office was not overly large, and it was easy enough to hear everything from his vantage.

"Did you not give him my message, boy?" asked the fellow, whom Robert guessed was the mysterious Mr. Pendergrass.

"Yes, sir." Mr. Osmet's voice faltered a fraction, though Robert was pleased the lad did not stammer or prevaricate as he was wont to do; the boy would never succeed if he quaked over demanding clientele. As their profession relied greatly upon those with money, and those of that class tended towards inflated egos, a strong backbone was paramount to a successful solicitor.

"Well?" Mr. Pendergrass barked the question, and Robert laid down his pen, his fingers drumming against the wood as he awaited Mr. Osmet's response.

There was silence for a moment, but then the clerk replied with more steel than before, "I gave him the message, as is my duty, but Mr. Bradshaw is master here. He decides how to respond to such matters."

"I see." Mr. Pendergrass's tone was low, and Robert could imagine the sour expression adorning the gentleman's face. The world was full of men who believed themselves lord and master of all they surveyed, but unbeknownst to them, the world was not large enough for all of them to rule and reign.

Footsteps sounded, warning Robert of the impending intrusion, and he took up his pen once more, turning his gaze to his work.

"Sir?" began Mr. Osmet, but his words were cut off by Mr. Pendergrass's cold voice.

"What is the meaning of this, Bradshaw?"

Robert may be a grown man of six and thirty, but there were times when it was impossible to hold back childish impulses. Giving into this one, Robert did not look up from his work, giving the intruder no hint that he'd been heard. Mr. Pendergrass moved across the room, coming to stand before Robert's desk, but still he did not look up. Once the gentleman was well and truly seething, Robert glanced up to Mr. Osmet and nodded for him to leave them be.

The older gentleman straightened his finely cut tailcoat and sat down on the chair opposite Robert. Mr. Pendergrass's expression looked as though he'd bitten into a lemon, his gaze taking in Robert with a barely contained sneer. But the satchel on his lap told Robert that for all the gentleman's pretensions, he was likely another man of trade.

"You ignored my summons," said Mr. Pendergrass with a narrowed gaze.

"I am not a dog to come at your bidding. Now, who are you and what do you want?"

Mr. Pendergrass's hands tightened on the satchel, his lips pinching even more than before. But with a haughty sniff, he replied, "I am solicitor to the late Sir Duncan Whiting, Baronet."

Robert held back a scoff. He ought to have known. Nothing bred condescension and arrogance quite like a connection to a title, even if Mr. Pendergrass was just another middle-class dredge.

"I hardly think someone who has passed on requires a solicitor," said Robert, turning his gaze to his work. "Sir Duncan must have more important things to do now than fret over legal matters."

Though he did not look up, Robert sensed Mr. Pendergrass's straightening spine and burning glare.

"I am here on behalf of his mother, the Dowager Lady Whiting."

"And I can hardly imagine why she requires my services when she has such a distinguished fellow as yourself to tend to her legal matters," said Robert in a dry tone.

"Sir Duncan's widow and daughter have taken up residence in this backward town. His mother is concerned their behavior might disgrace the Whiting name, and the Dowager Lady Whiting wishes to know the comings and goings of her daughter-in-law and granddaughter. As I cannot live both here and in Kent simultaneously, I require someone to serve as my eyes and ears in Lancashire."

Robert's brows rose. "You believe I fit the bill?"

Mr. Pendergrass shifted in his seat, his fingers drumming against the polished leather satchel. "From what I've heard, you are one of the best solicitors in the area."

"Spying doesn't require legal expertise."

"It doesn't, but no doubt your background has given you connections with men who can perform the duties admirably. I require you to hire and oversee their efforts, acting in my stead."

Robert placed his pen down carefully beside his papers and met Mr. Pendergrass's eye. "You think because I come from a poor background, I would not only have such connections but also no scruples against haranguing a widow?"

Mr. Pendergrass scoffed. "I am not interested in bothering her. We simply wish to know what she is doing with herself in case she does something to blacken the family honor. The chit doesn't know her place."

"And should the lady do something of which your employer does not approve, what then?"

He waved a vague hand. "Then we would take action to ensure it did not happen again."

Robert's gaze narrowed. "Forgive my ignorance, Mr. Pendergrass, as I am from such *humble* origins, but it seems to me that to 'take action' would most certainly be 'bothering' her."

With a heavy sigh that said he thought Robert a simpleton, Mr. Pendergrass replied, "Forgive me, Mr. Bradshaw, but it is only right that the Dowager Lady Whiting take action to protect her son's legacy, and we both fear his widow will ruin it if left to her own devices."

"And you must forgive me, Mr. Pendergrass, if I do not see it that way. The baronet is dead, and his widow is free to do as she pleases. Not only does your client have no legal rights over her daughter-in-law, but this course of action is repugnant. It may be difficult for you to comprehend, Mr. Pendergrass, but the gentry does not have a monopoly on honor."

Robert's jaw tightened, and he returned his attention to his work, dismissing the cad without another look. Mr. Pendergrass stood, and Robert did not look up, ignoring him altogether as the fellow stormed out of the office, the door crashing shut behind him.

Droplets of ink splattered across the page as Robert slammed the pen down and glared at the space Mr. Pendergrass had occupied. Insufferable twit. There was a reason he'd chosen Lancashire to set up shop. While some of his clients were difficult, the industrial town was home to many businessmen who'd worked their way into money. That was not to say they were never as irritating and pretentious as those who'd inherited their fortunes, but they were less likely to be. He preferred to be far from the obsequiousness that followed after the titled and ridiculously wealthy.

Letting out a heavy breath, Robert turned his attention back to the matter at hand, but as much as he tried to banish Mr. Pendergrass from his mind, thoughts of the mysterious widow pestered him. No doubt, she was as insufferable as the rest of her stratum, but for all Mr. Pendergrass's belief that Robert had no scruples, his honor needled him.

Robert doubted Mr. Pendergrass or the Dowager meant any harm. The more people blustered, the less likely they were to do anything of substance, and Mr. Pendergrass had proved exceptionally blustery. For all his airs, he was merely a bully. But that did not mean Mr. Pendergrass and his mistress were harmless.

"Mr. Osmet," called Robert while rubbing his forehead. When the clerk came to the door, he asked, "Do you know anything about Lady Whiting?"

While Robert wasn't familiar with the name, Greater Edgerton was small enough that a baronet's widow would dominate the local gossip, and Mr. Osmet's parents were well-versed in all the goings-on in town.

The clerk nodded and said, "She arrived about a month ago and resides with her sister, Mrs. Ambrose Ashbrook."

"The Ashbrooks?" Robert's brows furrowed. "I knew Mr. Ashbrook came from some money, but I hadn't thought his wife so well-connected."

Mr. Osmet shrugged and disappeared when Robert dismissed him.

Leaning back in his chair, Robert stared at the wall. As much as he wanted to ignore what had just occurred, there was no escaping the feeling that poked and prodded him to action. Even if Pendergrass meant no true harm, the lady deserved some warning. Besides, the Ashbrooks were good people, and they would wish to know if trouble was stirring.

Rising to his feet, Robert sighed and cast a glance at his work. He supposed Mr. Milton's contract could wait another hour.

Chapter 5

Shifting the pillow at her back, Lydia settled against the headboard with her book clutched to her chest. Windows sat on either side of the bed, and her gaze drifted towards them; though she could not see through the glass from her vantage, it was easy enough to see the light shifting and moving as the sun drifted across the heavens. She ought to emerge from her bedchamber, but the heroine's voice whispered to her, promising a few more hours of peace from the reality that lay beyond her door. Yet she had already passed the morning here, and duty pricked at her heart, telling her it was time to put aside her novel.

Lydia's eyes drifted to the leather and paper nestled in her arms, and she held the book tightly. The worlds created within those pages were terrible at times; heroines suffered countless indignities until all hope was lost, but all was made right in the end. Agonizing though it may be at times, the endings always compensated for the pains they suffered. There were always reasons behind the madness and misery. Some grand reward awaiting the poor heroine at the end of her story. A happy resolution that promised eternal bliss for her and her hero.

Leaning her head against the wood headboard, Lydia stared at the door, knowing that the world outside it was not so giving.

She shifted in her bed, reaching for the drawer in her side table, and retrieved the old handkerchief. Lydia ran her fingers over Mr. Marks' initials and placed a kiss on the worn stitches. Life had not been so kind to the pair of them, though she hoped her love had found more peace than she had. Surely at least one of them ought to be happy.

Replacing the handkerchief, Lydia set her novel atop the table and stepped out of her sanctuary.

Echoes of children's laughter rang in her ears, and her heart lightened at it, her feet moving quickly down the stairs to find the source. But as she passed the second floor, the door to the guest bedroom was ajar, and Lydia paused at the sight she saw there. Leaning away so she could not be seen by her sister and brother-in-law, she stared at the pair.

A table had been placed in the center of the room, angled to fit with the bed and wardrobe, and Ambrose stood hunched over it. Gears, springs, and bits of his machinery were strewn across the top, and Mary nudged aside some of the smaller parts to make way for the tea tray she carried.

"Are you going to remain cloistered here all afternoon?" she asked.

Ambrose did not answer at first, but when his wife repeated herself, he straightened and blinked at her, as though having only just realized he was no longer alone.

"I am so very close to finishing," he said, but when Mary glanced at the mess with an arched brow, he hemmed. "Near to being close."

But Mary gave him a knowing smile that said she did not believe that any more than his first statement. She kissed his cheek with a chuckle and turned to go, but her husband snatched her hand and pulled her back to him.

Lydia knew she ought not to stand there, but seeing the pair of them was like having the past come to life once more when she and Mr. Marks had stolen moments like this. She still felt the phantom memories of his hands resting on her hips and the feel of his fingers entwining with hers. Though the figures before her were those of Mary and Ambrose, Lydia saw herself and Mr. Marks, and she reveled in that blissful moment.

"And how is your day?" asked Ambrose, wrapping his arms around Mary. His wife sighed and shook her head, drifting into tales of all that she had done and what was yet to happen.

Holding her breath, Lydia inched away and snuck down the last few steps. For all that she ought to have been embarrassed by the displays of affection, the innocent conversation made Lydia feel like an intruder. Simple it may have been, but there was an intimacy to their words as they spoke of the little nothings of their shared life. It was the sort of conversation Lydia had never shared with Mr. Marks. Her heart pricked as she thought over their time together and realized just how little they had spoken, for propriety had not allowed them the opportunity.

But then, theirs was a connection far deeper than words.

Lydia snuck down the stairs as she imagined just what sort of discussions they would've shared as husband and wife. The same little insignificant conversations that wove together two independent lives into a single unit. Standing outside the parlor door, Lydia sighed and touched a hand to the wood, giving herself a moment to lock away such thoughts.

"Mama!" Isabella called when her mother finally opened the door, and to Lydia's delight, her little girl toddled towards her. Isabella's steps jerked and faltered as she compensated for her feet, but she did walk. Lydia could only imagine how uncomfortable it was for her to carry her weight on the sides of her feet, but Isabella only smiled and laughed, looking all the happier now that she was allowed to move about.

Scooping Isabella into her arms, Lydia kissed her soft cheeks and cooed over the child, though Isabella did not remain still for long. She wiggled free of Lydia's hold and returned to where her cousins played.

Vincent stood at the sofa's edge, holding tightly to that anchor, but when he saw Isabella coming close, he reached for her and took a few steps before bumping to the floor and crawling beside her. The pair drew close to Dottie and Esther, who sat among piles of clothes as they dressed and undressed their dolls. Isabella grabbed at one of the gowns, and Esther squealed, reaching for the stolen article, but Dottie handed the older girl a different gown, distracting her as the two babes entertained themselves by tossing about the rejected articles. Nurse Nunn sat with Lucas as they rallied their regiments to march on the enemy troops, and the nursemaid did a stellar job at keeping Isabella and Vincent from wreaking havoc in the battle.

This was where Isabella belonged, surrounded by those who welcomed her, and seeing her daughter so content lightened Lydia's heart.

But then Isabella plunked onto the floor beside her older cousins, which in and of itself was not remarkable, but the manner in which she sat had Lydia watching her daughter with a wary gaze. Shifting, Isabella tucked her feet beneath her, pulling at the edge of her dress to keep them covered and out of sight of the others as her old nursemaid had trained her to do.

Lydia's eyes filled with tears, and she stared at the child. Not two years old, yet the Whitings had left their mark. Stepping to her daughter's side, Lydia swept her up and sat down on the sofa beside the girls. She laid Isabella across her lap and reached for her feet, kissing the little toes as the child squirmed and laughed. There were so many things she longed to say to her child, but Isabella would not understand them, so Lydia showed her love in ways that words could not convey.

Isabella beamed and then wriggled free once more, moving to rejoin Dottie and Esther. But Lydia's heart fell when the child continued to hide her feet.

"Don't worry, madam," said Nurse Nunn, glancing up from her battle with Lucas. "She's still young."

Nodding, Lydia couldn't help but think the nursemaid was quite young herself to be giving such advice, but it seemed sound and gave her some relief, so Lydia chose to embrace it. Surely the damage the Whitings had done during that first year and a half of Isabella's life would heal with time. Though Lydia still did not know what to do about the shortsighted fools who grimaced and flinched at the sight of her beautiful baby girl.

The parlor door opened, and Mary stepped through and paused when she saw her sister. Lydia straightened, her hands twisting together as her gaze drifted away from Mary's pointed regard.

"I'm glad to see you've joined us, dearest," said Mary with a smile. "Ambrose is working on one of his machines at present, but when he is done perhaps we can take the children on a drive. The weather is quite fine today."

Lydia's expression tightened, though she fought against the grimace threatening to make itself known. Her insides clenched at the very thought of bouncing about the roads with the landau's head folded down, allowing every passerby to see them and gawk. A tremor took hold of her hands, and Lydia tried to breathe, but her heart wouldn't rest easy until she dismissed the offer in its entirety.

"My thanks, but I do not feel like going out today," said Lydia. "However, do not let that stop you. I am quite content to remain behind with Isabella."

Mary's brow furrowed as she stared at her sister, and Lydia prayed she would leave it be. "Lydia—"

"You have a mighty fine regiment, Lucas." Lydia turned her gaze to her nephew, and he held aloft one of his many soldiers with a smile. Then he threw it at Nurse Nunn's front line and laughed as the toys scattered. Hopping to his feet, he turned to his mother, pointing at the fallen and babbling about the battle they'd fought.

As Mary moved to the floor beside him, the parlor door opened once more. Mary turned to greet her husband but found the maid, Polly.

"Mr. Robert Bradshaw wishes to see you, the master, and Lady Whiting," she said with a bob. "He says it concerns an important matter."

"Who is Mr. Bradshaw?" asked Lydia.

"He's the brother-in-law of my friend, Mrs. Parker Humphreys, though I do not know why he would be calling." Mary paused, her brows furrowing. "Especially as he wishes to see all of us."

Turning to Polly, Mary said, "Show him to the library. It will be far easier to talk without the children underfoot."

And with that, the sisters left the safety of the parlor. Lydia did not know what the gentleman wanted of her, but the heavy feeling settling into her stomach warned her it was unlikely to be good news.

Chapter 6

From a single glance, Robert knew the library was a well-loved room. Too many families treated their library like a museum where one observes but does not interact with their surroundings, but the Ashbrooks intended this room to be enjoyed. There was a fireplace to his left with an arrangement of sofas and armchairs that was more efficient than organized; while most preferred straight lines, these seats were all angled towards the fire, allowing each proper access to the warmth.

Equally telling was the collection of books they kept, which spanned a variety of subjects. Novels sat beside thick treatises on industrialization, naturalism, astronomy, and history. Those who used their library as a symbol of their wealth and status would never keep Matthew Lewis and Ann Radcliff where anyone could see. Especially not next to a collection that would make any scholar proud.

If Robert had needed any more reason to like Ambrose and Mary Ashbrook, this room would've tipped the scales in their favor.

"Mr. Bradshaw." Mr. Ashbrook strode in with a hand outstretched and that easy smile of his. "I understand you are here to pay us a visit."

"Not precisely," he said as he shook the fellow's hand. "Something has come to my attention that you and your sister-in-law ought to know."

Mr. Ashbrook nodded, but before they could speak further, the ladies appeared, and Mr. Ashbrook ushered them all to the haphazard selection of seats. Robert chose to stand by the empty fireplace, which gave him a better vantage point from which to see them all. Most especially Lady Whiting.

She was not what Robert had expected, though he supposed that was his own fault. Though he was not especially close to the Ashbrooks, knowing Lady Whiting was Mrs. Ashbrook's sister had colored his image of her. The latter was no beauty by any definition (except her husband's), though she was one of those exceptionally capable people whose steel spine made up for her appearance. The former could not be more opposite.

Lady Whiting had the golden curls, features, and figure of a beauty. No doubt she had been highly coveted as a maiden, which was affirmed by the fact that she'd married a baronet. Yet there was a worn quality to her looks that belied her young years, as though she had withered, drying out like an autumn leaf. Matters were not helped by the fact that her complexion was dulled by the unrelenting black of her mourning clothes.

But still, she held herself with the haughty posture of one with a title, and Robert wondered why he had bothered to insert himself into this family squabble.

"You look excessively serious, Mr. Bradshaw. What is this about?" asked Mr. Ashbrook, pulling Robert out of his musings and to the subject at hand.

"I had a visit from Mr. Pendergrass concerning Lady Whiting."

That imperious facade cracked as the lady in question stiffened, her hand flying over to grasp her sister's. So, she had some feeling other than the haughtiness of a titled person.

As Robert thought about it, he realized that perhaps the most irritating people weren't the ones born to their high stations. Like Mr. Pendergrass and Lady Whiting, those who had no natural claim to a title clung tightest after having forged a connection to one, as though they felt an instinctive need to set themselves apart from others even if they were no better than the gentry and plebs they disdained. Robert had seen more than his fair share of such ridiculousness.

Though in many ways barristers and solicitors were partners, the former often viewed the latter with contempt, keen to put those of Robert's profession "in their place" simply because barristers claimed a higher social stratum. It was terribly shortsighted. After all, those "gentlemen" never deigned to dirty their hands with the business of billings and advertising their services, so they relied solely on solicitors to manage such gauche affairs. They hired out their services like any other working man, but that degree of separation allowed them to drape themselves in gentlemanly sensibilities. Yet it also made them dependent on solicitors. The opposite was not true, which was why Robert was so particular about which barristers he recommended to his clients.

But that was neither here nor there at present, so Robert abandoned such thoughts and focused on relaying his conversation with Mr. Pendergrass. Mr. and Mrs. Ashbrooks asked clarifying questions but otherwise left him to describe the interlude. The lady in question said nothing, though that cool composure crumbled as he spoke. Like ocean waves eating away at a sandy shore, his words stole away the little vitality she had, eating away at her until there was nothing left. How had such a fragile woman navigated life?

"Do you believe my sister-in-law to be in any danger, Mr. Bradshaw?" asked Mr. Ashbrook with a furrowed brow.

"Mr. Pendergrass is all bluster. I simply thought you should know he is lurking about."

Mrs. Ashbrook glanced from her sister to Robert. "And what of Isabella? Are they looking to reclaim her?"

Robert's gaze drifted to Lady Whiting and found her staring off at nothing, her hand still gripping Mrs. Ashbrook's. Rather telling that the aunt and not the mother asked the question, but that was to be expected; many of Lady Whiting's standing viewed children as a necessary imposition to be foisted off on nursemaids and governesses, and he doubted she spent much time around the child.

Eleanor would not have stood for such a thing. Had she been allowed the opportunity to raise her daughter, his wife would've been an attentive mother, engaged in Nell's upbringing and care. Robert had never experienced such familial bliss, but he often imagined all those little moments with mother, father, and babe and didn't understand why so many chose to forgo those simple joys.

"Mr. Pendergrass showed little concern about the child," said Robert. "His focus was on your sister."

Mrs. Ashbrook's shoulders relaxed, though Lady Whiting remained a statue. Again, Eleanor came to his thoughts, and Robert almost smiled at the thought of what she would have done had anyone threatened her child. He saw that same determination and courage mirrored in Mrs. Ashbrook, but Lady Whiting lacked that fire.

Thank heavens the child had the Ashbrooks to care for her interests. Robert doubted the widow could mount the fight necessary if the Whitings sought custody. Mr. Pendergrass's disinterest in the child likely echoed his employer's, but such things could change, and if Lady Whiting wished to keep her child, it would take a battle. One that she was clearly ill-equipped to mount.

Something Lady Whiting proved by rising to her feet and fleeing the room.

"I had a visit from Mr. Pendergrass concerning Lady Whiting." Mr. Bradshaw's declaration held Lydia in place. Her lungs refused to work, seizing until she was certain she would faint. The world was a jumbled mess she could not comprehend. Words flew about the room as Mr. Bradshaw explained what had occurred between him and Mr. Pendergrass, but Lydia could not lay hold of a single one. The conversation made no sense, and her useless mind could not set it to rights.

The Whitings despised the pair of them. During her flight from Elmhurst Court, Lydia's thoughts had been focused on evading her parents; never had she anticipated her in-laws caring what happened to them. Yet Mr. Pendergrass had gone to such lengths to locate them. To hire Mr. Bradshaw.

Clinging to Mary's hand, Lydia tried to breathe. Tried to think. Tried to calm herself. But all she could see were images of Sir Jude and her mother-in-law descending on Greater Edgerton to drag her back to Kent. Strapping Isabella back in those horrendous braces. Locking her dear little girl away in that cold and silent nursery.

Lydia forced herself to focus and meet Mr. Bradshaw's gaze, but there was such a hard quality to his eyes that she flinched away. His words were clipped, delivering his news with that unwavering certainty of one who is used to giving orders and having them obeyed. Though the fellow was much younger than her late husband, there was so much of Sir Duncan in that tone and expression—and it shouted that she had fallen short yet again.

The world pressed in on her, and she felt ready to drop. Shoving past the past and her panic, Lydia leapt to her feet and hurried out of the room. There was only one place that afforded her safety. One place where the world could not touch her. Taking the stairs two at a time, Lydia rushed into her bedchamber and slammed the door shut behind her. She leaned against the door and slid to the ground, wrapping her arms around her knees.

Would she never be free of the Whitings? That question haunted her as Lydia thought through the future. It seemed such a bleak thing, unraveling before her in a never-ending stretch of misery. Even away from their control, Lydia heard all those disdainful words and felt their disgusted gazes on her. The unwanted wife. The disappointing daughter-in-law. The young lady unfit to be a Whiting.

Useless.

A knock sounded at the door, and Mary called out to her. Lydia stilled and closed her eyes until her sister's footsteps retreated.

Getting to her feet, Lydia moved to the bedside table and snatched Mr. Marks' handkerchief. She slumped onto the bed, clutching the bit of linen to her chest, and allowed the ghost of him to steal her away to happier thoughts where Lydia could paint a happier version of herself. One as Mrs. Owen Marks. One where Isabella was his daughter, beloved by her papa and encircled by their love. How different her world would be if she'd been brave all those years ago and seized what she'd wanted. A perfect life where there was no need for tears, except those born from joy.

Her heart whispered that perhaps that fantasy could still be hers, but every instinct shuddered against that. Marriage would be different with Mr. Marks, but the thought of binding herself to anyone had her stomach twisting and churning until she was afraid she would make a mess on the floor. Lydia breathed in and out, but there was no calming the roiling revulsion. All she could do was embrace it as the tears fell.

Chapter 7

The world continued to spin along its heavenly axis, though Lydia wished it might stop for a moment. Not indefinitely, just long enough for her to gather herself. Lydia felt certain that a few weeks hidden away from the troubles and heartaches of this earthly plane would do her wonders. A chance to breathe. To clear her thoughts. To rest.

When Lydia had boarded that stagecoach four weeks ago, she'd believed distance from those who despised her and the freedom to choose her future was all she needed; Greater Edgerton would be her solace and put her life to rights again. Yet as Lydia stared at her bedchamber door, she felt as much a prisoner here as in Sir Duncan's household. Not that Mary or Ambrose held the blame for it, but the reality of her situation was vastly different from that of her dreams, and Lydia did not wish to face it.

But it had been far too many hours since she'd seen Isabella.

Lydia took a breath, squaring her shoulders as she glared at the wood. Her hand paused on the door handle, but she squeezed her eyes shut and stepped into the hallway. Wandering through the townhouse, Lydia sought the place where her family was bound to be, and sounds of their laughter and squeals drew her in. She opened the parlor door and found Ambrose in his shirtsleeves, lying on the floor. Children swarmed about him, leaping onto him while his wife assisted Vincent and Isabella into the fray.

Mary looked up and paused, though no one else noticed amidst the chaos. Lydia gave her sister a faint smile but skirted the edge of the gathering and sat on the far side of the parlor where she could watch while out of the way. Mary murmured something to Ambrose and joined Lydia on the sofa, leaving the children in his care.

"We missed you at church today," said Mary.

"I did not feel up to it. I hope Isabella was not a handful."

Mary smiled and glanced at her niece. "She is a darling, and it is no burden to help you. I only wish I could do more."

Those words wrapped around Lydia's heart, and the strain of the past day eased a touch; she felt like embracing Mary or holding her hand or showing some sign of her gratitude for all that she and Ambrose had done, but nothing felt right.

"Dearest, I am concerned about you," said Mary, her voice dropping low as she gazed at Lydia. "Please speak to me."

When Lydia did not reply, Mary sighed and shook her head. "I apologize for being so frank, but I keep hoping to see some hint of the Lydia I knew. When you arrived, I was overjoyed, but you spend more of your time in your room than with us, and when you do come out, you are listless or fretful. I've held my tongue, hoping you would speak to me, but still you remain silent, and I cannot stand by and watch you suffer alone any longer. I miss my sister."

Lydia's chin trembled, her eyes filling with tears as Mary took her by the hand.

"Please, tell me what I can do," she whispered.

Squeezing Mary's hand, Lydia gave a tremulous smile. "You are doing it."

"But surely there is something more," said Mary with a furrowed brow and a shake of her head. "I don't think you've left the house since you arrived."

Lydia's insides constricted at that, shrinking inwards as though trying to flee. Her bedchamber called to her like the sirens of mythology, but Lydia squeezed her eyes shut and swallowed to release the tension strangling her throat.

"I cannot stand all those people watching me, Mary," she whispered. "It is as though a sign hangs around my neck saying, 'Lady Whiting, Widow of Sir Duncan, Baronet,' and then they look at me and are disappointed with what they find. I am forever doing something wrong, and I can never measure up to their expectations."

Mary's jaw slackened, though her gaze grew more intense, clinging to every word her sister spoke. "What have they done to you, dearest?"

Tugging at her hand, Lydia tried to free herself while her gaze fell to her lap, but Mary did not relinquish her hold.

"And now, I've disappointed you as well…"

"Never!" Mary leaned close, her eyes so full of her aching heart that Lydia felt enveloped in her sister's love and concern. "The Lydia I knew was a bright spark of a girl who adored people. I was always in awe of your confidence and strength, and it breaks my heart to see that the Whitings' influence has transformed you into a frightened, doubting mouse."

Mary sighed and shook her head. "They've turned you into what I once was. I only wish I had known what they were doing to you. I might've done something—"

But Lydia squeezed her sister's hand with her own shake of the head. "There was nothing for you to do. And now, you're doing so much for Isabella and me." With a wince, Lydia dropped her head. "I know that something is broken inside me, but I do not know how to fix it."

Arms came around her, and Lydia burrowed into her sister's hold, reveling in the touch she so rarely received. Even if they'd grown to love her, the Whitings were never demonstrative, and her parents used affection as a manipulation. The Ashbrooks were the only ones who showed any sort of true and unrestrained love.

When Mary released her, both ladies were dabbing at their eyes, and Lydia's elder sister gave a curt nod of her head and squared her shoulders.

"I think the first step would be for you to accompany me on a walk through town. Just a simple stroll along the streets to get out of the house and into the air."

As much as her heart burned with shame, Lydia could not release her hold on her sister's hand. What sort of weak-willed fool would have such fear over a simple outing? And yet Lydia felt her muscles stiffen as though unwilling to allow her to move from that spot. Taking in a deep breath, she forced her head to nod.

...

Shifting the satchel on his shoulder, Robert smiled at Nell, who skipped along at his side. Bright blue stretched above them, unfettered and clear as they meandered along the street. There was no work to be done, no emergencies to address. Simply an afternoon free for him and his daughter to enjoy.

They passed the same corner as before, and Robert led her towards the vendors and a woman with a particularly fine array of strawberries, which called out to him with their vibrant red and sweet scent, promising juicy deliciousness. A few coins lighter, Robert rolled down the edges of his bag and offered the treat to his daughter.

Nell gazed upon the berries with a covetous eye, fairly drooling over their perfection, but she paused with her hand hovering over the pile, her brows pulling together. Robert moved the temptation closer, but Nell frowned and dropped her hand as she turned to continue on their way. With a sigh, Robert tucked the package in his satchel and took her hand once more.

"Have I ever told you about how much your mother loved to dance?" he asked, hoping that perhaps Prudence had correctly identified the source of Nell's unease of late.

His dear little girl beamed and nodded. "You never cared to stand up with anyone before her, but Mama was so perfect and elegant that you were entranced the moment you saw her."

Robert chuckled. "It seemed like everything she did was perfection, and I was forever in awe of her abilities. All Eleanor had to do was to set her mind to something, and she accomplished it."

Nell squeezed his hand and looked out towards the street as they moved along the pavement. She certainly seemed merrier at present, though she still refused the strawberry offering. Robert scoured his thoughts for new things to tell her.

"Have I told you the story of our courtship?"

With brows raised, Nell turned her gaze to him—those light eyes that were so like her mother's. There was such curiosity there that Robert knew he'd picked the right story. In truth, it was one he hadn't intended to tell her (as it did not reflect well on Eleanor's parents), but perhaps there was a way to spin the tale to keep Nell from viewing her grandparents in an unfavorable light.

"I moved to Greater Edgerton when I was a young man of twenty years. I had just finished my clerkship and was ready to begin my life as a solicitor."

Nell swung their joined hands between them, her gaze falling to the pavement as they meandered through the city, but her attention was fixed on his words.

"Sometime later, I decided it was time to venture into local society and attended a ball thrown by a client. I hadn't expected it to be anything out of the ordinary, but then I saw *an angel*," he said in a dramatic tone. With a slanted smile, Robert glanced at Nell. "She was surrounded by gentlemen all vying to catch her eye, but we saw each other from across the room and in that instant, I knew I had found my one true love."

"Really? In just one look?" she asked, fairly bouncing on her toes.

"Just one," he replied with a firm nod. "I spent a good hour gathering my courage, and when I finally approached her, she scolded me for taking so long."

Nell giggled.

"We spent most of the evening in each other's company, and the next day I called on her." Robert grimaced. "But her parents were not happy I did."

With a gape, she asked, "They weren't?"

Robert sorted through his words, trying to find the proper ones. Perhaps they did not convey the whole truth, but they were close enough to it.

"I was very young with hardly a penny to my name, and I came from a poor upbringing. I hadn't yet proved myself to be a steady, good sort of man. They had reason to be a little concerned." Robert nearly laughed at the fairy tale, but there was no helping it. His upbringing was more than poor, and the Humphreys had been more than a little concerned, but that was not the sort of story to be shared with his daughter.

"I needed time to establish myself, find us a home, and prove myself. So, we had to wait many years before we could marry," he said with a heavy sigh. "Many, many years. And all that time, I was so worried that some other fellow would win over Eleanor."

"But no one did."

"No, they did not," he said with a smile. "And that is what I loved most about your mother. She was the most loyal person I ever knew. Eleanor knew her heart, and she remained true to it and me, even though it took so very long before we could marry. She never wavered."

Nell bit the corner of her lips and slanted a look at her father. "Do you think I am like her?"

Pulling her to a stop, Robert crouched down before her. "You are the very image of her, Nell. You have her eyes and smile, and every day some new aspect of you that reminds me of her."

With brows pinched together and eyes filled with trepidation, she asked, "Truly?"

When Eleanor had announced their forthcoming joy all those years ago, Robert hadn't understood what fatherhood meant; he'd celebrated at the prospect, but his own experience with parents had left him ignorant of the simple but powerful joy that comes from that relationship. Though Robert did not care to see Nell's worries and fears on display, her tone was filled with all the sweetness and innocence of her young heart, as though his answer meant everything to her. It flooded his heart with warmth, and Robert smiled. His dear Nell.

"I would never lie to you," he said, chucking her under the chin. "You are so alike that I cannot miss my Eleanor with you around."

Light filled Nell's eyes, and she bounced on her toes before throwing her arms around Robert's neck. But she pulled back with equal speed and tugged at his hand, forcing them down the street. With a bright rapidity, Nell babbled about her young life, and Robert nodded and smiled, interjecting with the occasional question.

The pair reached the end of the street, and the buildings gave way to the riverbank that served as the boundary between the Olde and the New. From this angle, the mills, factories, and warehouses of Olde Towne looked like jagged river rocks edging River Dennick, the buildings pushing up to the very edge of the water. There was a beauty to it in its own right, even if most preferred the quaint rural look of New Towne.

The two sides of Greater Edgerton looked pasted together. And though it gave the town a disjointed appearance, Robert couldn't say it was bad, either. Too many villages were swallowed up, losing their country identity among the all-too-necessary progress the last few decades had wrought, yet Greater Edgerton managed to dance between the present and past.

"Papa!" Nell lurched forward, pointing at the river and dragging him after her as she rushed forward. But then she abandoned him entirely, sprinting after the ducks who were enjoying a leisurely afternoon at the water's edge.

Chapter 8

Surely a grown woman ought not to celebrate the meager accomplishment of having ventured out of doors four times in the past sennight. And surely she ought not to feel doubly thrilled that today marked the first time she'd done so without her sister accompanying her. Such paltry milestones were hardly worth lauding, and the elation Lydia felt only testified to her previous cowardice. And with Dottie skipping alongside her, Lydia reminded herself that she still had not managed a solitary foray into Greater Edgerton, but she tried to block out the insidious doubts and disappointment and focus on the pride she felt at having taken this step. Minor though this victory may be, there had been far too few of them of late for Lydia to turn it aside.

The day was far too glorious to focus on the pervasive gloom that poisoned so much of her life.

When she'd arrived in Greater Edgerton, Lydia had been surprised to find herself surrounded by large, unyielding buildings covered in soot and the thrum of machinery. Having never visited an industrial town before, Lydia's expectations had been more aligned with the quaint villages that populated the countryside. And now that she'd explored her new home more, Lydia was pleased to find that picturesque image wasn't wholly wrong.

Crossing the bridge that spanned the River Dennick was like crossing into another town. Buildings gave way to the water, and on the other side, trees and shrubs edged the dark water that rushed on by. Ducks waddled along the grassy riverbank, jumping in and out of the water at their leisure; the current was gentle here, and the creatures had congregated to sun themselves and hunt for luncheon. But their peace was short-lived as a torrent, in the shape of a child, blew through their ranks. They trumpeted their surprise, their wings flapping frantically as they fought to clear themselves from her path. But that only encouraged her to zig and zag with a great laugh.

"Nell!" Dottie tugged at Lydia's hand and waved with the other, and the whirlwind turned away from her prey and sped towards the pair of them.

Greeting each other with all the enthusiasm of their young years, the girls began jabbering about all that had happened since their last chat. The mysterious Nell looked to be around Dottie's age, though Lydia would guess the child was a year or so older than her niece.

Dottie tugged on Lydia's hand once more, nodding towards her as she grinned at her friend. "Can Nell join our lessons, too?"

Blinking, Lydia tried to understand Dottie's question, but the child clarified before her aunt had to puzzle it out on her own.

"The dancing lessons you said you were going to give me," said Dottie, fairly bouncing on her toes. "Nell wants to learn, too!"

The other girl hopped in place, her eyes wide as she nodded frantically. "Please!"

Lydia's brows drew together as her stomach gave a little flip; not as strong as it was wont to do, but still, an unhappy sort of twist. Not that she minded the addition of another pupil, but there was a great deal of difference between playing with her niece in the privacy of her home and giving instruction to a stranger.

"Papa!" Nell turned and waved at a gentleman standing at the edge of the greenery, and Lydia held onto her composed smile for a good second—before she recognized the fellow coming closer. Her stomach gave a stronger lurch than before.

There was such a stern look in Mr. Bradshaw's dark eyes and hardness to the lines of his face that made Lydia feel as though she was addressing her papa. Not that the fellow was of such advanced years (from their conversation, she gathered he was about Mary and Ambrose's age), but he had the look of someone far older.

Mr. Bradshaw's physique was broad and imposing, which was added to by the craggy furrows on his brow and around his eyes, which spoke of a man who found little joy in the world. Mr. Bradshaw was certainly not someone keen on seeing his daughter flying, nor would he have any inclination to allow her to join in Dottie's pseudo-lessons. No doubt the girl had a governess to educate her on all the proper refinements befitting a lady.

When he approached, Mr. Bradshaw met Lydia's gaze with the same dismissal he'd bestowed the last time they'd spoken, but he gave her a bow. "Lady Whiting."

"Mr. Bradshaw."

But Nell had no interest in such niceties, for she immediately began bouncing. "Dottie's aunt is giving her dance lessons, and I've been invited to join them."

Lydia's breath caught as she stared at Mr. Bradshaw, praying that whatever chiding remarks or disapproval he bestowed would be gentle. Nell did not deserve a sharp rebuke; she was only a child, unable to control her enthusiasm. There was little else Lydia could do but hope and pray that all would be well and the child's heart would not be bruised.

Mr. Bradshaw looked down at his daughter, that flat, polite look shifting into a wide smile. The angry furrows at his eyes crinkled, and Lydia swore she even saw something of a dimple emerge on his right cheek. She had never imagined him capable of showing any warmth, let alone this burst of emotion.

"Is that so?" he asked.

With a frantic nod, Nell beamed. "Then I can learn to dance just like Mama."

"And I am certain you will be as light on your feet as she was." Mr. Bradshaw chucked his daughter under the chin. His dark eyes rose to meet Lydia's, a question filling them, and Lydia realized she was staring at the fellow and quickly turned her gaze away from him.

"Might I take lessons, too?" asked Nell.

"We can discuss it later, poppet." Mr. Bradshaw slanted another look in Lydia's direction, which she pretended to ignore, choosing to stare off at the ducks bobbing along the river.

That shaking, quaking, frightened little girl she'd become whispered that she ought to return home to the safety of the known, but Lydia forced herself to remain calm. A deep breath allowed her to release the tension in her shoulders. There was no need to flee.

"Look." Dottie pointed a hand towards the river's edge, drawing the others' attention to the ducks, who were waddling back onto the grass, having grown bolder since their tormentor had disappeared.

Nell turned to her father. "Can I have the bread, Papa?"

Lifting back the flap of his satchel, he handed her a large chunk wrapped in a bit of linen. "They deserve a treat after your behavior."

The girl took the bundle and said to Dottie, "We can use it to lure them closer."

And the pair skittered off towards their quarry, leaving Lydia and Mr. Bradshaw alone. She shifted from foot to foot, watching the girls as they broke off chunks of bread and threw them at the ducks as though they were projectiles rather than offerings. Then Lydia glanced at Mr. Bradshaw and wondered what to do.

As they were both awaiting the girls, they had no other

place to be. They were hardly acquaintances, and Lydia couldn't claim a desire to deepen that relationship, but to stand apart from him felt like a snub. As much as Lydia wished for the distance, she didn't want to be cruel. After all, though he was stern and aloof, Mr. Bradshaw had gone to the trouble of warning her of her mother-in-law's continued interference.

If only he would walk away. Then Lydia would gain the solitude she desired without the added guilt.

The strictures the upper class placed on themselves were numerous and ridiculous, and Robert did not subscribe to many of their beliefs (most of which seemed only to exist as a way for them to place themselves apart from the lower orders), but that did not mean he was devoid of all manners. Treating others with decency and honor did not belong exclusively to the gentry. And many of that exalted class could use a lesson or two from those they deemed "beneath" them.

So, watching Lady Whiting standing there like a frightened sparrow, searching for some escape while unable to move, pricked Robert's conscience, demanding he do something to ease her nerves—though how to go about it when she possessed such a weak constitution was beyond him. The lady shifted again, straightening the shawl draped across her forearms. She looked close to fainting.

For a brief moment, he considered simply leaving her there, but to move away simply to avoid speaking with her was hardly the right thing to do.

"The weather is fine today," he said, tucking his hands behind him as he cast his gaze to the sky. Perhaps giving her an insipid but familiar subject would do the trick. But the lady merely nodded, and Robert held back a sigh. If she would not rise to such delicate subjects, he might as well choose something to his taste.

Robert kept his eyes turned to the girls. The young Miss Ashbrook had diverted Nell's attention from tormenting the poor creatures to properly feeding them, and the girls laughed as one bold duck came within touching distance, snapping bits of bread from their hands.

"Careful with your fingers, Nell," he called. Then, turning his attention back to Lady Whiting, he added, "I have made some progress in securing your bequest."

She straightened, meeting his gaze fully for perhaps the first time. They were a light blue with gray undertones that reminded him of the ocean on a stormy day. Rather fitting, as their mistress seemed constantly fretful.

"My bequest?" she asked.

Robert refrained from arching his brows, though the instinct struck. Luckily, he was used to hiding such emotions when dealing with difficult clientele.

"We discussed it last week when I came by the Ashbrooks' home." But the confusion did not clear from her gaze, so Robert added, "Your sister spoke to me about the money your husband left you and asked me to contact Mr. Pendergrass concerning it."

Though Robert had known prosperity for some time now, the time was not so distant that he'd forgotten the power of one hundred and fifty pounds. To his parents, it was a fortune (one his father would have gladly drunk away). To the young man who had dreamt of securing Eleanor Humphreys as his bride, it would've been a godsend. And there were many more who would view the news of such a bequest with rejoicing. No doubt, the widow of Sir Duncan Whiting, Baronet, viewed it as a pittance.

In her mourning clothes, Lady Whiting looked like an angry mark on the bright world around her. But at that moment, her expression shifted. Those stormy eyes cleared, lighting up as though the sun was finally shining on her. Her lips stretched into a smile, and the dark, sad lady transformed, leaving her looking far younger than before.

"That is wonderful news, Mr. Bradshaw. The best I've heard in some time." Lady Whiting's expression shifted, her lips pinching and her brow furrowing as she cast her gaze to the water. Though it was a troubled expression, it was a far cry from that which she previously displayed, for it held a spark of life. As though the lady he'd met before was a soulless shadow of the woman now before him.

The difference was quite startling, and it forced Robert to consider the entirety of who she was and to see that which he'd chosen to ignore. Lady Whiting was not a lady incapable of warmth, so it was clear that life and not nature had molded her into that listless creature. And Robert was all too familiar with such things.

His mother had never smiled. Perhaps she had at one point, though Robert could not recall ever seeing it. His elder sisters had been merry girls. They did not laugh and smile as often as Nell or his nieces, but his sisters' natural dispositions had been sunny once upon a time. Then they'd fallen prey to men all too like their father, and they shifted and changed, that light in their eyes dimming with each year until they looked all too like their mother. Women without hope. Simply existing until the toil and heartache of life finally ended.

"Then I am glad to have given you the news, Lady Whiting." And for the first time, Robert was happy Mr. Pendergrass had approached him.

The lady did not flinch, but there was a tightness to her eyes and lips that spoke of silent pain, and Robert was saddened to see it.

"Have you considered what to do with the funds?" Robert asked, hoping that a change in subject might return Lady Whiting to her previous spirits.

"I would like to give them to my sister, but I fear she won't accept them."

Nell and Dottie ran along the riverbank, putting some distance between them and their caregivers, so Robert turned in that direction, motioning for the lady to join him as they strolled after the pair.

"They have less need of it than you," he said.

Lady Whiting waved a dismissive hand. "I do not know what the future holds for me and my daughter, but they've done so much for me without asking for a thing in return. I do not know much concerning industry and finances, Mr. Bradshaw, but even I am not ignorant of the economic crisis that struck last year and its far-reaching effects throughout the country."

Robert nodded. "Several banks in the area have closed, and many businesses have been impacted, but I do not think Newland Mills is one of them."

"Perhaps not, but the funds my husband left me are not enough for me to be wholly independent, so why shouldn't it go to those who are caring for me and my daughter?"

"That is an admirable sentiment."

Lady Whiting frowned. "It is only what ought to be done."

Slanting her a smile, Robert shook his head. "Not everyone would see it that way—including the Ashbrooks. A widow with a daughter ought to keep whatever money she can find."

Especially when one was left such meager funds.

Sighing inwardly, Robert chastised himself for having been far more preoccupied with the inconvenience Mr. Pendergrass had presented than with opening his eyes to Lady Whiting's plight. He had ignored so many signs simply because he was irritated at the fellow's condescension and had assumed the lady in question was the same.

But what sort of man left his wife and child with nothing? From what Robert could surmise, Sir Duncan was not destitute, yet he'd consigned them to living off the mercy of others. And what more did it say that she fled the security of his estate? If Lady Whiting's mother-in-law was still so interested in her and the child that she sent a solicitor to spy on them, surely it indicated that the two were welcome to remain.

Robert knew what sort of man treated his wife so shabbily, and it was no wonder Lady Whiting looked like a startled rabbit in hunting season.

Chapter 9

Money. Lydia had never believed herself a greedy soul, but the thought of possessing any funds made her long to bury her face in the banknotes. Though part of her wanted to run to the shops and buy up all the little sweets and treats she wished to give Isabella, Lydia was filled with a lightness of heart at the thought of compensating her dear sister and brother-in-law for all the expense they'd taken on with the mother and child. Mary and Ambrose never complained. If anything, they were as likely to ply Isabella with gifts as their own children, and Lydia wished for once to give them something in return.

But it would not be an easy thing, and Lydia was grateful to have someone with whom to discuss it. Finances may not be Mr. Bradshaw's expertise, but he had a sharp mind, and as they wandered after the girls, they discussed the options before her.

In truth, Lydia was astonished to be having any sort of conversation with the intractable Mr. Bradshaw, who looked more comfortable scowling at the world around him. But here he walked alongside her, calling out the occasional warning or encouragement to his daughter while obliging a silly young widow on the matter of one hundred and fifty pounds. Likely, the fellow thought it strange to care so much about such a small sum, but it was far more than she'd had this morning.

Mr. Bradshaw smiled at something, and Lydia was astonished to see how warm it made him seem. There was a hardness to his features, as though life had weathered him more than others his age, but as they walked along, he relaxed, seeming more at ease and kindly than before, which allowed Lydia's nerves to ease. Still, he maintained that forceful aura about him. There was no ridding himself of the strength that seemed a very part of his soul, but it almost felt comforting. Protective.

Lydia shook her head at herself. Mr. Bradshaw's previous actions had proven him to be a considerate man. Few would have bothered to warn her about Mr. Pendergrass, and even fewer would have spent the amount of time he had discussing the issue at length with Mary and Ambrose. Lydia wished she recalled more of the conversation, but even now, it was a foggy jumble of emotions, driven by the fear of having her past life intrude into Mary's home.

And he was continuing to be of assistance. Lydia wondered if Ambrose had spoken to Mr. Bradshaw about payment for his assistance. Something in what he said made her think he had not. Did that mean he was doing so out of the goodness of his heart? Or was he simply wishing to charge them all the more after he secured the bequest? If Sir Duncan were standing beside her, Lydia would know the answer, but for all of Mr. Bradshaw's apparent hardness of character, the fellow did not seem the conniving sort.

No man who seemed so genuinely interested in his child could be as cold as Mr. Bradshaw appeared to be at times. Lydia couldn't think of a gentleman in her acquaintance who would even feign the emotion; being engaged with one's children hardly aligned with the general ennui the upper class cultivated and the middle class mimicked.

And it was then that Lydia realized precisely what had altered to make her feel more at ease. Mr. Bradshaw reminded her of Ambrose. Not that he shared her brother-in-law's affable air, but Lydia still marveled at how much time and energy Ambrose expended on his children. At home, her brother-in-law was as likely to be playing with them as he was to be tinkering with his beloved machinery.

"As I did not get the opportunity to do so before, I would like to offer my apology for distressing you the other day," he said.

Lydia blinked at Mr. Bradshaw for a silent moment as her distracted thoughts sought to catch the words and comprehend them. Turning her gaze to Dottie, Lydia watched her niece as the girls laughed at the ducks' antics.

"You were only the messenger, Mr. Bradshaw. I fear I am always distressed when the subject of my late husband's family is broached. And I ought to seize the opportunity—as I did not before—to express my gratitude that you went to the trouble of telling us Mr. Pendergrass is lurking about."

"From what I've heard, he has returned to Kent. He did hire a solicitor by the name of Peterson to do what I would not—"

Lydia straightened, her eyes swinging to Mr. Bradshaw, who held up a staying hand.

"Don't fret," he said with a wry smile. "All in all, it is a fine development. Mr. Peterson is the expensive, useless sort of solicitor who will send your husband's family massive bills without doing anything of value. He has no intention of stirring himself beyond sending vague, uninteresting reports. And as you seem keen to maintain a quiet life, I do not foresee Mr. Pendergrass causing you any more trouble."

Oh, it was a fine day for a walk, and it was made all the finer by Mr. Bradshaw. In a few minutes, he'd given her peace from the stresses of Mr. Pendergrass and the hope of funds soon to be in her barren coin purse.

"Thank you, Mr. Bradshaw," said Lydia, though those little words could not convey the relief she felt at his pronouncement. It was not comforting to know that someone was reporting her behavior to the Whitings (however inept their spy may be), but the weight of the past sennight lifted, leaving her rather giddy.

Mr. Bradshaw merely nodded at her expression of gratitude, as though the aid he'd rendered was of no significance, and he tucked his hands behind him, watching the girls scamper and play. Nell picked up a stick and swiped at tufts of grass while Dottie gathered a few wildflowers that were little more than weeds.

"I wish there was more I could do," he said. "A home ought to be a place of safety, but for far too many, it is a place of violence, and I know all too well how difficult it is to free yourself of it."

Lydia turned her gaze to her companion, her sympathetic heart stirring at that. Though Mr. Bradshaw appeared unaffected, Lydia had an inkling that he felt his words keenly, though she could not say if it was the confession itself or his memories attached to it. She longed to ask him more, to understand a little better the enigmatic man who had come to her aid on multiple occasions, all without fanfare or being acquainted with the lady he was aiding. But as much as that curiosity begged her to pry, Lydia kept her own counsel. If Mr. Bradshaw wished to speak more on the subject, she had no doubt he would.

Turning back to the conversation, Lydia said, "Sometimes the difficulty comes from recognizing the need to free yourself. Not all dangers present themselves clearly."

"A striking fist sends a clear message."

Lydia considered that and then shook her head as they wandered towards the girls. "Perhaps, but not all dangers are of a physical nature. My husband never raised a hand to me or my daughter, but he injured us all the same."

Pausing, Mr. Bradshaw turned to look at her. "Your husband wasn't a violent man?"

There was something in his gaze that had Lydia's eyes falling to the ground. "Not with his fists, but words can be weapons, too."

"As a lad, I would've welcomed a father who only used those 'weapons.' Yes, they can bruise and hurt, but only if the listener allows it. Words have little power on their own."

Lydia pressed a hand to her stomach as the light around her dimmed. She tried to swallow, but her throat was decidedly against it, refusing to allow anything past the knot that had formed there. Her shoulders rounded, and her heart shuddered, retreating in that old, far too familiar manner it had learned over her years as Lady Whiting.

Mr. Bradshaw turned away, continuing down the path with a grim dismissal that felt like a slap, and she heard the unspoken sentiments lying beneath the words he'd spoken: a stronger person would not be so easily undone. Useless, weak creature that she was, Lydia wanted to shrug off the sting of his disapproval but couldn't. It carried the memory of her husband bemoaning their marriage and his mother's never-ending harping. A constant disappointment and a good-for-nothing woman.

Her bedchamber called out to her, telling her to return to that safety, and to Lydia's shame, she turned her feet towards home. Her cheeks were flushed from the summer heat, and she was grateful that it masked the mortification spreading across her skin. Truly, she ought to be stronger. Stand firmer. Not be undone by one man's disapproval. But his voice joined with all the rest that pointed to her flaws and shortcomings.

Yet again, Lydia had been measured and found wanting.

But even as her cowardly heart thought to escape, Mary's spirit held her in place, begging her to remain strong. It was a buoy in the storm, giving her something to cling to as the waves battered her. Even if she was not strong enough at present, Lydia could borrow Mary's strength. That was enough for now.

With a cool shoulder, Lydia put distance between them. What had seemed indecorous moments before had become a necessity. Besides, she had no reason to fret about whether or not it made him uncomfortable, for Lydia did not spare him another glance to see if he even noticed.

Chapter 10

The older part of Greater Edgerton was by no means a beautiful development. It was about functionality and commerce, and no space had been wasted as the men of business expanded and built their empires. Beauty was left to the buildings of New Towne, and yet Lydia couldn't help but feel that even this dingier, plain portion of town was lovely to behold.

Though the Whiting estate in Hexford boasted fine prospects and the landscapes around her childhood home in Bristow were equally fine, Lydia could not help but feel Greater Edgerton was far superior. True, the air was not as sweet, and the buildings carried a fine layer of soot from the factories and mills. And there was not much landscape to be had. But there was a joy to the town; a vibrant, happy sort of feeling hung on the breeze, and Lydia adored it.

In the fortnight since she'd taken that first step out of Newland Place, Lydia had explored much of Greater Edgerton, even growing so bold as to do so without dragging poor Dottie or Mary along with her. She wished she could bring Isabella, but the child was too heavy to carry such a long distance and not strong enough to walk it on her own.

Perhaps she ought to speak to Mary about a picnic for the children. They could take the carriage and show Isabella a bit more of her new home. The idea seized Lydia, and a spark of something akin to excitement lightened her heart; it seemed such a silly, little thing, but Lydia's feet nearly skipped along as she wove through the streets.

Lydia opened the door and was met by quite the cacophony, as though an entire regiment of rowdy soldiers had descended upon the townhouse. But when she arrived in the parlor, she found Mary surrounded by something far more intimidating: the children had multiplied.

The parlor had been cleared of everything but the furniture, and Mary sat with the youngest horde, calling out warnings and instructions to the boys whose battalions of soldiers were growing into a frenzy; Lydia was fairly certain men on the battlefield did not fly, but more than a few found themselves flung through the air like cannonballs. A flash of skirts and hair ribbons flew past Lydia as a gaggle of girls leapt onto the sofa, while Mary warned them not to do that precise thing.

"Mary?"

Her sister looked over, her shoulders falling in relief. "Thank goodness. I fear I've made a terrible mistake."

Before Lydia could ask what it was, Mary heaved a sigh.

"I had intended to take the children to visit my friend, Prudence, but when I arrived, I found her in such a sorry state." Mary cast a look at listening ears and motioned for Lydia to draw closer. "The poor lady is worn to the bone. Her husband, Parker, has hardly been home for the last few days as he's been occupied with his patients, and little Hugo has been ill. Nothing serious, but he has been fractious, so she's hardly slept a wink and is in desperate need of some rest."

Lydia cast a glance at the uproar and knew the rest. "And so, you offered to take her children for a few hours."

Nodding, Mary grimaced. "And lent her Nurse Nunn to see to Hugo and assist with all the laundry to be done. The poor babe has made quite the mess, and their maid is struggling to stay atop it all."

With a chuckle, Lydia slanted a look at Mary. "I count nine children."

Mary's eyes widened, and she sighed. "I've managed it before, and they usually play well with each other, but they are in rare form today. Muriel is upsetting Ernest, who screams at her, which sets off Vincent and Isabella. Lucas shrieks if anyone so much as looks at his soldiers without his permission. And the girls..."

She motioned at the four who continued to jump on the sofa whenever Mary's attention wavered. At that moment, the girls caught sight of Lydia, and a familiar face came speeding over.

"Are you going to teach us to dance?" asked Nell, fairly dancing on her toes already.

"Now, I may be a bit slow at times, but I do not recall you being a Humphreys," said Lydia with an arched brow.

Nell's nose wrinkled, and she shook her head. "They are my cousins. I stay with Aunt Prudence during the day."

At that, both of Lydia's brows rose, and she slid her gaze to Mary. Though she could not claim a grand understanding of Mr. Bradshaw, he seemed well-positioned enough to afford a governess or nursemaid for his daughter, and yet he added to his sister-in-law's already great burden? Mary shrugged with a look that women had shared throughout the ages since the first time a man had done something so utterly senseless.

"Can we dance?" asked Nell as the other girls echoed her question.

Placing her hands on her hips, Lydia pretended to consider it. "I suppose I might be convinced to do so. But only if you are very obedient."

That was met with grins and nods, though Lydia knew such a promise was far too fleeting.

"That includes not leaping onto the sofa," she added.

Dottie's cheeks pinked, but the girls did as bidden. Lydia directed them to pick up the toys, and as much of the space had been already cleared, it was an easy thing to turn the parlor into a makeshift ballroom. Relocating Lucas and Ernest was a more difficult endeavor, but before long she had Dottie and Nell moving across the room with the basic traveling and setting steps. Though little Esther and Sadie tripped through the movements, they followed the older girls as they *chasséd* up and down the parlor while Mary occupied those unable or unwilling to join.

Dottie and Nell gobbled up every instruction, mimicking the steps with mixed results and utter joy. They had not the skill or numbers to form a proper dance, but Lydia beamed as the darlings threw themselves into the pleasure of it.

Humming a tune, Lydia led them into a round that was far more exuberant than organized, and the girls laughed and leapt about. Isabella toddled to her mama, and Lydia scooped her up, drawing her into their haphazard line. She could not recall the last time she felt so free, but that was the power of dance. No matter how miserable or lonely her life, when thrown into a reel or cotillion the world faded until her worries seemed naught but a distant trouble.

"I cannot wait to attend a ball," said Dottie as they were forced to catch their breath.

Nell sighed and dropped onto the sofa beside her friend as the other little misses wandered away. "My parents fell in love while dancing."

"It is easy to have one's heart stirred in such moments," said Lydia, nestling Isabella on her lap as she joined the girls.

"Is that how you fell in love with your husband?" asked Nell.

Lydia's smile tightened, but she shook away her shudder. Though Mary glanced at them with a concerned look, Lydia ignored the innocent mistake and shook her head.

"No, but I did fall in love with a handsome young man while dancing," she said with a wistful sigh.

"You did?" Nell sounded far too excited about the prospect, but it was Mary's startled expression that drew Lydia's attention.

"Who?" asked Mary, and Lydia dropped her gaze to Isabella, lifting the child to balance on her mama's knees.

"Mr. Owen Marks," she said in a dramatic tone, leaning close to Nell and Dottie with a sparkle in her eye. "He was my dancing instructor."

Nell sighed, dropping back against the sofa as though it were the most romantic thing her young heart could hope for.

"Don't fill your head with fantastical notions, little Miss Bradshaw," said Lydia. "You are far too young to be dreaming of love."

Nell shook her head. "But it sounds so delightful."

"Why didn't you marry him?" asked Dottie.

Lydia paused, her gaze drifting back to Mary, and she saw the understanding there. When she could think of nothing else to say to the girls, she said, "It was not meant to be."

Leaving the boys to their soldiers, Mary carried Vincent to the sofa, and though it was tight with the four of them, the girls made room for her.

"What was he like?" asked Nell. "Papa says my mama was the most beautiful lady that ever lived."

Lydia turned a smile to the young girl. "As every good husband ought. And my Mr. Marks was a very handsome man with broad shoulders and dark hair. And the most stunning blue eyes I have ever seen."

"And?" prodded Nell.

"And..." Scouring her thoughts, Lydia tried to describe him further, but her image of him had grown fuzzy over the years as time had stripped him away. "He was the finest dancer I've ever seen. So light on his feet and graceful. And he was so very kind to me."

Leaning close, she whispered in a conspiratorial tone, "I told him how much I wanted to taste ices, but my mother could not spare the time. So, while she was calling on a friend, he snuck into our townhouse and spirited me away to spend the afternoon gorging ourselves on them. And Mama was none the wiser."

"That was so kind," said Dottie while Nell gave another dramatic sigh.

"How wonderful," said Mary, though her brows were pulled tight together. "Though I am surprised Mama left you alone. From what I remember, she had your social calendar so filled that you hardly had time to sleep."

There was something in Mary's expression that had Lydia's neck prickling. It wasn't an open challenge, but there was such doubt in her gaze that Lydia felt her incredulity strongly enough. Lydia had relived the memory so many times, but she hadn't shared it aloud before. Now, speaking the words, there was something off-kilter about the details.

With utter clarity, Lydia recalled the sight of him calling to her from below her window, begging her to join him. She remembered creeping through the halls and slipping out the front door before the servants noticed. She could even recall the sweetness of the ices as they melted on her tongue.

And yet their townhouse was not near any shop that sold the treats, and she could not remember getting into a carriage. Of course, Mr. Marks did not own one, and Lydia had never ridden in a hackney—especially with a bachelor. To travel on foot would have taken far too long. And she would've been seen without a chaperone.

No, the memory was real. Lydia was sure of that. True, she did entertain herself by picturing delightful moments that hadn't happened, but she knew the difference between fantasy and reality. Yet the more details she tried to share, the less real the memory felt.

"Are you ready for more dancing?" she asked, hopping to her feet.

Dottie and Nell clapped, and Lydia smiled as she threw herself back into their impromptu dancing lesson.

Chapter 11

Some days stretched on interminably, and the only motivation to soldier on was the promise that the end would come and one would be allowed to return to the pleasures of their home. While such enticements varied from person to person, for Robert Bradshaw, that included an evening by the fire with Nell tucked beside him as they read and munched on toasted cheese and cakes in an entirely gauche manner.

Truth be told, Robert was rather eager to return to the book they'd recently begun. So many of the tales written for children were filled with endless lectures on morality; not that he begrudged a book teaching good lessons, but the virtue presented within those pages was rarely realistic and the sermons as laughable as they were blatant. But this new collection of folk tales was quite engaging.

Yes, the book taught loyalty and kindness, but those morals were wrapped in stories engaging enough to capture his attention, though they were a bit gruesome at times. British folk tales certainly had some gore, but the Germans reveled in it. Robert wondered if Eleanor would like their daughter to hear such things, but Nell adored the tales as much as Robert, and he couldn't bring himself to stop reading.

If she enjoyed this, perhaps she might enjoy Sir Walter Scott or Daniel Defoe. They were a bit mature for her, but with some editing and explanation on his part, she might be ready to expand beyond the juvenile works.

Robert kicked at a crumpled bit of paper that drifted into his path and sent it skittering down the pavement. For all his hopes of returning home posthaste, he was now forced to scour the town for his daughter. With a sigh, he trudged along, following a path he'd taken before. The Ashbrooks' home was so very far out of his way, and Robert only wanted to be in his own. His stomach gurgled in agreement, and he struggled against the rather uncharitable feelings.

Prudence Humphreys had been a godsend. Managing his business and infant after Eleanor's passing had been more than he could handle, and while other newly married ladies would've concerned themselves with establishing their home and their status as Mrs. Parker Humphreys, Prudence had spent her days caring for his babe and instructing her ignorant papa. He should not begrudge her a day to herself.

And he didn't. Not truly. But arriving on her doorstep to find that the mistress of the house was sleeping and Nell was still some distance away had not improved Robert's mood. The day had been long and trying, and he'd thought to be at home by now. Instead, he was trudging along in search of his daughter.

Robert's mood lightened as he turned the final corner and saw the Ashbrooks' door drawing closer. A moment later, he was ushered into the townhouse and found quite the happy sight in the parlor, which had his spirits lifting. The young girls were gathered together, attempting what looked to be a country dance; however, due to their inexperience and exuberance, it was more of a melee.

Though the maid had announced his entrance to Mrs. Ashbrook, the others did not notice. Nell beamed as she turned and hopped, weaving between the others as Lady Whiting clapped the rhythm and sang a wordless melody. Bending down, she scooped a babe from the floor and placed her on her hip as the pair spun, and the child laughed one of those joyous belly laughs that forced everyone within hearing to smile.

Lady Whiting turned and halted at the sight of him. Nodding at her, he smiled (as there was no other reaction to have when finding his daughter amid such happiness), and her wide eyes dropped away from him. Robert felt a flash of impatience at that overreaction; he wasn't a monster or brute or anything else that deserved such a discomforting reaction. However, he refused to give it a second thought. Lady Whiting may be a delicate, frightened little thing, but it would not sour the sudden improvement of his mood.

"Papa!" Nell paused in the dance and rushed to his side.

"Miss Bradshaw." Lady Whiting spoke the name with a hint of admonition, though the smile that accompanied it was warm.

Nell paused and gave him a curtsy that was more deferential than skilled. "Mr. Bradshaw, how lovely to see you today."

The girl's gaze flew back to Lady Whiting, silently seeking approval as the lady gave her another beaming smile and nod. Manners were promptly forgotten as Nell bounced on her toes. Lady Whiting whispered something more to Nell, and the girl nodded, coming forward to introduce Robert to the others in the room with the poise of a grand society lady, even when she stumbled at times. In turn, each of the children gave their curtsies and bows with varying degrees of success. With each, Lady Whiting gave little instructions. Always giving some prod or correction with a heaping portion of praise for the good they did.

This was perhaps the first time Robert understood why the late baronet chose to marry a lady with little dowry or connections, for this Lady Whiting was far different than the unhappy creature he'd met before. Yes, she was still timid and quaking whenever she met his eyes, but when turned to the children, she beamed. Lady Whiting had a natural beauty, but it was that light that drew the eye.

"And this is Isabella Whiting," said Nell, motioning at the child on Lady Whiting's hip.

Robert's brows rose of their own accord, though he supposed he ought not to be surprised. Most aristocratic mothers spent some time with their children, even if it was for a short period, but Lady Whiting looked far more comfortable with her babe in her arms than most of her class.

The child's mama watched him with wary eyes, and Robert forced himself not to roll his eyes. Did she think he would hurt her child?

Taking Isabella's hand in his, Robert bowed over it with all the gentlemanly poise befitting a grand lady and received a toothy grin and giggle in response. Rocking, Isabella pulled at Lady Whiting, who set the child on the floor with another wary look at Robert.

And it was then that he realized why. Lady Whiting kept a steadying hand on her daughter as she took her first few, wobbling steps. Though Isabella was old enough to be mobile, she was unsteady on her feet and walked with a jerking gait. The hem of her gown rose, allowing him to see her limbs as he hadn't before.

Those little feet were twisted up under her so that the poor child had to walk on the sides of them, with her right foot so curled that most of the weight was pressed right onto the ankle. The steps looked so painful that Robert felt sympathetic twinges in his own feet, though Isabella merely grinned as she stumbled along, eventually abandoning walking to crawl quickly across the rug to her cousins.

Robert's gaze rose to meet Lady Whiting's, but there was none of the timid mouse showing there, as the wariness had been replaced with an outright challenge. The lady's chin lifted, her eyes hardening as she met his gaze, a clear warning issued. Robert blinked at that, and he hid the smile that wanted to emerge at the sight of the protective stance; he doubted Lady Whiting would appreciate that expression, but it was hard to feel anything but pleased at the sight of it.

A child in Isabella's position needed a protector. The world did not view such abnormalities with a favorable eye, and too many parents preferred to ignore or despair over them. Lady Whiting seemed hardly capable of taking care of herself, but Robert knew if he said the wrong thing, Lady Whiting would not let it stand.

Good for her. She was finally showing some spirit.

Robert gave her a nod. "She is a sweet child. You must be proud."

Lady Whiting's expression shifted, her brows drawing close together. "She is, and I am."

The girls wandered off to their dolls, leaving the pair staring at each other, and Robert felt like sighing. Without the protective energy thrumming through Lady Whiting, she returned to that quailing little creature who looked at him as though he was a wolf from one of Nell's fairy stories, looking to gobble her up at the slightest provocation.

"I apologize if I offended you the last time we spoke." Robert didn't like to prostrate himself when he wasn't in the wrong, but he found he cared more about Lady Whiting's discomfort. Clearly, she still harbored bruised feelings over their last interlude, and if a simple apology cleared the air, Robert was willing to make the sacrifice.

Lady Whiting blinked at him, her brows pulling closer and closer together as she studied him. "I don't know why you are apologizing. You find me lacking, sir, and according to your philosophy, it is my fault if I am hurt by such an appraisal. After all, it is the listener's fault for being wounded."

Robert held back a sigh. Why were women so sensitive? It was as though they lived to find fault and then nurse the wound for the rest of their days. Thinking through the various manners in which to soothe this flighty lady's bruised pride, Robert realized they had an audience. It was no surprise, as the room was small and there were many people about, but seeing Nell's gaze fixed on them rattled him.

A Tender Soul

It was not as though he'd wished to offend Lady Whiting. His father was a brute who thrashed about without thought of his actions, and Robert had no desire to follow in his footsteps. However, he didn't care to bow and scrape to those who viewed him as their inferior—as most in Lady Whiting's station required. And placating sensitive souls was a futile endeavor; their feelings were forever injured.

But for one reason or another, Nell had taken to Lady Whiting, and his daughter was keenly aware of every word spoken between them.

"I am truly sorry if I offended you, madam. I was simply expressing an opinion based on my own experience. I hadn't meant to hurt you," he said, meaning every word. Though he did not understand why she felt so (nor did he believe it was his responsibility to heal her imagined wounds), Robert didn't like the thought of having upset her. Flighty, nervous, and delicate she may be, but Lady Whiting seemed a kind person, and he was sorry if his words—however unintentional—had caused her pain.

Even if it was her fault for taking offense where none was intended.

Lady Whiting considered him, watching him with an expression that held more than a bit of puzzlement for several long moments before she nodded.

Robert nodded, glad that it was over, and turned to look at Nell. "We ought to return home, poppet."

His daughter's expression crumpled the moment he spoke the words, but before she could give any protest, Lady Whiting spoke.

"Please, might she stay a little longer? The girls are having such a grand time, and the Humphreys will be here for the rest of the evening. I hate the thought of Nell leaving so soon."

Lady Whiting's gaze begged with him to agree, which added to Nell's silent pleas and those of the rest of the girls.

"If you wish, you may stay for supper," said Mrs. Ashbrook. "My husband will be home before long, and we will have a grand indoor picnic with all the children. Adding another two to the party shan't be an inconvenience."

Robert considered the invitation and Nell's wide, begging eyes, and with a silent sigh, he nodded. There was no point in fighting a losing battle.

Nell beamed and turned her attention to the pile of dolls and clothing the other girls had gathered together. More interestingly, Lady Whiting seemed equally pleased, giving Robert a wide, shining smile before she joined the group. His brows rose as she sank to the floor, tucking her feet under her as she joined the girls.

When Robert drew closer, Nell shifted over to make space for him, and he sat beside her. Lady Whiting watched him with wide eyes, though he didn't know why it was any stranger than the widow of a baronet doing so. But any such thoughts were quickly swept away as Nell dropped a doll into his lap. With a few instructions, Dottie and Nell had the group organized into a grand ball with the dolls moving through the various steps the girls had learned that afternoon.

Chapter 12

Some books were written to enlighten the reader's mind, and even works of fiction could educate and broaden one's understanding of the world. Some books were nothing but entertainment, giving the reader an escape from reality. Lydia's current novel fell squarely in the latter category, and she adored it all the more for it. Kidnappings and assassinations were not a part of her life, and those dark times promised light at the end: a joyful reunion of separated lovers and a guarantee of unending happiness. Life was not so kind, and ugliness did not always lead to such beauty. Lydia reveled in every last word, losing herself to the drama on the page that was ofttimes ridiculous but engaging, nonetheless.

The parlor door opened, drawing Lydia's attention before her sister swept inside with a narrowed gaze. Mary stood before her with a hand on her hip as she dropped a handful of coins into Lydia's lap.

"Did you think I wouldn't notice extra coins in my reticule?" she asked with a wry smile.

Scooping up the coins, Lydia held them up to her sister. "When you refuse to take them outright, it forces me to use more covert methods."

Mary shook her head at that and sat on the sofa beside her. "You and Isabella have more need than Ambrose and I."

Lydia sighed and tucked the coins into her pocket as she sorted through other options. This had become a game of late, and Mary was proving far more skilled at discovering the money than Lydia was at hiding it among her sister's funds.

"Isabella and Vincent are still asleep," said Mary with a sigh.

Glancing at the clock on the mantle, Lydia frowned. "They ought to be up by now."

Mary nodded. "But as Nurse Nunn is unlikely to return with the other children for another half an hour, I think we ought to enjoy the quiet while we have it. We'll have to start dressing for tonight soon enough."

For the first time in longer than she could remember, Lydia felt a frisson of excitement run down her spine, settling inside her with a happy flutter. When the invitation for the dinner party had been issued a fortnight ago, Lydia had felt uncertain, which was unsurprising. However, as the days had passed, the thought of an evening engaged in friendly conversation had grown more appealing.

All in all, Lydia was quite proud of herself for it.

"Are you certain you wish to join us tonight?" asked Mary, and when her sister sent her a questioning look, she added, "Your improvement of late is astonishing and makes me so very happy, but I do not wish you to go only to please me."

"In all honesty, Mary, I am looking forward to the evening. It is an intimate gathering that can hardly be called a party. And I have met most of those in attendance. I think it will do me good."

Drawing closer to her sister, Lydia rested her head on Mary's shoulder, as she had many times as a girl. With each day drawing her further from her time in Kent, Lydia felt more like herself, and never did she feel more at home than with her sister. Mary had been as much of a mother as their own. Perhaps more, for their mother had been more preoccupied with neighborhood politics and jockeying for a better position than her daughters.

For a brief moment, Lydia's mind wandered down that old, familiar path, and she wondered why it was that she and Mary, both of whom had been raised by people fixated on status and money, had no desire for either.

Mary had done well for herself. Ambrose was not a landowner with as vast an income as the highest echelons of Bristow's society. Certainly, his wealth did not match that of his brother-in-law, Simon Kingsley, but Lydia would hazard to say Ambrose Ashbrooks' coffers were healthier than Papa's. Not a small feat for a younger son. However, Mary never aspired to wealth and certainly did not seek after being one of the well-to-do families of Greater Edgerton, though Lydia knew she was.

And though Lydia had married well by society's standards, she'd never aspired to do so. Her parents' ambitions had driven her to accept Sir Duncan. From her childhood, her life had been shaped by the expectation of an exalted marriage. The Haywards' hope for a better future lay in their lovely Lydia, and she had known better than to deviate from that plan.

Yet she had utterly failed. Widowed and penniless, there was little in Lydia's life that could be deemed a success except for Isabella. And few outside Lydia and the Ashbrooks would call her daughter a blessing. Fools that they were.

And now, what lay ahead for her? What did she desire from life? Without her parents' dictates, what course would she choose?

"That was a heavy sigh," murmured Mary.

"It was the sound of a lost soul, set adrift without a final destination." Lydia hadn't meant to sound so bleak, but she could not help it.

Mary straightened to meet Lydia's eye. Though instinct had Lydia shying away from sharing all, the hopeful glint in Mary's eye eased some of the fears that begged her to hide. This was a safe harbor in which to rest. In quick succession, Lydia shared her thoughts and finished with something she had not truly considered until the words emerged from her lips.

"I have longed for freedom, yet I do not know what to do with it," said Lydia. "I haven't the money to establish myself, and I haven't the foggiest notion how to remedy that. I feel as though I am coming back to myself, but I do not know what to do once I've found my footing."

Bringing her arm around her sister, Mary gave a sad little sigh of her own. "Do not fret about that yet, dearest. When you are ready, Ambrose and I will help you sort it out."

The knot in Lydia's chest loosened, and she gave a contented smile. Mary would know what to do when the time came, and there was no point in muddying the present with those future concerns.

"But we do need to decide what gown you'll wear for tonight," said Mary.

Lydia huffed. "They're all drab, so it makes no difference."

Mary rose to her feet, pulling Lydia along with her. "You may think them drab, but you look lovely in anything."

"Mourning clothes are intended to be unattractive," said Lydia with an arched brow as the pair made their way to her bedchamber.

"And mourning is intended for those who are missed."

Lydia wasn't sure if she should laugh or cry at Mary's flippant remark, but the saucy glint in her sister's eye kept her from dwelling on what she ought or ought not to do.

Mary tugged Lydia forward, and the pair stood before her wardrobe. Lydia longed to shove aside the dark colors and embrace the bright hues she preferred, but she was simply grateful to have her choice of gowns.

Mr. Bradshaw was an odd character. He was opinionated, unyielding, and thought poorly of her, yet he had gone to the trouble of sending for her things from Elmhurst Court. Lydia had left with the clothes on her back and a small portmanteau, abandoning the large wardrobe befitting the baronet's wife. Of course, the Dowager Lady Whiting hadn't sent the jewels she'd been gifted, but the clothing alone was worth more than the funds Sir Duncan had left her and would ensure Lydia needn't expend any funds on dressing herself for quite some time; and once her mourning was over, she could sell those dresses. That was a blessing indeed.

Mary sorted through the gowns and lifted one out of the wardrobe. Fashion was moving away from the slim silhouette of the past few decades, and now the shoulders and sleeves puffed outward like balloons in an unflattering manner. Luckily, Sir Duncan had shown no interest in her clothing, and though the Dowager wished her to be the height of fashion, the lady hadn't cared for the new style any more than Lydia, leaving Lydia's gowns free of that distorted shape that was slowly taking over the fashion plates.

Stretching out the skirt, Mary held the dress up to her sister, but Lydia shook her head. If she was to go out tonight, she needed a gown that felt more like an old friend and companion. One that adored her as much as she did it. Joining her sister at the wardrobe, Lydia sorted through the options until she found the perfect choice.

Though it was a dark mimicry of the gown she truly wished to wear, the black color didn't feel as oppressive as her other mourning clothes. The neck was wide and scooped with a band of braiding along the edge that was mirrored with three wider strips along the hem. The sleeves gave a nod to the fashion without being overly large, and a hint of lace ringed the cuffs, décolletage, and the bottom of the skirt. Lydia could almost pretend she was wearing the original with its white silk and gold accents.

Mary brushed a hand across the skirt. "That is lovely—"

A knock sounded at the door, and Polly entered with a tray of letters. Mary sorted through them, laying the majority back on the salver for later. Polly bobbed and left, and Mary held out a missive for Lydia.

"I am glad to see your friends from Kent have written," she said with a smile before turning her attention back to the dress and musing over the rest of her sister's toilette.

But Lydia's gaze was fixed on the envelope in her hand. She had no acquaintances in Kent who would bother with the cost and effort of writing, except to offer an olive branch of friendship in order to gather gossip. However, Lydia recognized the handwriting. Casting a look at her sister, Lydia broke open the seal and unfolded her mother's missive. Forgoing the usual greetings, the letter arrived straight at the heart of matters.

Do you have any idea what you have put us through? Your father and I have been out of our minds with worry after you disappeared. You left no note or word of where you'd gone. You simply snuck away before dawn like some common thief. We've been combing your home and ours, hoping for some sign of you, and with every passing day, I feared something terrible had happened to you. How could you behave in such a manner?

Her insides squirmed like eels caught in a net, and though she pressed a hand to her stomach, there was no quieting the unease. Perhaps she ought to have left a note for her parents. Lydia could imagine how anxious she'd be if Isabella went missing. Whatever else had passed, they were her parents, and they loved her. Though it had seemed like the proper course of action at the time, it was hard to cling to that certainty when reading through sentence after sentence of Mama's worries and fears.

Never once did I expect to find you staying with that woman.
I do not know what pains me most—that you vanished without a word or that you chose her home over ours. What have we done to deserve such mistreatment? That you would betray us in such a manner wounds me to my very soul. We've done everything we can to give you good prospects and a fine future, and now you are casting aside all of our sacrifices and

embracing someone who abandoned us all in favor of her selfish desires.

Perhaps your sister's betrayal is deserved, for we never hid the fact that you were our favorite. I should've seen the signs long before that fateful night she rejected us. She was always jealous of how much we love you and all we did to ensure your bright future...

Lydia moved backward until her legs hit the bed, and she sank to the mattress. Her heart warned her to turn away from the letter, but her eyes refused to listen, and they gobbled up every word like a puppy presented with a treat. That destructive eagerness reminded her of little Pepper, who had a fondness for sweets, though they did not agree with the poor dear. If not watched properly, he was bound to eat anything he shouldn't and make himself sick afterward. And she was following her puppy's example.

Pausing, Lydia straightened, her mind leaping from the present to the past. Pepper would be eight years old, and still alive if properly cared for. She wished she knew where he had ended up, but once the Dowager had decided Pepper was a nuisance, Sir Duncan had sent her beloved companion away. But as her husband had given only vague answers to her questions, Lydia clung to the hope that Pepper had been given to a proper family with a warm home and boundless affection for the excitable bundle of fur.

Lydia pulled away from that line of thought, turning her attention back to the letter as her insides twisted.

Please forgive your dear Mama. I understand our discussion must have shocked you mightily, but can you not see that it is the only way forward? Your father and I have beggared ourselves to give you the proper education and ensure you married well. Your husband's dishonorable behavior has given us no other recourse but to try again. Surely you understand that without your aid, we will be ruined. Only you can save us...

The letter continued in that vein, alternating between begging and blaming, each word striking at Lydia's gentle heart; her cheeks glowed pink, her skin flushing and prickling as though the air around her had warmed. If her parents' salvation lay within her power, was she a horrid, unfeeling daughter if she cast them aside? Could she abandon them to their own devices? Lydia's thoughts raced through all the many things they'd done for her. Their trip to London and her debut into Society had cost them dearly, and Lydia had left them without even the one hundred and fifty pounds.

And then Lydia's eyes fell to her mother's farewell.

Perhaps if I had been a better mother, we would not be facing this current fracture. Please tell me I am not too late to heal that breach. All our future happiness depends on you. Please do not fail us.

Shoving the missive aside, Lydia covered her mouth and took a deep breath, but her stomach continued to churn.

"Dearest, what is the matter?"

Lydia stood and moved to the door, but she was already inside her bedchamber; there was nowhere else to retreat to. And then Mary was there, pulling her back to the bed and fluttering about as Lydia attempted to explain. She held up the letter, and Mary snatched it up, her eyes sprinting across the page for no more than a second before she cast it aside.

"Pay them no heed, Lydia," said Mary, taking hold of her sister's hands as her gray eyes shone with shared pain. "This is what they do. They twist your actions to paint you the villain, but do not allow them to manipulate you any longer."

"But they've done so much for me," whispered Lydia.

"No." Mary's voice was little more than a growl, her expression hardening as those gray eyes of hers burned. "They did no more than what any parent ought to."

"My Season..." Lydia's gaze grew unfocused, her thoughts sifting through all the bills they'd incurred. Mama and Papa had never been quiet about the expense they were undertaking, and each pound spent felt like a physical weight on her.

"That was for their benefit. Not yours. Everything they do is for their own sake."

Lydia shook her head and moved to stand, but Mary grabbed her by the hand and pulled her back to her seat.

"Do not retreat, Lydia. Please, do not. You have come so far. Do not allow them to ruin your happiness."

"They will have nothing if I abandon them. What sort of ungrateful child treats her parents in such a manner?"

"What sort of parents treat their child like this?" Mary shook her head, her eyes blazing as she took the letter and shook it. "These are the same words they used on me. The same poison that nearly cost me that which I love most in the world."

Crumpling the letter, she threw it across the room and took Lydia's hands once more. Mary's brows twisted, her eyes glistening as she continued. "I nearly gave in to them. I believed Mama when she said I was selfish for doing as I wished, and as much as it pains me to admit it, I would've cast Ambrose aside for their sake. If not for you."

Lydia's eyes widened.

"I sat up all that night, thinking and fretting about my future. Then you came to my bedchamber—"

"I was wretched to you," whispered Lydia.

Mary shook her head but paused and sighed. "You lashed out because of your pain, and it was that anguish that helped me to see our parents were selfish creatures. Their lives were focused solely on their wants and needs, and we were nothing more than tools to them. They were selling you into matrimony and shackling me to their side, and all because they aspired to greater social standing and refused to practice economy in our household."

Taking in a deep breath, Mary's mouth pinched, her gaze growing pained. "My only regret is that I did not rescue you from their machinations, too. I shouldn't have left you behind, Lydia."

"But I owe them so much—"

"Anything you may have owed them was long ago paid when you married that horrid man."

Lydia shook her head. "It gave them nothing."

"And that is their fault."

"But I did not give him a son..." Pain jabbed at Lydia's temples, and she winced, pressing a hand to her head. The room was stifling, and she could not seem to breathe. Then Mary's arms came around her, and Lydia felt like shoving her aside. She needed air.

"Do not give in now, dearest," whispered Mary. "Please do not leave me again."

Lydia struggled to get her lungs to work properly. They drew in breaths at a rapid pace, yet she still felt as though she was suffocating.

And Mary continued to hold her close, murmuring sweet and gentle things. "We will weather this together. We will find a way."

Those words settled into Lydia's chest, easing the pain and allowing her lungs to relax. Her arms came round her sister, clutching her as though she was a lifeboat in a storm-tossed sea.

"Do you promise?" whispered Lydia.

"I promise."

Though she could not relax entirely, Lydia felt the tension seep out of her. For once, there was someone at her side who would know what to do. Mary would sort it out.

Chapter 13

Though not one to seek out grand parties, Robert enjoyed an evening spent with good friends and good food. As the Fowlers guaranteed a ready supply of both, he found himself quite pleased to have been granted an invitation to their table. It was bound to be an entertaining dinner.

Robert didn't understand why so many of the tradesmen aspired to be counted among the gentry. Their attempts to affect the wealthy's air of ennui made them more tedious than sophisticated. And even when they had the income to join the lofty ranks of the elite, only an exceptional dose of obsequiousness would overcome their low breeding. To Robert's thinking, that was a poor exchange, indeed.

But then, there were people like the Fowlers, Leggats, and Pughs, who simply embraced their station for what it was. Others viewed it as an unenviable limbo between the poor and the wealthy, but to this merry group, it was a beautiful blending of the benefits of the lower class with the wealth and ease of the upper.

What surprised him more was how comfortable the Ashbrooks and Rushworths were among them. Having been born of the gentry, they were used to dining in finer circles than this.

Here, the people talked and laughed a little too loudly, did not stand on ceremony, and generally did whatever made them merriest, and yet the couples did not flinch at the occasional faux pas. It was one of the reasons Robert liked them.

The scent of the room was heavenly, and it pushed him to fill his plate to the brim with stewed breast of veal, roast turkey with lemon and liver, pickled vegetables and fruit, stuffing with white gravy and bacon, and a smattering of other delectable dishes begging him to partake. To say nothing of the sweets that awaited them.

With a wide grin, Mr. Ashbrook leaned over as Robert tucked into his meal. "I apologize for being an inferior substitute for my sister-in-law. She makes for a far prettier dinner companion."

"You do yourself a disservice, sir."

Mr. Ashbrook barked a laugh at the dry tone. "My wife would not thank you for inflating my pride."

Taking a sip of his drink, Robert shrugged. He was far more pleased than if his companion had been as Mrs. Fowler intended. It had not escaped his notice that the only unattached people in the company were paired, nor how crestfallen their hostess had appeared when the Ashbrooks arrived without Lady Whiting. Even now, Mrs. Fowler slanted the odd disappointed look at Robert. She had been on him to remarry for too long to allow such an opportunity for matchmaking to slip her by, even if the lady in question was still in mourning. Thankfully, fate (or rather, Lady Whiting's delicate nerves) intervened.

"I hope Lady Whiting is not unwell."

Mr. Ashbrook's brow furrowed. "She is well enough, though she received some disturbing news this afternoon. She felt it best to remain at home."

Turning his attention to his roasted turkey breast, Robert nodded. "That is understandable with her weak constitution."

The gentleman huffed. "What do you mean?"

Robert considered that a moment. "Only that she seems a fragile sort of creature."

"She has earned the right to be," said Mr. Ashbrook before taking a drink.

"Yes, she mentioned her troubles during her marriage."

Mr. Ashbrook's brow rose at that. "I do not care for your tone."

Robert held up a staying hand. "I meant no offense."

"Then you ought not to speak in such a dismissive manner, sir. Especially considering you have some intimate knowledge of how detestable her situation was in the Whiting household. Her husband's spurning her from beyond the grave is proof enough that she was mistreated."

"True," Robert conceded with a nod. "A husband ought to provide for his wife and child, and it is cruel of him to have left them at the mercy of others."

Mr. Ashbrook's gaze narrowed, and he waited a moment before saying, "And that is not enough for you?"

Robert tried to smile. "I truly do not mean any offense, Mr. Ashbrook, and I do not wish to belittle her suffering, but the streets are full of those whose circumstances are truly horrendous. Lady Whiting will not be forced to work all hours of the day to provide for her child. Her marriage may have been difficult, but it has not left her scarred. She has come out the other side a pauper. Nothing more."

With a halting huff, Mr. Ashbrook shook his head. "I've heard similar things said before, and it never fails to surprise me how much people adore ranking heartaches, either to claim that only the most heinous of agonies ought to be acknowledged or to count themselves lucky that their trials are easier than others'. Either way, it does neither themselves nor others any good."

"A bit of perspective is a good thing," said Robert, taking a bite of boiled potatoes.

"At times, it can be. But far too often, it is used to degenerate another's pain or to wrap oneself in a cloak of superiority while they thank the heavens that they are not as bad off as their fellow man."

Robert considered that with a smile. "That is an interesting perspective, and not one I have heard before."

Mr. Ashbrook gave him a slanted look. "I can tell you are not convinced."

"As one who works with privileged people who are far too quick to think themselves martyrs, I cannot help my opinion. It has been proven far too many times."

"And I would think a solicitor would understand that the world is not so absolute as to allow only one opinion to be the entire truth." Mr. Ashbrook skewered a carrot and leveled a chastising look at his companion.

Robert chuckled. "You are right, sir, and I concede the point. Truly, I meant no offense towards your sister-in-law, and I do hope she fares better tomorrow."

Mr. Ashbrook took a sip of his drink and considered that. "I hardly knew Lady Whiting before she appeared on our doorstep, but my wife assures me she is doing better each day."

Silence stretched out for a moment as the gentlemen enjoyed their meal, but before long, Mr. Ashbrook set down his fork and gave Robert a pensive look.

"Might I ask your professional advice?" he asked.

"Certainly."

"Lady Whiting's parents are keen to exert power over her once more, and though I know she is a free agent now, I would like to know if I ought to be concerned. Do they have any legal rights over her?"

Robert's brows rose. "What do they want from her?"

Scowling at his plate, Mr. Ashbrook replied, "They view her as their fatted calf to offer up in sacrifice to Society. It was they who arranged her marriage to the baronet, and since it proved fruitless for their social and financial aspirations, they are determined to find her a new husband."

With a shrug, Robert bit into his stuffing and gravy. "That is easy enough to answer. Not only do they have no legal right over Lady Whiting at present, but they couldn't have forced the first marriage. Parents may object to and forbid marriages, but they cannot speak the marriage vows for their children. Lady Whiting chose to marry the baronet."

"Unfortunately, her parents are quite determined, and I fear they may go to great lengths to ensure their daughter's cooperation."

Robert straightened, his blood chilling at Mr. Ashbrook's furious tone. There was a world of meaning beneath it, and Robert did not care for the implications.

With a narrowed look, he asked Mr. Ashbrook, "Is she in danger?"

Mr. Ashbrook considered that for far longer than Robert cared for. "I don't believe so. The Haywards are determined, but they are more subtle in their machinations. Her parents prefer insults and manipulation to outright threats."

Robert relaxed and smiled. "Then she shall be fine. Simply do not give in to their entreaties, and there is little they can do to her."

"Again, if it were only that easy," said Mr. Ashbrook. "Is there a way for us to deny them contact? Now that they've located her, I feel certain they will pester her relentlessly."

"I know of no legal manner in which to do so, but there is a simple solution. Ignore them. If all they have are words, then she is in no danger."

Mr. Ashbrook chuckled, though it was not a happy thing. "Again, as a solicitor, I would think you of all people would understand the power of words."

"Only to those unwilling to stand their ground," said Robert with a swig of his drink.

Mr. Ashbrook scoffed. "Life is not always that simple."

"It seems simple enough to me." Robert tried to modulate his tone to something less dismissive than the one he wanted to use. Mr. Ashbrook seemed a sensible fellow, and yet he subscribed to the same thinking as his flighty sister-in-law.

"Though they exerted pressure upon her, she would've been beyond their power once she turned one and twenty. Now that she is well past that age, she need only ignore them, and they can be nothing more than an annoyance."

With a sigh, Mr. Ashbrook turned back to his meal. "I see we shan't agree upon this, but that is the way of things. Not everyone can slough off the influence and mistreatment of others, and those who can view that sensitivity as a failing in those who can't. I only hope you never come to understand that words bruise as easily as any blow and leave their mark long after a physical wound heals."

Robert took a few bites, allowing his own words to slip into silence. Though he knew Mr. Ashbrook was inherently wrong, it would not do to tell the gentleman so. He may not be as delicate as Lady Whiting, but clearly, Mr. Ashbrook was a tender soul as well.

"That aside, I do not doubt her parents will do everything they can to gain control over Lady Whiting once more," said Mr. Ashbrook. "They poured all their hopes into her making a grand match, and though they may not resort to violent means, they will fight to get her under their thumbs again. Letters won't be the end of it."

That thought settled uneasily in his stomach, as Lady Whiting was not suited for battle, and Robert did not care to think of any woman standing alone against such foes.

"If you need any assistance, do not hesitate to send word. No doubt you have a solicitor on retainer, so I do not know what good I will be, but I offer my services all the same."

Mr. Ashbrook nodded. "My thanks. My man is good for affairs at the mill, but I do not care for the barrister he engages."

"Who is it?"

"Mr. Hockering."

Robert grimaced. "Yes, he's a bit hopeless."

Mr. Ashbrook shrugged. "As I've not had much use for a barrister, it hasn't been a concern."

The pair fell into more familiar territory, speaking of business and other matters that occupied their days before being pulled in other directions by the other guests. Yet the conversation lingered in the back of Robert's thoughts. Mr. Ashbrook didn't seem the sort to be easily swayed by the opinion of others; he was a decisive, outspoken sort of fellow. While he was a bit of a people-pleaser, Robert couldn't imagine him being overcome by self-doubt or giving credence to the opinions of others, yet he had strong words in defense of those like Lady Whiting.

No doubt it was a reaction to Robert's hard assessment of his sister-in-law, which was admirable. Robert hadn't meant to insult her. While he could not comprehend her fractious state, he didn't like that she was so overwrought by her parents. Something about her called to Robert, begging him to help her. It wasn't the sentiment Mrs. Fowler wished to rouse in him, but he couldn't deny that he was rather preoccupied with the young widow.

Such thoughts followed him as they finished the meal and made their way to the drawing room. Mrs. Fowler had tables set up for cards, and Robert joined in a hand or two. The company shifted and moved about here and there, but as the evening progressed, Robert became aware of Mrs. Ashbrook. Or rather, aware of how aware she was of him.

The lady kept slanting him looks. Establishing oneself as an independent man of business was not an easy prospect, and a solicitor only thrived when he was able to read his clients and clerks. Robert's instincts told him Mrs. Ashbrook was gathering her courage to talk to him, and when it seemed as though she had finally rallied, Robert moved to the edge of the gathering to allow her a bit more privacy in which to approach him.

"Mr. Bradshaw, might I have a moment of your time?" she asked, and Robert nodded, motioning to a pair of chairs set off to one side.

The lady attempted some light chatter before Robert finally struck at the heart of the matter. "You needn't worry, Mrs. Ashbrook. Your husband spoke to me of your sister's possible legal troubles, and I assured him I am at your disposal—"

"Legal troubles?" Mrs. Ashbrook straightened and blinked.

"Mr. Ashbrook spoke to me of Lady Whiting's concerns about your parents and the lengths to which they may resort to get her under their thumb once more."

Mrs. Ashbrook gave him a soft smile, her gaze brightening as she turned it to her husband, who was in the midst of a hand of cards and trouncing everyone soundly. But she turned her attention back to Robert and shook her head.

"It is comforting to know we have an ally in you, Mr. Bradshaw, but I wished to speak to you about your daughter."

Robert cocked his head to the side. "What about her?"

Mrs. Ashbrook clasped her hands tightly in her lap, and though she was plainly uncomfortable with the situation, she forged ahead. "My sister enjoyed the dancing lesson she gave the girls the other day, and as Nell seemed equally enthralled, I thought I would ask if you would allow your daughter to spend her afternoons at our house, where Lydia can teach her dancing and etiquette and the like."

"If your sister is so keen on the idea, why isn't she the one asking me?"

Considering that, Mrs. Ashbrook spoke carefully. "I think you are well aware of how timid she has become. Though she expressed much delight over the idea, I fear it will take some time before she would dare to ask you herself, and I fear I am not patient enough to wait for her. It pains me to see her so withdrawn."

Robert gave her an assessing look. "That is not her usual temperament?"

"Not at all," she said with a vehement shake of her head. "Before her marriage, my sister was effervescent. She adored people and had a sunny disposition. It breaks my heart to see her so downtrodden."

With a furrowed brow, Mrs. Ashbrook held Robert's gaze with a spark of hope burning within. "That dancing lesson was the first time I saw my sister as she once was. She has continued to teach Dottie, and it has helped some, but I thought I would speak to you about Nell as well. It is easier with more students, and it would ease some of Mrs. Humphreys' burden."

Robert straightened again, meeting Mrs. Ashbrook's worried expression with one of his own. "What is the matter with Prudence?"

Mrs. Ashbrook stared at him for a good long moment before answering. "You haven't noticed how much she is struggling of late?"

Robert shrugged. "She is tired, but that is nothing out of the ordinary. She was much the same after the birth of each of her children."

With a sigh that spoke of a woman's frustration with the shortsightedness of men, Mrs. Ashbrook shook her head. "Your sister-in-law would never say a word to you, for she adores you and Nell, but she is worn thin. Hugo is far more difficult than her other babies, and Muriel is struggling with the new addition to their family and causing all sorts of trouble. With your brother-in-law's busy schedule of late, Prudence is at her wits' end. Meanwhile, she believes she can manage it all and refuses to say a word to you about it."

"And Nell is a burden to her?" asked Robert with a frown.

Mrs. Ashbrook huffed. "That is why she did not wish to speak to you about it. The present situation has naught to do with whether or not Nell is a burden. She is a lovely child. But many women take on more than they can manage and refuse to speak up when they're overwhelmed. Prudence doesn't wish to offend or hurt you."

Robert's shoulders fell as he considered that. "It's long past time for Nell to receive more formal education than what Prudence has given her, and I've thought about hiring a governess, but I am not keen on the idea. I've tried to hire help over the years, but I find too many of them are too strict or are more interested in catching my eye than fulfilling their duties."

"Our eldest, Dottie, is attending a fine school—one I would highly recommend. My sister has taken to walking Dottie to and from school, and if you wish it, she could bring Nell home as well. Then Lydia can teach the girls together about dancing, etiquette, and the like."

"That sounds like a fine solution," said Robert with raised brows. "Nell would have the education she needs, Prudence would have one less child underfoot, and Lady Whiting would be allowed to do something she loves to do."

Mrs. Ashbrook nodded. "It would be beneficial to all involved."

Robert gave a sharp nod. "That is a fine plan, Mrs. Ashbrook."

"I thought so," she replied with a smile. "Though I would thank you not to speak a word of my part in it to Prudence as she may take umbrage with my interference."

Waving a dismissive hand, he said, "You came to me to speak about Lady Whiting teaching my daughter. Nothing more. If it has other benefits, then all the better."

Mrs. Ashbrook smiled and nodded, rising to her feet. With a quick word of thanks and farewell, the lady strode away, looking quite pleased with herself. Robert thought it quite strange that she and Lady Whiting were so very different, but then, if Mrs. Ashbrook were to be believed, Lady Whiting had not always been the quivering mouse she was. Memory wasn't always a reliable thing, and perhaps Mrs. Ashbrook merely thought her sister very different in the past than she was at present, but Robert spent many minutes pondering if it were true.

And if it were, what had happened to Lady Whiting to alter her so completely.

Chapter 14

Though she loved novels, Lydia was not one to read anything more strenuous than a tale of adventure or romance (preferably both), and certainly, she had never read a book on the finer points of dancing. Thanks to dear Mr. Marks' efforts and her years of practice, Lydia was well-versed in the subject; however, there was a vast difference between knowing and teaching. Honestly, she would never have thought to find such joy while combing through stuffy treatises, yet she scoured every page for tidbits that would aid her curriculum. In many ways, Lydia felt silly for going to such lengths, as she was only teaching two young girls, but even knowing that, she returned to the instruction books again and again.

Isabella grasped the edge of the sofa, tugging at the edge of Lydia's dress while calling "Mama" again and again. Setting aside the book, Lydia lifted her daughter onto her lap and kissed the soft spot just below Isabella's jaw until the child giggled and squirmed.

"No!" she said, pushing at her mama, though her laughter and smiles belied her protests.

The girl went limp, and Lydia smiled down at her beautiful little daughter. "Mama loves you so very much, my darling."

Isabella grinned and patted Lydia's cheek. Shifting the girl around, Lydia picked up her book and read aloud, "'Every species of dancing, from being an art in which the limbs collectively considered, are indispensable necessary to the production of a required effect, are consequently susceptible of caricature, and of an improper, indecent levity, in the execution. Waltzing in its performance is particularly so...'"

But Isabella did not hold still for long and squirmed free of her mother's hold, wandering off to the other side of the parlor. With Dottie at school, Esther accompanying her mama on errands, and the boys tramping the riverside with their nursemaid, she was free to explore without her cousins bumping into her. Walking was difficult enough for Isabella, but with four other children running and crawling about, she could scarcely go more than a few steps before someone knocked her down.

Lydia turned her attention to her book, and though this particular work had little to offer her young students (she could only imagine what Mr. Bradshaw would say if she taught Nell the waltz), it was fascinating to read a dancing master's instructions and analysis of that dance. A waltz step was not a foreign concept, as it was part of many country dances, but Lydia had little experience with the French or German variety, though they had gained more acceptance in the past few years.

Blushing to herself, Lydia wondered what it would be like to take lessons with Mr. Marks nowadays when such dances weren't nearly as scandalous as they had been when she'd debuted in society. Moving around the room in those delicate steps, fixed to your partner's side for the entirety of the dance. It sounded marvelous. Her cheeks became so heated that Lydia reached for her handkerchief and pulled it free of her pocket.

Several coins spilled out, and Isabella turned to watch as one hit the floor and rolled. The child gave chase, but Lydia was quicker than she, snatching it up before her daughter could put it in her mouth. Gathering the coins, Lydia counted through them, though she knew exactly how much she would find, for these were the same ones she'd secreted into Mary's pocket a few days ago. Lydia smiled and chuckled to herself. Her sister would not surrender their game but neither would Lydia, and one way or another, she'd find some way to get them into the Ashbrooks' coffers.

"Come here, my darling." Lydia reached for Isabella, but the child turned and scuttled away. Again, she was not as fast as her mama, but Isabella attempted to escape all the same. Scooping her up, Lydia wandered from the parlor, musing over where she might hide the coins this time. As the game had progressed over the weeks, it had become as much about finding unique hiding places as it was getting the coins into the other's possession, and Lydia thought through the possibilities.

"What do you think, Isabella?" she asked, climbing the stairs to reach the bedchambers. When Lydia arrived at the second-floor landing, she paused.

"Perhaps the library?"

Isabella rocked forward, spurring her mama to move while babbling a string of sounds that occasionally matched proper words, though Lydia doubted they were an answer to the question as much as a command for her mama to move. Stepping into the library, Lydia searched the space and landed on Mary's end table. Opening the drawer, Lydia lifted the novel inside and placed the coins beneath it. As the Ashbrooks spent their evenings with Mary reading aloud, it wouldn't be long before her sister discovered the treasure.

"There we go," she said, bouncing Isabella on her hip as the pair strolled back down the stairs.

"Madam," said Polly with a bob, holding up a letter. "The post has just arrived."

Taking it in hand, Lydia knew the script in an instant, and it had the same effect it always did. Heat swept through her, and her muscles grew weak and shaky. The letter was like a stone dropped into her heart, weighing her down, and Lydia tried to breathe. Moving to the sofa, she put down her daughter and dropped onto the cushion, her hands clasping the bit of paper.

Lydia squeezed her eyes shut and breathed through the

anxiety coursing through her. She sent out a silent prayer that Mary would return. Her sister always set things right again. Yet even as Lydia hoped for rescue, her cheeks burned, sending a wave of shame to chase away the anxiety. Could she truly not face a simple letter on her own? Did she need aid in even such a little thing?

Mr. Bradshaw's stern judgments came to mind, and though she could not countenance his wholly unyielding view on the matter, Lydia longed for a dash of his self-possession. She could only imagine what he would think about her cowering in such a moment. This was not the first of the letters to arrive, nor was it likely to be the last. Would she forever be crying and gnashing her teeth whenever they appeared? Could she not attempt to be strong on her own without leaning wholly on Mary? Could she not stand on her own for once?

Cracking the seal, Lydia steeled her nerves as much as she could and stared down at the flowing script. It would not overtake her.

After everything we have done and sacrificed for you, I cannot believe you are betraying us in such a manner...

Mama's words rambled on in that fashion for some time. They pricked at her, echoing fears and doubts she harbored, but Lydia forced herself to focus on that which was true: she had done more than any child ought. She had sacrificed everything for her parents, and the fact that it amounted to nothing was none of her concern. Mary's logic and comfort wrapped around her, and though Lydia could not stop herself from feeling Mama's words, she did not allow them to wound her.

But everything shifted at Mama's concluding words:

As you refuse to do your duty, we are forced to move against you. Know that we are only doing it for your good, as you will fall into ruin without our guidance. And so, we will petition the Court for guardianship of your daughter. Perhaps that will give you some incentive to return home and follow your parents' counsel.

Lydia's eyes rested on those words, and she read them again and again, though they refused to make any sense. They held her prisoner in that moment as she tried to comprehend just what Mama was saying.

Her heartbeat picked up its pace, pumping ice through her veins as she stared at the letter. The anxiety of moments ago came back in full force, threatening to swallow her in its terrifying abyss. But Lydia's gaze moved to her dear Isabella, who sat on the ground next to a doll Dottie had given her when they'd first arrived, and with absolute clarity, she realized two things.

That threat was not hollow: Mama and Papa would do what they could to get Lydia under their control again. And Lydia could not allow them power over Isabella: she would become their new Mary.

Her older sister had always been intended for servitude. Though Lydia had never understood why gentlemen overlooked Mary, it was clear to their parents that she would not be their financial salvation. Mama and Papa may not have thought of Mary as their servant—not overtly at any rate—but there was no disguising the fact that they wanted her to remain their spinster daughter, who would nurse them in their waning years. Someone whom they could order about without having to pay her.

So, not a servant, rather a slave.

Lydia saw Isabella's future if she were raised in her grandparents' household. With her feet as they were, marriage was not a given, and Mama wouldn't waste a penny on a girl with an uncertain matrimonial future.

As much as Lydia wished to hide away from these troubles, she could not. Escaping the Whitings' house had been as much to protect Isabella as it was to free herself, and she would not fail her daughter now. Though she had been unable to save Isabella for the first year and a half of her life, Lydia would do everything in her power to protect her now.

Chapter 15

The day had been a quiet sort, but Robert ought to have known better than to trust the calm. These were the precise moments when chaos enjoyed creeping up on him, pouncing without warning and sending his world into a dither. Not that Robert was one to get swept up in the resultant tumult.

His clerks were another matter.

With guidance, Mr. Biller had learned to adapt to such goings-on, but a young man in his early twenties did not have enough experience to handle the whirlwind that swept into Robert's office the next moment. And Mr. Shirley was naught but a lad and was still rather terrified of the fairer sex.

The main door opened, and Robert didn't look up from his paperwork as he'd long ago learned to ignore such distractions and left Mr. Biller to handle it. But the general agitation that accompanied the newcomer traveled from the front room into his private office, past thoughts of wills, trusts, and property conveyances just moments before the whirlwind swept into his sanctuary.

"Mr. Bradshaw," was all Lady Whiting said before launching into a rambling and incoherent stream of words.

Mr. Biller stood in the doorway with wide eyes, and in the distance, Mr. Shirley hid behind the stack of books sitting on his desk. Robert waved a hand at the young men, instructing them to go back to their work, and approached the tempest. And there was no other way to describe her because Lady Whiting was in a fine temper—though she was more akin to a conflagration. Standing there with her daughter on her hip, the lady was ablaze with a fire he hadn't thought her capable of. Though a hint of hysteria clung to the edge of her voice, Lady Whiting's blue eyes burned with determination.

The child began to cry, and that did more to calm her than Robert's words. Lady Whiting stilled, rocking her daughter with soft and tender words as Robert divested her of her bonnet and cloak before ushering the lady to a seat.

"Now, what is the matter?" he asked while taking his own.

"I cannot allow them to do it, Mr. Bradshaw," she said, placing a kiss on her daughter's temple. "You must help me. You are the only attorney I know." Lifting her hand, Lady Whiting gave him a crumpled letter. "It is from my parents, sir. They are threatening to take my daughter. Please tell me they cannot do it."

Robert scanned through the words and felt a stirring of sympathy for the young widow. Her mother's words were hard and unyielding, critical and condemning, though with just enough heart and kindness to make them all the more manipulative. Having known a wide swatch of humanity, Robert was familiar with those sorts of people who viewed themselves as the pinnacle of humankind, deserving of everything they desired regardless of what it cost others.

Slanting a look at Lady Whiting, Robert examined her, but she met his curious gaze with a desperate one.

"Can they take Isabella from me?" she asked, and Robert forced himself back to the letter, coming to the crux of the matter.

With a sigh, he placed the letter aside. "Unfortunately, yes."

"But I am her mother!"

Isabella fussed, arching her back, and Lady Whiting shifted her hold until the child was resting against her mother's shoulder. Rocking back and forth in place, she rubbed Isabella's back and cooed at the child. When her gaze met Robert's again, Lady Whiting's eyes were filled with a mixture of anger and agitation, pleading with him to tell her that it was all untrue.

"I will not allow them to take my daughter, sir. They only want her to force my hand, and I shan't allow her to be under their thumb."

Robert relaxed into his seat and felt more than a touch surprised by the passion with which she spoke the words. Lady Whiting held his gaze without flinching, and Robert tapped his fingers on the arm of his chair as he considered the situation.

"Would you care for something to drink or eat?" he offered. "And should I send for your sister and brother-in-law? I think they ought to be part of the conversation."

"I only need answers, Mr. Bradshaw. How can they take my child? What can I do to stop them?" Lady Whiting's voice broke, and she winced. With a few breaths, she seemed to gather herself, but there was a hint of tears in her eyes. "I shan't give her to them."

Robert's gaze softened, his heart stirring unexpectedly. He wouldn't have thought it possible for him to feel such warm sympathy for Lady Whiting, but with her pleading yet unflinching gaze fixed on him, Robert couldn't help but feel a modicum of pleasure: though the lady seemed beaten down, she had some fire left in her.

Robert nodded. "Good. You will need that sort of determination, for we have a fight ahead of us."

But before he could delve into the heart of the matter, Mr. Shirley appeared at the doorway and announced that Mr. Ashbrook had arrived, which was nothing short of providential. Though Lady Whiting said she did not need her brother-in-law there, she would need the Ashbrooks' support through this ordeal if they were to succeed.

"Lydia?" Mr. Ashbrook came to his sister-in-law's side, casting a glance at Robert before turning his entire attention on her. "What is the matter? Polly came to the mill and told me you were distressed. Why have you come to Mr. Bradshaw's office?"

In quick succession, they had seated Mr. Ashbrook and explained what had brought her there. When Robert offered up the letter to read, the fellow merely shook his head.

"I can well imagine what is in there, sir, and have no desire to read it for myself." Turning to Lady Whiting, he added, "Should we send for Mary?"

"I need answers, and I cannot wait another moment, Ambrose." And then she turned her attention to Robert once more, her gaze begging him to speak.

Clearing his throat, Robert began to unravel the mess that was custody law. "It is a father's duty to name a legal guardian for his children in his will, and he can choose whomever he wishes to oversee his child's upbringing and inheritance, though in most circumstances, it is a male relative or friend of the father. As your husband did not name one, Lady Whiting, you—the child's natural guardian—can take stewardship of Isabella."

Lady Whiting relaxed a fraction, and Robert's insides churned at the thought that it was his duty to dispel that relief.

"Unfortunately, that doesn't mean your parents cannot petition the Court of Chancery to gain control of Isabella, and they will be granted it. The Court's main consideration is the financial security of the child, and as your parents have property and income, and you have none, they will be given Isabella."

Mr. Ashbrook leaned forward with a pinched expression. "But you told me the other day they had no legal manner in which to gain control over Lydia."

With a hesitant nod, Robert added, "They cannot directly, but that doesn't extend to her daughter, unfortunately. Using their grandchild to force her mother to do their bidding hadn't factored into my answer when we last spoke."

Perhaps it ought to have, but treating a child like leverage wasn't a commonly used legal tactic, and Robert could not countenance what sort of people would do so.

Lady Whiting's complexion paled, and Robert straightened. "Are you certain I cannot get you something to drink? Or perhaps—"

"No, Mr. Bradshaw. Please continue." The lady gathered herself once more and met his gaze with a nod.

"Normally, Chancery doesn't bother with guardianship issues of children without title or inheritance, like your Isabella, and luckily for you, the Panic of last year sent ripples through the legal world as well as the economic one, and the Court is overwhelmed with petitions. With so many more pressing matters, it is highly unlikely Chancery will bother with your daughter. Without the Court dictating the guardianship, you are free to claim it."

Lady Whiting held her daughter tighter, pressing another kiss to her temple, and Robert's insides knotted, knowing that what he had to say next would not help matters, though Lady Whiting needed to know the breadth of her troubles.

"But if your parents are as unscrupulous as you fear, they needn't bother with the courts. They can simply take the child."

"Pardon?" Mr. Ashbrook straightened and gaped. "How can they do that?"

Robert sighed. "Until twelve years ago, the law did not consider kidnapping as anything more than a minor issue. Stealing a child's clothing could lead to prison or even transportation, but to steal the child itself incurred nothing but a rather minor fine."

Lady Whiting gaped, holding her daughter closer to her.

"The law has changed to include more stringent penalties, but those punishments mean nothing if not enforced, and many constables and squires would not view your parents taking your child as a crime. You could petition the Court for her to be returned to you, but you would face the same difficulties I enumerated a moment ago. I cannot say with any certainty that Isabella would be returned to your care."

Closing her eyes, Lady Whiting took in a breath, resting her face against her daughter's fine baby hair. She took a moment before meeting his gaze again. Fear and courage shone in the depths of her blue eyes, and Robert was in no doubt that the conversation pained her. Yet still, she was not fleeing.

Good for her.

"What are my options, Mr. Bradshaw?"

Robert sifted through his legal knowledge; though he had limited experience with guardianships, he knew enough to be of some use. Unfortunately, what he knew of them was the precise reason he avoided the Court of Chancery as much as possible.

"To my thinking, you have three options, though I regret to say none of them will be appealing," he said.

But Lady Whiting nodded for him to continue.

"The first would be to wait. Perhaps your parents may abandon their plans—"

"They will not, sir," said Lady Whiting, her gaze falling to her daughter. "Not until I am beyond the age where I can catch a man's eye, and even then, I do not believe they will give up hope that I can bring them another wealthy son-in-law."

Robert's expression tightened, and he turned his scowl to the desk. There was no good unleashing it now, as those who deserved it were not in the vicinity.

"And the other options?" asked Mr. Ashbrook.

"Immigrate," said Robert, though he knew it was a poor option indeed for a young widow with a child and no income. "If you are not in the country, there is little they can do. It would be easy enough to disappear."

"Neither my wife nor I will countenance such a thing," said Mr. Ashbrook.

Robert gave him a challenging raise of his brow. "It is your sister-in-law's decision."

Lady Whiting's eyes widened at that, though they glinted with a hint of gratitude. She shook her head. "I have neither the income nor the skills to provide for my daughter in such a situation."

Robert gave an appreciative nod at that and continued to his final point. "The most obvious solution would be for you to marry again."

Chapter 16

The air thinned, and it felt as though her head had begun spinning in place as Lydia clung to her daughter. The gentlemen continued to talk, but their voices faded from her thoughts, leaving her alone with Isabella. Everything around her slowed, and time felt like a caramel pulled until it was stretched impossibly thin.

And then the world coalesced around her, slamming into her as Lydia realized what was happening.

Marriage? Heavens above. Her stomach soured at the very thought, and that old, familiar panic started to seize her. Her heartbeat quickened, but Lydia rested her cheek against Isabella's head and forced herself to breathe, allowing her daughter's scent to fill her lungs; the child was growing so fast, yet she still had a touch of infancy about her, and that sweet fragrance wrapped around her heart, anchoring her to this moment.

Isabella needed a mother who could face such difficulties. She needed someone to protect her, and Lydia could not do so if she fell to pieces. Strength. Courage. Determination. She needed to be all those things if she hoped to save her daughter.

"I understand this is not an ideal solution, Mr. Ashbrook. I am simply giving you the facts as they are," said Mr. Bradshaw with strained patience. "Upon her marriage, Lady Whiting's husband would be granted legal guardianship of her daughter, *and* it would remove her parents' incentives to pursue this further."

Mr. Bradshaw was right. As loath as she was to follow that course of action, Lydia was no fool. Marriage would nullify her parents' motivation for claiming Isabella. And surely a marriage of convenience of her choosing would be far better than one her parents chose for her as their only requirement was a healthy bank account.

At the very least, this marriage would be *her* decision.

"I can marry," she said, though Ambrose did not seem to hear her as the gentlemen bickered about her future. Mr. Bradshaw's gaze swung to her, and he held up a hand, quieting Ambrose. Lydia repeated herself.

"You cannot be serious, Lydia," said Ambrose with a hard frown. "Mary and I will find a way to protect you—"

"Perhaps. But perhaps not. I am not willing to risk my daughter."

Mr. Bradshaw's brows rose, and he gave an appreciative nod. Ambrose opened his mouth to reply, but Lydia spoke first.

"I appreciate your concern, Ambrose. I do," she said with a thin smile. "However, I do have a..."

She stumbled over what to call Mr. Marks. A candidate? A former beau? At times like these, words felt too small and simple to convey her thoughts and feelings.

"I know of a man whom I can marry," she concluded. "We almost married once."

Ambrose straightened. "Your old beau?"

Lydia's cheeks pinked. "I see Mary has been telling you my secrets."

Turning in his chair, her brother-in-law faced her fully. Ambrose opened his mouth and closed it, seemingly rethinking what he was going to say before continuing, "I know you two harbored a tendre years ago, but do you not think he might've married someone else?"

Giving a vehement shake of her head that set Isabella fussing once more, Lydia calmed herself and her daughter before answering in an even tone. "It was so much more than a flirtation or passing fancy, Ambrose: he asked me to marry him. I loved him with all my heart, and I know he felt the same. I rejected him because I had to, but that does not alter how fiercely and entirely we loved each other."

"A love like that is not easily overcome," murmured Mr. Bradshaw. Lydia's gaze met his, and she was surprised to find a warm heart shining in his eyes. Mr. Bradshaw hadn't seemed a romantic sort, but it was clear that he felt such things deeply, and Lydia smiled at him.

"I know that." Ambrose frowned, considering his words before adding, "But it has been seven years."

"Seven years is not such a long time to heal from a lost love," said Mr. Bradshaw.

Ambrose shook his head with a huff. "And you were both so young—"

"Love does not belong solely to those of mature years, Mr. Ashbrook," said Mr. Bradshaw.

Despite the chaos of the moment, Lydia found herself smiling yet again. And towards Mr. Bradshaw of all people. She hadn't thought to find an advocate in him or to agree with him so thoroughly on any subject, and she was pleasantly surprised to find herself wrong at this moment.

Turning her gaze back to Ambrose, Lydia added, "We were young then, and we are young still. His proposal was a foolhardy thing, for he couldn't have afforded a wife at that time, but we were so in love, and we could not bear to be parted. Even if he relinquished those feelings and decided to marry another, it is unlikely he could've afforded to. Many a young man has put off having a family of their own until their thirties or even forties."

"True," Ambrose conceded, though his tone conveyed utter doubt.

Holding Isabella close, Lydia rested her hand on the child's back and held her brother-in-law's eyes, willing her heart to show through her gaze. "Trust me, Ambrose. I love Mr. Marks, and he loves me. Though I hadn't thought to remarry so soon, I know we are meant for each other."

Then, dropping her eyes to the floor, Lydia shook her head. "However, I do not know how to find him."

"I can make inquiries as to his whereabouts if you wish," said Mr. Bradshaw.

Lydia paused. "I appreciate your assistance, but I cannot afford—"

Mr. Bradshaw waved her words away. "This requires little effort on my part, Lady Whiting. Think nothing of it."

Blinking at the fellow, Lydia found herself smiling yet again. "That would be lovely, sir."

Nodding, Mr. Bradshaw retrieved a fresh sheet of paper. "What is his name?"

"Mr. Owen Marks. He was my dance instructor while my family was staying in London."

If the fellow found that shocking, Mr. Bradshaw gave no hint of it, merely taking note of what she had to say, though Ambrose looked extremely unhappy with this development. And if she were to be honest, Lydia was none too pleased about being forced into this situation. The thought of marrying for any reason had her insides churning, but she forced the roiling mess to calm.

This wasn't some stranger. This was her Mr. Marks. Memories and fantasies of him had been her only comfort throughout her marriage, and however wretched those seven years had been, a life with Mr. Marks would be equally blissful. This was her one true love.

Turning to Mr. Bradshaw, she added, "I would ask that you do not send word to Mr. Marks as of yet. I fear I hurt him greatly when we parted, and I ought to be the one who speaks to him."

Though Lydia had no thought as to how she would broach that subject. The memory of their final moments together still pained her. Though they had known her path was set, they'd both harbored too many hopes that they could change it for the parting to be anything but agony.

Mr. Marks had so little in the world, but one of the greatest gifts she'd ever been given was those loving words he'd used in his marriage proposal. Something the Whitings could never understand was how much more precious such sentiments were. No amount of riches or fine clothing had comforted Lydia during those dark years; only Mr. Marks' whispered declarations gave her the strength to continue.

And she had turned that gift aside for her parents' sake.

Mr. Bradshaw gave another nod, and Lydia contemplated what she would put in a letter. How did one contain all that had happened and all that might be in a few pieces of paper?

"I think I ought to see him in person," she said.

Ambrose's brows rose. "That would be quite the ordeal, Lydia. The trip would take several days and would cost a pretty penny."

Lydia straightened. "I have the money Sir Duncan left me. You and Mary refuse to take it, so what better way to use it than to help me free myself of my parents?"

"Such a journey could be dangerous for you to take on your own," he added with a grimace. "I fear I cannot spend so much time away from the mill at present. A letter will suffice, Lydia."

Her brother-in-law glanced from her to Mr. Bradshaw, and Ambrose's expression hid none of the disapproval and uncertainty he felt. The light around her dimmed as Lydia considered his words. Perhaps he was correct. Though she had no inkling of how to compose such a letter, the difficulties of traveling to London seemed insurmountable. Her trip from Kent to Lancashire had been born of desperation, and she felt certain that journey had been divinely blessed, for those days had passed uneventfully. Lydia doubted she would be graced with such easy travel a second time.

"I can accompany Lady Whiting to London," said Mr. Bradshaw, and Lydia's gaze snapped to his. "I have business there and can wait to leave until we have found Mr. Marks' location."

Her heart burned, filling the whole of her, and Lydia could hardly countenance the kindness Mr. Bradshaw was bestowing.

"You would do that?" she asked.

Mr. Bradshaw fidgeted with the quills and papers on his desk before nodding. "It is nothing. I assure you."

Not being one to blush easily, Robert knew his face did not show how uncomfortable Lady Whiting's gushing gratitude made him. He rather wished his visitors would leave and allow him to return to his work, but he did enjoy the swell of pleasure he felt at seeing the young widow so animated. Luckily, there was little more to discuss until they received word of Mr. Marks, giving her and Mr. Ashbrook no reason to linger.

Lady Whiting rose to her feet while bouncing her daughter on her hip, and she moved to the door with a wide smile and a plethora of thanks. Mr. Ashbrook followed her out but paused at the threshold, sending his sister-in-law to the carriage before shutting the office door and facing Robert once more. The fellow looked grim, and Robert guessed the source of his disquiet; Mr. Ashbrook had made his objections known.

"I appreciate your kindness to my sister-in-law, Mr. Bradshaw, but I think this course of action is unwise."

"As you've made clear."

With a sigh, Mr. Ashbrook dropped onto the chair once more and drummed his fingers against the arm. "I know nothing of this Mr. Marks, except what she has told my wife, which is not much at all. After all Lydia has suffered, I do not wish to see her crushed if this Mr. Marks is not the paragon she thinks him to be."

With a nod, Robert considered that. "True. There is a strong possibility that this trip to Town will come to naught, but that doesn't mean the journey will be wasted."

Robert considered the fellow for a moment. Mr. Ashbrook was not an overtly handsome man, though he was one blessed with a charisma that drew the eye. Robert knew little of him beyond his reputation, but the time he'd spent in Mr. Ashbrook's company confirmed everything he'd heard. Mr. Ashbrook was a good sort, and though he was being a fool at present, it was born from worry and fear on his sister-in-law's behalf.

"I have made the journey many times, and I give you my word I will do everything to protect her," said Robert. "At the very worst, Lady Whiting will lose some money, and though she has precious little of it to risk, the trip shan't cost her the whole of her funds."

"But I would rather see it invested or put to some better use," said Mr. Ashbrook.

"And I cannot think of a better way for her to spend it. Did you see her when she spoke of her plan?"

Mr. Ashbrook sighed again. "It is rare to see her so enthused about anything."

Robert nodded. "By your own admission, Lady Whiting has been allowed no freedom in her life, and even if this proves to be a disaster, isn't it time she is allowed to decide for herself? I, for one, wish to encourage her."

In all honesty, Robert was impressed by Lady Whiting's backbone. Buried beneath the fears and worries was a woman with a will of her own if allowed to use it. If not, life would likely wear her down until she was beyond assistance.

Unbidden, memories of his mother came to mind, though Robert brushed them aside as quickly as they came. There was no good to be had recalling his final conversation with her. He'd done all he could to protect her, but no amount of aid could help someone who wouldn't take it. His father had her under his thumb in every sense possible, and there was nothing Robert could do to free her.

Crossing his arms, Mr. Ashbrook sighed and shook his head as the wariness eased from his gaze. "I am properly chastised, sir. Though I still worry about what will come of this, you are correct. If this helps her find her own feet again, it is a price worth paying."

Rising, Mr. Ashbrook stuck out his hand and gave Robert's a firm shake. "My thanks, sir."

With a nod, Robert ushered the fellow out, leaving him alone in his office once more. He took his seat and sighed, welcoming the quiet after that interlude. Picking up his quill, Robert glanced at the paper that held the scant information Lady Whiting had given him, Robert picked up his quill. For good or ill, Lady Whiting had decided her course of action. Now, all he had to do was find this Mr. Owen Marks and plan a trip.

Chapter 17

Though Robert avoided London, he'd made the trip many times since Nell had been born. His colleagues would likely think him a sentimental fool for disliking the time apart, but leaving his daughter behind always brought him a slight pain—even if Nell seemed eager for it. She made a good show of being disappointed as well, but all thoughts of her papa were forgotten when the Ashbrooks opened their door. With hardly a kiss goodbye, she scurried after Dottie to see where she'd be staying.

"Are you certain she will not be a burden?" he asked as Mrs. Ashbrook ushered him into the parlor, where Lady Whiting was giving her own farewells.

"Not at all," said Mrs. Ashbrook with a wave of her hand. "We are very grateful for your assistance with my sister. Besides, Dottie has been in alt for the past sennight over having a guest and has planned quite the to-do while Nell is staying with us."

Robert nodded, though a small part of him still worried about the imposition. He batted that away, as it was the only solution. Prudence was still struggling with her brood, and the Ashbrooks were the best option. Besides, Nell would prefer staying with a playmate closer to her age; she adored her cousins, but they were so much younger than she.

Lady Whiting stood in the parlor with her daughter held close. Surely the child was too young to understand what was happening, but she sensed her mother's distress and began to fuss.

"We will watch over her, Lydia," said Mrs. Ashbrook, placing a hand on Isabella's back. "We shan't let her out of our sight."

The lady nodded, though she made no move to release her daughter.

"Are you certain this is the right course?" asked Mrs. Ashbrook. "I am certain we can find some other way."

Robert glanced at Mr. Ashbrook, who stood with his youngest in his arms. But the fellow needed no prodding. Drawing closer to his wife, Mr. Ashbrook put a hand on her back and murmured something to her that Robert could not hear. She nodded and sighed but gave no other protest.

"We need to be on our way if we are to make the coach," said Robert.

Lady Whiting nodded, but still made no move to release her hold on her daughter. Though Mr. Ashbrook put more effort into schooling his expression, his wife watched her sister with a fretful scrunch of her brow. Thankfully, she remained quiet as Robert silently willed Lady Whiting to be strong. With deliberate care, the lady handed the child to Mrs. Ashbrook, giving Isabella one final kiss.

"I shall miss you, my darling," she whispered. Turning her gaze to her sister, Lady Whiting smiled. "Don't fret, Mary. I am certain this is the proper course. All will be well now."

Mrs. Ashbrook attempted a smile, though it was no more convincing than Mr. Ashbrook's, and Robert ushered Lady Whiting out before their worries convinced her to abandon her course. In short order, they were bundled into their coach, which deposited them at the inn from which their journey would truly begin. And Robert braced himself for the four days to come.

Plans were tricky things. In the abstract, they were a checklist of items needing to be done before success was achieved. But too often, details were either overlooked or overly complicated, making the plan simpler or more complex than needed. Either way, a plan rarely unfolded as anticipated.

When settling the details for this trip, Lydia had focused on thoughts of Mr. Marks, Sir Duncan, and her parents. It was those worries that had kept her up until the wee hours of the morning as she fretted about what was to come. It wasn't until the hour of their departure that Lydia comprehended the full breadth of what she was doing.

In the abstract, she hadn't expected her parting from Isabella to pain her so very much; she would be gone little more than a sennight—a fortnight at the very most. But although the Whitings had curtailed Lydia's time in the nursery, she'd stolen away time every day to see Isabella. Yet now, she faced several days without her.

As the carriage rolled away from the inn, Lydia found herself wondering if she ought to have insisted Isabella come with them. Surely they could've included her in their journey, and they needn't be parted. As if strengthening that argument, her thoughts raced with all the many things that might go amiss while they were separated, and Lydia tried to breathe as her chest tightened.

Mary and Ambrose would watch over her. There was nothing to fear. Truly.

"All will be well, Lady Whiting."

Lydia's eyes darted from her lap to Mr. Bradshaw, and she found him watching her with something akin to sympathy.

"I would prefer for our daughters to join us, but I have no doubt the Ashbrooks will care for them in our absence." Mr. Bradshaw spoke with such certainty that some of the tension in her chest eased, allowing a bit of common sense to work its way past her fretting. It was silly to assume the worst. If anything, Mr. Bradshaw had more reason to fear, as he was leaving his child with another family altogether, yet he felt assured of Nell's safety and comfort. And why shouldn't he? Mary and Ambrose would watch over the girls as if they were of their own brood.

With a sigh that eased the last of her fears, Lydia turned her attention to the window.

In her younger years, the only trip she had ever taken was to London that fateful Season. In her married years, Sir Duncan had brought her to London a time or two, but he mostly left her in the country whenever he set his mind to travel. Though she had made a similar journey with Isabella some two months ago, the fear driving her escape and the unknown prospect of what awaited her in Lancashire had made the journey seem but a blink of an eye. Lydia had always thought traveling was an exciting prospect, but the more experience she had with it, the less exciting the prospect seemed.

The first few miles weren't terrible. They were the usual bumping, thumping, rattling experience one expected of carriages. And though Lydia had fretted over what to say to Mr. Bradshaw, by silent agreement, they'd chosen to hide behind their respective books, and any additional travelers they procured during the varied stops seemed content to allow that silence to linger on.

But good luck never holds. If anything, bad fortune follows quickly upon its heels, guaranteeing to balance whatever good its kinder brother bestowed.

Lydia gave Mrs. Crenshaw a genuine smile when the lady climbed into the carriage, but alas, the happiness of having another woman aboard was quickly quelled as words spewed forth from the woman's mouth; she was kind enough and full of good-natured observations about anything and everything that crossed her mind, and though it was not enlightening or interesting, Mrs. Crenshaw was a merry sort who imbued every syllable with good cheer. However, the woman managed to speak a full hour while never pausing long enough to allow anyone else to speak a single syllable. Lydia would be content to simply ignore her, but whenever she attempted to disappear behind her book, Mrs. Crenshaw directed something at Lydia, forcing her to engage once more or be monstrously rude.

And as much as rudeness had its appeal at times, Lydia couldn't bring herself to act so when the recipient was a well-meaning and minor annoyance.

Besides, focusing on Mrs. Crenshaw allowed Lydia to ignore Mr. Crenshaw. Almost.

Lydia nudged the fellow's foot, which had once more drifted forward to tangle in her legs. As there was little space to be had in the vehicle, there was nothing to be done about limbs encroaching on another passenger's territory, but one must do what one could to minimize the impact one's person had upon another; Lydia had thought all travelers had an unspoken agreement upon entering the confined space. Apparently, Mr. Crenshaw did not think such politeness applied to him.

From the moment he took his place across from Lydia, his limbs moved wherever they pleased. It was bad enough that he insisted on wiping his muddy boots on the edge of her gown (yet another unfortunate byproduct of travel), but the fellow took up far more than his allotted space. Whenever Lydia attempted to nudge his feet or knees, he simply spread further. It was like sitting across from Napoleon, taking territory bit by bit that did not belong to him. Where was Wellington when one needed him?

With a sigh, Lydia turned from the gloomy overcast sky and glanced at Mr. Bradshaw. His book remained clutched in his hand, though he had his eyes fixed on Mrs. Crenshaw, who was giving a remarkably detailed account of all the plants in her garden.

Mr. Bradshaw's gaze met Lydia's, and there was a silent groan pleading for her to save him. With a quick widening of her eyes, she sent back sympathy and understanding, but she could do nothing more for the situation than he; after several attempts to break through Mrs. Crenshaw's monologue, Lydia surrendered herself to the tantalizing hope that perhaps the next stop would see the husband and wife depart. For that brief moment, Lydia shared a silent laugh with Mr. Bradshaw, commiserating together in the only manner allowed them. Then she gave a pointed look at Mr. Crenshaw's offending limbs, and they shared yet another moment of sympathy.

It wasn't until the moment was over that Lydia realized just how odd it was to share any sort of understanding with Mr. Bradshaw. She hadn't thought they shared much in common.

Mr. Bradshaw's words spoke of his low opinion of her, yet his actions testified differently. He entrusted her with his daughter and escorted her to London. And he had defended her to Ambrose. Lydia knew the gentlemen hadn't intended her to overhear, but Mr. Bradshaw's support of this plan (no matter how foolish he might think it) was astonishing. It was said that actions speak louder than words, yet the phrase was usually attached to unkind actions and honeyed words—not the opposite.

That confusion only increased after the next stop on their journey. Lydia lingered longer than the others, unwilling to return to the coach a moment sooner than necessary, and approached to find that Mr. Bradshaw was not waiting to help her in as he had before. Instead, he'd followed Mr. Crenshaw's example and entered first. Perhaps Lydia might've overlooked that startling behavior, except it placed him directly across from Mr. Crenshaw, saving her from battling the fellow's wandering limbs. Mr. Bradshaw's action was too out of character to be anything but a purposeful choice to take her place.

Unfortunately, the next few hours of travel left Lydia with little else to focus on than deciphering Mr. Bradshaw's inscrutable behavior. With mixed company, she couldn't ask him directly, and Mrs. Crenshaw wouldn't allow Lydia the opportunity to focus her thoughts on a book, so Lydia was left to pick through all the nuances of his actions and words—which, with a fellow like Mr. Bradshaw, was like trying to sort out a riddle with only half the lines.

By the time they arrived at the inn for the night, Lydia felt knotted up in more ways than one. Her legs and back begged to be stretched, and her thoughts longed for answers. More insistent was her stomach, which demanded a proper meal.

Stepping free of the carriage, Lydia surveyed the place which was to be their lodging for the night. She supposed that being the only inn for some miles granted the proprietor a measure of security, but she would think the fellow himself would wish to live in a better place than this. Perhaps it was only the dying rays of light that gave the place a forlorn look, but Lydia swore the walls sagged.

Had she been alone, she would not have entered, but with Mr. Bradshaw at her back, Lydia felt her nerves slip away into nothing. Not that she was naive enough to think that a solitary man might serve as protector if true trouble was afoot, but it was difficult to believe Mr. Bradshaw could not handle whatever may come.

In quick order, he had them situated in the pub, though the building did not improve upon closer acquaintance. It was dark, small, and had only a passing familiarity with soap and water, but as it did little good to bemoan this temporary situation, Lydia took her seat and awaited their dinner. She hoped it was edible.

The barmaid dropped two bowls of stew before them, and the hunks of bread that had been balanced on the rims fell to the tabletop. But to Lydia's surprise, the food smelled quite delicious. Or perhaps her empty stomach had conjured more appetizing aromas. But if that was the case, it was a blessing, for this bowl of stew may be one of the best she'd ever eaten, and Lydia tucked into it with a fervor that would have raised her mother-in-law's brows.

"Now, would you be looking for a room tonight?"

Lydia looked up from her meal to find the innkeeper standing beside their table.

Reaching for his coin purse, Mr. Bradshaw said, "We require two rooms—"

But the fellow shook his head. "I'm terribly sorry, sir, but I'm afraid we have only one room for you and your lady friend."

Mr. Bradshaw paused and turned a gimlet eye on the proprietor. "I am a solicitor, and this lady is my *client*."

The fellow held up his hands. "I meant no disrespect, sir. I only mean to say that we don't have accommodations unless—"

"If you have a pallet somewhere, I will take that, but she requires a proper bed."

The two haggled prices for a moment, and Lydia stared at Mr. Bradshaw as he dropped a few coins into the innkeeper's hand and returned to his meal. He seemed to give her no more thought as he tucked in with the same fervor she'd shown a moment ago.

"Why are you being so kind to me?" she blurted.

Chapter 18

Mr. Bradshaw paused with his spoon halfway to his mouth and gave her a furrowed brow.

"For all that you call me your client, I have not offered you a farthing of compensation, yet still you assist me in my troubles. You've sent out petitions on my behalf, are accompanying me to London, and have given up a proper bed for my sake." With a sigh, Lydia shook her head. "You even surrendered your seat so I would have a more comfortable situation. I cannot comprehend it."

Dropping his spoon to the bowl, Mr. Bradshaw narrowed his eyes. "I assure you that even lowborn men are capable of manners and treating a lady with respect."

"Of course they are, but this is more than that, Mr. Bradshaw. You've made it clear you hold me in low esteem, yet you defended my plan to my brother-in-law."

Mr. Bradshaw cocked his head. "And how do you know that?"

"I overheard you two speak after I left, and I cannot countenance why you would go to such lengths to assist me."

"It seems I need a better door," he muttered.

Lydia's cheeks reddened, and she attempted to cover her response by speaking low and quick. "I may have pressed my ear to it."

"Then I need better clerks."

Her brows drew together, and she shook her head. "Do not blame them."

Mr. Bradshaw shook his head as well and gave her a small smile. "I do not. Nor am I sorry you overheard it. I meant what I said. I am pleased to assist you in this matter."

"I know you do not think well of me, sir." His brows rose, but Lydia shook her head. "Do not deny it. You made it quite clear you do not hold me in high esteem."

"I assure you I do not leave my daughter in the care of people whom I hold in low regard."

Lydia scoffed. "I cannot comprehend why you allow me to teach her, but you have made your low opinion clear on many occasions."

Robert was not prone to megrims, but he was certain to have one tonight, for its human embodiment was seated before him. After that wretched day of travel, he simply wanted to collapse on a proper bed and get a good night's rest, though he knew that was not in his future.

"I've already apologized to you concerning that," he said.

Lady Whiting's gaze dropped to her dinner, and she pushed the chunks of mutton and vegetables around. "As I've said before, it is not so easy to erase the damage done by words, sir. I have accepted your apology, but that does not mean your words no longer pain me." Abandoning her spoon, Lady Whiting raised her gaze to meet his and added, "That is the problem with words. They are easily spoken, but their influence is not so easily forgotten."

"If you choose to allow the wound to fester, it is not my fault."

"True," she conceded with a nod, "but wounds do not heal in an instant, either. Have you never been made to feel worthless?"

Robert turned his attention back to his meal and nodded. "That is my point. I've always been treated poorly because of my birth, yet I have not allowed that to hurt me."

Silence followed though the other patrons of the pub kept the air filled with chatter and laughter. Robert took another few bites of his food while Lady Whiting considered his words.

"You've never felt the sting of those low expectations?" she asked.

Robert stared at his bowl of stew and wondered if the cook knew salt and pepper existed as he gave that question proper thought. "Certainly, but I dusted myself off and ignored them."

"How?"

Lady Whiting's question was nearly lost in the din around them, but that single word drew Robert's gaze, and he found her watching him with wide eyes.

"I simply do not listen," he said.

The lady sighed, her shoulders slumping as she turned her gaze to her stew, churning about the chunks with her spoon. As she seemed finished with the discussion, Robert returned to his meal, though with less gusto than before as his thoughts churned over that question.

Robert didn't think much of his younger years. There was little reason to do so, for they were hardly worth remembering. But something in Lady Whiting's tone drove him to cast his thoughts back through those early days and remember that which was better left forgotten. He found himself wondering if his father was alive or dead; though the brute was young enough to still be among the living, his lifestyle spoke of one destined for a shortened life. More than that, Robert wondered if he even cared to know. If living, his father was far from here. If dead, the man deserved no mourning. So, Robert supposed his father's current state was of no concern to him.

Mr. Ewings was more of a proper father, and though it had been a year since that dear man's passing, Robert mourned him still. Memories of those early years he'd spent as Mr. Ewings' clerk flooded his thoughts. It was a testament to how kindhearted the gentleman was, for no matter how many mistakes his young, bumbling clerk had made (and Robert had made plenty), Mr. Ewings never lost his temper.

Perhaps he ought to write Mrs. Ewings and see how she was faring. Her husband had more than aptly provided for his widow, but Robert knew just how lonely a house could be without one's spouse to fill it.

"There is something to be said of surrounding yourself with good people," said Robert.

Lady Whiting slanted a look at him from under her lashes, though she kept her face turned to her dinner.

"I was perhaps a bit hasty to say it was solely a matter of not listening to the condemnations," he clarified. "Your question got me thinking about my own life, and the man who changed my life."

Though the lady attempted to feign nonchalance at his enigmatic statement, there was too much curiosity in her gaze to ignore, so Robert continued.

"Mr. Ewings was the gentleman who trained me to be a solicitor," he said. "My father worked the fields as a day laborer and expected me to follow in his footsteps as my brothers did, but I spent my time hounding the local schoolmaster, learning all I could. Eventually, I caught the attention of our town's solicitor, who recognized my potential and took me on as his clerk."

Robert glanced at the room around them, his eyes meandering the space as his thoughts sorted through the past. "Though I have a natural determination. I can in all honesty say I would not have achieved my success without Mr. Ewings' efforts. Few would've assisted a young man with nothing to offer in return."

"That is quite the blessing," said Lady Whiting. "Not everyone finds that sort of aid."

"You have your sister and her family," he said, turning his gaze to her once more.

Lady Whiting nodded, though her eyes remained lowered to her stew. "But I fear there are far more voices telling me to surrender."

"Then you must ignore them," he said with a shrug.

She sighed. "It is not that simple."

"Whyever not?"

Lady Whiting's brows drew together, and her gaze bored into her bowl for several long moments before she spoke again. "Imagine someone claimed your Nell told a fib."

"She doesn't fib."

She waved that protest away. "Imagine someone claimed she did. What would you do?"

Robert shrugged again and took a bite of his soup. "I would trust my daughter, for she has earned it."

Lady Whiting nodded. "And if someone else also came forward to say she fibbed?"

Considering that, Robert replied, "I suppose I would investigate it further, but I would still believe Nell until I found evidence to the contrary."

"And if more people said she had?"

Robert paused, examining the lady, though she hardly looked up from the table.

"What if they all said the same thing?" she asked. "Wouldn't you believe them? Even if Nell claimed to be telling the truth?"

"Perhaps," said Robert, though he knew it was likely more than a 'perhaps.'

Lady Whiting's blue eyes finally rose to meet his once more, and there was a pain inside them as she said, "Imagine those voices are pointed towards you, saying you are a disappointment and beneath their contempt. Do you not think it would be easier to believe them more than the one or two that are claiming the opposite?"

Robert almost smiled and huffed at that, for Lady Whiting's argument was as sound as any he'd heard in his years in the legal profession, though she would likely take his mirth as derisive rather than surprising. Lady Whiting was fascinating.

"I concede the point," he said. "Though I will say it is important to pay better heed to the sources. What does it matter if an acquaintance thinks poorly of you compared to someone who knows you well?"

Lady Whiting scoffed, though it held more exhaustion than derision. "I assure you that hearing anyone say the world would be better without you is a mighty blow that cannot be easily shaken off."

Robert scowled at her, though he softened his expression when she shrank away from it. "Who said such a thing to you?"

There was no reply, so Robert waited in silence as she pushed around her dinner. At times like these, patience was a virtue, and though Robert couldn't claim he possessed it, he could summon it at times.

"Your husband," he concluded.

Lady Whiting gave him a wan smile. "That particular quote belongs to my mother-in-law, though Sir Duncan expressed similarly uncomplimentary opinions. It was the last thing she said to me, though I believe her precise words were that the world would be better off if it had been me and not my husband who had perished."

"No doubt they were the words of a grieving mother," Robert said, though he doubted it.

"They were not. Nor were they the opinions of mere acquaintances. Both my husband and his mother have long regretted our marriage. Though not more than myself."

With furrowed brows, Lad Whiting dropped her gaze to her dish and pushed it aside. Her voice lowered, and Robert was forced to lean closer to hear her over the crowd. "Perhaps I might ignore all the things they said, but it was not only them. The villagers and servants dismissed me. My husband's guests and friends mocked me. What little kindness I received was only due to my beauty, and when it became clear I had not the skill and training to step in as the baronet's wife, my only value was that of a broodmare. And even that role I could not perform to their satisfaction."

Robert watched her as she seemed to shrink down into the chair.

"Only Mary and her family believe I have value, and as much as I am grateful for that, it is difficult to trust a few voices speaking kindnesses when so many others say the opposite. Who does one believe? The one voice or the many?" Lady Whiting shook her head, turning her gaze to the fireplace; despite the full room, the summer's day had been a gloomy, damp thing, and they could've used a fire there, but the innkeeper had kept it empty.

"You should trust those who know you best," said Robert.

Lady Whiting's eyes met his once more, and she gave another wan smile. "But friends and family are freer and more generous with their compliments than their criticisms. Kindness can be driven by pity, but hard words are usually unvarnished truths."

Robert frowned. "That is a bleak assessment."

"But true enough. Would you believe the single overly kind witness when so many others are saying otherwise?"

Shoving aside his meal, Robert considered that and the lady before him. He'd never given much thought to words before, yet Lady Whiting's logic was infallible—even if it sat uneasily with him. Robert was not given to fits of embarrassment, but he felt a swell of it at that moment, realizing how readily he'd judged her.

And so, he told her.

"Though I have said so before, I do apologize for adding my voice to the many who have hurt you. It was not my intention. And I assure you I am not saying so because of pity or a false desire to smooth over the past. I truly regret that I caused you any pain."

Lady Whiting studied him with a furrowed expression for several long moments before she nodded.

"And to answer the question that started us down this conversational path, I will freely admit I haven't had the highest opinion of you in the past," he said, laughing to himself that perhaps Lady Whiting was fully correct in her assessment of kindnesses, for he'd wanted to soften that truth. Instead, he'd given it to her unvarnished. "However, as to why I am aiding you, it is entirely due to the changes you are making of late. It gives me great pleasure to see you taking charge of your fate."

Pausing, Robert considered that and realized there was a bit more to his motives than he'd realized before. "And I suppose I would like to be your Mr. Ewings. Though I like to think of myself as a self-made man, he helped me to become what I am. I can think of no better way to honor him than to do the same for another."

But there were other thoughts that he did not care to share. Even with their growing camaraderie, there were certain truths Robert wished to remain hidden. Like how much Lady Whiting reminded him of his mother and sisters, how little he'd been able to do for them, and how nice it was to have someone accept his assistance.

Lady Whiting straightened, watching him with wary eyes for several long moments before she said, "I think I believe you, Mr. Bradshaw."

Robert opened his mouth to give a smart reply but paused as he realized she had ample reasons to disbelieve overtures of kindness; he'd reacted much the same when his mentor first offered his friendship, so he could not fault her for feeling the same.

"Thank you, Mr. Bradshaw," she said with a faint smile. Turning her gaze to the bowl of stew, she nodded at it. "I cannot decide if this is the best or worst meal I've ever had."

With a chuckle, Robert nodded. "Hunger can make even the most unpalatable meal a feast."

Lady Whiting's brow wrinkled. "Are you certain you do not wish for the bedchamber? I hate to be such an imposition, and you already delayed your trip to London on my behalf. No doubt you would be there by now if not for me."

Robert ignored the itch at the back of his neck. There was no need to tell her that his trip to London was mostly unwarranted. There were items of business to conduct, but the majority could've been completed through correspondence, and the rest could've waited until something critical forced him to Town.

"It is no imposition," he said. "And I cannot countenance taking your bedchamber. I doubt you'd fare well in whatever lodging the innkeeper will scrounge for me."

Shaking her head, Lady Whiting huffed. "I would fare better than you think. It would not be the first time I had to sleep on an inn floor."

Robert tilted his head, watching her with a twisted smile. "And when would you have ever done that, Lady Whiting?"

Straightening, she gave him a smile that held some of that brightness of spirit she'd shown of late. "When I left my husband's home, I had only my daughter, a portmanteau, and hardly enough funds to pay for the journey." Before he could ask further questions, she held up a hand and continued, "I hadn't planned to take the journey until the night before, when I knew I must free myself and my daughter from my parents and the Whitings. But I could not delay, so I took what pin money I had left and boarded the first coach that pointed me towards Lancashire."

Robert's brows rose as he considered that.

"It took me considerably longer than if I had decided on a route beforehand, and there were several nights when I was left with no option but to sleep where I could." Lady Whiting's smile widened, and pride gleamed in her eyes. "But I found my sister."

Leaning back, Robert shook his head. "There are not many ladies who would have undertaken such a journey."

Lady Whiting dropped her gaze to her stew. "I had no other choice."

"Yes, you did. And for your and your daughter's sake, I am glad you took it." More than she could understand, for his family was filled with examples of those who had not. Though in his childhood, his mother hadn't had a safe place to land like Lady Whiting had, Robert's later offers of safety and support had been met by deaf ears.

Robert's expression softened, and he added, "But there is no reason for you to suffer such a rough journey again."

Lady Whiting smiled at him. Not a wide, bright thing, but a soft, pleased grin that shone with an earnestness one did not often find among titled ladies. Of course, Lady Whiting was proving to be vastly different from most of her class. In considering his dear wife, Robert tried to think of whether she would do as Lady Whiting had. Eleanor had spirit—the sort that would fight against the imprisonment Lady Whiting had faced in her marriage. But if Eleanor had landed herself in such a difficult situation, Robert didn't know if she would be willing to surrender the creature comforts she adored.

Warmth settled into his heart as he considered the coming trip. The first day of travel had left much to be desired, but Robert felt that Mr. Ewings would be quite pleased with the efforts he'd made on Lady Whiting's behalf. Whatever came of this journey, Robert felt certain it would help put Lady Whiting to rights.

Chapter 19

Heavens above. Six and thirty was not such an advanced age, but Robert felt like a steam locomotive on its last lump of coal. In his twenties, missing a night's sleep would be irritating but not problematic. Now, after a wretched night, he was faced with overwhelming evidence that he was not as young as he once was. Add to that the rocking motion of the carriage, and Robert hadn't any chance of staying awake, though it was hardly a worthwhile sleep since he was jolted awake constantly as the coach bumped over the uneven road. And his already sore neck was only growing stiffer from the odd angle at which he propped his head against the side of the carriage.

Not all innkeepers were unscrupulous. Many were good-natured sorts who ran their business with dignity and honor. Unfortunately, too many fell into an unenviable category: lazy. Cutthroats and misers could be dealt with in quick order, but those who simply couldn't be bothered were harder to wrangle. It was near impossible to inspire effort in someone who did not care.

And so, Robert had spent a cold, hard night in the stable, counting the minutes until morning.

Honor dictated he keep awake to watch over Lady Whiting as they traveled, but it was a losing battle. If he could snatch a full hour of rest then he might manage to be alert for the rest of the day. Robert shook his head, rubbing at his face as he straightened, and the movement knocked a bundle to the ground. Lady Whiting dove for it and caught the bit of linen before it spilled its contents, and she offered it to him.

"What is this?" he asked, and she pulled back the covering to reveal a hunk of bread and cheese. They were simply made, but the loaf was fresh, and the scent set his stomach gurgling.

"You slept through lunch, and the coachman said there isn't going to be refreshment before our stop for the night," she said. "I thought you might get hungry before then."

Staring at the food, Robert felt the stiffness of his muscles ease. With the weather in a sour disposition at present, their journey had been chill, but that bite in the air eased as warmth flooded through him. Her offering was such a little thing, yet it struck Robert with far more force than was warranted. But then again, he could not recall the last time someone had taken care of him in such a manner.

Robert breathed in the aroma and smiled. "Thank you."

Lady Whiting blushed and turned her gaze to the window. "It is nothing."

"I assure you it means a great deal to me," he said.

"I am in debt to you with little hope of ever repaying your kindness, Mr. Bradshaw."

Taking a bite of the bread, Robert gave her a slanted smile as he chewed. "I would say this makes us even."

"You are so easily bought?"

Robert chuckled. "You have not tasted this bread. And my mother was fond of saying that nothing pleases a man like a full belly."

They lapsed into silence, and Robert glanced at the pair opposite. The gentlemen (whose names he had long forgotten) were occupied with their own pursuits, one with his newspaper, and the other situated as Robert had been moments ago.

Most roadside fare was hardly worth noting, and perhaps it was only his hunger making it seem so, but the bread and cheese were delectable. The loaf was the hearty sort with a crusty outside hiding a soft and airy inside, and the cheese was sharp and flavorful—the perfect pairing for a simple meal.

Robert's lids slid closed again, and he forced them open once more. With the day fast approaching its close, it would do him no good to sleep at present. Glancing at his companion, Robert seized on the first subject that sprang to mind.

"What are you reading?" he asked, nodding at the book on her lap.

"At present, it is Thomas Wilson's *An Analysis of Country Dancing*." Lady Whiting tapped the cover with a bright smile. "I've been educating myself so that I might better teach your daughter and my niece."

Robert stared at the lady and found himself supremely grateful Mrs. Ashbrook had spoken to him about the dancing lessons. Anyone who saw the pride in Lady Whiting's eyes would know how much it meant to her. And though it was a simple thing, Robert knew too well what joys could be found in small victories when one was forging a new path.

"And you enjoy reading about such things?" he asked.

Lady Whiting clutched the book and gave a contented nod. "It may seem strange, but though I am familiar with dancing, there is so much more to it that I could not appreciate before. It is quite a fascinating subject."

Though Robert could not agree on that point, he would not begrudge her the pleasure she found in it. Certainly, she was not as keen as he to delve into his world of wills, trusts, and money scrivening.

"But, sir, I must admit," she said, leaning forward to whisper, "more often than not, I delve into some lurid tale. I just finished *The Forest of Valancourt* and was enamored with it, and I have at least one more Gothic novel tucked in my valise."

The gentleman across the way glanced over the top of his newspaper and met Robert's eye with a look that revealed far more about the person giving it than it did of the subject of his derision; it conveyed a clear irritation for female chattering as though he and all men preferred the ladyfolk remain silent. But that exasperation was no less irritating than Mrs. Crenshaw's incessant conversation the day previous.

Giving the fellow a narrowed look, Robert turned to Lady Whiting and nodded. "I am fond of that novel as well."

The lady straightened, meeting that confession with a blank stare. "You needn't mock me."

Giving her a chagrined smile, he shook his head. "I am in earnest. I am not ashamed to admit I enjoy Gothic tales."

That confession earned him a scoff from the other passenger and a roll of his eyes before the gentleman disappeared behind his newspaper, which didn't bother Robert in the slightest. But the look on Lady Whiting's face said she believed him no more than the gentleman.

"Why is that so shocking?" asked Robert. "It is perfectly acceptable for a fellow to read Sir Walter Scott, yet many of his stories are no less ridiculous than those of Mrs. Smith, Francis Lathom, or Matthew Lewis."

"Though I doubt Sir Scott employs much romance."

Robert waved that argument away. "Perhaps not as much as his Gothic counterparts, but there is nary a story that does not have a fair maiden who entrances the intrepid hero. Have you not read him?"

Lady Whiting shook her head. "I admit I am only slightly familiar with his novels."

"I have all his works at home, should you wish to read them. If you are a fan of stories with adventure and a smattering of romance, then you would enjoy them."

With a faint smile, she studied him. "I do not know many men who would admit to enjoying stories where love plays a role."

Robert shrugged. "Perhaps not, but it's telling that most stories written by men and aimed at a male audience have some hint of romance to them—no matter how small. Even if the hero spends the majority of his time defeating the forces of evil, there is mention of a damsel, and he will win her heart by the end. Men may not own it, but everyone wishes to love and be loved."

That smile broadened as she stared at him. Her eyes flashed with warmth and mirth, making the blue sparkle despite the cloudy day. "Mr. Bradshaw, you are a romantic."

Slanting her a twisted smile, he shrugged once more. But that was met with silence as Lady Whiting stared at him.

"What is the matter?" he asked.

Lady Whiting shook her head, but when pressed, she admitted, "You are not at all what I thought you were, Mr. Bradshaw. The man I met nearly a month ago seemed more apt to sneer at my literature choices."

Giving Robert a pointed look, she turned her gaze to the gentleman behind the newspaper and back again with far too much emphasis for him to miss her meaning.

"My demeanor when we first met was befitting a fellow having been pulled into a situation not of his own making. And I was at your sister's home on business, not a social call." Lady Whiting raised her brows, and Robert recalled their other meetings and nodded. "I suppose I have not presented myself well."

That was met by a sad smile. "The same could be said of me."

Robert liked her all the more for admitting it. Neither of them had been at their best during their first few meetings, but what had happened was not nearly as important as what would come next, and they both could—and would—do better.

Leaning closer, Robert whispered to her, "Is there any possibility you might read aloud some of whatever *lurid* tale you've got secreted in your valise? I fear I am not enjoying the novel I brought on the journey."

Lady Whiting gave him a brilliant smile—one that chased away the shadows in the carriage and brightened the world around her. And Robert couldn't help his responding grin at having inspired such a look.

...

Having an amiable traveling companion made a world of difference. The silence they'd shared before may have been amiable, but it was silence nonetheless. That melted away as the miles passed, making the next few days fly by with far more speed than before. Lydia's education and knowledge of the world were sadly lacking compared to Mr. Bradshaw's, but it was as interesting to hear him explain the finer points of his work as it was to debate literature. Though truth be told, the nuances of his profession were tedious at times, but his passion for the topic made them more intriguing than they'd have been otherwise. Lydia had never thought of contracts and wills as interesting business before.

Mr. Bradshaw was such an odd man. At first glance, he seemed so aloof and rigid, yet here sat a man who not only had read books like *The Venetian Sorceress* but enjoyed them enough to discuss the plots and characters. Lydia wished she had a quill and paper on hand to write down the many suggestions he shared, but she would simply have to pester him for those recommendations when they arrived home.

But that drew her up short.

Once upon a time, home had meant Bristow, but her parents' roof was no longer a welcome refuge. Lydia couldn't even claim to feel like a visitor inside her husband's house—an interloper or poor, unwanted relation perhaps, but there was nothing hospitable for her there. Yet despite her short stay, Greater Edgerton had become a home to her. Even though she was in fact a visitor and a poor relation, Mary's house was a haven to her. A welcome oasis in her life.

And if all went as planned today, Lydia would not remain there.

Her heart was constricted, tightening into a ball. The sentiment was not overpowering or painful, but more like a pressure that settled in the center of her chest. All would be well. Lydia knew it, yet restless energy took hold of her, wanting her to take some action, but she was shut inside the carriage, unable to make it move faster. Lydia was stuck, waiting and watching as the countryside gave way to the city.

"What is the matter?" asked Mr. Bradshaw, and she turned to meet his worried gaze.

Uncertain how to answer that, Lydia lay hold of the first pressing issue. Leaning forward, she whispered to him so as not to allow the others in the carriage to overhear; luckily, those gentlemen were engaged in their own conversation and not paying her any heed.

"What if Mr. Marks does not forgive me? We have come all this way, and I do not know if he will even hear me out."

Mr. Bradshaw took a moment to consider that, as he was wont to do. The fellow rarely gave hasty replies, though many in his situation would've been quick to assure her, and Lydia appreciated his thoughtful responses all the more for it.

"If he cannot forgive you, then he is not the man you thought he was," said Mr. Bradshaw. "But I doubt it will come to that. Love is not so easily ignored, and if Mr. Marks truly cared for you, he may be hurt, but he will forgive."

"You sound certain of that."

Mr. Bradshaw shrugged. "If the woman I loved appeared on my doorstep, begging my forgiveness, I would freely give it. I would hazard to say there is no happier outcome than a quarrel to be mended and lovers reunited."

Lydia watched him for a silent moment. "You truly are a romantic at heart, Mr. Bradshaw."

"After having lost my love, I learned to seize happiness when I can, Lady Whiting. I would give anything to have my wife back once more."

Lydia examined his profile and found herself saying, "I understand you lost her when Nell was born."

The fellow nodded and said nothing further.

Though perhaps she ought not to ask it, Lydia found herself compelled to do so. "You loved her so very much?"

Mr. Bradshaw gave a sad smile. "She was the best of women. How could I not love her?"

Lydia smiled faintly, her gaze drifting to the window, though she did not see the passing buildings. "That is a beautiful sentiment, Mr. Bradshaw."

Those words were too small for what Lydia felt at his declaration. Mrs. Bradshaw had been absent from this world for some eight years, yet the fellow spoke with the conviction of a newly married man, determined to love and cherish for the rest of his days. Lydia had been wrong to say Mr. Bradshaw was a romantic, for such devotion displayed more than merely a loving heart.

"Do not fret, Lady Whiting. One way or another, we shall make things right."

Lydia nodded, and she clung to his certainty as they arrived at their lodgings, deposited their luggage, and set off for their final destination.

Chapter 20

This last leg felt far longer than the rest, though it took a fraction of the time. Of course, the streets were far more difficult to traverse than the rest of their journey, for they were clogged by the evening exodus for home. Despite their slow progress, the timing of their arrival seemed precipitous, for Mr. Marks was guaranteed to have arrived home for the day; Lydia could not imagine waiting another wretched hour.

But those happy thoughts fled her as the world outside the hackney's window moved from townhouses to tenements. The driver stopped before a dilapidated building that bore the distinction of being the finest on the street, though that meant little in this neighborhood. Lydia stood on the pavement and stared at it, unable to believe someone of Mr. Marks' standing would be forced to live in such a place. The fellow may be a lowly tutor, but that was a world above someone who belonged in the slums.

Mr. Bradshaw gave orders for the driver to wait for them and came to her side as she stood transfixed. He did not speak the words aloud, but Lydia felt the silent question. Giving him a nod, she moved towards the building and followed the directions to Mr. Marks' rooms. Lydia steeled her nerves, forcing her hand to remain strong as she knocked at his door, but the swirl of anticipation and anxiety set her insides quaking.

A woman opened the door, and Lydia blinked at her and the child sitting on the woman's hip.

"Yes?" the woman asked. Lydia's throat tightened and her heart gave several erratic thumps.

"We are here to see Mr. Owen Marks," said Mr. Bradshaw, though his gaze turned to Lydia.

She examined the pair on the doorstep and nodded, shutting the door most of the way; through the crack, Lydia saw several children running about the small room.

"His sister," whispered Lydia.

Mr. Bradshaw looked at her with raised and disbelieving brows.

"Mr. Marks spoke of his youngest sister. Quite often, in fact. I don't know why he is living with her. But it is no matter," she said with an airy wave as though casting aside Mr. Bradshaw's doubts.

The door opened once more, and a man filled the doorway.

"Yes?" he asked.

Lydia blinked. "We are looking for Mr. Owen Marks."

The fellow nodded and held out his arms as though presenting himself. But it took a long moment before Lydia could see the young man she knew in the figure before her. His dark hair lacked the easy manner in which it had swept across his head, and his blue eyes were grayer than she recalled. But more than that, his elegant hands were roughened and cragged. He hardly resembled the handsome figure that had captured her heart.

"If you are simply going to stand about gawking at me, I'll return to my dinner," he said, moving to shut the door.

Lydia stepped forward, pushing against the wood. "Am I so very altered that you do not recognize me?"

"Papa!" One of the children launched herself at Mr. Marks' leg, latching to his calf and plopping herself onto his foot.

"Papa?" whispered Lydia. Her thoughts raced through scenarios in which that title could be applied to Mr. Marks without him having married, none of which soothed her heart. Especially when the woman came up beside him and touched his back with a familiarity that was more than a sister would display.

Pressing a hand to her stomach, Lydia stepped away from the familial scene of husband, wife, and children. She counted four little ones—the eldest of which couldn't be more than six years old. Lydia spun in place and hurried back towards the hackney. Mr. Bradshaw kept pace with her, keeping a hand at her elbow to keep her from slipping in her haste.

"Miss Lydia!"

Though she did not want them to, Lydia's feet paused of their own accord, turning her to see Mr. Marks rushing after her.

"What are you doing here, Miss Lydia?" Mr. Marks paused. "Though I suppose that is not your name any longer."

Lydia opened her mouth, but words did not emerge.

"Lady Whiting," supplied Mr. Bradshaw, and Lydia nodded, though she could not raise her eyes from her feet.

There was silence for a moment before Mr. Marks asked, "Would you come inside and tell me what has you on my doorstep after so many years?"

Lydia's gaze met Mr. Bradshaw's, but his expression held no hint of whether he thought it the right course of action. He merely met her own puzzled look with a questioning glance of his own, making it clear the decision was hers alone.

With a nod, she allowed Mr. Marks to lead them back to his tiny flat. The children seemed to have multiplied, and the woman watched them with a questioning look as Mr. Marks ushered them in and sat them around the kitchen table that occupied the majority of the room. Quickly, the woman cleared away the food, moving aside their dinner so their guests could sit.

"Lady Whiting, might I introduce my wife, Mrs. Mary Marks," he said, drawing the woman closer. Mrs. Marks' eyes widened at the sound of the title, and she glanced between her husband and her visitors.

Lydia's mouth dried, her tongue sticking to the roof of her mouth. She nodded, ignoring the prickles of pain radiating from her heart.

"My elder sister is also Mary," she finally managed. "It is a good name."

Mrs. Marks gave a tremulous smile and a bob. "Thank you, my lady."

Shifting the babe on her hip, the woman ushered the other children forward, giving their names in rapid succession as each gave an approximation of a bow or curtsy, though Lydia's thoughts could hardly grasp what she was seeing, let alone their names. The chair beneath her wobbled, adding to the disorientation she felt. It was as though the entire world was off-kilter, and she was stuck in the midst of it, unable to right it.

Mrs. Marks fluttered about, offering refreshments, but Lydia could not countenance eating a morsel, though she accepted a cup of tea made with leaves that had been steeped so many times, there was hardly any flavor left in them. Given their humble lodgings, it was a miracle they could afford such a luxury. Though Lydia did not wish to take such an offering, her mouth was too dry for her to turn it away.

Especially when Mrs. Marks took her seat beside her husband. Though both they and their offspring were as clean as one could expect in their surroundings, there was a ragged quality to them, as though they wore exhaustion like a shawl. Yet they shared little, silent moments that spoke of contentment. Touches and looks that displayed no overt emotions but were the signs of a husband and wife who were more than mere partners.

Lydia did not fault Mr. Marks for finding his happiness, yet her heart ached at the sight of it.

"Now, what has brought you and your husband to my doorstep?" asked Mr. Marks.

Straightening, Lydia shook her head. "This is Mr. Robert Bradshaw. He is my solicitor and friend."

The gentlemen exchanged nods and handshakes as Lydia struggled with what to say.

"My husband passed away nearly three months ago," said Lydia, and Mr. Marks glanced at her mourning clothes with a solemn nod.

"I am sorry to hear that," he murmured.

"I am not," she said, the words slipping out before she could rein in her tongue.

Mr. Marks' brow furrowed. "Then I am even sorrier to hear that. I'd hoped your marriage would be better than you feared."

Lydia's gaze dropped to the table as she fiddled with her teacup. She didn't know what to say to that, for it had been far worse than she'd anticipated. Nor did she know how to complete this conversation while holding onto her dignity. Though she'd cobbled together a manner in which to broach the subject of their marriage, Lydia hadn't anticipated his wife being in attendance; as that subject was no longer applicable, she didn't know what ought to replace it.

"I wanted to see how you were faring," she said, which was honest enough.

"Well enough," he said, taking his wife by the hand. "The past year has not been kind to us, but we have weathered it."

"What happened?"

Mr. Marks gave an unhappy laugh. "No one is stingier with their bills than the wealthy. I always struggled to collect from my clients, but with the Panic setting so many in a dither, it became impossible to get what I was owed. In the end, I decided to change professions. Luckily, my father taught me cobbling when I was young, so I was able to find employment in a shop."

His wife set down their youngest, who toddled after his siblings, and she straightened, placing a hand atop her husband's. No words passed between them, yet Lydia felt the understanding and strength they gave and took from each other. It was just the sort of moment Lydia had imagined with her Mr. Marks.

"Have you settled in London?" he asked, and Lydia fought against a blush.

"I am living with my sister in Lancashire," she replied, struggling to know how to respond without letting him know the whole of her shame. "I am in Town for business."

Mr. Marks nodded, seeming none the wiser, but Lydia felt Mrs. Marks' gaze and saw the understanding dawning there. And though she did not speak a word, Mr. Marks noticed his wife's expression and his brow furrowed.

"I hate to be a bother," said Lydia, getting to her feet and moving towards the door. "We have intruded on your dinner and should leave you to it—"

"Miss Lydia—Lady Whiting, please," he said, and Lydia shuddered. It was bad enough having that name forever tied to her, but to hear it from *his* lips in a tone steeped in pity was more than she could bear.

Mr. Marks stopped her at the door, and though the others gave them some distance, the room was not large enough to afford more than a passing nod at privacy.

"You came for more than that, didn't you?" he whispered.

Lydia's back pressed against the door, her gaze falling to her toes. "I know I hurt you, but I had hoped you would still be free."

Mr. Marks straightened, standing before her in silence for a long moment. "You did not hurt me, Miss Lydia." Shaking his head, he corrected himself, "Lady Whiting."

"I prefer Miss Lydia," she murmured. With the last bit of her courage, Lydia met his gaze. Those eyes that had seemed like bright beacons in her dreams were dimmed with sorrow.

"As do I," he said with a slight smile.

Lydia's throat dried out, constricting until she struggled to get out a syllable. "I have often thought of our final words. They were a balm and comfort. Now that I am..." But Lydia couldn't finish that statement. Closing her eyes, she winced at her stupidity.

Ambrose had been right, and she'd been a fool.

"I do not wish to distress you," he whispered, "but though it broke my heart to see you marry that man, any sentiments we may have harbored would've come to naught. There was no future for us."

Lydia's shoulders drooped. "But surely love would've found a way."

Taking her hand in a brotherly hold, Mr. Marks shook his head. "I mean no disrespect, but we didn't love each other. Not truly. I cared for you deeply, and teaching you was a pleasure, but any feelings we shared were little more than a flirtation born from spending so much time together in an intimate setting."

Lydia shook her head. "You proposed."

Straightening, Mr. Marks blinked at her. "I did not. I may have been too bold in my attentions and expressing my adoration, but marrying a student would've been disastrous. I would've ruined my reputation and destroyed my business." Pausing, he cast a look at his humble dwelling. "What little good it did me."

Lydia tugged at her hand, dropping it to her side as she stared at the floorboards. "I see."

Mr. Marks stepped closer, his voice dropping to a whisper. "I am making a muck of this, aren't I? I do not wish to hurt you, but I fear you made more of us than what was truly there."

Swallowing, Lydia tried to clear her throat, but it was getting so very difficult to breathe in the confines of this tiny place. She gathered what little courage she had left, nodded at Mr. Marks, and turned her gaze to Mr. Bradshaw.

"I think it time we leave them to their dinner," she said. With a curtsy to both Mr. and Mrs. Marks, she added, "I apologize for having intruded. Thank you for your hospitality."

And then she turned away before the last of her composure broke.

Chapter 21

It was a mystery how something could be both divine and dreadful at the same time, but Lydia found herself locked in that paradox, swinging between relief and anguish. Having concluded his business far quicker than anticipated, Mr. Bradshaw had somehow secured them last-minute tickets inside an empty coach, which meant Lydia was not only pointed home the next day but traveling in a prime situation. Though that could be counted a great blessing indeed, it meant she was forced into tight quarters with someone who had witnessed her folly and she had four days to fret over her return to Newland Place and the troubles that had driven her to Town.

This trip had been as pointless as Mary and Ambrose had predicted.

Mr. Bradshaw had hardly looked at her since they'd left the Marks' home, and Lydia could not blame him for it nor the silence that hung heavy between them; if the weeping, frightened creature was beneath his contempt, surely the flighty, silly thing she'd become was no better. Shielding her face behind the rim of her bonnet, she closed her eyes to give them a rest after a restless night and far too many tears. The street was a sharp cacophony of people, carriages, and animals that surrounded her like a fog, the noise sending a stab of pain to her temples; as much as she wished for some powders to ease it, Lydia knew she deserved that constant pricking.

Had she truly thought Mr. Marks would be her salvation? Lydia's heart constricted, her breaths coming in short pants as she relived that awful scene once more. The years she'd spent worshiping Mr. Marks' memory joined the throng, mocking her with every fantasy.

How had she been so foolish? That question plagued her. It poked and prodded, giving her no rest from its incessant demand. But even as she tried to sort through her memories, Lydia swore all the various imaginings were true. She and Mr. Marks had been more than a flirtation.

Hadn't they?

But even as she tried to cling to the fantasy, Lydia saw the truth peeking through the rosy facade, making it clear that her dreams had leaked into her memories, twisting them into something far grander than the past had been.

Placing a hand over her eyes, Lydia tried to shake free of the shame weighing her down, but this trip had been such a foolish undertaking. She ought to have known better, but it was no wonder she would make such a ridiculous decision; Mama had predicted as much in her letters.

"...you will fall into ruin without our guidance..."

As much as Lydia wished to deny it, Mama's fears had come to fruition.

"We will sort it out," murmured Mr. Bradshaw.

Lydia straightened, her eyes snapping open to find him watching her with that same driven, hard look he so often displayed. Her cheeks pinked, and she dropped her gaze once more.

"You wish to help the foolish woman who ignored her sister and brother-in-law's sound advice and spent her meager funds to chase after a love that never existed?" she mumbled.

Silence followed that, and it was several long moments before she risked a glance at him—and found that unyielding stare of his. While in the past, it had seemed a cruel sort of look, Lydia realized there was no disgust or judgment in his expression. It was merely a window to Mr. Bradshaw's heart and the tenacity that defined him.

"From the very beginning, this journey had a strong possibility of being a fool's errand," he said, "but that is of no importance."

Lydia tried to remain upright, but the weight of all that had happened, her mistakes, and what was to come pressed down on her, and she struggled to ask the question he waited for her to speak.

"And what is important?" she asked.

Mr. Bradshaw's gaze was as strong as steel as he replied, "That you tried."

Lydia's shoulders fell. "What good is it if I make such poor attempts?"

With narrowed eyes, he watched her. "It is one thing to have a moment of self-pity, but wallowing is not worthwhile."

"It's only been a day since I found out everything I believed and clung to for the past seven years is a lie."

"And you have every right to be distraught, but there is a vast difference between feeling that pain and surrendering to it. I have worked with many who had similar upbringings to my own, and though the details of our lives are different, the one attribute we shared was our determination. Everyone falters and falls at times, but only the successful pick themselves back up and try again."

On the surface, Mr. Bradshaw had reminded Lydia too much of her husband—a fact that had only made it all the more difficult to keep her composure when he was about. And while their trip together had shown her a gentler side of him, Mr. Bradshaw remained a commanding man to his core. Yet, Lydia didn't feel the urge to shrink away from his authoritative air. If anything, his words roused an echo of that strength within her, making her feel the truth of his words.

"So, do you wish to hide away once more, Lady Whiting? Scuttle back to Lancashire and cower in the shadows? Or are you going to try again to free yourself and your daughter?" Though there was a bite to Mr. Bradshaw's words, there was something to his tone that spoke more of curiosity than condemnation.

Lydia considered that.

In truth, Lady Whiting's answer shouldn't matter so much to him. Whatever course she chose for her life was her decision, and Robert ought not to be so invested. But to see her go to such lengths only to surrender at the first sign of trouble was disconcerting. Lady Whiting was proving to be far more interesting and enjoyable than he'd anticipated, but the fire that had begun to burn in her eyes was sputtering out, and Robert couldn't bear to see it extinguished. And so, he counted the seconds as she thought through her answer.

But as much as he wanted her to speak, Robert was pleased to see her take his question seriously. Far too often, people leapt to give the desired answer with little thought or true commitment to their words. But Lady Whiting was not giving such a hasty response.

Yet another reason to like her. It was becoming a rather lengthy list.

The carriage rocked back and forth for several long moments as they wound their way into the countryside. Thank the heavens that he'd decided to purchase the extra seats; such a conversation was better without an audience.

"I understand why you disliked me when we first met," she said.

That wasn't anything close to what Robert had anticipated hearing, and he watched her with wary eyes, allowing her the time she needed to gather her thoughts together.

Glancing down at her hands, as though they might hold the answers she sought, Lady Whiting clenched them with a frown.

"There was a time when I was not afraid to speak out. Though my efforts came to naught, I defended Mary to my parents without worrying about their wrath. I was not the bold, do-as-she-pleases sort, but neither was I the quailing, wretched creature I am now."

Before Robert could respond, she released her clenched hands and met his gaze with an unflappable certainty.

"I despise what I have become, Mr. Bradshaw, but I do not know how to change it." Her light brows crumpled, her eyes pleading with him. "I want to be stronger—not only for my daughter's sake but for my own. Yet every time I think I have a grasp on my world, it is upended, leaving me at odds once more."

She dropped her gaze once more to her hands, twisting them in her lap. "I cannot help but wonder if Isabella mightn't be better off with someone else as her mother."

"That is ridiculous," he said.

"I do not believe so, sir. Why else would she have been born with such twisted feet if not for the shortcomings of the woman who bore her?"

Robert blinked at Lady Whiting, and his heart stirred for her. Those words were far too similar to ones he'd thought when Eleanor was taken from him. It was all too easy to shoulder the blame and believe that all the unexpected or unpleasant aspects of fate were engineered by one's failing or flaw.

"I assure you that illness and hardships come to everyone—saints and sinners alike," said Robert. "If it was merely a matter of being good and receiving health, wealth, and happiness, everyone would aspire for perfection."

"And I assure you my family's physician was not of your thinking," she murmured. "He said being born with such maladies was a clear sign of divine retribution."

"Then he was a crackpot. My brother-in-law is a physician and has never espoused such beliefs. Life is too imperfect a thing to attach meaning to every aspect of it."

Lady Whiting's brows rose. "You do not believe the Divine is in the details?"

Robert contemplated that and replied, "I don't believe God is a puppeteer controlling every aspect of our lives, but that He can give meaning to hardships if we allow it. And I refuse to believe that your sins—if you can even call them that—are laid upon your daughter's head. Where is the justice in that?"

Blinking, she turned her gaze to the window, though her eyes did not track the passing landscape.

"So, Lady Whiting, as you are determined not to surrender, what is it you wish to do with yourself?" he asked.

"I wish to not be called Lady Whiting, for one," she mumbled.

Robert's brows rose at that, and she waved his reaction away.

"It is a silly desire I cannot indulge as it would raise eyebrows if I insisted on being referred to as Lydia, but I abhor my title." With a slight shudder, the lady shook her head as she stared at the world beyond the carriage. "I became Lady Whiting the moment I married, and in all the years I was Sir Duncan's wife not one person ever addressed me by my given name. Even my parents refer to me by that title, although it no more belongs to me than it does to you. It's a meaningless, cold affectation that reminds me of my husband every time I hear it."

Giving that confession due consideration, Robert asked, "Then if I may be so bold as to ask, would you prefer it if I referred to you by your given name in private? I suffer from no pretensions that require me to stand on such ceremony when alone—though I know well enough that it would be inappropriate to do so in public."

The lady's cheeks pinked, but she gave him a tiny smile that brightened her eyes. "That would be delightful. Though I fear it will seem strange to refer to you as Mr. Bradshaw when you are referring to me so informally. Should I take the same liberties?"

Robert gave her a regal nod. "You did claim me as your friend yesterday."

"I believe I said you were my solicitor first." There was just a hint of laughter to her words, and it eased away the shadows that had clung to her eyes for the past day. It lightened Robert's heart to see it.

"I concede the point," he replied with a chuckle. Then, reiterating his previous question, he added, "So, *Lydia*, what do you wish to do with yourself?"

The lady's expression scrunched as she thought this through, her eyes fixed to the window as the world passed outside it.

"I do not know." Though the words were spoken quietly, Lydia's tone was filled with frustration. Turning to face him, she threw her arms wide. "How am I to know? My parents decided my fate before my marriage, then my husband did so after. The only thing I clung to was a fantasy that does not exist. How does one choose one's path?"

Robert nodded. "Standing on the threshold of possibilities is a beautiful and terrifying thing. But perhaps together, we might sort it out."

When Lydia faced him again, her eyes were bright and wide, watching him with such tentative hope. Her mouth hung slightly agape, as though meaning to speak but unable to gather her thoughts enough to do so. Watching him for several long moments, her eyes blinked again and again before she finally spoke.

"You've been so good to me. I do not know what I have done to deserve such generosity..." Her words broke, and her gaze began to shine. She tried to continue to talk, but her tears gathered in earnest.

Robert stared at her, inching back into the seat with a wince. "There's no need for tears."

Lydia wiped at her eyes with a dismissive wave and tried to argue with him, though her words became indecipherable. Patting at his pockets, Robert hunted for a handkerchief and held one out to her. Lydia dabbed her cheeks with it while continuing to ramble on.

"It is nothing, I assure you," said Robert.

But with a deep breath, she shook her head. "And I assure you it is not."

Leaning forward, Robert patted her knee with a jerky movement. "All of us need assistance from time to time. I am only glad that I can be of aid to you."

And before the lady could begin weeping anew, Robert prodded her back onto the subject of her future and what she wanted it to be.

Chapter 22

Carriages were a ridiculous expense. Not only were horses costly to maintain, but even if one were to forgo a coachman, one needed a groom to see to the day-to-day care of the animals and vehicles. Then there were constant repairs to be made and taxes to be paid, and when all was said and done, the price outweighed the benefit. After all, Greater Edgerton was not a large town and the distance between the Ashbrooks' home and his was not that great.

However, Robert couldn't deny that there were times when he'd welcome that luxury.

Nell skipped next to him, but he merely trudged along, grateful he could put one foot in front of the other. There was no single culprit behind Robert's exhaustion, but the three days since he'd returned from London had been filled with a never-ending list of demands. Though only gone for less than a fortnight, the work that had greeted him upon his return would take nearly as long to resolve. Luckily, his clerks were capable of handling the minor tasks, which eased some of the burden.

The back of his neck tickled as a phantom instinct had Robert slowing, though Nell tugged at his hand to force him along. Swinging his gaze around the street, he scoured the passing people and carts for the source of his unease. His eyes swung wide until they connected with the Ashbrooks' door behind him and then back the other way while Nell called out for his attention.

"One moment, poppet," he mumbled, his attention fixed on the world around him.

A man stood across the street, leaning against the brick face of the building opposite; with arms crossed, he watched the comings and goings, though his gaze kept returning to a fixed point. From his current position, Robert couldn't confirm his suspicion, but intuition reared its head, shouting at him that something was amiss.

"Stay here, Nell," he said in a tone that commanded her attention even more than his words, and Robert stepped into the street, holding the fellow in his sights as he wove through the traffic.

The movement drew the man's attention, and he gave Robert a narrowed look before turning and sauntering down the street in the opposite direction. Picking up his pace, Robert followed after, but his quarry darted into an alleyway and scaled a wooden gate stretching across the pavers; his thin frame snaked up and over the edge with enough speed that Robert knew it was pointless to follow.

Turning around, he moved to the man's original position to see precisely what the fellow had been watching—Newland Place.

"Papa?" Nell's voice carried over the clattering of the carts, and Robert dragged himself away from the unpleasant reality that stood before him. Crossing the street, he took Nell by the hand, and they set off for home once more.

"What happened, Papa?" she asked.

"Nothing, poppet."

And that was true enough. All Robert had were impressions to guide his assumptions, and though he didn't care to jump to conclusions, he trusted those instincts. Someone was watching the family, and Robert could think of only one member of the household who would warrant such attention. Perhaps the man had been employed by the Whitings' solicitor, but Robert knew all of Mr. Peterson's spies, and it was unlikely any of them would quit such a lucrative and simple position. This new fellow must've been the Haywards' spy.

That thought followed him as they walked the familiar path home, and Robert sorted through the possibilities. Likely the man's presence was merely an intimidation tactic, but Robert could not dismiss him out of hand. There was no need to worry Lydia or the Ashbrooks unduly, but perhaps it was time to hire his own set of eyes to watch over them.

"Papa!" cried Nell with an impatient tone that said this was not the first time she'd attempted to gain his attention.

"My apologies, poppet. I have a lot on my mind."

"Such as?"

Robert glanced at his daughter, wondering if he ought to tell her the truth. "I am concerned about Lady Whiting. Some people wish to take away Isabella, and I am helping her."

Nell's happy footsteps paused as she stared at her father with wide eyes. Before she could speak her worries aloud, Robert added a portion of the truth. "I've written to someone who might be able to aid her, but I don't know what more I can do."

Watching him with a furrowed brow, Nell seemed to consider that statement before giving him another bright smile. "I am certain you will sort it out, Papa."

Robert gave a responding grin, though he felt none of its warmth, and they continued on their way. Nell bounced beside him, her skipping steps moving with far more lightness than Robert felt at present. Now that he'd taken on the responsibility of aiding Lydia in her troubles, he felt them pressing down on him like a satchel laden with bricks.

At present, he wasn't even certain he could be of any assistance to her and Isabella. Their legal options were few, and though the Courts were preoccupied with other matters, that was only a stay of execution. If the Haywards pressed their suit, they would eventually win, and Robert had no doubt Lydia would do as they bid to protect her daughter. To say nothing of this new development; Robert could only hope and pray that her parents would content themselves with spying on the household and nothing more.

Lady Lydia Whiting was a fascinating creature. Such an odd mixture of strength and weakness. Having witnessed the changes wrought in her during the past few weeks, Robert knew she had the potential for both—and that he greatly desired to foster the former. That determined light in her eyes was becoming a familiar friend, and Robert wished to see it grow. When accompanied by that unrestrained smile of hers, he was hard-pressed to turn his back on her.

To say nothing of the shuddering revulsion that took hold of him whenever he thought of seeing Isabella given to her grandparents' care. He couldn't bear to see her in the power of people who would treat her shabbily.

With great animation, Nell chattered about all the many lessons Lydia had taught her that day, hardly drawing breath as she spoke of all the details of each moment they'd been apart.

"She is so elegant, Papa!" said Nell, tugging on his hand as she skipped beside him. "And she knows so many things. She promised to teach us a quadrille, though we shall need a fourth as Mrs. Ashbrook is often occupied and isn't a strong dancer and Esther is too young. Lady Whiting says I have mastered the Boulangère and dance it perfectly!"

Nell gave a twirl and continued to rattle on about all the many pearls of wisdom Lydia had bestowed upon her. Robert smiled to himself, his heart swelling as he saw all the little ways in which Nell had altered since receiving Lydia's tutelage; that fractious, worried part of her that had been taking precedence of late was fading once more.

What had begun as a means to an end had grown into something that was blessing his dear little Nell. For that reason alone, Lydia deserved Robert's aid.

Nell continued to chatter on, her conversation never wavering or pausing as they made their way back to Pembrooke Place, and when he opened the front door, the scent of roasted beef and vegetables had his stomach gurgling loud enough that Nell giggled.

"Are you laughing at me?" he asked with a mock growl, and Nell hid her smile behind her hands, giving him a shake of her head. Robert dropped his satchel beside the door, casting off his hat as he raised his hands and lunged for her. Nell squealed and sped down the hall, rushing into the parlor. With all thoughts of his fatigue forgotten, Robert followed after her, and the pair startled the maid, who gave a shriek and dropped the bundle in her arms.

"Sorry, sir," said Jenny with a bob, snatching the package and offering it to him. "This was delivered this afternoon."

Nell ducked behind a sofa, and Robert took the soft packet tied up in brown paper and twine.

"Mrs. Bunting says dinner will be ready any minute," said Jenny with another bob.

With a nod, Robert dismissed her and sat on the sofa that hid Nell. Popping up, she hung over the back, staring at Robert's bundle.

"What is it, Papa?"

With a tug, Robert loosened the twine and unwrapped the package to reveal a note nestled atop a waistcoat. Though a true connoisseur might note that the fabric was not as fine as some, it had a refined sensibility to it—something that perched upon a perfect balance of good quality and good price.

Glancing at the paper, he saw a few scant words:

My deepest thanks for all that you have done and continue to do. — L.

It was no great leap in logic to know who had sent it, and though Robert had seen the lady in question less than an hour ago, it was no great surprise that she preferred to send it ahead so she could not see his reaction to her gift.

Lydia needn't have worried.

What efforts Robert had made towards being fashionable in the past had been due to Eleanor's influence. His wife had spent an inordinate amount of time ensuring that his outfits were *à la mode*, but since her passing, he'd expended naught but a cursory effort to ensure he was properly dressed. Keeping oneself abreast of the latest fashions seemed such an unnecessary effort and expense, though Robert did appreciate a good piece of clothing.

Lydia had chosen a simple style that suited his sensibilities. There were no extreme points to the lapels or outrageous embroidery to draw the eye. Though Robert tended towards blacks and browns, this waistcoat was a rich blue of the sky when the last rays of light were dipping beneath the horizon.

"Who is it from?" asked Nell, leaning over his shoulder, and Robert slid the note out of sight and tucked it in his pocket. Receiving such things in lieu of payment was entirely respectable, but it wouldn't do to chance Lydia's reputation being besmirched by such things—especially as theirs wasn't a wholly professional arrangement.

"A friend," he replied.

"You must try it on." Nell scurried around the sofa to stand before him, and Robert was left with no choice but to do as ordered.

The waistcoat fit far better than expected, and he buttoned it up, straightening it for his daughter's inspection.

"It looks beautiful on you," said Nell, and though Robert smiled at that enthusiastic description, he agreed that it looked quite fine on him. Examining himself in the mirror above their fireplace, Robert felt like a peacock strutting about the parlor, but the blue waistcoat suited his brown eyes so perfectly that he couldn't help a second and third look at himself.

"You need better clothes." Nell spoke in such a prim tone that Robert held back a huffing laugh.

"Then I am blessed to have a friend to watch over me in such matters." And he truly was, though Robert had never expected to feel so about Lydia. An unexpected friendship had formed between them, and he was supremely grateful fate had dropped her into his life.

But thoughts of the mysterious man outside the Ashbrooks' home had Robert's smile fading. The more he came to know her and her past, the more determined he felt to keep Lydia and Isabella free of her parents' control. Staring at his reflection and the gift her hands had wrought, his muscles tensed as though ready and waiting to do what needed, though Robert didn't know what that was.

One way or another, he would find a way to keep Lydia and her daughter safe.

Chapter 23

There were some days of such unparalleled beauty that the mere sight of the world left one breathless, and though gray clouds were usually not of interest, the heavens above were not an unyielding wall of dingy hues. Little shafts of light peeked through the veil overhead, turning them into puffs of dappled gold. The light and dark contrasted perfectly, making each seem all the more vivid and captivating.

No doubt it would rain tonight, and the scent of the promised moisture filled the world around her. Lydia took a breath and let her feet carry her along the riverbed. Though she had no pocket watch to guide her, she knew she still had some time left before it was necessary to make her way to Dottie and Nell's school, and Lydia was determined to enjoy the moment to its fullest.

Her thoughts meandered like her footsteps, sorting through the same subjects she'd contemplated ever since her return to Lancashire a fortnight ago. Lydia smiled to herself—something that was more common by the day—and wondered what good she'd done in her life to deserve such a friend as Robert, for there was no other way to view his presence in her life than as a blessing. Even if she hadn't thought so a month ago.

There were still too many things to be sorted before her life would be settled properly, but she felt it coming together little by little. The incident with Mr. Marks had been a disaster in many ways, but it had altered her life for the better in others, and Lydia couldn't say she was disappointed with—

"You aren't where you ought to be."

The voice pulled Lydia from her musings, and her gaze focused on the path before her to see a thin man with a grim expression. Lydia blinked, uncertain of where he'd come from or to what he was referring (or if he was speaking to her), but she moved to step around him, and he moved with her, forcing himself into her path.

"Leave me be," she said, taking a step backward.

"You aren't where you ought to be," he repeated, his dark eyes narrowing as he pushed closer. "They've given you every opportunity, and you're not listening. Go home, little girl, before something nasty happens."

No matter how much she tried to distance herself, the man did not relent. Stepping backward, her foot caught a root, and Lydia stumbled, her back colliding with a tree. Before she knew it, the man loomed over her, pinning her to the trunk. He laid not a finger on her, but darkness radiated from his gaze, seeping into her in a cold wave that chilled her through.

"Your parents have been patient until now, but you'd best listen to their letters, or they might just send me to fetch you home." The man whispered the words in a gentle tone, his lips curling into a smile, and Lydia shuddered at the sight of it.

Instinct told her to nod. To remain silent. To simply do as bidden without a word of complaint. And though her heart thumped in her chest and her voice shook, Lydia managed to whisper, "Leave me be."

The man leaned away with a chuckle that sent a shiver of revulsion down her spine, and his gaze lingered in a manner that had her cheeks scorching and her stomach turning, but Lydia kept herself propped up against the tree, waiting as he sauntered away.

Her breaths came in ragged pants, and she pressed a hand to her stomach, forcing away the edge of panic that tried to take hold of her. She closed her eyes for a moment, taking hold of the fear that pushed her to run and cry, and forced it deep down inside. Falling to pieces would solve nothing, and Lydia could not bear the thought of letting it get the better of her now.

They were just words. A threat, certainly. But in this instance, Lydia couldn't help but recall Robert's statements in the past. Words had no power except that which she gave them, and threats were along the same vein. But no matter how she tried to cling to that certainty, it was impossible not to imagine all the possibilities that might come if her parents made good on it.

Lydia's heartbeat picked up its pace, and she tried to breathe. Shoving aside the emotions that threatened to overwhelm her, she clung to logic; it may not always be of assistance, but in this instance, it eased the edge of panic as she thought through her present circumstances. Mama and Papa were serious and would not give up. That was true. However, they were not violent. If they had wanted to force the issue, they would've done more than send warnings. She still had time to sort things out.

Pushing off the tree, Lydia hurried along the street, allowing the afternoon routine to settle her nerves as she fetched the girls and led them home. Though she wished she could so easily shake off the encounter, it lingered, following her as she led the girls home and began their lessons. Thankfully, the task at hand distracted her enough to put aside her worries temporarily. Soon, Robert would arrive to fetch Nell, and together, they would find a solution.

Clapping her hands together to mark off the beats, Lydia led the girls back and forth through the parlor.

"*Chassé*," she prompted, punctuating each step with a clap of her hands as she called out the movements of their feet. "And *jeté assemblé*."

Lydia moved through the steps without any thought, her feet skipping along with the familiarity and grace of one who had performed them more times than she could count. Usually, the girls followed her instructions, but today, Dottie's expression couldn't be more of a frown if she tried, and Nell's brows were so furrowed that she looked to have only one. Though her experience with teaching was not of a long duration, Lydia had quickly learned to read such moods. Her charges were not of a mind to continue, yet Lydia could not stand to abandon her lessons and return to her fretting.

All would be well. It would. She knew it to be true, but her limbs dragged with exhaustion born of too many restless nights and the persistent alertness she'd been feeling of late; one could not be on edge for such a length of time and not feel its effects. And the encounter that afternoon had only added to her dragging steps.

Stopping, she gathered her last reserves and donned a bright smile; sometimes feigned enthusiasm engaged the girls' waning attention, but before Lydia could say anything to raise their spirits, Dottie sighed, her shoulders slumping.

"I am tired. Can we not stop?"

Lydia glanced at Nell, but the girl paid Dottie no heed; moving about on her own, she scowled as she continued to stumble through the steps. Lydia stared at the pair, thinking through her options before she finally surrendered. It wasn't as though her wages would be docked if she released the girls from their lessons earlier than intended.

Dottie sighed and collapsed onto the sofa, and Lydia joined her, though Nell continued to move back and forth.

"We can continue tomorrow, Nell," said Lydia, but that was met with a shake of her head.

"I must get it perfect." Hopping and gliding back and forth, Nell forced her feet to move through the steps, but if she got it right one moment, the next she stumbled. With a scowl, she stomped her foot and began again.

"Nell, there is plenty of time for you to master these steps," said Lydia, patting the sofa beside her. "Come have a rest."

But the girl shook her head and returned to her practice. Nell moved with determination, her flare of temper growing once more, which did nothing to aid her grace. Lydia had seen hints of that grim resolution here and there, but the girl was now clearly in the grip of it, forcing herself to keep moving with mounting frustration.

"Nell, leave it be—"

"No, I must get it right!" Nell stomped again, her expression crumpling as she tried it again.

Lydia turned to Dottie, who was staring at her friend, and said, "If you'd like, I shall teach you and Nell how to serve tea. Perhaps you can persuade Cook to organize some treats to go with it, and we can have a proper spread to share with your mama and the other children."

Dottie straightened with a happy gleam in her eye. Nodding, she hopped from the sofa and scurried off in search of Cook and Mary. Only once the parlor door was shut did Lydia move from the sofa to join Nell. The girl paid her no mind, continuing to struggle through her movements. Nell had proven herself a dedicated student, but there was something more to her relentlessness that spoke of a troubled heart.

"Nell, what is the matter?"

Pausing, the child turned with a scowl. "I don't want to give up."

Lydia blinked and shook her head. "No one is saying you must. But you have only just begun learning to dance and cannot expect to master it all in such a short time."

With drooping shoulders, Nell's gaze fell to the floor. "My mama did. She danced like an angel."

Giving Nell a gentle nudge, Lydia led her to the sofa and sat beside her. "And you are quite talented as well, but you mustn't be so hard on yourself. This ought to be enjoyable."

Nell's chin trembled, and Lydia's heart broke as the child tried to remain composed. Though she did not know the source of Nell's heartache, Lydia knew she was in distress and did not know what she could do about it. When no other option presented itself, Lydia followed her instincts and reached for Nell, folding her into her arms.

"There is nothing to fret about, Nell."

The child held still for a moment before melting into Lydia's hold.

"But I need to be better," whispered Nell, her voice hitching. "I need to be perfect."

"Why?" Lydia held fast to Nell, rubbing her back as the child shuddered.

"Mama was so good and beautiful and elegant, and I try so hard to be like her, but I cannot seem to manage."

Lydia's mind leapt forward, seizing at Nell's meaning before she had the chance to speak the words, and she tightened her hold on the girl, as though that might protect her from that pain. Nell gave another few shuddering breaths before she continued, and Lydia's thoughts churned as to what she could say.

"Mama was kind and talented and perfect, and if not for me, she would be here."

Squeezing her eyes shut, Lydia shook her head, placing a kiss on the child's head. "No, darling, that is not true!"

Nell leaned back and wiped at her cheeks with a fierce nod. "It is. If not for me, she would be here."

There were so many trite things to say in such a moment, assurances that all was well, but Lydia did not wish to give words that could easily be shaken off. With a silent petition, she hoped she could settle on the right thing to say. Lydia had not known Mrs. Bradshaw, so there was little insight she could give into the girl's mother. Instead, she drew on her own.

Reaching forward, she tucked a curl behind Nell's ear and gave her a gentle smile. "Your mother's death is not your burden to bear. It is the risk every woman takes when bringing life into this world. Some of us succeed and some fail, but I can tell you with utter certainty that I love my Isabella more than anything, and I would not hesitate to surrender my life for hers if necessary. I do not doubt your mother felt the same."

Nell watched her with wary eyes, her doubts tainting not only Lydia's words but how she valued herself. Yet hope hid beneath that pain. Lydia's heart twisted anew, for she knew all too well how painful such fears could be and that desperate longing to be free of them. Though Lydia wished to take the girl in her arms again, she kept her eyes fixed on Nell so she could see the truth in Lydia's expression.

"I may have only known you a short time, but you are a dear girl," she said, taking Nell's hands in hers. "You are courageous and daring, and you have such a kind heart. I would be honored to have a daughter like you, and I am certain your mother is proud of you."

Nell's chin wobbled, her eyes filling with tears, and she dove into Lydia's hold, her little body shaking beneath the tears. The parlor door behind her opened, and Lydia met Mary's wide eyes. While rocking the poor dear, Lydia motioned for her sister to give them another few minutes, and Mary herded the other children away before Nell noticed they were there.

Lydia murmured sweet words, giving her the tenderness hurting hearts needed to hear again and again and hoping they might drown out the angry and critical voices that haunted Nell. Buried beneath those thoughts, Lydia let out a prayer of gratitude that she'd been in a position to aid the sweet child at such a time.

It was several long moments before Nell calmed, and she remained in Lydia's embrace for longer than that. A noise sounded from the hall, and Nell straightened, wiping at her cheeks. Lydia straightened the child's braids and straightened the hem of her dress, doing what little she could to aid the girl in collecting herself. But the parlor door burst open, and Lucas bolted into the room with Esther on his heels. Mary hissed at them to stop, but there was little more to be done as Nell's moment had already ended. Pulling Lydia close, Nell gave her one final embrace before thoughts of tea parties and treats had her hurrying after Dottie.

Chapter 24

Handing his hat and gloves to the maid, Robert smiled as the sound of laughter echoed from the parlor. Such merry noises were a welcome thing, but more so when joined by the unrestrained glee of children. Because he had come to the Ashbrooks' home so many times now, the maid wasn't surprised when Robert raised a finger to his lips and nodded for her to be on her way without announcing him. Inching the door open, he found the parlor empty and followed the sounds as they drew him to the adjoining dining room.

Mrs. Ashbrook and Lydia sat among the children at the table, a tea set spread out in front of them. Though the older girls attempted gentility, the Ashbrook boy stuffed his cheeks full of cakes and made faces, which encouraged the others to do the same. Mrs. Ashbrook gave a half-hearted attempt to minimize the mess, but any authority she had was undermined when she laughed at his antics.

Only Lydia noticed his entrance. She held a cup of tea to her lips, her eyes alight with mirth. The lady had quite fine eyes that were made all the lovelier as they sparkled and shown with her silent laughter.

"Papa!" Nell flew from her chair and grabbed him by the hand, dragging him to an empty seat. "Lady Whiting is showing us how to serve tea."

Allowing himself to be ordered about by his daughter, Robert sat beside Lydia as directed and reached for the cream.

"Papa, no! We do not put the cream in first." Nell swatted his hand away, and Lydia cleared her throat, giving the child a look of gentle reproof.

Pausing, Nell straightened and gave her father a demure smile. "I do beg your pardon, sir, but please allow me."

Lydia gave her a regal nod, and Nell beamed. Though the lady watched the young girl's movements closely, she did not rush in to handle the teapot for her when Nell poured him a cup. Adding the appropriate sugar and cream, she handed it to her father with a smile.

Robert took a sip. "That is a perfect cup of tea, Nell."

With a jolt of joy that had her nearly bouncing out of her seat, Nell abandoned the airs of hostess to show him what she had learned. Reaching for a small tea caddy, she turned the key and opened the lid.

"Mrs. Ashbrook allowed me to choose," she said, showing him the compartments full of tea. "A proper hostess mixes a special blend for her guests."

Glancing over at Lydia, Nell awaited the answering nod before continuing. "And we do not put the cream in first."

"And whyever not, poppet? That is how I have always made my tea." Though Robert had never been much of a tea drinker he was certain he'd been told it was imperative to add the cream first.

With an affronted look, Nell shook her head. "One only puts the cream in first to protect the porcelain from cracking from the sudden heat, but only poor-quality porcelain does so. Adding the cream before the tea can alter the flavor and tells your guests you are serving them from inferior teacups."

Robert wasn't certain about that, but he gave his daughter a nod and listened as she chattered on about the nuances.

Nell leaned forward and whispered to him, "We gave the children milk because they do not know the difference. They only care about the cake."

The manner in which she said "children" was so very wise and matronly that Robert had to hold back the laugh that begged to be released. He gave her another solemn nod, not trusting himself to speak at present. Turning his gaze to his right, he met Lydia's eyes as they both shared a smile. It was a sweet, nothing sort of moment, but it filled him with such warmth, and Robert could not think of another place he'd rather be than at this little tea party.

Lydia's gaze dropped to his waistcoat, and her eyes softened at the sight of her gift on display while Robert straightened the gift with a grateful grin. This was hardly the first time he'd worn it, yet he never tired of seeing the pleasure shining in her eyes at the sight of him wearing her offering.

"Do you like Papa's new waistcoat?" asked Nell, appearing between the pair of them, and Robert nearly spilled his tea at the interruption.

"It is very fetching," said Lydia.

"A friend gave it to him," added Nell, returning to her seat to sip at her tea.

Robert's cravat strangled him, and he held onto his smile, though his gaze darted to Mrs. Ashbrook and all the little listening ears. Lydia's cheeks pinked a touch, and she turned her attention to her drink. Though Robert tried to ignore it, he caught a speculative look from Mrs. Ashbrook. Luckily, her son began making a mess in earnest, diverting her attention to more pressing concerns.

"I apologize," he whispered, leaning closer to Lydia. "Nell does not understand the insinuations that might arise if someone were to suspect the giver of my gift."

Lydia shook her head. "Think nothing of it. I am not afraid of a bit of gossip, and I could not allow all your kindness to go unpaid. Though I do apologize for the fit. I had to guess at your measurements."

Robert waved that apology away. "It fits quite well, and I am grateful for your thoughtfulness. It has been some time since I owned such a fine article."

Hiding behind her teacup, Lydia chuckled. "I imagined that was the case, as you do not seem the sort to enjoy shopping."

With Mrs. Ashbrook casting furtive glances in their direction, Robert straightened and spoke in a louder voice. "I've been looking into properties that might serve as a location for a school."

"School?" asked Mrs. Ashbrook, and Lydia dropped her head.

"I mentioned it only in passing, Mr. Bradshaw," she said, rubbing at her forehead.

Robert frowned. "But you enjoy teaching the girls. Why not do something more with it?"

Lydia fiddled with her teacup and frowned, though there was a gleam to her eye that testified of her hidden desire. "I haven't the skills to manage something like that. And it would cause a scandal for Sir Duncan's widow to become a schoolmistress."

Turning to Mrs. Ashbrook for support, Robert added, "We spoke of some plans for your sister during our trip home from London. She wants something to do and needs an income, and education seems the best option."

Mrs. Ashbrook nodded and smiled. "That would be just the thing, Lydia. You have done such a wonderful job with Dottie and Nell, and there are plenty of families in the area who would pay dearly for their daughters to be educated in the social graces by someone as proficient as you."

"But—" Lydia began, though her sister cut off her protests.

"If you do not wish to do it, then I shan't force matters, but if you wish to pursue it, then I and Mr. Bradshaw will do all we can to aid you in it." But then Mrs. Ashbrook turned a wary glance in Robert's direction as though uncertain if she'd taken liberties in adding him in her promise.

"Certainly," he said with a nod.

"And if my mother-in-law discovers I am blackening the family name by earning my bread?" Lydia rubbed at her forehead and her shoulders dropped. Something in her expression pinched, her eyes darkening as she stared at a spot on the tablecloth.

"Then we shall deal with her interference if it comes," said Robert. "But there is no reason to borrow trouble."

"I fear trouble is already here," she murmured.

Mrs. Ashbrook did not hear her response, but the despair in her tone had Robert straightening.

"Might I have a word with you in private?" he asked, and Lydia nodded, though she did not meet his gaze. Mrs. Ashbrook waved at them to leave her with the children, and he led Lydia into the adjacent parlor, helping her to the sofa.

"What is the matter?" he asked, his eyes falling to her hands as they twisted in her lap.

"I had an unpleasant visit with someone as I was going to fetch Dottie and Nell from school."

Robert shifted in his seat to look at her more fully. "With whom?"

"A man my parents hired to deliver a message in person as they are no longer content with only letters."

Shooting to his feet, Robert stared down at her. "Did he hurt you?"

Lydia's brows rose at that, and she shook her head. "He didn't lay a finger on me. It was only a warning that I ought to do as bidden."

Robert's pulse thrummed, his blood heating as he considered that. Her tone made it clear that there was much Lydia wasn't saying—none of which was pleasant. Robert was well familiar with the sorts of men who had no scruples about threatening a woman, and though Lydia held onto her composure, there was an edge to her movements and words that spoke of an unsettled heart. And it was no wonder.

What would have happened if the man had been more aggressive in his delivery? Robert rubbed his face and banished the thought, for it did no good for him to contemplate it; he needed a clear head at present, and such imaginings only added to his agitation.

Standing before her, his feet itched to move, and Robert allowed himself to pace as he thought through what he ought to say. There were many words he could speak, but he did not wish to upset her. The more he dug into the meat of the law surrounding her situation, the less hope he felt that all would come to rights if they were forced into a legal battle. And none of it would do any good if the Haywards took unsavory paths to victory.

Tucking his hands behind him, Robert wore a path in the rug as he contemplated another possibility he'd settled on some days ago. There was an easy solution to Lydia's woes. He paced the parlor and wondered if it was foolhardy to mention it. Not that Robert Bradshaw was one to be foolhardy nor was this idea was of the spur of the moment variety. The situation before him was clear. Lydia needed freedom from her husband's family and her own, and there were few opportunities for her to gain it—at least where Isabella was concerned.

Lydia's eyes followed him as he walked, her expression tightening as the silence drew out, and yet Robert did not know how to broach the subject. She had consumed much of his thoughts for the past fortnight, and with each day, it became clearer what ought to happen, but that did not make it any easier to express it.

"I'd hoped for more time, but if your parents are resorting to such tactics, it may be time for us to consider other alternatives. As much as I hope to find some other legal solution, I fear the only option before you is to marry."

Straightening, Lydia nodded. "You said as much before we set off for London. Do I need to remind you how fruitless that avenue proved to be?"

Tucking his hands behind him, Robert shook his head and continued to pace. "But we have not discussed other marital possibilities since then."

It was silent for a heavy moment, and Robert chanced a look at Lydia; she stared at him as her complexion grew ashen, her brows knitting together.

"You think it time for me to settle for a marriage of convenience?" she asked in a whisper.

A flush of heat had Lydia's head spinning, and she clung to her composure as the wave swept through her. She worked through all the little ways she'd learned to control the anxiety coursing: breathe, clear her mind, ignore the past and focus on the present. With those defenses in place, she was able to fight back the panic that threatened to overwhelm her. Yes, she wished to flee, but Lydia knew she was stronger than the impulse. Even if her nerves were already frayed.

Robert paced before her, rattling off the various reasons she ought to consider this course of action, but Lydia focused on her breathing. She did not understand why it helped so, but in such moments, one of the strongest weapons against her nerves was forcing air in and out. It could not eradicate the sentiment, but something about it allowed her to calm and wash away much of her discomfort.

It did not help that Robert was speaking with that commanding air of his. Though he was altogether different from Sir Duncan, that similarity struck her at the worst moments, making it all the harder to remember that this was Robert—her friend. Yet Lydia forced that unfair comparison aside and focused on how those times were often tied to some work to be done or issue to sort out when Robert was determined to set things to right; that hardness was not the whole of him, and he had many kind and tender dimensions to him. Something Sir Duncan had never possessed.

And that helped to calm her as well. Instincts were well and good at times, but they could not be trusted in their entirety, and though they begged her to flee, Lydia knew Robert was not the enemy here. And that his heart was far warmer than his current temperament displayed. He was her ally, and one did not flee from one's allies.

Only when Lydia had herself well under control was she able to truly listen to what Robert was saying.

"With my protection, you would be free to pursue your school or any other path you choose, free of your parents or husband's family—"

Lydia straightened. "You?"

Robert paused, turning to look at her with a raised brow. "Of course. You cannot think I would suggest you marry a stranger. That could be worse than marrying whomever your parents choose."

A burble of laughter escaped before Lydia could stop it, and she slapped a hand over her mouth as her posture relaxed. Robert stared at her.

"I apologize, but for a terrible moment, I thought you were in earnest," said Lydia.

Robert straightened, his expression tightening. "I was. As much as it pains me to admit it, you and Isabella have few options, and I cannot bear to leave you unprotected. Marriage would be the most complete solution, and I can think of no one better suited to be your husband."

A chill swept through her, moving from her very core to the tips of her fingers; it settled within her as Lydia struggled to grasp the truth staring her in the face. But Robert continued to ramble concerning the reasons why this was the best course of action, and Lydia was forced to accept it was not some figment of her imagination.

Chapter 25

Lydia gaped at him, trying to sort out which of the many things she wished to say was the most pressing. "But surely you do not wish to marry for convenience's sake. You are still young enough to find a proper wife."

Robert huffed. "And who do you think could replace my Eleanor? There is not a woman alive who could ever hope to compare."

Nor would he find one willing to marry a man so intent on clinging to his wife's memory. But that was best left unsaid. Yet Lydia could not leave that statement wholly uncontested. Nell's tearful words came to mind, and Lydia suspected her father's stubborn blindness held much of the blame. Perhaps a more innocuous question might spark a deeper conversation without her having to address it directly.

"But do you truly think you could never love again?"

Robert waved that away, and Lydia's insides clenched. Apparently, she would not have such an easy go of it.

"I understand better than most how much appeal a memory can have, Robert, but do you not think that perhaps you might feel differently one day?"

But Robert looked as ready to dismiss that question as easily as the first. Unfortunately for Lydia's sake, something more blatant was required.

"It is easy to conflate reality with fantasy." Lydia's hands twisted in her lap, and she forced them to still. She shifted in her seat, and though she tried to keep her voice steady, it lowered as she added, "And Nell has told me stories of her mother that make me think you have done so."

Robert gaped at her for a moment before turning to pace again, his hands tucked behind him. "I am not here to discuss my wife or daughter. We are speaking of you and your daughter."

Arguments came to her lips, but Robert's posture and expression were rife with dismissal, and as much as Lydia liked to believe she'd developed some courage over the past three months, she was very much disappointed to realize that it snapped like a biscuit when presented with opposition.

"We can marry at once and send word to your parents," he continued, speaking as though the whole ordeal was decided. "You shall be free to do as you please once they have abandoned their plans. Open your school, leave Greater Edgerton, or whatever you wish to do. Our arrangement would be purely to offer my name and protection, though should you need more support, I have funds enough to care for you and Isabella."

Those words sent a new chill through Lydia that worsened as he spoke, making her feel as though she were lost in a winter storm. Her throat knotted so she could not swallow or breathe as she saw what was to come. Another husband to control her. A life of being the unwanted addition. A burden to her husband. She'd be the interloper once more.

There must be some other solution, but Lydia's thoughts spun out of control. Some rational part of her said that Robert could be trusted, but the past sprang into her thoughts, shouting out dire warnings. Lydia forced her throat to open, but then her breath came in short pants, quickening until she felt faint. It felt as though someone had reached into her chest and squeezed her heart, and Lydia touched a hand to her forehead, forcing herself to focus.

"I only wished to be of assistance," he said with a frown. "I will not run roughshod over you."

Lydia met his gaze and tried to speak, but though she wished to give him comforting words, she could not keep a hold of her tongue. "I know, but a husband is—"

A jerk of a sob broke her words, and Lydia shook her head, holding a hand to her mouth and closing her eyes to gather her strength, but the sentiments roiling through her were more powerful. Tears sprung free, and she tried to assure Robert, though the words came out in a garbled mess. His eyes widened, and he glanced at the dining room door with an expression that said he hoped Mary would appear. When she did not, he came to sit beside Lydia on the sofa and handed her a handkerchief.

"I know," she murmured, mopping at her face. "But what if—"

And that thought dissolved into more tears, and Lydia curled inwards, covering her face. Too much had happened today, and the battle for control was long over; she could only embrace the fears and anxieties coursing through her. A hand touched her back. Lydia's blurry gaze turned to Robert, and before she knew what she was doing, she leaned towards him, and his arms were around her.

"All will be right in the end, Lydia," he murmured, though they both knew that was a hollow promise. Yet she clung to that assurance, hoping it might chase away the panic gripping her.

It was several long minutes before Lydia calmed enough to attempt speech. All the while, Robert held her, offering her what little comfort he could.

"I did not mean to distress you."

Wiping her face, Lydia paused at something in his tone. It was the sort of emotion she hadn't expected to hear from him, but she recognized the hurt buried beneath the apology. Though she was loath to return her thoughts to the moment that caused so much pain, Lydia thought through his proposal.

"It is not you, Robert," she said with a shake of her head. "You may not believe it, but I am touched you offered yourself up as the solution."

He gave her a raised brow that held a touch of humor, and Lydia responded with a watery chuckle. Though peace was not something she would find so easily at present, certainty took its place. With the fog of emotion clearing, Lydia saw the truth of his declaration. Robert truly meant to aid her, and he would not be like her husband. That certainty settled into her, giving her a buoy in the storm to cling to.

"I apologize for my reaction. I did not mean to fall to pieces, but I have been exhausted of late, and it has been an especially trying day," she whispered with a wince. "You are being so very kind to me. Please do not think me ungrateful. You simply surprised me."

Robert huffed and muttered with a wry smile, "I surprised myself."

Twisting Robert's handkerchief, Lydia stared at it and contemplated the options before her. Or tried. At present, her mind was fixed on the fact that she still had the handkerchief he'd previously bestowed on her the last time she'd turned into a sobbing mess.

Her time with the Whitings had deadened her, leaving her listless and beyond feeling, only to find all those emotions rushing into her at once when she'd been faced with her parents' plans. Now, it felt as though her feelings swung between being that dull murmur in the background and screaming at her. Even now, she felt that edge of hysteria threatening to stir it all up again.

And then Robert patted a sympathetic hand on her shoulder. The movement was hardly comforting, but the awkward attempt at consolation had Lydia smiling. The poor fellow looked so at odds about what to do with a weepy female that it was hard not to find some humor in it.

This was Robert. Lydia did not understand how he had transformed from a disapproving stranger to a welcome friend, but she could not deny the change that had been wrought in their relationship. He was pigheaded and unsympathetic at times, but he was honest and had a good heart—the sort of fellow who'd been determined to help a poor widow he hadn't known. That knowledge helped to clear the fog that filled her thoughts, though Lydia could not dispel her nerves altogether.

Whether or not Robert would be a brute of a husband, a marriage of convenience was something to be feared. And mourned. Lydia's heart grew heavy as she considered the future he was presenting. Though she was in no state to welcome romance and courting, buried beneath the fear was a flickering hope that she would one day find love. This course of action would make that an impossibility.

But what of Isabella? What price was too high to ensure her comfort and safety?

Her chest rose and fell in quick succession, her muscles tightening as she stared off at the far wall. "A marriage of convenience might be the only solution."

Robert patted her shoulder once more, though Lydia did not feel like smiling at it anymore. "I fear it might. I've spent countless hours researching the issue, and I fear Isabella shan't be safe without a husband. I cannot change the law, but I can give you that."

Nodding, Lydia dropped her gaze to the linen in her hands. "Might I have some time to consider it?"

"Certainly," he said, rising to his feet. "The sooner it is settled, the better, but the situation isn't so dire that it cannot wait."

Lydia cast him a glance, though her gaze did not linger on him. "My thanks, Robert."

"You are most welcome, Lydia."

Giving her a formal bow, he swept out the door, and the room felt empty with him gone. Robert had such a presence about him, like a bonfire on a winter's night. Something that chased away the frost and darkness and warned off the dangers that filled the night. Lydia found herself once more sending out a silent prayer of gratitude that he had found his way into her life.

Whether to protect her daughter's future or her own was no real debate at all, but Lydia sent out a silent prayer, begging for divine intervention to give her some other course of action.

Chapter 26

Fidgeting spoke of a mind ill at ease with one's situation and decisions, and Robert never indulged in it. He knew better than to allow base emotions like self-doubt to cloud his judgment. A hint of uncertainty was one thing, but only a fool allowed his emotions to take control—though Robert quickly amended that thought, for Lydia was no fool, even if her heart held more sway than it ought to. Perhaps he'd thought her weak or silly once, but beneath that tender soul of hers was buried a stalwart heart, one that continued to dust itself off when thrown to the ground again and again.

Lady Lydia Whiting was such an odd contradiction of strength and weakness, determination and doubt. A woman who left comfort and safety with little more than the clothes on her back to travel halfway across the country. Who faced a marriage of convenience to save her child. Who fought for her freedom, despite the fear and uncertainty that surrounded the future. There were few— male or female—who would do such things. People were far too comfortable with the status quo, regardless of how undesirable it was. They accepted their lot, but though crippled by inexperience and self-doubt, Lydia had done what many others wouldn't dare.

And he'd made her cry.

Robert frowned at himself. His offer had been well-intentioned, and he knew her reaction was her own doing and not his, yet he could not banish the worm of guilt that had wriggled its way into his thoughts. It burrowed deeper every time he recalled her bright eyes shining with tears. Lydia had suffered enough in her life, and Robert hated that he'd added to her burdens.

Especially with such a foolhardy declaration. At the time, Robert had thought it the wise course of action, but at present, he was at a loss to understand what had possessed his good sense and pushed him to make such a hasty offer. Their options were not yet exhausted. The Haywards may be intimidating Lydia, but that only required more diligent protection. Yet he had blundered into asking her to marry him. Or telling her, rather. As he thought about the conversation, he wasn't entirely certain if he'd ever actually posed it as a question or if he'd simply told her she ought to marry him.

For all his pretensions towards intelligence and thoughtful deliberation, Robert Bradshaw was a fool of the highest order.

"What is the matter with you?" asked Parker, watching his brother-in-law with a furrowed brow as they stood on the Ashbrooks' doorstep.

Shifting from one foot to the other, Robert shrugged the question off. "Nothing."

"If I didn't know you better, I would say you are fretful."

Robert leveled a narrowed look at Parker, but the fellow was unperturbed and unrepentant.

"I might even think it has something to do with the young widow we're visiting," said Parker with a smile.

"I don't care for your insinuations," said Robert with a scowl.

Parker's grin fled, and he straightened as his eyes widened. "It was only a jest, Robert, but something in your tone makes me think I wasn't far from the mark."

"Don't be ludicrous."

"I'm not," said his brother-in-law, his fingers tapping against the edge of his valise. Giving Robert a faint smile, he asked, "You care for Lady Whiting, don't you?"

With a huff, Robert reached up to knock again. What was taking the maid so long? Newland Place was not such a large home that it ought to take so much time for the girl to answer.

"I readily admit Lady Whiting is a friend but my feelings do not extend beyond that."

"It would be understandable if they did," said Parker with a vague wave. "She is pretty and seems like a fine woman. And Nell adores her."

Robert frowned. "You needn't construct wild fantasies about the pair of us, Parker. She is a friend and a client. I am not interested in pursuing her in any other capacity—"

And thank the heavens, the door finally opened. With a few quick words, Polly deposited them in the parlor, and Robert hoped the interruption might be the end of it, but Parker watched him with a contemplative gaze. Once the maid went in search of Lydia, his brother-in-law continued their conversation as though no time had elapsed.

"While it is admirable for you to remain true to my sister's memory, you are still young. There is no need for you to sentence yourself to a solitary life. There is nothing shameful—"

"We are here in an official capacity only."

Parker's brows rose. "I was not aware solicitors undertook the hiring physicians for their clients. It seems I have been neglecting a lucrative avenue for finding new patients."

Robert shifted in place once more and wandered over to the mantle. "You are a peace offering to a friend."

With a chuckle, Parker shook his head. "And what did you do to require an apology of such grandeur?"

Shifting from foot to foot once more, Robert tucked his hands behind him to keep from fidgeting. "I offered to marry her."

A weighty silence followed that, and Robert glanced over his shoulder to find his brother-in-law gaping at him.

"I—" began Parker, but he stopped, his brows drawing together.

Robert waved the reaction away. "It was a practical arrangement to protect her and her daughter. That is all."

The parlor door opened, and Robert snapped his mouth shut as Lydia appeared with Isabella on her hip.

"Mr. Bradshaw?"

Turning to face her fully, Robert bowed and motioned for his brother-in-law to come forward. "Allow me to introduce Parker Humphreys."

The fellow gave the proper bow, but when he straightened, he faced Lydia with a wide grin. "I am here as an apology."

Robert hid his wince and then leveled a narrowed look at the man, who had not the sense to look chagrined; Parker merely grinned back at Robert's scowl, and Lydia watched the pair with a furrowed brow as she bounced Isabella.

"He is a physician," said Robert. "I asked if he might take a look at Isabella—"

"No." Lydia's hold on her daughter tightened, and she stepped away as though Parker might snatch her child. "I will not allow another butcher to touch my child."

Parker moved away, raising his free hand in placation. "I understand, my lady."

The use of that title did nothing to soften Lydia's posture. She stood, poised to flee the parlor while watching Robert with a mixture of confusion and betrayal. Giving her a gentle smile, Robert motioned for her to come with him to the far side of the room. He sent Parker a silent command, and his brother-in-law nodded, giving them as much space as he could and turning his attention elsewhere.

Drawing close to her, Robert dropped his voice. "I did not mean to upset you."

"I shan't allow Isabella to be tortured again. My husband and his mother subjected her to their physician again and again, and none of it did any good."

Ignorant of her mother's distress, the child gave Robert a toothy grin, and he held out a hand, taking hers in his with a gentle brush of his thumb against the back of the child's hand.

"I know that Isabella's feet are a concern, and my brother-in-law is an excellent physician. He believes he might be able to help her."

Lydia's posture softened a touch, but she held tight to Isabella. "You trust him?"

"I give you my word that I shan't allow him to hurt her. He is a good man."

Glancing past Robert, she watched Parker as he studied a painting on the far wall. When her gaze returned to Robert, Lydia studied him with equal intensity.

"Why did Mr. Humphreys say he was an apology?"

Tucking his hands behind him, Robert rocked back on his heels with a sigh. "I know I upset you during our last visit."

Lydia straightened with a half-smile. "It is not your fault I fell to pieces. If anything, you deserve praise for what you have offered us."

Robert shifted in place once more, clearing his throat. "That may be, but I do not like having caused you such distress."

Though he'd come to understand Lydia far better over the past month, Robert could not discern the look she gave him. There was some intensity of emotion stirring beneath the placid facade, and he could not tell whether it was a pleasant feeling. And that made him shift in place once more. Ought he to assure her again? Apologize? What words might he offer to make her smile once more?

"You needn't rush to a decision, Lydia. There is time for you to decide." Robert cleared his throat, his smile tightening. "My offer was earnest but hastily given. We have not exhausted all our options yet."

Her gaze dropped to her daughter, who had leaned forward to rest her head on her mama's shoulder. Rubbing a hand along Isabella's back, she said, "Marriage is the surest course of action."

Robert nodded. "But we needn't go through with it immediately. I simply want you to know it is there, and I will make certain you are never in their power again."

Lydia's eyes gleamed as she gazed upon him with a warmth that echoed in his heart. "Thank you, Robert. I do not know what I would do without you."

Offering up his hand, he motioned to the sofa beside Parker. Robert stood with it extended, silently waiting to see if she accepted. Slowly, she lifted her hand and placed it in his. A surge of energy flowed through him, making his heartbeat quicken until he felt certain he was capable of slaying dragons and battling whatever foes might come. Though tentative, her touch held the entirety of Lydia's trust, giving it to him in a manner that awed and humbled him.

Robert led them over to where Parker stood, and Lydia stiffened, though she seemed to hold firm to the faith she'd demonstrated in him as she held firm to his hand. He couldn't think of another person who trusted him so implicitly, especially when she had so many reasons to distrust. Certainly, Eleanor hadn't, for she'd been an independent sort who did not place her trust in another. Some thought her headstrong. Others thought her excessively capable. But either way, she rarely looked to her husband for support. She hadn't needed it.

His stomach clenched at that thought, and Lydia's hand tightened around his, drawing his attention back to her. An unspoken question rested in her gaze as he met it, asking what was amiss, and Robert smiled, banishing those thoughts from his mind. But they weren't so easily dismissed as he helped her to the sofa.

His thoughts mixed with the words Lydia had spoken during their previous discussion before her tears had flowed. Robert couldn't recall her exact wording, but her meaning was quite clear. Perhaps he was a tad more generous than necessary towards Eleanor's memory, but that did not mean he was confusing fantasy with reality. No doubt Lydia was speaking from her own experience, but there was little similarity between his situation and her past with Mr. Marks. Lydia had hardly known her old dancing instructor. Eleanor had been his wife, and they had courted for nearly seven years before that. It was not a fair comparison.

He released Lydia's hand and straightened to find Parker scrutinizing him. Robert refused to rise to the bait or feel the slightest bit flustered, for he was doing nothing wrong in assisting a friend and client. Sighing at his ridiculousness, Robert ignored those troubling thoughts of Eleanor. It was all a bit of foolishness, and he needed to pay attention to the work at hand.

Chapter 27

Only the strength of Robert's convictions kept Lydia from running from the parlor. Shifting Isabella around so she rested on her mama's lap, Lydia watched Mr. Humphreys as the fellow gave her a warm smile she did not return.

"Well, aren't you a darling?" asked Mr. Humphreys, squatting before Lydia and offering his hand to Isabella, who leaned back into the crook of Lydia's arm, though there was more coyness than timidity to the movement.

Turning his gaze to Lydia, he added, "During my studies, I aided in treating a child with a severe case of clubfoot. I cannot guarantee to heal your daughter entirely, but I am certain we can improve her current condition."

"Allow me to fetch you a chair," said Robert, stepping into the adjoining dining room.

Flicking back the latch on his valise, Mr. Humphreys opened it, and Isabella stiffened. Lydia rocked and cooed at her, but Isabella's little lips quivered, her dark eyes fixed on the physician's bag for a long moment before she let out a sharp, desperate scream. Twisting in Lydia's hold, she wrenched away from Mr. Humphreys, burying her face into her mother's neck as she wailed for her mama again and again.

A crash sounded in the dining room, and Robert rushed through the doorway between the parlor and dining room with wide eyes as Isabella babbled into Lydia's neck, alternately saying "no" and calling Mr. Humphreys "bad." The fellow in question raised his hands and stepped backward with a frown, his gaze locked on his little patient as Robert closed the distance in a few steps, placing a gentle hand on Isabella's back. But the child cringed, burrowing deeper as she hid her feet deep under the edge of her dress.

Lydia's heart felt as though it would crack at Isabella's agony. Rising to her feet, she walked the room, bouncing her daughter in her arms.

"Mama is here, darling," she cooed, rubbing Isabella's back as she sent an apologetic look towards Mr. Humphreys. "It is not you. Isabella has a terrible history with physicians."

"I do not blame her for her reaction," said Mr. Humphreys with a sad smile. "There are plenty in my profession who terrify me, and far too many innocents are made to suffer at their hands."

"I had hoped her memories were fading." Lydia pressed a kiss to her daughter's head.

Robert stood at the ready, watching her as she paced, his gaze flicking between Isabella and her. Lydia gave him a grateful smile.

"Might I ask what has been done for her?" asked Mr. Humphreys.

Speaking in a calm, even tone that helped to calm Isabella, Lydia said, "There were a number of foul concoctions they forced down her throat and ointments they rubbed onto her feet, though I cannot tell you what they were. But the worst was a wretched harness that forced her feet to straighten. My husband insisted she be kept in it all the time, but it never seemed to do anything but hurt her. I swear it nearly broke her little bones with all the wrenching it took to get her feet into them."

Lydia cringed at the memories of that butcher twisting Isabella's little feet to attain the proper shape, and she clutched her daughter all the tighter for it. Surely there was something she could've done to spare her child that pain, though Lydia knew there was not. Any protests she'd mounted had been ignored or resulted in some censure for her or Isabella.

"Forgive me, dearest," she whispered to Isabella.

"Scarpa's shoe," muttered Mr. Humphreys in a tone that sounded more like an oath. With hands on his hips, he scowled at the floor for a moment before turning his attention to Lydia once more. "Though not widely accepted, enough believed Scarpa's claims and used the horrendous thing on their patients. It is amazing what physicians will believe simply because it is published in a medical treatise, even if no one else has been able to replicate the man's findings. They do not bother to use their good sense to look at a claim and realize it is ridiculous—"

Mr. Humphreys cut short his tirade and gave her a weak smile. "I apologize, but it is astounding how insensible people can be."

Isabella began to calm, going limp in Lydia's arms as remnant shudders had her breath coming in shaky pants. Mr. Humphreys and Robert both watched the child with worried gazes, though Robert returned to his previous task and fetched the chair he'd abandoned in his rush. Out of Isabella's sight, Mr. Humphreys reached into his valise and pulled out a beautiful bit of marzipan shaped like a strawberry.

Inching closer, he held it out to her. Isabella kept her face buried, though she turned just enough to watch him with narrowed eyes. For a long moment, she studied his offering and him before she reached out with a cautious hand and snatched the confection. Her sniffles calmed a touch as she munched on the treat.

Carefully, Mr. Humphreys moved closer, and Isabella did not cry out as before, but she squirmed in Lydia's hold. He straightened and retrieved another treat from his valise, luring her in with another promise of sweets. Nodding at Lydia, Mr.

Humphreys directed her back to the sofa, and though Isabella did not relax, she did not complain at the change—not even when Mr. Humphreys sat opposite Lydia in the chair Robert had procured.

"We needn't try anything during this visit," said Mr. Humphreys. "I would simply like to examine her feet to gain a better understanding of what Isabella requires. I shall need some time to research a bit further before I wish to attempt any treatments."

Lydia nodded, rocking side to side before she shifted her hold to turn Isabella around, but the child whimpered again.

Mr. Humphreys held up a staying hand. "There is no need. It would be better if I could examine her feet upright, but if we can just get them free of her dress, I can take a look while she is in this position."

Leaving Isabella resting against her shoulder, Lydia inched up the hem of the small gown, and though she expected Isabella to squirm, the child chuckled instead. Lydia looked down and found Isabella smiling hesitantly, her eyes fixed off to the side. And that was when Lydia noticed Robert standing there, directly in Isabella's line of sight. Puffing out his cheeks, he wrinkled his nose, and Isabella's hands flew to her mouth to cover a laugh.

Mr. Humphreys took hold of Isabella's right foot, and she stiffened, squirming around to see who had hold of her. Before she could let loose a cry, he held up another confectionery, which Isabella took with a wary look before Robert drew her attention once more. Lydia watched the physician as he took the misshapen foot in his hand and, with gentle touches, turned it, casting glances at Isabella, whose attention remained on her treat and Robert's silly expressions.

"Her right foot is worse than the left," said Mr. Humphreys, "and I do not know if it can ever be set to rights entirely, but there is no reason it cannot be straightened to a degree. If nothing else, it will ease some of the pain of walking."

Lydia's thoughts drifted as Mr. Humphreys continued to talk to himself about the various options available. For one who had spent so many years at odds with herself and the world around her, the peace that nestled into her heart was a startling thing—though not unwelcome. The more distance she gained from her life among the Whitings, the more tranquil she felt. Her skin tingled as a flush of warmth followed on its heels, sweeping through her and settling into her chest like a well-tended kitchen fire. To have gone from being entirely alone to having so many willing to aid was a severe shift in her world, and Lydia hoped she never acclimated to that joy.

Gaze drifting towards the source of much of her present contentment, Lydia found Robert shifting his features in a manner that would likely leave his clients aghast if they could've seen it. Isabella giggled and smiled around bites of marzipan, unaware of Mr. Humphreys' work.

Then Robert's eyes met Lydia's; those rich, dark depths shone with mirth, his lips curled into a pleased smile that she matched. Yet again, he was doing so much for her. Sacrificing his time and dignity to entertain a small child—to say nothing of the great gift he'd brought in the form of Mr. Humphreys. Lydia held his gaze, pouring all the gratitude she felt into that look, hoping he could feel just how much this meant to her.

How much he meant to her.

Lydia pressed a kiss to Isabella's head, using the movement to rip herself free of Robert's gaze. Her heartbeat increased until it felt like a hummingbird was trapped in her chest. Clinging to Isabella, Lydia focused on her daughter, allowing that to anchor her to the here and now, though her thoughts sorted through her feelings.

She could not love Robert. She couldn't. It was just a twisted sense of gratitude blurring the edges of reality. But the strength of her panic testified to the truth: Lydia would not fear so greatly if it were only a flight of fancy. Resting her head against Isabella's, Lydia tried to focus on her daughter, but it was an impossible feat with the child laughing and drawing her mother's attention back to the man who inspired it.

Lydia wanted to scold and mock herself in turn. Surely she was making more of her feelings than they were, and even if that weren't true, Robert had made it abundantly clear that his heart was full of his wife and no one else. She simply had to keep her silly heart in check.

That thought ought to calm her, but it only served to stir up her agitation. Keeping her head next to Isabella, Lydia drew in a deep breath. The scent of infancy had long faded, but still, holding her daughter close helped to focus her. There was little room left in her life for anything else but Isabella at present.

Chapter 28

To his knowledge, Robert had never whistled a jaunty tune. Not that he was unable to do so, but it wasn't a habit he'd developed. So, he was rather stunned when the impulse seized him as he wandered down the street. The sky above was choked with clouds, though they did not look to bring rain; it was odd that he felt such brightness of spirit when the world around him looked so bleak. There was even a bit of lightness to his step that felt entirely foreign. Robert was no dour creature, but such ridiculous displays were unusual for him. Until now, apparently.

But it was no wonder that he felt that joyful burst of energy coursing through him. Nell was happy with her new school and afternoon lessons with Lydia. Parker was certain he could do much for Isabella, who was showing less and less inclination to scream whenever she saw the physician, though she was likely to drive Parker into the poorhouse with her demands for sweets whenever he visited. And even Lydia seemed more at ease.

Moving through the streets of Olde Towne, Robert considered the buildings around him. Though Lydia had not yet arrived at the point of letting rooms for her school, he had spent some time researching the options available to her. Though space was more plentiful in this part of town (and it was closer to Lydia's lodgings), the vast majority of her potential clientele lived on the other side of the river.

There were the rooms above Mr. Raymond's shop. Though the fellow hadn't felt the direct sting of the financial collapse of the banking industry, like so many others he was capitalizing on the situation and snapping up better situations as others were forced to retrench; Mr. Raymond had purchased a proper house for his growing family, leaving the rooms above his shop empty. Perhaps Robert ought to speak with the fellow and see if the tailor had found a tenant.

Of course, Robert was getting ahead of himself, for Lydia had not made a decision on that front, but she was warming to the idea. He knew it was trepidation and not disinterest that kept her silent on the subject, and her learned timidity was easing with each passing day. She may not know how to begin such an undertaking, but between himself and Mr. Ashbrook, there was no reason they could not get her school running.

Taking the final turn, Robert quickened his pace as he approached the Ashbrooks' door. The maid had him inside in a trice, and Robert grinned at the sound of Lydia's steady voice counting out steps in the parlor. Inching open the door, he peeked inside, hoping not to disturb the girls in the midst of their lesson, but he was only superficially successful.

"Papa!" cried Nell, abandoning her studies to come over to him, bouncing on her toes with a rapid string of details about what had occurred during their lessons. She spoke without breathing, and once finished, she turned away and ran back to Dottie as the pair continued to practice their steps.

"I apologize for interrupting your lesson." Robert smiled at Lydia, and she gave him a vague nod of acceptance.

"It is no matter, Mr. Bradshaw. We were nearly finished."

Using his surname in mixed company was the proper thing to do, but there was a degree of formality to Lydia's tone that sounded strange coming from his friend. Though slight, her words felt distant. Something more akin to the Lady Whiting he had first met and not the Lydia he'd come to know. Lydia kept her gaze fixed on her pupils, watching them with far more determination than warranted.

"Is something amiss?" he whispered.

Lydia gave him an airy smile, shaking her head. "Certainly not, Mr. Bradshaw."

And yet she did not meet his gaze when she spoke, nor was her tone any warmer than before. If not for little ears, Robert would push the subject, but as things were, it was best to ignore it for now, though he found that difficult. Lydia did not seem agitated, so he did not think her current mood had to do with her parents or the guardianship of her daughter, but something was the matter.

"Can we practice a country dance, Aunt Lydia?" asked Dottie.

Nell's eyes widened, and she beamed. "Papa can stand up with me!"

Lydia ran a hand down her skirts, her eyes still not meeting Robert's when she said, "I doubt Mr. Bradshaw cares for dancing, girls."

Robert's brows rose at that. "That is a spurious accusation. I adore dancing."

"Papa never cared for dancing before Mama. She was so perfect and elegant that he was instantly entranced by her." Nell gave a heavy sigh at the end of that speech, as though her eight-year-old heart could think of nothing grander. Robert's own heart, with six and thirty years to its credit, agreed.

"Your mama was the finest dancer I've ever known," added Robert, giving his daughter a warm smile. "I've never seen anyone so light of step and graceful. I doubt the grand muse and goddess Terpsichore herself could rival your mama's talent."

It was only then that Lydia met his eyes, and Robert was puzzled at the frown she gave him. Her expression pinched, and he felt like a schoolboy facing his old schoolmistress.

"My mama enjoys dancing, too," said Dottie, completely unaware of the irritation thrumming from her aunt. "But she is too busy to join our lessons and stand in as our fourth. And Papa is at the mill."

"Please, might we do a country dance?" asked Nell.

"That sounds diverting," agreed Robert, joining in with the young girls to pester their schoolmistress.

Something inside Lydia seemed to sigh, releasing some of her aloofness, and she asked, "Do you know *Sherbourne Castle*?"

Robert shook his head. "But I am a quick study."

Lydia considered the girls and asked, "Perhaps *Duke of Clarence* or *Doctor Lushington*?"

Each of the girls clamored for her choice (which was the opposite of the other's), and Lydia turned questioning eyes to Robert.

"*Doctor Lushington*," he said.

With a nod and a few words, she arranged the girls in their proper positions, taking the man's part opposite her niece while Robert stood up with Nell. Though he enjoyed the sight of his daughter standing before him with a great beaming smile on her face, his gaze drifted to his left, where Lydia stood opposite Dottie. The lady paid him no mind, giving the girls a few counts before the dance began in earnest. Without a pianist on hand, Robert had to focus on the beat Lydia counted and the silent music echoing from his memories.

Moving forward, Lydia and Dottie swung around each other before weaving around Robert and Nell. The dance itself was simple, the steps not as quick or intricate as some, though Lydia occasionally called out little instructions for the girls. When it came time for the two couples to *poussette* together, Nell reached for the wrong hand, and her cheeks blazed, although Lydia's correction was subtle and gently done.

With only two couples and no accompanying music, the dance was far shorter than what one would find at an assembly or ball, and Robert was as eager as the girls for another. Launching into the next, Robert smiled as Dottie and Nell did an admirable job keeping pace with the adults. They stumbled and faltered at times but fared far better than he'd done during his first few forays into dancing.

But then Nell scowled at herself, stamping her foot. "I cannot get it right!"

Before Robert could say a word, Lydia crouched before her. "Nell, you are doing beautifully. You and Dottie have only been practicing for three months. You cannot hope to be an expert so quickly."

Nell's shoulders drooped. "But I want to be perfect at it."

"Dearest, none of us are perfect," she said, chucking the girl under her chin.

Nell nodded without being appeased, but when Robert moved closer, Lydia straightened and nudged his daughter back into place, beginning the dance once more before he could say a word. Robert sent a questioning look at Lydia, but he received only a narrowed gaze in return. Though he spent the rest of the dance puzzling over the strangeness of that interlude, he had no thought as to why Lydia was so put out with him or why she behaved as though he was the source of Nell's frustrations.

With a few smiles, Robert had Nell's mood back to its usual sunny disposition by the time Lydia ended the dance.

"Perhaps we might try—" began Lydia.

"The waltz!" Nell's enthusiasm was echoed in Dottie's beaming grin, the pair nodding and pleading with Lydia.

Their teacher blushed, though Robert held in a silent laugh. He did not care for the thought of his daughter dancing with any young man in such a manner, but it was hardly scandalous any longer. The country may be slow to adopt fads, but few now gave the previously shocking dance any thought. Looking at Lydia's expression, Robert wondered if she was of a more traditional bent.

"You and Papa could demonstrate," said Nell, and Dottie nodded vigorously.

"Please, Aunt Lydia," she added.

The lady gave Robert an inscrutable look, studying him without meeting his gaze for a long moment before she gave the girls a faint smile. He felt certain Lydia would not have agreed had her pupils been any less demanding.

"If you insist," she said, ushering the girls to the sofa so they could observe. Moving to the center of the room, Lydia had Robert stand beside her as she addressed the pair. "This is only to be a small demonstration, and there are far too many variations on the waltz to show you all of them."

She held out her left hand to him, and Robert took it while placing his right on her back. Stepping into their positions, the pair promenaded for a few steps before Lydia turned to face him, her hand still in his. As she hummed a slow count of three, Robert knew she intended them to do the Pirouette, and he raised the hand clasped in his so it arched above their heads, his right hand shifting to her shoulder blades as the pair drew closer.

Without missing a beat, they moved together with delicate steps, turning around the parlor in as much of a circle as the rectangular space allowed. Their situation had them standing so very close to each other, and Robert's gaze was fixed on his partner (as was proper), though she kept her face turned away.

"This is a popular position many dancers take," said Lydia, maintaining the steps while explaining the nuances of the dance. "Though it is by no means the only option. Nor do you have to remain in that embrace."

Lydia cleared her throat as she fumbled over that final word, her cheeks turning a light shade of pink. But despite that awkwardness and the lack of music, the pair did not struggle to keep in time with each other. They stood no closer than a couple ought, yet Robert found himself trying to put some distance between them. His tailcoat scratched at him, making him want to fling the wretched thing off, and it was far too warm in the room. He was certain it had not been so unbearable just moments before, and the windows were already flung wide open.

His heart gave an erratic beat, yet his steps did not falter. He sensed every move she made, felt her intention as she transitioned them from one position to another without pause. Releasing his hand, Lydia turned to stand side by side, shifting her steps so that she moved backward as he forwards. His right hand remained at her waist, and after only a moment's hesitation, she rested her left arm on his shoulder.

It felt as though facing her directly would be a more intimate position, but though they stood abreast, the space between them lessened until their hips rested against each other, bringing them together like one entity. Lydia's gaze turned from the room at large to meet his, and he realized just how close together they stood. Her face was mere inches away from his, her blue eyes holding his as the air fled the room.

Chapter 29

Robert cleared his throat and gave a shaky smile as Lydia's soft voice filled the room in a steady count while they turned. His hand tightened at her waist, and he forced his fingers to relax as he struggled to breathe. Her pale eyes held his, and Robert wondered if she was flustered as well. He ought to drop his gaze—he knew it—but once that connection had formed, Robert couldn't pull free of her. More than that, he didn't want to.

She called to him, drawing forth a question he hadn't expected to consider, but neither could Robert deny it coalescing in his thoughts. Was it time for him to consider a different path or would he cling to the past? He'd chastised Lydia for doing just such a thing, and she was rising to the challenges of her life; for him to continue as he had would make him a hypocrite of the highest order.

That desire whispered for him to seize the moment. To seize her for his own.

Why was he fighting it? Somewhere in the back of his mind, Robert knew there was an explanation, but lost in Lydia's gaze, he could only see the vast difference between the two of them. This lady did not allow the past to wholly dictate her future.

Certainly, she struggled against its bindings, but still, she was attempting to shape her world into something better than what life had given her. Robert had allowed himself to remain mired in the past, forgoing any possibility of a life beyond that of a widower.

But as much as logic played a large role in his life, it failed him while in the midst of such longing. Now was not the time for thinking, when she was so very close. Robert's gaze fell to Lydia's lips as they turned about the parlor, and they drew him in. Standing so close to her, he felt her breath catch, though her heart beat a rapid pulse, matching his beat for beat.

They were so very near, and Robert couldn't stop himself as he leaned in—

Eyes widening, Lydia straightened and pulled free of his hold, turning to her pupils. "And that is the Pirouette or Slow Waltz. There are the Sauteuse and Jetté as well, all three of which are used together in varying combinations to form a single dance, alternating between one, two, or all of them as the conductor's prerogative..."

And so she continued, explaining the dance to the pair of young eyes and ears that had been watching their every move. Robert straightened his tailcoat, turning his gaze from his daughter to stare at the fireplace, but the ridiculous article did not want to sit properly on him at present. It felt all too tight and askew, so he tugged and shifted it several times, wishing he could be rid of the tailcoat altogether.

How had he forgotten their audience? Robert longed to feign ignorance and claim his behavior had been nothing but friendly regard. Fraternal, even. Yet it was never wise to ignore the truth when it was standing right before him.

Slanting a gaze towards Nell, he found her attention fixed on him and not her lesson. Her gaze held no malice or anger, merely the curiosity of a child puzzling out what she'd witnessed. Robert had never been prone to blush, but he felt his cheeks warm under her regard. Eleanor's eyes stared at him, making silent retribution for this betrayal. But there was no honor to defend, no wrong to right.

There was a reason so many had viewed the waltz with distrust, for it was hard to remain aloof from any woman held in such an intimate embrace. Lydia was a lovely creature, and it was only natural that she inspired an inkling of desire in him, but it was the byproduct of the moment. Lydia was merely a companion and friend. Nothing more.

Good heavens, Lydia hoped and prayed her words were sensible, for she could not turn a single thought towards Dottie and Nell. Her cheeks felt ready to burst into flames, and Lydia strained to keep hold of her composure as she rambled on about the writings of Payne and Wilson.

For goodness' sake! She was a grown woman! More than that, Lydia was a widow who knew all too well how terrible marriage could be, and here she was fairly throwing herself into Robert's arms. Had she nearly kissed him? And in front of the girls?

Lydia's legs were weak, and she felt like collapsing onto the floor and covering her face, as though that might hide her. Robert stood there, silent and aloof, his gaze turned to the fireplace like it held all the wonders of the universe, though it was clear from his posture that he was no more at ease with what had passed than she.

Was he shocked at her behavior? And yet he had drawn closer than necessary. At the moment, she would've sworn that she was not the only one affected by their dance, but the fellow had made it clear many times that his heart still belonged to his wife. She supposed it did not matter, for it did not loosen the knots that had formed inside her. No answer would ease the fractious energy winding her up like a child's tin toy whose springs were about to burst.

On one extreme along the spectrum of possibilities, Robert had recognized her behavior and did not welcome it, in which case she would fairly perish from her embarrassment. On the other, he'd been an equal participant, but that brought no solace. As intoxicating as the moment had been, Lydia's stomach roiled at the thought.

A marriage of convenience was one thing—a necessary evil. Something that hardly warranted being called a marriage, as it would be nothing but a formal arrangement to protect Isabella. A signature in the wedding registrar and a new name only. They wouldn't even share a home.

But love...

While she desired it in the future, Lydia didn't know what she felt about the sentiment at present. The thought of marrying in any true sense of the word was terrifying. Years of fantasizing and hoping for Mr. Marks had made the prospect tolerable, but subjecting herself to a true marriage made her pulse race—and not for any pleasant reason.

Sometime during her rambling discourse, Nell and Dottie had risen from the sofa and began moving in a circle with their invisible partners, mimicking the steps Lydia had demonstrated. Robert stood to the side, straightening his tailcoat, and for once, she hoped he would leave posthaste. Given some time apart, no doubt her feelings would settle once more. And then she would avoid dancing with Robert again.

"It is time for us to return home, Nell," said Robert, moving towards the parlor door.

His daughter did not pause in her steps, merely calling over to him as she stared at her feet, "But Dottie and I are going to practice."

"You can do so tomorrow," he replied.

Nell frowned at her feet, and Lydia saw her frustration return in force. As much as Lydia longed to have the Bradshaws gone, she knew there was something far more important that needed doing. Her heart clenched, and she held onto that discomfort, which was preferable to the embarrassment that colored her cheeks a deep pink. Whether or not she wished to broach the subject, someone needed to speak with Robert.

Lydia drew his attention and waved him to the far side of the parlor, leaving the girls to their practicing. Robert met her gaze, though it was not her friend staring back at her. He was such a bizarre duality; quite warm and caring at his core, yet when faced with some issue or concern, he donned a stoic air that, though aloof, held the promise of a capable mind ready and willing to be of assistance. More and more, Lydia was coming to think of the two as Robert's "friend" and "business" aspects.

When broaching sensitive subjects, it was preferable to deal with the latter and not the former. However, it was far easier to deal with that practical side of his at present, for it allowed her to pretend the waltz had not happened.

Forcing herself to remain still and not broadcast the nerves that begged her to flee from the room, Lydia said, "Might I speak with you a moment?"

It was not the most intelligent question to ask, as her motioning for him was a clear indication she wished to speak to him, but it was a good place to begin.

"I am concerned about Nell," she added, dropping her voice low enough so the child could not overhear, though with the concentration Nell was giving her dancing, Lydia doubted the child noticed the hushed conversation.

Robert blinked at her with a furrowed brow. "What is the matter?"

Lydia gathered her hands in front of her, and she considered her words for a moment, tentatively choosing which to use. "I have seen her again and again get overly frustrated when she falls short of her unrealistic expectations. Her need for perfection is troubling."

His stiff posture eased, and he waved a dismissive hand. "Nell is high strung, it is true, but she is a happy child."

"Yes, she is." Lydia spoke slowly, trying to feel her way to the right words. "Nell is a good girl and gives her all to whatever she is doing, but there is a desperate edge to that dedication."

"She has been in a mood of late, but she will grow out of it soon enough." Robert turned to the girls, clearly intent on leaving the conversation where it was, and though instinct warned Lydia to leave it be, that frantic energy coalesced into words.

"It is more than a mood. Nell is convinced she is not good enough, and that imagined inadequacy will fester and grow if it is not addressed."

Straightening, Robert met Lydia's eyes for the first time since their dance, and the tightness in her chest eased at the concern in his gaze. "You truly think it such a great concern?"

"I do."

Robert's brows furrowed, his gaze drifting off as he considered that. "What is to be done?"

But that minuscule peace fled as Lydia knew it was time to broach the subject he did not wish to discuss. "It would help if you were circumspect in the stories you tell your daughter about your late wife."

When the fellow merely stared at her, Lydia added, "I fear you've given your daughter the impression her mother was perfect in every manner, and Nell is attempting to live up to that impossible standard."

Robert huffed, turning away to move to his daughter. "Thank you for bringing it to my attention, but I must get Nell home."

Everything from his tone to his expression and posture spoke of disbelief and dismissal, and Lydia's hands shook as she realized her warning had done no good. The girls continued to dance, unaware of the tension on the other side of the parlor, and Lydia watched as Nell grew more agitated at her attempts.

Clenching her hands, Lydia raised her chin to stare at the man's back as he walked away. "The past is never as perfect as we remember it, Robert."

Chapter 30

Robert paused, and Lydia stared at the stiffness of his shoulders before he turned to face her with narrowed eyes.

"You did not know my wife." There was no threat in his tone, but it was impossible to misunderstand the edge to his words that warned her to tread carefully. But Lydia did not quiver or quake, though instinct begged her to be silent. She could never match his height, but she straightened to face him with all the dignity she could muster.

"I know no woman can be as perfect as you claim her to be. Nell is forever telling us the tales of her accomplishments, each more impressive than the next. What do you think that does to the child who feels responsible for her death?"

Robert scowled. "Nell is not responsible—"

"We know that," said Lydia, jabbing a finger at the pair of them before gesturing to the child who stood on the far end of the parlor, "but *she* sees her father pining for this perfect, angelic creature, believing her mother would still be in this world if not for her. Nell feels her mother's death keenly and is trying to be worthy of that sacrifice."

With a sigh, Robert turned away again with another dismissive wave of his hand. "I have never once given her any reason to think that way."

"You don't have to say it directly!" Lydia's voice rose, stopping Robert in place as the girls stared at her. When Robert deigned to face her again, she forced her voice to lower, though there was no softening the hardness to her tone. "As I have said before, words have power, and to someone who is hurting, the wrong ones can cause significant damage and pain. Nell is trying to be like her mother to atone for the loss, and you telling her how impossibly perfect the lady was makes her feel like she will never measure up."

Robert's expression tightened as he crossed his arms, his words coming clipped and succinct as he glowered. "You've known Nell for a few months, and you think to lecture me about what she needs? I cannot resurrect her mother, so I am giving our daughter the only opportunity she has to know that dear lady. My Nell is not so weak-willed as to fall to pieces over a few words."

Lydia jerked back, blinking at the hard man staring at her as the full weight of his words battered against her fragile defenses. Her shoulders rounded, and she instinctively backed away, though she stopped as her gaze drifted to Nell. The two girls were no longer practicing. Though Lydia couldn't be certain they'd heard or understood the argument, they knew full well it was taking place. Nell's light eyes darted between her father and teacher, her hands wringing before her, and Lydia could not believe Robert was so blind as not to see the state his daughter was in and what she would become if this continued.

But Lydia did, and she could not stand by and remain silent. Luckily, her voice remained steady as she spoke.

"I am well aware you thought me silly and weak when I first arrived, and it is clear that though your opinion has improved, it has not altered." Lydia ignored how her heart writhed and twisted as she said those words. "But though you have good intentions, you are hurting Nell by clinging to this fantasy. Your daughter will spend her life chasing after that epitome of perfection, only to be disappointed again and again when she falls short."

"I—"

"I am not finished, sir!" A spark flared in her chest, lighting the kindling that had been laid there year after year, untouched and ignored until it was a mighty pyre of suppressed emotions ready to burn.

Robert paused, his brows raising, though the anger did not dim from his eyes as she continued.

"You have no notion of what it is like to be surrounded by expectations you cannot hope to meet." Her jaw clenched, her muscles straining as she stared him down. "You cannot hope to understand what that does to a person. Forever feeling like others are tolerating your presence—"

"I have never treated my daughter in that manner!" Robert swung his arm wide, pointing at Nell, who shrank beneath their regard. "I have done everything I can to be father and mother to her—"

"And I am not saying you've done so on purpose! You're trying to be good, but you are careless with your words!" Lydia felt like shaking the wretched fellow until his good sense returned to him. "You see it as weak to be swayed by the opinions of others, but I assure you it is not strong to be dismissive of others' feelings. It takes strength to be surrounded by this world with all its cruelty and choose to feel and empathize, even though it causes you pain."

Stepping closer, Lydia dropped her voice, holding Robert's gaze as she added, "You strive to be a good papa to your Nell, and I am merely trying to tell you that such tender souls cannot always protect themselves from self-doubt and criticisms—real or imaginary. The unfortunate truth is that you cannot feel so deeply without being easily bruised from time to time, for it is impossible to turn your heart on and off like some machine. As you grow, you learn to protect it, but Nell is too young to do so."

Lydia stood there, staring at the fellow as he stared back.

The muscle of his jaw tightened, his teeth clenching before he said in a low voice, "As you are so delicate, I will keep my words to myself, Lady Whiting, and take my leave."

Giving her a shallow bow, Robert turned and motioned for Nell to walk through the parlor door. The child glanced at Lydia, her eyes full of concerns and questions, though it was a testament to her father's foul mood that she did not voice them.

Mary appeared at the doorway, staring at the Bradshaws as they continued through to the front door, but they were gone in a trice, leaving her gaping at Lydia.

"What has happened? I heard raised voices."

Shaking her head, Lydia strode out of the parlor and up the stairs, grumbling to herself about foolish, stubborn men.

Heaven save him from interfering women! Robert's teeth ached from the pressure of his jaw, but it was better to keep it locked tight than to allow all he was thinking to spill out into the world. Lydia would crumble beneath the weight of his frustrations, and whatever else she may think of him, Robert did know when to be cautious with his words.

How dare she speak of Eleanor in such a manner! Lydia had not known her, so how could she think to cast judgment on his memories of her? But then, she dared to claim she understood Nell better than her own papa, so it was hardly a surprise Lydia would be so presumptuous. She claimed a friendship with him, yet she thought him a fool who did not know truth from fiction. As if she were a proper judge of such a thing. Robert Bradshaw had grown from a scrawny, poor child to a successful solicitor with a comfortable house, servants, and more income than his father had dreamt of. One did not achieve such accomplishments if one did not have a good head on his shoulders.

"Papa."

Robert pulled free of those swirling thoughts to look at his daughter, who clung to his hand. Nell was breathing heavily, her expression pinched as her legs moved at a clipped pace to keep up with his. He slowed to a moderate pace and forced the frustration from his voice as he apologized.

"Are you angry at Lady Whiting?" she asked.

That was precisely what he was, though Robert knew admitting such a thing would not be prudent. Regardless of what Lydia said, he was circumspect in his words.

"We had a disagreement, but it is nothing of concern, poppet," he said. "Friends argue at times."

Nell frowned, though some of her disquiet eased as she gazed at the street as they walked along. "I've never heard Lady Whiting raise her voice before."

Despite all the frustration and irritation boiling inside him, Robert found himself smiling. It was a faint, small thing, but it was a smile, nonetheless. He hadn't ever thought to see her in such a rage. If he hadn't been the focus of her anger, perhaps he might've enjoyed the display a bit more.

"Mama wouldn't have raised her voice like that." Nell spoke with authority, as though it was an undeniable fact, though her brows pulled low.

"What makes you say that?" he asked.

Nell looked at him and, with wide eyes, replied, "Because she was so very kind and patient—a proper lady. And a proper lady doesn't lose her temper."

"Lady Whiting is all those things." Despite the simmering anger and resentment, the words came in quick reply to that indirect aspersion upon Lydia's character. Growling at himself, Robert batted away that sympathy; she had hardly shown him the same courtesy when she'd attacked his behavior towards his daughter.

With a frown, Nell gave a hesitant nod and added, "But Mama was even more so. She would never shout at you."

Memories quick and vivid flashed through his mind, and it was as though he heard Eleanor's voice echoing around him. True, Eleanor was too much a lady to have allowed her temper to flare in public, but she'd had no qualms about doing so in private. More than a few of their delicate decorations had met an unceremonious demise when she was in a temper.

"Your mama loved me very much." The words came without bidding, springing from his lips with a life of their own, though Robert did not know what they had to do with what Nell had said.

"And Mama was so very beautiful and kind," she added with a nod. "When she was a young woman she was crowned the May Day Queen because everyone loved her so much. She was the best of women."

Robert frowned at that and the accompanying internal whisper that followed, repeating the accusations Lydia had laid at his doorstep. Shaking his head and dispelling such ridiculous thoughts, Robert turned his attention to their path home as he growled and grumbled to himself about all the reasons Lydia was entirely and utterly wrong.

Chapter 31

Many men only viewed their children as a necessary link in the family chain to carry on their name, bloodline, and fortune. Having fulfilled their duty in bringing their offspring into this world, those fathers felt little more was required of them—except to ensure that the legacy bestowed upon them remained intact until the next generation rose to take their place. But from the moment Eleanor had announced he was to be a father, Robert had felt a keen connection with his child, which had only grown when Nell entered this world.

Overwhelmed at times he may be, but Robert had always done his level best to give Nell the affection she needed. Seeing her happy gave him more satisfaction than Robert had thought possible, and thus, he'd always thought himself an attentive father. Yet Robert had spent the days following his row with Lydia fixated on Nell to a stronger degree.

The child paid it no mind, which was for the best as only a Bedlamite scrutinized every action and word—especially when it was clear that Lydia had spoken out of turn. Yes, there were moments of concern, but they were mere moments. No child is joyful at all times. Nell was in a stage of life where she was stuck between childhood and adolescence, and that was bound to cause some confusion and frustration.

Robert's eyes followed the print on the page, the words flowing from his mouth as he read the story aloud, though his attention rarely strayed from his daughter. Curled up on the sofa beside him, Nell rested her head against him, her eyes staring into the fireplace. They'd enjoyed the first volume of German fairy tales so very much, and Robert was pleased to discover another collection had been published in English that very year, though it had taken some effort to secure a copy.

The tales were a bizarre blend of gruesome and innocent, and though Robert didn't care for his daughter to hear the tales in their entire unadulterated horror, it was a bit disappointing to discover that the translator had taken it upon himself to sanitize some of the more disturbing portions. More often than not, the omission eliminated some important detail. But as Nell did not notice it, Robert supposed it was for the best.

"'...as the little boy stooped down to reach one of the apples out of the chest, bang! She let the lid fall, so hard his head fell off—'" Robert's brows rose as he gave the page a rueful smile. The translator's definition of "disturbing" was certainly inconsistent. To his thinking, a stepmother murdering her young stepson in such an imaginative fashion warranted such a description, but as Nell gave no shudder or shriek, he continued with the story, for his curiosity was far too piqued to let the tale go. And it only grew more confusing and bizarre as the story unfolded.

A few pages later, the fictional world was set to rights, including the villainous stepmother receiving her just rewards and the poor stepson resurrecting to live happily ever after, and Robert found himself wishing the world was that simple. Not that the story itself could be called thus as it was complicated and meandering, but in the end, all was as it should be. The wicked received their punishment, and no wrong could not be righted. Though Robert was supremely grateful for his life, part of him envied the sweet innocence that believed everything would be perfect in the end. Perhaps the eternal happiness stories promised was a symbol of the hereafter, but Robert knew this world was too flawed for anyone to receive such unparalleled perfection in this life.

"It's time for bed," said Robert, placing a kiss on Nell's head before shutting the book. He braced himself for a protest, but she merely nodded and rose from the sofa. With a furrowed brow, he watched her walk out of the library and up the stairs to her bedchamber.

A mood. Nothing more. The child laughed and smiled as much as any other, and a melancholy moment did not mean Nell was struggling with some invisible burden like Lydia suggested. But as the days passed, Robert's anger sputtered, allowing him to admit there might be some truth to Lydia's assertions. Possibly. Perhaps. But like everyone, her view of the world was colored by her experiences, and just because there was some truth to Lydia's warnings did not make them entirely correct, either.

As Nell was more than capable of handling her nightly ministrations on her own, Robert remained on the sofa, scrubbing at his face. A yawn sprouted, stretching and expanding to fill his entire lungs.

Why were women so obstinate? Though even as he posed that silent question, Robert knew it wasn't in earnest, for he didn't want Lydia's newfound strength dimmed. He'd never thought to see her in such a temper; that cowering, quailing woman of the past had been replaced with a warrior, bent on protecting his Nell at any cost. Lydia had not retreated, and that was admirable.

Even if she was wrong.

Robert drummed his fingers against the arm of the sofa as his thoughts dredged up all those passing signs that were all too easy to ignore or overlook except when another drew special attention to them. As a whole, Nell was a happy child. That was not feigned or imagined. The young girl was a bright ball of joy that bounced through her days with little care or troubles, and surely that would not be the case if Lydia's claims were wholly true. Yet her accusations picked at Robert, demanding he acknowledge something was amiss with his daughter.

Crossing his arms, Robert leaned his head against the back of the sofa and stared at the ceiling, contemplating the current situation. Her cool reception the last four afternoons made it clear she was nursing bruised feelings. His heart sat uncomfortably in his chest as he contemplated his behavior during their disagreement. Robert hadn't meant to imply Lydia was weak. Whatever disparaging sentiments he'd harbored in the beginning had long since faded, and he did not view her in such an unflattering light anymore. Quite the opposite.

Sinking lower into the sofa, Robert stared at the ceiling and sighed. What good would it do to acknowledge his guilt? True, it might give Lydia a moment of relief, but Robert would be made to suffer far more than penitence required. His misstep would be trotted out as proof of his fallibility in every disagreement. From now until they parted ways, he would be punished for it again and again. Never allowed to forget the wrongdoing he'd committed.

Luckily, his fatherly duties demanded he abandon such dark musings, and he went in search of his daughter. Robert didn't understand why so many parents surrendered such simple joys to their nursemaids and governesses. There were times when having a servant on hand was useful, and heaven knew that getting Nell to sleep was not always so simple, but like anything that brought true happiness, it often required much effort and sacrifice along the way. A hard-won battle made the victory all the sweeter.

Of course, it didn't help that his experiences with nursemaids and governesses had been soured by women more interested in becoming the next Mrs. Bradshaw than caring for Nell. It seemed as though every time he'd attempted to hire one, the woman fell into one of two camps: flirty or dour. Neither of which was the sort he wanted rearing his daughter or in his household.

A Tender Soul

Slowly climbing the stairs, Robert sent out a silent prayer of gratitude. Despite his irritation, he knew he was blessed to have Lydia taking such a hand in Nell's education. The school Mrs. Ashbrook had suggested and Lydia's lessons were just the sort of influence he wanted for Nell.

Robert paused at the first-floor landing. Despite his accusations (the memory of which sent an itchy skitter down his spine), Lydia was such a good example for Nell. Timid the lady may be at times, but she hadn't surrendered from saying that which she thought needed to be said. Lydia had been assertive in her confrontation yet not shrill or belligerent. There were no names thrown about—or dishes, for that matter. A heated disagreement, yet it had not devolved into something petty.

For all that Nell believed a lady would not behave in such a manner, Robert could not think of a more perfect example of what a lady ought to be when faced with pigheaded men. Direct action without cruelty. Honesty and determination. "Ladies" were either the fragile creatures Lydia had once appeared to be or feigned timidity in public while being tyrants behind closed doors, and neither type held any appeal.

By the time he arrived at Nell's bedchamber door, Robert knew precisely what his course of action ought to be. Whether or not his apology ended as poorly as he expected, Lydia deserved one. Truth be told, Robert could not fathom why he had been so very unyielding. Whatever the circumstances, Lydia hadn't deserved his derision and anger. Her intentions had been pure (even if they were misguided), and his temper had gotten the better of him.

Robert's stomach gave an unhappy turn; it was not a wholehearted objection, but a weight settled inside it as he contemplated their argument once more. It was naught but a disagreement between friends. Nothing more. It wasn't the first nor last time such strife would occur, and it was nothing of note. A quick apology and all would be right once more.

The whole thing was ridiculous. If Lydia had kept her own counsel, there would be no need for such discomfort between them. But if a resolution required him to put aside his pride, then so be it. Robert was not such a stubborn fool as to allow things to fester on as they were. If Lydia was determined to receive an apology, then he would give it, and they could be done with the whole messy business.

Giving Nell's door a knock, Robert poked his head inside and found the child already lying on her pillows, staring up at the canopy above her. He came to her side, smoothing out the bedclothes as he contemplated her silent state.

"Does a proper lady not speak before bed?" he asked with a smile.

The candle on her bedside table flickered, the light glinting off Nell's blue eyes as she held his gaze for a silent moment. Then she rolled onto her side, giving him her back. Robert straightened and blinked at that.

"What is the matter, poppet? I was only teasing."

That was met with silence, and Robert sat on the edge of her bed, staring at his daughter's back.

"Did something happen during your lessons?" Though Robert could not imagine Lydia taking out her foul mood on her pupils, he could not think what else might've gone astray for her. Nell had seemed perfectly amiable this morning. "Or at school perhaps?"

Nell burrowed into her blankets, and Robert tugged them back. "Speak to me, poppet."

With a gentle hand, he turned her and was met with tear-filled eyes. Nell's chin trembled, and she shook her head. Her shoulders tightened, her lower lip jutting out as her expression crumpled into a sob. Robert had her in his arms as she began to cry, pulling her onto his lap as she buried her face in his shoulder. Rocking her back and forth, he held her as the tears flowed, wetting his shirt.

"I am never—" she blurted, though her words broke as she fought to get them out, "going to master—" she gulped and shuddered, "the dances!"

Robert let out a huff, a chuckle quickly following as he smiled to himself. "Is that all?"

Her cries grew more frantic, and Nell shoved at him, pulling away to curl into a ball at the edge of her mattress.

"Poppet?" Robert reached for her, but when his touch grazed her back, Nell buried herself into her blankets.

Her voice broke as she continued to babble about the dances and her apparent inability to learn them, and Robert sat there blinking like a fool as he tried to understand. But even his muddled brain made the connection between Lydia's warnings and his daughter's tears. He felt the ghost of "her" lingering beneath Nell's sorrow—the mother who danced like an angel, who mastered every step with ease, who entranced the whole room with every movement.

Robert's heart wrenched, his head dropping as he clutched the bedclothes. "Oh, poppet."

Nell's head rose, turning to gaze at him over her shoulder with wide, wet eyes. Her chin wobbled, and Robert cursed himself for those tears. Gathering her into his arms again, he joined her on the bed, leaning against the headboard as she rested against his shoulder.

"Every time I see you and the girls dancing with Lady Whiting, I am awed by how quickly you are learning it all. You mustn't be so hard on yourself when you do not master it in an instant. I promise you it took your mother years."

Raising her head, Nell met that with a frown. "But Mama was the best dancer in town—"

Robert nodded. "Yet she did not learn it all in a few weeks. Nor was she flawless."

Nell straightened and moved to turn away again, but Robert wrapped an arm around her and held her in place. His heart sent out a petition, hoping the proper words might come to his mind. As he'd spoken the wrong ones in the past, Robert did not trust his tongue at the moment. But a long-forgotten memory made a sudden appearance.

Robert opened his mouth and paused as the words stuck in his throat for a silent moment. If not for Nell's tears, he wouldn't even contemplate sharing something Eleanor preferred to have forgotten. However, Lydia's arguments surfaced once more, spurring him to give his daughter a truth to heal her heart.

"Have I never told you about the Michaelmas disaster?" Robert asked, though he knew full well he had not.

Giving him a narrowed look, Nell wiped at her cheeks and shook her head.

"It was not long after I first moved to Greater Edgerton." The memory had faded some, but as the tale unfolded, the images became clearer. "I was already entranced—"

Robert paused at the glowing description that came so readily to his lips; Nell should hear such things, but speaking of how thoroughly enamored he'd been with Miss Eleanor Humphreys likely wasn't the best course at present. He hadn't meant to say such things, yet they had come without bidding, and a niggle of worry had him wondering why the words had been such an instant response.

So, he stopped and began again.

"I was settling into town when Michaelmas arrived. The townsfolk organized a grand assembly to celebrate; villagers and townsfolk from all around attended it, and all the young ladies were aflutter," he said with a smile, though Nell did not return it. "Your mother was set to be the belle of the ball and had most of her dances secured before the night arrived."

"Including you?" The question was quiet, but Nell rested her head on his shoulder as he answered.

"Yes, I was fortunate enough to have received that honor, but that is not the point of this story." Robert shifted his arm, bringing it around his daughter. Nell gave a sniffle or two but otherwise remained quiet, accepting his embrace.

"Her father paid a small fortune for her gown, and it was made from a gauzy fabric so light that it seemed to float around her. Your mama was a sight, and she knew it, reveling in all the attention she garnered from the gentlemen and ladies in attendance."

Robert pressed a kiss to his daughter's head. "All was right in Eleanor's world for the first dance, but when the pace of the next proved a tad too rapid, she discovered that wearing such a delicate gown to a lively assembly had been a mistake—especially as she'd insisted on wearing a particularly elaborate set of heels that were far too unsteady for such dances. Her foot caught on her hem, ripping the fragile fabric."

Nell straightened, meeting his gaze with wide eyes.

"But that was not all," he added before she could interrupt. "Many a lady has torn a hem or ripped a seam and left the dance floor to see to the damage, but Eleanor refused to relinquish her place in the dance, insistent that she was graceful enough to overcome that hindrance. She tried to compensate, but during a particularly tricky bit of footwork, she toppled right over, spilling onto the floor in the middle of the assembly."

Nell gasped, her hands flying to her mouth.

"There was no hiding it," Robert said with a groan. "Her partner helped her regain her feet, but your mama's pride wouldn't allow her to surrender so easily. She laughed it off and resumed her dance, but her dress had torn even more in the tumble, and it was not five minutes before she ended up on the floor again."

"Poor Mama," said Nell with a furrowed brow.

But Robert gave his daughter a mischievous grin, hoping to lighten her somber mood. "It was some time before the ladies stopped teasing her about it, but it was good for her. Your mama needed people to twit her from time to time: she took herself far too seriously."

The sorrow faded from Nell's expression, her lips pulling into a faint smile as the light in her eyes sparked to life once more. "That happened to Mama?"

"I give you my word," he said with a solemn nod. "After the second time, she cried retreat and left the dance floor. Unfortunately, she'd done too much damage for the gown to be salvaged, and she returned home shortly after."

"And you were heartbroken you did not get your dance?"

Robert nodded.

Nell settled once more, resting her head against him for a quiet moment before she said, "I haven't fallen in a dance."

"Not yet, but you are bound to at some point. I've had my fair share of stumbles. And regardless, it doesn't matter if you are a perfect dancer or an abysmal one, Nell. You can only try your best and not worry about the rest."

The pair sat like that for several long moments as more memories filled Robert's thoughts. It was strange that he'd forgotten so many little things, though he often thought of his wife.

"Can you tell me another story, Papa?"

Robert pressed yet another kiss to her head, and Nell snuggled close as he asked, "Have I told you about the time she got lost in the woods when she was your age?"

Chapter 32

With autumn officially underway, it ought to have been too chilly for a drive in an open carriage, but the landscape around Greater Edgerton hadn't realized that summer was quickly fading into the distance. The edges of the leaves showed the occasional hint of yellow, but the world was still awash in greens with the only touch of gold to be found was the sun shining above them.

Lydia had been too hasty to leave Isabella at Newland Place; she would've enjoyed the outing. Surely she would be safe while surrounded by Ashbrooks, but with Mama's latest missive still bouncing around in Lydia's thoughts, she couldn't rest easy with her child out in public. Lydia felt eyes on her, but she banished the thought. There was little chance that whatever spies they'd hired would be following the carriage as it bumped along the road.

Shaking her head at her foolishness, Lydia turned her attention to the passing scenery. Isabella had to remain at home. Not only did she require her nap, but the landau could hardly fit the entire Ashbrook family with both Isabella and Lydia. Ambrose and Mary sat on the seat opposite with Lucas on his papa's lap while Dottie and Esther squeezed in next to Lydia—

though the children hardly kept their seats, despite their parents' warnings. If Vincent and Isabella had come, it would've been a chaotic ride that would leave their mothers feeling worn to threads afterward.

Perhaps she could borrow the carriage another time and take Isabella out to see the countryside.

"But do you like it?" asked Ambrose.

Mary's canted her head as she watched the passing city. "I admit it is a beautiful house, but it feels wrong to profit from another's misfortune."

Ambrose shrugged. "There is nothing we can do for the Wilsons. With the sale of Oak Hall, they should be able to retrench and weather their current downturn. I am certain we can purchase it for a reasonable amount."

"But Newland Place is our home, and it would be so much work to move to New Towne," said Mary with a touch of vinegar to her tone.

Lydia pretended not to listen to their conversation, though it was impossible not to overhear. When she had first met Ambrose Ashbrook, Lydia had thought him as shallow as a puddle; a thoughtless fribble who cared only for his own pleasure and joy. Yet he surprised her again and again with how well he understood Mary and saw beneath her all too often prickly demeanor. Providing yet more evidence that Ambrose understood far more than he let on, the fellow lifted Mary's hand to his, placing a kiss on the back of it.

"Our family is our home, no matter where it is. Should it be Oak Hall, Newland Place, or a hovel, it will feel like home if we are there together," he whispered. "But wouldn't you like the children to have a proper garden in which to play? A larger nursery and better rooms for us all? And the library..."

His sentence drifted off, and Mary's expression warmed, her eyes shining as she added, "It does have a very fine library."

Lydia kept her gaze turned to the side, ignoring both the personal conversation in front of her and the children who bounced around the carriage, but her gaze kept drifting to

Mary's hand wrapped around her husband's. It was a little thing, one of many little nothings that bespoke two people joined in more than holy matrimony. There were plenty of husbands and wives who shared little more than a surname, and Lydia's heart lightened each time she saw the signs and confirmations that Mary had found herself a happier situation.

"What are your thoughts, Lydia?" asked Ambrose with a sly smile.

She straightened, her cheeks pinking. "I did not mean to eavesdrop."

Mary swatted at her husband and shook her head. "We are hardly in private, and it is hardly secret, as we just showed you the house."

"I do not think her thoughts are on Oak Hall," mumbled Ambrose with another sly smile that had the color in Lydia's cheeks deepening.

"Ambrose," warned Mary, though there was a hint of a laugh in her gaze that nullified the chiding tone.

"I cannot think what you mean," said Lydia, though no one (not even she) believed it.

"He is a good man," said Ambrose with a sharp nod, as though that decided things.

Lydia gave a pointed look to her brother-in-law and then at Dottie; though the child paid the adults little mind, small ears had a knack for hearing things they ought not to.

"He is a good friend. That is all," said Lydia. Her gaze narrowed as it turned to the passing world. "Even if he is a pigheaded fool."

"As you have said for the past sennight," said Mary with an impish smile that proved her husband had far too much of an influence on her.

"All men are pigheaded fools at times," said Ambrose. "We can only hope to find wives who knock some sense into us when necessary."

"I assure you I have no interest in such an old man," said Lydia in a dry tone.

Mary's gaze sharpened, her attention turning from teasing to indignant in a flash, as Lydia had hoped it would. "The man is my age."

With an innocent smile, Lydia nodded. "And there are a good many years between us, dear sister."

Ambrose huffed, not bothering to cover the snort of laughter as Mary narrowed her eyes.

"Nine years, Lydia. There are only nine years between us." But there was a hint of mirth in her gaze as Mary shook her head. "But do not think you can distract me with your teasing."

Lydia's gaze fell to her fingers, which twisted into knots. Then Mary's hand was there, resting atop them and drawing her gaze to her sister's gray eyes.

"There is nothing to be embarrassed about," said Mary. "He is a good man, and if he has captured your heart in any manner, then you ought to pursue that possibility. You deserve to be happy."

With a sigh, Lydia shook her head. "I do not know what I feel."

Ambrose's lips pulled into a slanted grin. "That is a sign of good things to come."

But he quieted when Mary gave him a narrowed look. Shifting the children around, she joined Lydia on her side of the landau, leaving the unruly masses to their father's care.

"He is a good man, Lydia," she said. "And he is good for you."

Lydia shifted in her seat, smoothing her black skirts and fiddling with the edges of her shawl as her eyes roved the floor of the carriage. Words she'd thought so many times before came to her mind, but they were no more useful than when she'd first thought them; how could she describe her feelings when she did not comprehend them? Anger and frustration were easy enough to identify, but Lydia could not give voice to the longing she'd felt once the initial hurt faded.

She missed Robert—that much was certain. But as a friend? Confidant? Beau?

Just thinking that last word sent a cold chill down her spine, filling her with fractious energy that demanded she alight from the carriage and walk to Newland Place. And yet a frisson of warmth settled into her heart as she recalled the argument they'd shared. Infuriating, yes. And even hurtful at times. Yet Lydia could not recall another time she had argued with anyone in such a fashion, let alone a man.

What had taken possession of her tongue? Despite much time spent pondering the moment, Lydia couldn't comprehend how she'd been so assertive. Robert shared Sir Duncan's authoritative air, which brooked no refusal or opposition, yet she had stood against him, demanding he listen to her.

Certainly, there was an answer that flitted around her thoughts, but Lydia could not countenance it nor comprehend what it meant, except to know that for all his bluster and stubbornness, she did not fear Robert. True, he'd been dismissive and curt, but it was a stark difference from any disagreement she'd ever had with her parents, her husband, or his family.

And then there was her reaction to his harsh treatment. Not a few weeks ago, hearing him speak about her condescendingly as though she was fragile and delicate would have sent her fleeing for her bedchamber. Yet she had stood her ground. A tickle of a smile played at the corner of her lips as she recalled it.

But a pain pricked at her temple, and Lydia rubbed at it, shaking her head. "Mary, as much as I wish I could speak to you about such things, I fear I cannot even begin to understand what I am feeling at present. One argument does not constitute a permanent fracture in our friendship, and as infuriating as he is at times, I do wish to heal the breach. Beyond that, I do not know."

With a squeeze of her hand, Mary smiled and relaxed into the squabs beside Lydia with a nod. "Figuring out one's heart is not always easy—even if it is your own. Luckily, there is time enough—"

"Hello, there!" Ambrose stretched in his seat, calling out before them, drawing the attention of his companions. Polly stood on the doorstep to Newland Place, her hands wringing before her as she stretched to search the road. When her gaze fell to their carriage, her eyes widened, and she waved at them, rushing forward to meet them as they pulled to a stop.

"Thank heavens you've returned. I sent some lads to find you, but I didn't know when you'd return. I didn't know what to do," the young lady babbled, gesturing at the front door and the carriage and turning in place, as though searching for the boys of which she spoke.

Ambrose gave the ladies a hand, helping them and the children out of the carriage as Mary stared at the maid and asked, "Whatever is the matter, Polly?"

Her expression crumpled, and with wide, tear-filled eyes, she shook her head. The maid stifled a sob and pressed a hand to her middle. "I couldn't stop them. I tried, but they pushed past me. You must believe me. I did my very best, but they were too big and strong—"

"Polly!" Mary snapped, halting the rapid babbling. "What happened?"

"Two men took Isabella."

Chapter 33

There was never enough time. Life seemed to be nothing more than a series of minor issues that needed attending, drawing Robert away from what he wished to do. Today might be a day at home, but there were household accounts or correspondence here that stole away time from Nell, reading, or some other leisure activity.

During the week, Robert preferred his office desk to be free of distractions, but at home, his desk faced a window, allowing him to look out and see the swaying branches of the trees and the puffs of clouds in the sky; with the window open, he heard Nell playing in the small patch of garden behind their house. They served as reminders of what awaited him when he was finished and made slogging through the work all the easier—even if it taunted him at times.

Staring at the papers before him, Robert sifted through the lists he'd made. The first consisted of various stories and details he might share with Nell. Having shared a few of Eleanor's mishaps, it was becoming all too clear that his daughter wanted more, but Robert was finding it difficult to recall all the many things he'd long ago known. Then there was the list of apologies he could give Lydia. The time was fast approaching when he'd have to speak to her, and he needed an offering. And as difficult as it was to populate the previous list, this was all the more difficult.

Though he'd been a poor excuse for one, Robert was her friend, and he owed her greatly for giving him the swift kick that he'd needed. There were plenty of things Lydia required, but though her clothes were of fine quality, Robert did not think her enamored with expensive things; no doubt they were more a reflection of her husband and his family than a true manifestation of herself.

Pausing, Robert turned his ear to the garden and heard Nell humming a tune. He wondered if she was practicing again. Until their conversation two days ago, Robert hadn't noticed just how much effort his daughter put into her lessons, but now, it felt as though every quiet moment was filled with it.

Turning to the list of stories, he wrote, "*Broke Parker's arm while climbing a tree.*" Robert didn't know if that would be particularly helpful in this instance, but perhaps it would do Nell some good to know that her mother spent her younger years getting into many scrapes with her twin. Robert drummed his fingers against his desk, staring at the pane of glass, and turned to the second list to scratch out, "*Shawl at Mrs. Hannigan's shop.*" Perhaps that was too personal a gift to give, but it was such a lovely shade of blue that would flatter Lydia's fine eyes.

A knock sounded at the parlor door, and Robert turned to see Jenny enter with a bob.

"Lady Whiting is here to see you, sir," said the maid.

"Send her in," said Robert, coming to his feet.

The maid scurried away, and he pulled on his tailcoat and straightened his waistcoat as he thought through what he would say. At least he would be saved the humiliation of approaching her first, even if he did not have the offering he intended to give her.

With hurried steps, Lydia swept into the room. "Robert, I am so sorry, but—"

Robert held up a hand and shook his head. "Think nothing of it. We both said things we regret."

Blinking at him, Lydia stared for a quiet moment before beginning again, "But you do not understand—"

"I do," he said, giving her a magnanimous look. This was far easier than he'd anticipated. Perhaps he would not need to give her a token after all, for she seemed quite determined to mend things. "It is better if we simply forgive and forget, as they say."

"Robert!" His name shot from her lips, and he straightened, pulling himself free of his thoughts to give her his full attention. It was only then that he saw how red her eyes were, and the tremble of her chin.

"What is the matter?" he asked, taking her by the arm to lead her to the nearby sofa, but Lydia shook him off.

"You must help me. I don't know what to do. Ambrose has gone searching for her, but I cannot sit at home waiting," she said, babbling on in broken sentences as Robert gently guided her to a seat before her legs gave out.

Crouching beside her, Robert looked into her tear-filled eyes. "What has happened, Lydia?"

"They took Isabella," she said, her voice breaking as she clung to his hand. "We left the little ones behind so that they might nap while we went out on a drive, and when we arrived home, we discovered some men had forced their way in and taken her. Nurse Nunn and Polly did their best, but they couldn't stop them, and now, she is gone..."

Her words were clear enough as she began, but Lydia dissolved into tears at that, and Robert embraced the impulse that had him pulling her back to her feet and into his arms. Lydia buried her face in his chest, shuddering and weeping, and Robert held her tight, giving her the little comfort he could. His thoughts raced through the possibilities, but he knew the most likely scenario—her parents were playing their hand.

Robert held back a scowl, though he dearly wanted to unleash it upon himself. He ought to have employed someone strong to serve as protector and not merely his eyes and ears. If he had been wiser, none of this would have happened.

"We will make this right," he murmured, and though they were trite words, Robert knew they were true. One way or another, he would make certain of it.

Lydia nodded. Straightening, she wiped at her cheeks and put a few steps' worth of distance between them. His heart sank, and Robert looked down at his empty hands as though that might provide some explanation as to why they felt so bereft. Clearing his throat, he shook off the instinct that pushed him to take hold of her once more and straightened.

"We knew the Haywards might take a drastic step like this." Robert usually avoided speaking useless words, but for the life of him, he couldn't think of anything sensible to say while Lydia watched him with pleading eyes as though he were the source of her salvation. Thankfully, his wits returned to him, and he turned to his desk, sifting through the papers there. "I believe it is time we take a dramatic step of our own."

"But how are we to find her?"

There was too much pain in Lydia's voice for Robert to ignore. He had enough sense to avoid acting the fool and drawing her into his arms again, but he held onto her hand, hoping that the efforts he'd put forth on her behalf may bear fruit. Lydia had been through enough and deserved some happiness.

"I've had a few spies of my own keeping watch on Newland Place," he said. "They'll know precisely where Isabella is."

Lydia nodded, though she looked no more comforted than before, and Robert's insides gave an unhappy twist. Despite the irritation, anger, and frustration that had arisen between them, he could not bear to see her so very unhappy. Muscles tensing, he focused on the task at hand. There were no physical battles to fight, only turmoil and pain, both of which he couldn't beat into submission for her.

The echo of their argument played in his mind again, recalling that which Lydia had spoken concerning her unique sort of strength. He'd dismissed the sentiment before, but watching her face down yet another heartache determined to break her, Robert couldn't deny the truth of her assertion—opening one's heart to the world as she did was not weak. It took strength to face such bruising again and again without closing oneself off. It had been many years since Robert had thought of his mother and sisters with any frequency, yet he still recalled their hopeless gazes; anyone looking at them knew in an instant that they had surrendered to life, breaking beneath the unfortunate burden they'd been forced to bear.

And it was at that moment Robert realized he didn't allow himself to think about them, for it caused him too much pain. Surely that wasn't an act of strength but cowardice.

Lydia still stood there, staring at him, and he knew he needed to say something—anything—that would erase the sorrow dimming her eyes.

"I've been looking into other courses of action for you and Isabella that don't require you to marry an obstinate widower who does not always recognize good sense when it is waved in his face." His self-deprecating tone earned him a faint smile, so he continued. "Do you trust me?"

Without hesitation, she nodded and gave him another wan smile. "Even if you are a pigheaded fool at times."

Glancing down, Robert realized he still held her hand in his, and he squeezed it before turning to the desk and sorting through his papers. Upon finding a clean page, he began scribbling a note to Mr. Peterson.

...

Pigheaded he may be at times, but Robert was no fool, and only a fool approached such a precarious situation without a healthy dose of trepidation. As he had never met the other party, the Haywards were unknown entities, and though Robert felt confident he understood them well enough, he couldn't rid himself of the hint of fear that had his pulse quickening. Desperation often drove people to erratic behavior. He supposed that described Lydia and himself as much as it did the people with whom they were meeting. Not wholly desperate, though, as he was fairly certain the Haywards would capitulate to his terms.

Lydia stiffened, and Robert threaded her arm through his. It was a tad too familiar of him, as she did not require assistance and their connection was not of a romantic sort, but the touch calmed her, and Robert could not deny her that as they stared at the inn's front door. The sign proclaimed to all around that it was The Royal Oak, with lettering far too ornate for a simple country inn, but it did not surprise him that of all the places in town, the Haywards were staying in this self-important location.

All would be well. It would. In short order, Lydia and Isabella would be reunited and the Haywards would skulk back to Essex. Though every time he comforted himself with such assurances, a dozen possibilities flooded his mind, reminding him of all that might go amiss. Desperation brought with it a slew of unforeseen consequences.

Rubbing the back of his neck, Robert warned that strange, worrisome feeling not to make itself known. Lydia was anxious enough for the both of them. But as much as he tried to calm himself, he couldn't help but think that her and Isabella's futures relied on this plan of his. Robert shuddered to think what would happen should the worst occur.

"We will make this right, Lydia," he whispered. "I give you my word."

She worried her lip for a moment before giving him a nod. Shifting so that he stood before her, Robert waited until she met his gaze, and then he held it.

"I will, Lydia. Even if I have to steal Isabella back myself." Gathering all the determination burning through him, Robert held her eyes, meeting her bright ones with his dark, hoping that she saw his certainty. And though he would not risk speaking of his plans in a public place, Robert comforted himself with the knowledge that it was no false promise. He knew of more than a few men who would eagerly serve as additional muscle during a rescue, and they could be counted upon to come at a moment's notice.

No, it was not an idle promise, and Robert willed Lydia to believe it.

A fraction of his own fears eased a bit at that thought. They had alternatives. If they had to rush to the marriage altar, then they would do it. If he had to hire a slew of men to steal Isabella back, he would. Yet still, that flutter of anxiety would not leave him completely, and Robert felt all the more off-kilter for its presence.

"You truly believe that don't you," she whispered.

"With all my heart, Lydia. I swear it. I will make certain you and Isabella are together and safe."

Before he knew what was happening, Lydia wrapped her arms around him, and though a brief flash of propriety warned him this was a public place, Robert could not force himself to step away as she held him. And when she finally released him, his heart lightened at the sight of her quiet confidence in him. She gazed at him as though he was a hero from one of their novels, pledging his life to the cause of righteousness, and in some ways, Robert supposed that was true. For his words were a promise and a pledge as strong as any that had been given.

He tucked her arm in his once more, and the pair strode into The Royal Oak, ready to do battle.

Chapter 34

The world dimmed as they stepped through the entry, and Lydia's gaze swept the pub, searching for her parents. Robert spoke a few hasty words to the innkeeper, and they were led into a private parlor. Clinging to his arm, Lydia forced her breathing to slow, though her lungs strained against the control. It had been a short time since they'd discovered Isabella gone, but those minutes felt like an eternity.

"All will be well," he whispered, and Lydia clung to his promise and his arm.

Clearing the horrid thoughts that whispered dire warnings of what was to come and what might have happened to Isabella, Lydia focused on the man at her side. It was at times like these that she felt her cowardice keenly, for there was no mistaking its hold on her, and a sad part of her wondered if she would have the courage to face down her parents if not for Robert's presence.

As it was, Lydia wished Mary had accompanied them. Her sister had a fiery temperament that sloughed off her parents' manipulations with ease, but even as Lydia wished for another ally at her side, she knew Mary's absence was for the best; having their disavowed daughter present would only increase the tension. Besides, Robert was a strong support, and with his promise ringing through her thoughts, Lydia felt ready to face down the demons.

Mama and Papa sat on the sofa with a tea service sitting before them, looking as though nothing was out of the ordinary. Until their gazes fell to Robert. Mama held onto her poise far better than Papa, whose expression tightened, and Lydia was all the more grateful he was at her side, which in turn made her feel all the more helpless. The muscles in Robert's arm tightened, and Lydia turned her eyes to meet his. He gave her a faint nod, his gaze radiating such conviction that her heart lightened in response. It was as though she heard his voice in her thoughts, promising her she could manage this.

"My dear Lydia," said Mama, her lips pulling into a frown. "I do not understand why you have treated us in such a fashion. Your papa and I have been beside ourselves ever since you disappeared from Elmhurst Court."

"Where is Isabella?" A surge of pride flooded Lydia's heart as she managed the question with poise.

Mama gave her a hint of a smile that held more than a bit of reproach. "I imagine you are in quite a tizzy—like we were when we discovered you missing. We were left to fear the worst, and you sent no word. Even after all this time, you refuse to respond to our letters, forcing us to take drastic measures."

There was so much anguish in her mother's eyes, and it pierced Lydia's heart. "I did not think what it would do to you. I apologize for any hurt I may have caused."

"We have only ever tried to do our very best," said Papa. "We have sacrificed and struggled to give you the best life we can. What have we done to deserve such cold treatment from our daughter?"

"It is a terrible thing to be so ill-treated by those we love. I've hardly slept a wink since that awful day." With a shake of her head, Mama retrieved a handkerchief from her reticule and dabbed at her eyes. "You've forced us into this horrible position.

Making us behave in such an underhanded manner. If you had simply spoken to us directly or even written a few lines—"

Mama sniffled, leaning into her husband as Lydia felt the weight of their accusations pressing down on her. A simple letter. What would've been the harm in that? Instead, she'd remained silent. Her heart clenched as she thought of all the terrible minutes she'd passed since Isabella had been taken. Not knowing where she was or what would happen. And Lydia had done that to her parents rather than simply speaking to them. That guilty weight grew heavier, making it difficult for her to stand upright. Her shoulders drooped as she lowered her gaze to the floor.

"Enough." Robert's voice cut through the room, and Lydia straightened as though that one word freed her from the spell her parents had woven.

She did not understand how they had managed it once more, but with a few accusations, she'd reverted to a cowering mouse. With a crumpled expression, Lydia looked at Robert, but there was no disgust or judgment in his gaze, only his silent support. Though she harbored doubts, his eyes said he believed in her strength, and that allowed her to gather her wits about her once more.

"Give me Isabella," she said, straightening as she stared down at her parents.

Papa watched her with narrowed eyes before nodding at someone in the corner behind Lydia. She turned to see the man who had approached her in the street. Robert tensed beside her, and Lydia knew he was recalling Nurse Nunn's black eye she'd received at the cad's hand when she'd tried to protect the children. The fellow knocked on the door beside him, and it opened to reveal a bruise of a man that looked precisely like the brute the nursemaid described as the fellow's partner. But all that was forgotten at the sight of her daughter clutched in his arms. The child arched back, pushing against the man.

"Mama!" she shrieked, and Lydia lunged forward, but the wiry partner barred the way.

Robert's hand came down on her shoulder, and he stepped forward, putting himself between the men and her as much as he could while Lydia reached for Isabella.

"Give her to me!" Lydia spun to face her parents.

Papa waved a dismissive hand. "You have no right to make demands on us, young lady. It is your fault we are in this unfortunate position, so do not think you can swan in and get your way."

The anguish and disappointment in her mother's gaze called forth Lydia's instinct to drop her shoulders once more, but before they could make more than a cursory movement, she straightened again. With Isabella's whimpers and whines ringing in the air, Lydia found a hidden reserve of strength and faced down her parents, jabbing a hard finger at them. Borrowing Robert's demand, Lydia felt his certainty and strength settle over her, stoking her own.

"Enough!" she barked. "My fleeing Elmhurst Court and ignoring your letters was a clear enough sign of my feelings. I am not interested in marrying for your sake again. I gave you one marriage. I shan't give you another. And for you to use my daughter against me is unconscionable. Have you no shame?"

"Have you no honor or sense of duty?" retorted Mama, straightening to stare her down. "We have sacrificed everything for you, and yet you would deny us this? You selfish, unfeeling creature!"

Lydia sucked in a deep breath, gathering her righteous anger. "I was a fool for ever allowing you to control me as you have. Know this: I will marry a pauper just to spite you before I will ever marry whatever horrid, wealthy man you have intended for me."

The door Lydia and Robert had used opened, and a fellow of middling years and features peered into the room. Robert motioned for him to join them, and the stranger shifted the documents in his hand and shut the door behind them. In the interim, Lydia smiled at Isabella, hoping that might calm her somewhat (even if it did little to calm her mama).

"This is Mr. Peterson," said Robert, not bothering to give her parents the decency of a proper introduction. He glanced at Lydia and drew her attention back to the business at hand. There was a question in his gaze, and he nodded at her parents as though asking if she wished to deliver the news. But Lydia shook her head, giving him free rein to deliver the details of his plan; he knew them better than she.

"He serves as the Whitings' solicitor in Greater Edgerton," said Robert, tucking his hands behind him as he examined Mama and Papa; there was a sneer to his expression that testified to his low opinion of the pair. Robert nodded at Mr. Peterson, and the fellow picked up the narrative.

"My client has been made aware of the situation that has arisen between you and her daughter-in-law, and she is not well pleased with it," said Mr. Peterson with far more glee than one ought to have when working for the Whitings. Mr. Pendergrass would be horrified at the breach in decorum, and it made Lydia like the fellow all the better for it.

Papa paled, though he maintained a stoic facade. "I do not see how our family matter has anything to do with the Whitings."

Robert gave him a pitying smile. "You may be a fool in many ways, Mr. Hayward, but I hardly think feigning ignorance at present will serve you well."

"And who are you, sirrah, to speak to me in such a manner?" said Papa, puffing up his chest, though he deflated a touch when Robert gave him an unimpressed look in response.

Mr. Peterson continued, "The Dowager does not wish for you to drag her family name into the courts, so she is offering a settlement in exchange for your signing a binding document that relinquishes any legal hold you have over Miss Isabella Whiting in perpetuity."

"How much?" asked Papa with a raised brow.

"Fifteen hundred pounds."

Mama huffed, throwing her hands wide. "That is a pittance."

Hearing the others debate about the worth of her child was too much for Lydia to bear. Turning away from the haggling, she focused on her daughter, wishing she had tens of thousands of pounds to give the pair if it meant Isabella would be free of them. Robert moved to her side, pressing a gentle hand to her back, though she sensed his attention remained on the debate. Lydia gave Isabella a wide smile, calming her with funny faces and cooing words. The child still whined and wriggled in the silent man's hold, but she stilled as her mother gave the only comfort she could from a distance.

"Are you ignoring us, Lydia?" demanded Mama. "You would stand there silently, ignoring your duty to your family?"

"Isabella is my family," said Lydia.

"I gave you life, and you have given me nothing but heartache!"

A flash of guilt had Lydia cringing for a moment, but she closed her eyes, gathering her hard-won strength before meeting her mother's gaze. Perhaps if she'd been met with cool disdain or anger, Lydia might've met it with composure, but it was resentment that shone in her mother's eyes—and that fed the temper that had been quietly smoldering beneath her fear and self-doubt.

"You have never cared about me as anything other than an investment, and you dare to say I owe you anything?" Drawing herself up, Lydia glowered at the pair as that flickering fire grew. "Do you have any thoughts of anyone's heartache but your own? Can you even feel the slightest bit of sorrow for all the deprivations I suffered as Sir Duncan's wife? I've done everything you've asked of me, and it is never enough!"

"How dare you speak to us—" began Papa, but Lydia shouted over him.

"How dare you treat your children like objects to do your bidding! How dare you treat us like slaves and doxies to be used or sold off in pursuit of your happiness! How dare you use your granddaughter as a pawn to fill your pocketbook!" Lydia's voice rose, and Isabella whined, but there was no containing the bonfire burning through her veins as Lydia unleashed all she'd longed to say. "Sign the document, take your money, for you will not get a better offer. Whatever else I do, I will make certain you have no power over me and my daughter. If I have to flee the country, I will, if it means we are free of your influence. I am done with you both! Now, leave us be!"

Chapter 35

With Robert's attention divided between the various threats surrounding them, he couldn't truly appreciate Lydia's fury. The man holding Isabella was by no means rough with her, but watching the child struggle to free herself had Robert's muscles strung taut. Despite the years that separated him from his childhood, some instincts never died, and his had Robert studying the two brutes and his surroundings, aware of anything and everything that could be used as a weapon should it come to that.

And then there were the Haywards. Those slippery, selfish, wretched, horrid... There were not insults enough to describe those two. Seeing them in the flesh proved far worse than anticipated, and the more they spoke, the more Robert wished to toss them from the inn and take Lydia and Isabella far from here. The husband and wife worked together, thrusting and jabbing at their daughter, twisting reality until it matched their warped view of the world; if he hadn't known better, Robert might've been convinced they were the poor, downtrodden parents of an ungrateful daughter they claimed to be. It was impossible to watch the conversation unfold and not marvel that Lydia had shaken free of their manipulations.

His gaze drifted to her, and Robert's heart swelled at the sight of her standing firm and defending herself and her daughter. Lydia was radiant, burning bright with a fury born from that passionate heart her parents had callously broken again and again. Though her strength was not of the quiet sort at present, Robert understood precisely what Lydia meant about the fortitude it took to withstand such treatment and not surrender. It was a miracle Lydia hadn't become bitter or simply faded into nothing, as his mother and sisters had done.

"You think you can simply cast us aside?" demanded her father. "We shan't be thrown over until we have received our due!"

"Lydia, do not do this," added her mother, trotting out her tears and handkerchief in a manner that would make any actress proud. "I fear for you, my dearest girl. What will you do without us to watch over you? You are too trusting to be left on your own. We may not have been the perfect parents, but we tried our best to take care of you. And now..."

The woman burst into tears and reached for Lydia. Robert wanted to step between them, but it was entirely unnecessary. Lydia stood firm on her own. There was no weakening of her resolve or even casting furtive glances at Robert; she stared them down.

"You are too weak to face the world alone and will not survive without us." Her father puffed himself up, sending a scorching glower at his daughter and then Robert. "Or are you hoping to secure a protector by handing out your favors—"

Robert didn't realize he'd moved until he had Mr. Hayward by the cravat. Thankfully, he had enough sense not to break the cad's nose. Twisting the linen in his fist, Robert drew Mr. Hayward close, the fellow's eyes widening as he held up his hands in surrender.

"You will not speak to her in such a manner." Robert was rather surprised his tone was so even, for his fist itched to punctuate his warning. Had Mr. Hayward been a man in his prime,

Robert wouldn't have hesitated to teach him a lesson in manners, though it was probably for the best as Lydia and Isabella did not need to see such a display.

Mr. Hayward squawked like a flustered chicken, but Robert held his gaze, promising him all the things his good sense would not allow him to do at present.

"Have you had your fill?" asked Robert, glancing at Lydia. She watched him with wide eyes, though a hint of a smile quirked the edges of her lips as she considered his question. Lydia nodded, and Robert's attention slid back to Mr. Hayward, who remained fixed in place.

"You are going to sign the document. You will take the Dowager's offer, for it is the best you are going to get and far more than you deserve. Then you will do as your daughter bids and leave her be." Robert spoke in a low tone, his burning gaze showing just how serious his words were. "Should you choose to do otherwise, our next conversation will not be so congenial."

Only when Mr. Hayward nodded did Robert release his cravat, and the fellow stumbled back a step. Leaving Mr. Peterson to handle those details, Robert rounded on the large man who held Isabella. Having spent a youth among a rough crowd, he knew how to discern those who take orders from those that give them, and this man was certainly in the former category.

"Give her to me," he said, reaching for Isabella.

The man paused, and Robert forced himself to remain strong, holding his gaze in unflinching certainty; the other could certainly best Robert in a match of physical prowess, but there was more to winning a battle of wills than such mundane attributes. He poured all his dogged determination into his eyes, making a clear promise that should a fight begin, Robert would not surrender easily—which was more than could be said of hired muscle.

Stepping forward, the man dropped Isabella into Robert's arms, and the child wrapped her arms around his neck, burrowing into his hold with a desperation that made him want to pummel the lot of them, but he was satisfied with another long, challenging look at the thinner man that had both him and his partner edging towards the door.

Lydia's breath caught as Robert stared down the brutes while clutching Isabella with a gentleness that was at odds with the murder in his eyes. Though she had thought she'd seen him in a temper, it was nothing to match the scorching fire blazing through him now. A vague instinct whispered that she ought to be worried, but calm swept through her, settling into her heart with a certainty that Robert would never turn that temper on her or Isabella.

He was a tempestuous fellow—the stubborn sort to stare down a much larger man and not flinch—but at his heart, Robert Bradshaw was kind. A protector who stood as her second when necessary, allowing her to fight her battles and only stepping in when necessary. Neither smothering nor abandoning. A solid, steady presence at her back.

Only when the physical threats skulked out the door did Robert turn to face her. Isabella was buried in his hold, clinging to him with a ferocity that made Lydia's heart hurt.

"Isabella," she whispered, stepping closer.

Light blue eyes lifted at her voice, and Isabella wriggled in Robert's hold, reaching for Lydia with a desperate cry. And then she was in her mother's arms, held so close that Lydia feared she might hurt the child, but she could not release her.

"We have you, darling," she said, rocking Isabella as Robert moved to stand between the Haywards and them while Mr. Peterson finished his work.

Lydia gave them her back, not caring what they were doing. Robert would ensure all was right, just as he'd promised he would, and she trusted in his word and ability. Ignoring Mama's protestations, she hummed a tune as Isabella relaxed in her hold. Soon the parlor was empty, and Lydia felt a twinge, though she could not say if it was sorrow that she was unlikely to see her parents again or guilt for the gratitude she felt at that prospect.

Perhaps a bit of both.

"How is Isabella?" Robert drew close, placing a hand on the small of Lydia's back, and she wondered if he'd even realized how often he was doing that of late—or how much she longed for that touch.

Isabella was resting against her shoulder, whimpering but otherwise calm, and Lydia gave him a grateful smile. "I cannot say for certain without checking her over, but she seems only frightened."

Robert nodded and moved to the doorway, calling out to the innkeeper to summon the coachman and ready Ambrose's carriage. But then he was back at her side, his hand resting on her back in that familiar fashion.

Turning her gaze to his, Lydia gave him a tremulous smile. "I don't know how I can ever thank you, Robert."

"I assure you it is entirely unnecessary. I am simply pleased to know I was of some assistance." Reaching forward, he brushed a gentle touch to Isabella's head. She didn't move, but his eyes brightened in response to her contented smile.

Without giving herself a chance to rethink her impetuousness, Lydia leaned forward, wrapping her free arm around him and pulling him close.

"You may think it unnecessary, but I assure you it is not." Lydia wished she could explain the myriad of emotions coursing through her, but she was feeling too much all at once to describe the individual feelings, and there were not words enough to do them justice. "I would've been lost without you."

Robert straightened and met her eyes. "You are strong and determined, and I have no doubt you would've managed it, Lydia. I am merely honored I was allowed the opportunity to assist you."

His arms drifted down her back, and Lydia knew she ought to step away. But she didn't. And neither did he. Her side was pressed to him, and Lydia knew no other's touch filled her with such peace and joy. His face was scant inches from hers, but it was not their proximity or his touch that held her attention. It was his eyes.

They were dark. Not the stormy variety that so many Gothic characters seemed to have, but a velvety brown that gleamed when he was happy and burned when he was in a temper. At present, they reminded her of a well-worn leather that had been polished to a shine, but there was a contented brightness to them that she'd never seen before. Then his expression softened, and a hint of desire colored his gaze, calling to a buried part of her that longed to lean forward and press her lips to his.

Robert would never be counted a handsome man, but his features were arresting. They were strong like the man beneath them, making him look more mature than Ambrose but in a dashing manner that was all too appealing. More than that, the man himself drew her in like a lighthouse in a storm-tossed sea, promising her the safe harbor she longed to find.

The distance between them lessened until his lips feathered against hers.

His hand drifted from her back to rest on her hip, and Lydia's muscles tensed, jerked away as Sir Duncan's phantom fingers squeezed her skin. The memory of his cologne filled her nostrils, choking her with their bitter scent, her throat tightening as his ghost fairly ripped them apart. Lydia drew her arms tight around her daughter as Robert blinked rapidly as though stirring from a dream. His mouth hung open as though he wanted to say something, and Lydia's head shook back and forth, her body reacting before she could think better of it. Turning on her heel, she fled the inn.

Chapter 36

Stubbornness was not a bad thing. Fierce determination and an unwillingness to surrender had given Robert the power to claw his way out of the gutter. Every blessing in his life, from his profession to his daughter, was a byproduct of that trait in one form or another, and Robert felt no need to apologize for it. But he also knew such undeviating conviction could be ruinous when combined with obtuseness, so he tried to maintain clear judgment and a level head. Unfortunately, his blindness tended to make itself known at inopportune times, and as Robert trudged through the streets, he finally accepted that he'd allowed it free rein when it came to Lydia.

As she'd taken her brother-in-law's carriage after her sudden departure from The Royal Oak, Robert was left to wander through New Towne, but it was for the best. He needed some time to ponder, and sitting in an enclosed space with the person who inspired such emotional conundrums would've been counterproductive.

Friend was such a wonderful word, and Robert cherished those few people who embodied it. In many ways, the fact that Parker was his friend meant more than his being a brother by marriage. Familial titles often meant little more than a shared history; his actual brothers shared little with him, other than their parentage.

And Lydia was his friend. Yet that word no longer held enough meaning when applied to her. The sentiment had been creeping up on him for so long that Robert did not know when things had altered between them, but the fact that he'd intended to kiss her twice certainly painted their relationship in a different light. He cared for Lydia in a manner that engulfed a far greater title than "friend" while maintaining the perfect essence of it.

As this revelation was so new, Robert wasn't ready to claim it as love, but neither could he cling to the ignorance that had kept him from seeing that truth for what it was.

Heavens above. He adored Lydia.

Even now, a part of him longed to give chase and follow her to Newland Place simply so he could spend the afternoon with her. And the next day. And the day after that. In all honesty, Robert could not think of another (save Nell) whose company he desired so readily. Lydia was like a gentle breeze blowing on a brilliant summer day, calming and cooling the world with its delicate touch.

Glancing at the sky, which had shifted from its azure hues to the blazing oranges and yellows that marked the sun's rapid descent, Robert realized the afternoon was passing far quicker than he'd realized. Pointing his feet towards the Humphreys' home, Robert continued to muse over this development while his head and heart battled between elation and horror until he was so twisted in knots that even a sailor couldn't have untied him.

The Humphreys' maid ushered him in when he knocked, but rather than climbing the stairs to the parlor, where Nell was certain to be, Robert found himself moving past the staircase and into Parker's examination room. As the majority of his patients were seen in their home, the space mostly served as his herb garret and study, though Robert never understood how the fellow endured the heavy scent of medicines choking the air; he supposed a tolerance of the smells was a byproduct of Parker's profession.

Bundles of plants hung from the ceiling to dry, and dozens of jars filled the shelves lining the walls. The man in question stood to one side with mortar and pestle in hand, pulverizing a small collection of ingredients into a powder. Glancing up from his work, Parker frowned and paused.

"Did it go poorly?" he asked.

Robert straightened and dropped onto an armchair that had been shoved to one side of the cluttered room. Scrubbing at his face, he tried to affect a calm air and smiled at his brother-in-law. "It went exactly as planned, and the child is at home with her mother."

Parker set down his medical implements with a nod and took off his apron, hanging it on a peg before joining Robert in the chair's twin. "Then what has you looking like the worst has happened?"

Mouth agape, Robert thought through how to respond to that, but he couldn't think of what to say. He didn't even know why he was here precisely; his feet had chosen for him.

"Does it have anything to do with your feelings for the lovely Lady Whiting?"

Robert huffed, his hand dropping to the arm of the chair with a thud as he stared at Parker, but before he could say a word, the fellow held up his hands and shrugged.

"I've had plenty of time to watch you and her mother during my visits with Isabella. It's clear your feelings extend beyond platonic."

Dropping his head back against the chair, Robert sighed. "Have I been making a fool of myself without knowing it?"

Parker chuckled. "Certainly, though not in the manner you mean."

Any other time, Robert would answer that jest with a quip of his own, but his humor was failing him at present, so he remained silent. He stared up at the ceiling and heard Parker lean forward, though Robert did not meet his gaze.

"Would it be such a terrible thing?" asked Parker. "Though I cannot vouch for the lady's feelings, I do not believe her unaffected."

Robert's eyes traced the swirls of plaster adorning the ceiling as his thoughts wandered.

"I would think that as my wife's brother, you wouldn't be so eager for me to abandon my vows to your sister," he mumbled.

"Robert..." From the edge of his vision, he saw Parker shake his head with a sigh, letting his words drift into silence.

"As there is no point in denying the truth, I will admit I care for Lady Whiting." Robert paused and considered that, though he decided to refrain from quantifying just how deep his feelings went. "But I cannot help but feel Eleanor's loss at such a time. If not for fate, she would be by my side, and there would be no question as to where my affections lie."

"As much as it pains me to say it, Eleanor is not here," replied Parker in a low tone. "There is nothing wrong in finding joy with another."

Robert sighed, his eyes continuing to follow the streaks of plaster overhead as he thought about that. "Though I hope she has found something better to do with her time in the great beyond than to sit around watching me, I cannot help but feel like she is there, and it seems unnatural to court another with her looking on."

Parker said nothing in response, though Robert felt his attention as the fellow's thoughts tried to churn out the proper thing to say. Robert's mind drifted back to the variations of this argument he'd had with himself over the years, and an old, common refrain came to his thoughts. He'd not given it much weight before, but perhaps it might just be true.

"I suppose I am being overly hard on myself," he mumbled. "Eleanor would want me to find happiness again—"

A bark of laughter, sharp and scoffing, cut Robert's musings short as he straightened and stared at his brother-in-law. Parker's brows were twisted in disbelief, his hands held up in surrender, though the gesture did not soften the expression on his face.

"I loved my sister dearly, but I can say without hesitation that she would never be so magnanimous," he said with a shake of his head.

Robert frowned, staring at the fellow, though Parker did not stumble over his words, flush over the implications, or show any sign that he felt the slightest bit of remorse over impugning Eleanor's character.

"How can you say such a thing, Parker?"

"Quite easily, I assure you," came the quick response. Leaning forward, Parker held Robert's gaze and added, "Eleanor had many good qualities, but she enjoyed attention far too much to be that giving. She wouldn't surrender your affections and would likely prefer it if you continued to pine for her the rest of your life."

Shoulders drooping, Parker sighed and dropped his head. Pinching his nose, he took a moment before continuing. "I have longed to talk to you, Robert, but you won't see reason. You've twisted your memories of Eleanor into something that doesn't resemble the woman you knew, though I do not comprehend why. The stories you tell of her are a warped version of who she was, and you cling to the fantasy that your marriage was this grand romance when the truth is far from it."

A spurt of anger drove Robert to his feet, but the space was far too small for pacing. Turning about in place, he felt like lashing out, though there was no target at which to aim, so he forced the impulse down. The last time someone had spoken thusly, Robert had not reacted well, and regardless of how obtuse Lydia thought him at times, Robert was willing to learn his lesson.

As his thoughts leapt to Lydia, Robert found that fractious energy fading, and he dropped back into the chair opposite Parker. "She said something similar to me."

Parker's brows drew together before he asked, "Lady Whiting?"

Robert nodded. "I didn't listen."

"That doesn't surprise me. I've tried so many times, but you will not face the truth. I will go to my grave adoring Lady Whiting if she has been able to make you see sense."

Robert stared sightlessly as he thought through the past, sorting through the wealth of memories he'd stored in his head. And though his heart continued to beat against the knowledge, the sinking in his stomach testified to the truth he'd hidden from for so long.

"Eleanor was my sweetheart," Robert murmured, but it felt as though the world beneath him dropped away, and no matter how he tried to cling to the certainty of that statement, his dread grew. Having been silenced for so long, its voice was faint and shaky, but it was there, telling him what he hadn't wanted to face.

Parker winced and shook his head, his right foot bouncing on its ball. "In all fairness, Robert, I think you both were more determined to be sweethearts than you were in truth."

Robert's head jerked back, and he stared at Parker. "Whatever lies I might have told myself since, we did love each other."

"Eleanor was as stubborn as you, Robert. Once our parents forbade your courtship, she was determined to have you. Can you truly say you didn't feel the same?"

"I loved her."

Parker's head bobbed back and forth as he considered that. "Yes, but you two were never right for each other. The pair of you were happy at first, but it was quickly apparent you did not suit. In theory, Eleanor liked the thought of marrying a self-made man, but the reality is she wanted a higher station in society and adored all the social thrust you detest. You two wanted vastly different lives, and that was bound to make you both miserable."

Again, Robert rose to his feet. He took the two steps to the fireplace and back; it was a poor excuse for pacing, and it made his head spin after a few moments, so he contented himself with standing in place as he thought.

Tucking his hands behind him, he recalled those happy moments they shared. They were true. Weren't they?

But even as Parker continued to talk about what he'd witnessed of their marriage, Robert's memories supplied images and conversations that came to his thoughts with more clarity than the others he'd so often shared with Nell. Where the latter were hazy and unfolded like a play being performed for him, the former sprang from his own perspective, seeing Eleanor through those old eyes in stark detail.

There were good times. There were. Yet for every happy memory, another followed filled with malcontent and anger. And though he knew it was wrong of him to compare the two, it was impossible not to think of his disagreements with Lydia. Raised voices, yes, but no insults or petty grudges. The argument with Lydia had been a passionate disagreement between two people that, though not entirely civil, had not caused irreparable damage.

"I did not want Eleanor to perish," whispered Robert.

Parker's head jerked back, and he gaped. "I never said you did."

"Whether or not we were unhappy, I wouldn't have wished that to happen."

With brows raised, Parker stared at him for several long moments. "Of course you wouldn't."

Robert dropped his gaze and turned to the fireplace. Rubbing at the back of his neck, he tried to ignore his ribs constricting, squeezing his insides. He felt Parker's attention on him, but Robert couldn't think of the proper words to explain. Not that there was any explanation. His stomach roiled and soured, and he moved back and forth in the very small space in which he could pace. But it did no good.

The last few days of her life played again and again in his head. Robert still recalled with perfect clarity those long hours he'd waited as she battled to bring Nell into the world. Then the babe's cries broke through the night air, echoing through their home. A brilliant moment that filled his world with unimaginable joy, followed by the long, somber vigil they'd held at Eleanor's bedside as she wasted away.

"Speak to me, Robert. I do not understand what you are trying to say."

Scrubbing at his face, Robert felt the pressure in his chest grow until it forced the words out. "What sort of man feels relieved when his wife dies?"

Chapter 37

The silence was palpable; like a miasma filling the room, it choked out the sound and dulled the world around him. But Robert felt Parker's gaze burning holes in his back, and though he had never felt the inclination before, he began to babble. It was difficult to describe. Robert hardly understood it himself, though as he thought of the days following Eleanor's passing, he remembered little sorrow. He mourned the loss, of course—he was not a monster—but not as a husband ought to.

What sort of man felt a flash of gratitude that he wouldn't have to spend every evening in endless dinner parties when the cost of that freedom was his wife's death?

"That is ridiculous," said Parker.

Robert nodded, his head hanging low as he leaned heavily against the mantle. "I ought to be flogged, I know."

"No, you are ridiculous!" Parker shoved against Robert's back, forcing him to turn and meet his eyes. "It is only natural for you to feel relief at not having to suffer through a marriage you knew would make you both miserable in the end, but that doesn't mean you wished her dead or aren't saddened by her loss. Being grateful that your life is once more your own is not the same as wishing her dead."

In a flash, Robert saw Nell's face looking at him with such trepidation and uncertainty, and he felt keenly that same fear; of hearing that which one wants to hear, but not knowing if it is truth or merely placation.

"Things were not terrible between you and Eleanor before she passed, but it was clear your marriage would not be a happy one," said Parker. "Neither of you was willing to admit the truth of it, and so, I was forced to simply watch as things devolved. It was easy to see that it would sour further as the years passed until it became some twisted, poisonous thing. I adore you both, but you were a terrible match. And if our parents hadn't tried to push the pair of you apart, you two would've realized the truth instead of stubbornly clinging to each other."

Robert shifted from foot to foot, unable to drop Parker's gaze, for it held firm and unwavering as he spoke. Crossing his arms, Parker shook his head, his eyes breaking from Robert's to gaze sightlessly at the room.

"My sister was an incredible lady in many ways. She was effervescent, full of life and energy that revitalized everyone around her. She had a talent for making others happy."

Robert huffed and smiled to himself. "Eleanor made you feel as though you were the most captivating and brilliant person in the room. And she could make even the grayest days sunny when she put her mind to it."

Parker gave him a wide grin and nodded. "It was a marvel to watch her work her way through a room. Bouncing about like a honeybee, stopping here and there to spread a little of her joy to everyone."

The pair stood there, silently considering that past, but as time wore on, Parker's smile faded, his eyes dimming when he spoke again.

"But she was stubborn and uncompromising, Robert."

"The same can be said of me."

Parker gave him a hesitant nod. "Yes, but there was a fundamental difference between the pair of you that guaranteed you'd never be happy together. It may take time for you to realize your faults, but you are willing to acknowledge them and improve. Eleanor was not. She never could."

Folding his arms across his chest, Robert considered that as he examined the floorboards. "I was not the husband she needed in life, but surely I can honor her memory."

A hand came down on his forearm, drawing his attention back to his brother-in-law. Parker's brows were scrunched, his gaze full of sorrow, though his voice held the mixture of certainty and comfort that made the fellow such a fine physician.

"There is no shame in finding happiness now that she is at peace," said Parker. "Nor is there any good that comes from twisting Eleanor's memory into a lie. You hold no blame for her death, nor is it wicked of you to move forward with your life."

It was as though Robert heard Nell's voice echoing in his head as the word slipped out. "Truly?"

More than the assurances Parker offered, Robert felt his brother-in-law's certainty in his expression. Honesty shone in Parker's eyes, begging him to trust in his words. Though little more than a whisper, comfort settled inside Robert, allowing him to hope as he hadn't since Eleanor had passed.

"Good heavens, man. Have you truly been carrying that around with you for so long?" whispered Parker. "Why didn't you say something?"

Robert's brows pinched and pulled, his gaze boring into the floorboards as he considered exactly what he'd said and the truth of the matter. "I didn't fully recognize it until now, and I couldn't bring myself to admit aloud the few inklings I'd had."

Pinching his nose, Parker shook his head and motioned them back to the seats, and with his restless energy spent, Robert needed to sit, for his legs could not hold him much longer. Dropping heavily, he sank and leaning his elbow on the arm of the chair, resting his forehead against the tips of his fingers so he could rub at the pain that was beginning to manifest.

"Guilt is a tricky thing," said Parker. "When harnessed, it is a harbinger of change and a painful but necessary part of one's evolution. It brings to light one's shortcomings, driving a person to improve with the promise of a better future. Yet too often, people lock it away, allowing it to fester until it twists itself into dark mimicry of what it can be, bringing with it despair and hopelessness. Guilt becomes shame, and nothing good comes from that."

Robert nodded absentmindedly, his thoughts sifting through all that Parker had said and all that had passed. It was difficult (if not impossible) to focus on anything when the entirety of the last decade had been upended in one short conversation.

"I know I promised to retrieve Nell, but is it possible for her to stay the night?" he asked.

"Certainly," said Parker. "Though we appreciate you lightening Prudence's load of late, we do miss having her around."

Robert rose to his feet, brushing off his trousers. "My thanks. I have quite a bit on my mind at present, and I need some quiet in which to think."

With a narrowed look that held a hint of a smile, Parker nodded. "As long as that also includes a conversation with a certain lady."

Straightening, Robert watched his brother-in-law and friend for a long moment, but Parker merely stood and clapped him on the shoulder.

"It is time you let go of the past, Robert. I don't know if your future includes Lady Whiting, but it'd be a shame not to explore the possibility."

Robert gave another vague nod and turned to the doorway, leaving Parker to retrieve his apron and return to his work. With the past so disheveled, it was difficult to consider the future, but as his feet led him out of the Humphreys' home, Robert couldn't help but notice how often his convoluted thoughts turned to Lydia.

Peace was an odd concept, for it encapsulated a world of contradictions. Its touch was gentle, yet it was filled with power, ushering in a flood of gratitude and joy that was overpowering at times. Both enigmatic yet all too recognizable when it appeared. It could materialize amid chaos and flee when the world was silent. It slipped into one's life without bidding at times yet required effort to maintain.

The Ashbrooks' parlor was filled with the squealing giggles and shrieks of children, which grew exponentially when Ambrose waded into the midst of it, throwing himself into the fray as only a father could. Yet peace settled into Lydia's heart, drawing forth a surge of such unadulterated gratitude that she was overcome by the strength of it. Tears gathered in her eyes, yet they were unlike any she had shed in a very long time, for they were the product of utter joy.

Isabella walked with her halting gait to Ambrose, leaping onto his back as several of the other children baited their captive, harrying him with determined force. The little ones ended up on their bottoms more often than they were on their feet, but Ambrose was always mindful and saved them from harm.

With her heart burning like an ember, Lydia felt as though her spirit expanded until it spread out farther than the confines of her body, filling the entire parlor with that warmth emanating from her chest. Isabella was home and seemed unaffected by the whole ordeal, and they were safe.

"I am so happy for you, Lydia," said Mary, repeating the words she'd spoken at a regular interval since Lydia had arrived home.

"I am fit to burst," she replied with a broad grin. Lydia couldn't keep it off her face, for it truly felt like a world of options was available to her. She did not know what she wanted to do with the opportunity, but the fact that it was there made her heart expand even further. Lydia had time to decide what to do with it.

Because of Robert.

It was astonishing how quickly one's heart could turn from celebration to dread. Like a rock tossed into a calm pond, it set the still waters rippling and sank to the bottom with a muted thud. Cheeks heating, Lydia shifted in her seat and straightened her impeccable skirts. Eyes riveted to the black fabric, she picked at the stray bits of lint and dust that had accumulated over the day. But even as she tried to distract herself, her traitorous thoughts replayed her parting with Robert. A flush of heat crept through her, though it held none of the joyful radiance she'd felt moments before.

"I will be forever grateful for Mr. Bradshaw. He has done so much for our family," said Mary in a tone that made a passing attempt at nonchalance. But only a slight one.

"He is the best of men." Despite the uproar of their parting, she could not deny just how good a man he was.

There was a long silence while the ladies watched the children attack Ambrose, though Lydia sensed Mary's attention was turned almost entirely on their conversation, waiting to pounce on the subject she wished to broach.

"With your newfound freedom from our parents, you are granted the opportunity to marry for love—should you wish it." Mary's tone was gentle and cautious, as though terrified she might just leap from the sofa and run away at the slightest provocation, which Lydia supposed was understandable as she'd been wont to do that very thing before.

"Do you trust my judgment after the debacle with Mr. Marks?" Lydia tried to keep the bitterness from her tone, but it was impossible to erase it completely. But more than that, phantom shivers ran down her spine as she recalled her near kiss; the pleasure of having Robert so close mixed with foul memories of her husband's touch, mixing until she struggled to separate the two.

Dropping her head, Lydia sighed. "Even if I were to take the chance, I fear Sir Duncan is not done with me: his ghost haunts me still."

Mary turned to face her sister better. "The past is not so easily erased, Lydia, but it needn't dictate your future."

Gaze fixed on her hands, Lydia swallowed, though her throat was far too dry to manage it. Her sister's hand came to rest atop hers, and it helped to ground Lydia in the here and now, even as memories of her husband threatened to drag her down dark paths.

"I am well acquainted with fear and self-doubt, and I wish I had a simple solution or word of wisdom to undo all the damage your heart has suffered, but I'm afraid it's something you must overcome yourself. Time can heal such wounds but only with effort." Mary sighed. "But I will say that if you have any desire to love and be loved, you must open your heart to it—frightening though it may be. I promise that it is well worth the risk."

Lydia nodded, though she could not meet Mary's eyes. Her sister sat there for a silent and all too awkward moment before adding, "Mr. Bradshaw seems like a fine man—"

But she was saved from whatever Mary was going to say when Polly opened the parlor door with a bob. However, it was at this moment that Lydia learned with absolute clarity just what was meant when people said "out of the frying pan, into the fire," for the maid announced Mr. Robert Bradshaw was here to see her. Her cheeks certainly felt ablaze, as though she were roasting quite thoroughly in both the proverbial frying pan and the fire.

Fate, which had always been a fickle acquaintance, had decided to interfere in her life once more.

Chapter 38

Lydia and Mary rose to greet their visitor. Ambrose paused only briefly to acknowledge him before the children attacked him with a vigor that had the others wincing on his behalf, though he only grunted, rubbed at his ribs (which were likely now bruised thanks to Esther and Vincent's knees and elbows), and threw himself back into the fray.

An irritating flutter of weakness made Lydia wish to leave the parlor, but she mustered her courage and greeted Robert with equanimity; in truth, she was quite pleased with herself, for she was as calm and collected as though they hadn't nearly kissed that afternoon. Timid was not a word she associated with Robert Bradshaw, but Lydia could think of no other way to describe his smile at that moment. It startled her enough that she made the mistake of meeting his eyes.

Robert's gaze had a magic all its own. Before him, Mary was the only person who had ever truly seen her. The Whitings, her parents, and all the rest only looked at small pieces, never seeing the entirety of who she was. But Robert saw not just the beauty of her face nor the goodness with which she tried to face the world, but all the hidden parts of her. Like strokes of a paintbrush, each aspect came together to form the portrait of Lady Lydia Whiting, and Robert saw them all.

Mary said a few things to him, but Lydia did not hear the particulars. Robert answered in kind, though his attention did not deviate from Lydia. Glancing between them, Mary smiled to herself and bowed out of the conversation, and though Lydia knew she ought to feel embarrassed at the implications, it was hard to be worried about such silly things when trapped in Robert's unflinching gaze.

"I brought you a gift," he said, holding up a brown paper package.

Staring at the offering, Lydia shook her head. "After all you have done, I would think it more fitting for me to give you something."

Robert scratched at the back of his head, his gaze slanting to the side. "I treated you poorly not long ago, and whatever I may have done since then to earn back your favor, I still must acknowledge I did not behave in a manner befitting a friend and said things I ought not to have said, and it is time that I offer some recompense for that previous offense, and though I know an offering will by no means erase what has passed, I hope it may ease any lingering pain our altercation might've caused..."

Lydia's brows furrowed as he stumbled through his words, dancing close to the important subject without saying anything of value that helped her to understand his meaning.

Finally, he stopped and nodded at the package. "Open it."

Moving to the sofa, Lydia sat and tugged at the twine that bound the paper around the misshapen package. She pulled back the paper and found a set of boots.

"As winters in Essex are far milder than here, I thought you were unlikely to have proper footwear for the coming snow," said Robert, tucking his hands behind him. "You'll need proper boots if you wish to continue your daily walks."

Lydia blinked at the gift. The boots were by no means lovely, but they were of good quality and sturdy enough for their intended purpose. A tickle of a smile quirked up her lips as she looked at them, and a flood of warmth filled her once more, bringing with them a slight sheen of tears, though she did not allow them to take hold.

Ambrose would've purchased her some, but now she did not have to pester him with such things or suffer the discomfort of bringing yet another financial burden to her family. That Robert had saved her that frustration made the simple gift all the more meaningful. No doubt the Whitings and her parents would disdain such a utilitarian offering, but the gift was a prime metaphor for the man who'd purchased them—useful and thoughtful wrapped into one.

"This is perhaps the most perfect gift anyone has given me," said Lydia. Rising to her feet, she clutched the boots to keep from embracing Robert once more; she'd done so several times already today, and it was best not to make it a habit. Even if it seemed entirely natural to do so.

Besides, they had an audience. Robert's gaze darted to those eyes and ears that, though not pointed in their direction, were aware of what was happening on the other side of the parlor.

"I wanted to purchase ones for Isabella as well, but with her condition, I thought it best we take her in person," said Robert. "The cobbler is certain he can fashion something to protect her feet, but he will need to see her in person to determine how best to make them."

And that only added to the perfection of the moment. Lydia found it more difficult to keep her tears from spilling out. Luckily, she had one last reserve of self-control to keep herself from devolving into a silly mess again. After all she had suffered today, she didn't think she could withstand much more.

"Robert, I don't think I can begin to express how much this means to me," said Lydia, squeezing the boots tight to her chest.

Robert scratched at his head again and his eyes darted from her to her family and back, and for the briefest of moments, Lydia could've sworn he blushed.

"I'm pleased they meet with your approval. I had wanted to speak to you sooner about the unpleasantness that has persisted between us..." And so, Robert continued to mumble on in vague and confusing manners about the gift and the "unpleasantness," leaving Lydia to stare at him for several long moments as she tried to piece together his meaning; though she understood bits, she was mostly bewildered, for he was speaking many words yet saying nothing, which was entirely unlike him.

"Might you accompany me on a stroll?" he finally asked, casting another look at her sister and brother-in-law. "I was hoping to speak with you alone."

Lydia nodded, and he led her towards the door, but at the threshold, she paused and glanced at Isabella. After the day they'd shared, instinct told her not to leave, and Lydia felt a jolt of panic at the memory of what had happened the last time she had left her daughter in another's care.

"I've been assured that parents left town immediately following our discussion," said Robert, his gaze softening as he considered her. "No one else has any designs on your daughter."

"Because of you," she whispered.

Robert shifted, his eyes dropping away, and another hint of pink stole across his cheeks—enough so that Lydia couldn't deny the blush this time. The sight of it made her want to laugh, for she had never thought to see Robert Bradshaw discomposed.

Turning her attention back to the issue at hand, Lydia watched as Isabella toddled among her cousins, laughing and clapping with a light and joy that had been missing from her life in Essex. And Lydia was all too aware of how much of that was due to Robert's efforts. Her eyes drifted from her child to the man beside her, and Lydia's heart burned inside her chest, setting her eyes aglow with the warmth that pulsed through her as she met his gaze. This dear man who had done so much to secure the happiness and safety of herself and her child, and she could admit without caveat that nowhere did she feel so safe as she did by his side.

Lydia faced him and nodded, and Robert tucked her arm in his, leading her from Newland Place and out into the darkening evening. The sky had grown black with a hint of orange light marking the last dying rays of the day, though the gas lamps on the buildings provided enough light for them to see as they meandered to the river's edge. The man at her side fidgeted, though Lydia did not understand what had him in such a state. Holding Robert's arm, she hoped some of her hard-won peace might seep into him.

"I miss reading together," she whispered, for that seemed the proper volume when the world was so silent around them. The mills kept the daytime so noisy, making the night seem all the quieter. The workers were tucked in their homes, and the masters were readying themselves for their evening entertainments; though there were a few others about, it felt like they were alone in the world.

Robert huffed and gave her a hint of a smile. "I do as well. I couldn't wait any longer and finished *The Forest of Valancourt* myself. Though I did not enjoy it as much without you there to gasp at the shocking parts and swoon at the romantic ones."

With a chuckle, Lydia shook her head. "I did not swoon, sir."

"I beg to differ. You let out more than a few heavy sighs at the various declarations."

"That is not the same as swooning."

Robert led them over the bridge spanning the river and onto the expanse of green that edged the New Towne side. They wove between the trees, whose leaves shuddered in the evening breezes, and Lydia turned her face to the moon, which hung high in the sky, its silvery light bathing the world around them.

"Perhaps I could stay after Nell's lessons," he said. "We could read together while the girls play."

Words emerged from his mouth, though Robert could attest to what they were. Lydia paused and turned to face him, her eyes aglow in the moonlight. She was lovely no matter what the situation, but bathed in the shadows and starlight, Lydia looked like an ethereal creature, her golden tresses white in the darkness.

"I would like that," she said.

What had he been saying? Robert struggled to keep his attention from straying, but Lydia smiled at him, her eyes sparkling with silent laughter as he stood there, gawking like a fool. He cleared his throat, his gaze drifting towards the river as they continued along the edge of the water.

"Do you truly like the boots?" Robert struggled to keep his voice calm. For goodness' sake, what was happening to him? He felt like a lad again, awkward and squeaky-voiced, struggling to get the courage to speak to a lady. He was a grown man with a thriving business, a good reputation, and a healthy income, yet every look from Lydia had him stumbling over himself.

"Very much so."

"I am glad," he said with a nod of his head. "I do regret the discomfort that has arisen between us of late."

Lydia glanced at him with a considering look, and Robert weighed his words.

"I suppose it is not only of late," he said with a frown. "I fear I misjudged you in the past and didn't fully comprehend just how wretched your parents are. Added to our recent disagreement, it seems as though I might have quite a few...issues..." But that was not quite right. However, "sins" was too great a word for it. "I suppose you have every right to have been unhappy with me, and I regret having given you reason to feel so..."

Pulling him to a stop, Lydia turned to face him. "Are you trying to apologize, Robert?"

He stiffened, though he tried to keep his expression calm. "I merely wish to acknowledge that perhaps I might've handled things in a less than ideal fashion..."

Lydia let out a low chuckle, and her hand rose to cover it. "I never thought to see you so flustered and uncertain. Is it so difficult to simply admit fault? For instance, I would like to apologize for my part in it. Though I do not regret speaking out, I might've done so in a more politic manner."

Robert scoffed. "And I wouldn't have listened. It has been made very clear to me of late that I have a talent for stubborn blindness."

"You are masterful." Even as she spoke the words, Lydia stiffened, covering her mouth once more. "I do not know what possessed me to say that."

But Robert took that hand in his, lowering it with a shake of his head and a smile. "I love when you tease me, Lydia."

They stood there, toe to toe, bathed in the moonlight, and Robert felt that same pull settling in his heart, whispering to him again and again that this was the woman for him. And his palms began to sweat in earnest.

Chapter 39

"Why are you so afraid to apologize, Robert?" she asked, in a low tone that did nothing for his equilibrium. "You have done so before."

A few dismissive remarks came to his thoughts, but as much as his instincts drove him to speak them, Robert's good sense and his heart kept him in check. This was precisely why he was here. Try as he might to sort through his thoughts about Eleanor, he could not make sense of them. He hadn't even realized what he was doing until he knocked against the Ashbrooks' door. But outside of Parker, there was no one else with whom he could speak of such things; it was in her very nature to empathize with others, and Lydia had a unique perspective and keen understanding of human nature that Robert desperately needed.

"I am not afraid to apologize in most circumstances."

Lydia's brows rose. "Just now, then? Why?"

He opened his mouth, but years of denials held his tongue in check. Closing his eyes, he took a deep breath and forced himself to speak.

"Because my wife always made me pay for such admissions." Robert winced, shaking his head with a sigh. "That sounds terrible."

"It sounds truthful." Lydia took him by the arm and forced him to move again, and Robert allowed the steady movement and the beauty of the nightscape to settle into his bones and calm his troubled heart.

"Eleanor was often a difficult woman." And thus he began unraveling all he'd spoken to Parker. As much as he valued his brother-in-law's opinion, something in Lydia invited and inspired him to speak. From the few initial words, more came with them, bringing forth everything he could recall about their courtship and marriage.

"I didn't know I could have a disagreement with a woman without it devolving into a horrid mess," said Robert.

"And I did not know I could speak my mind without being belittled or bullied," replied Lydia. "I think we both have received far too much mistreatment from those closest to us. But I am pleased to find evidence that you have a far more tender soul than you give yourself credit for."

"In all honesty, I am not even certain any longer how many of my memories are true," said Robert with a frown. "I've told myself so many stories and ignored so much of the truth that I feel as though I cannot trust myself."

"How well I understand that feeling. It is difficult to trust one's judgment after such an unsettling revelation. But when I discovered my true love was nothing but a myth, a good friend helped me through it. I felt ready to surrender, and he pulled me from the brink." Lydia gave him a faint smile, though her light tone deepened as she added, "You did what you could, Robert. Do not blame yourself or feel foolish for having made the best of a difficult situation."

Stopping her once more, Robert faced her directly, holding her gaze as he said, "Lydia, I apologize for not listening to you when you advised me about Nell. You were entirely correct, and I am ashamed of how I behaved—"

"It was nothing—"

But Robert took her by the hand and shook his head. "No, Lydia. Do not excuse it. My pride was pricked, and I lashed out at someone who did not deserve it."

Lydia opened her mouth to respond, but he spoke over her. "You did not deserve it, Lydia. You were being a friend to me and my daughter, and I am truly sorry for how I reacted. It was unkind, unjust, and undeserved. As were my hard words about your past, both then and when we first met. I spoke from my limited viewpoint without any consideration for you and your feelings."

Stepping closer, Robert held her gaze, willing her to believe his words, for he meant every syllable. "Please, forgive me."

With a hesitant smile, Lydia squeezed his hand. "Of course."

Robert's brows rose at that. "Surely I should give some stronger form of penance before you offer that up so freely. I hardly think an apology alone suffices."

Lydia's smile grew. "As one who has heard so few apologies in my life, I assure you it is not a small thing. Thank you, Robert."

"And my many thanks for confronting me when I needed it, Lydia. Promise me you will continue to do so."

With a chuckle, she shook her head. "What man wishes to keep company with a woman who harps at him?"

"I would hardly say what you did was harping. You helped me see that which needed to be acknowledged. As loath as I am to admit it, I fear I need someone of good sense to give me a swift kick when I need it. Besides, I enjoyed seeing you in a temper." When Lydia scoffed at that, he added, "That is the whole, unadulterated truth. I may not have liked being on the receiving end of your anger, but I liked seeing that fire. It is more true to who you are than the timid creature you were when we first met."

Watching him with wary eyes, Lydia considered that, her expression softening as she watched him, and Robert held onto the truth of his words, letting it shine in his expression.

"Thank you, Robert," she whispered. "Thank you for your aid today and all that you've done for me—including making me feel comfortable enough to express my opinion so forcefully. If I have felt free to be my true self, it is due in large part to you."

Robert's cravat tightened around his neck, and he fought the urge to fidget as he weighed her words. Parker had certainly felt as though there was something brewing between them, and Robert's instincts agreed, but Lydia kept spouting words of gratitude. Was that all she felt? Or was there more beneath it?

Smothering a burble of laughter, Robert shook his head at himself, wondering why his courage failed him at such a crucial moment in his life. But with Lydia looking at him, he felt none of his usual certainty. His mind was awash with doubts and worries, examining every word and expression for the true meaning beneath it.

Robert puffed out his cheeks, cursing this ridiculous behavior, and forced out the question before he could think better of it. "Is it only gratitude you feel for me?"

Holding her gaze, he tried not to think about the silence that stretched out as he awaited her answer. Lydia's brows rose, her mouth slackening as she stared at him. As his mother had been fond of saying, in for a penny, in for a pound.

"We almost kissed this afternoon." Her eyes widened, and Robert hurried to add, "At least, I almost kissed you. And you seemed keen on the idea at first."

Lydia swallowed, her mouth forming words though no sound emerged. Biting down on her lips, she dropped her gaze from his, and though the light did not allow him to see the variations of color, he sensed the blush rising to her cheeks while his memories supplied the exact shade of pink that was so terribly becoming on her.

"Yes, I was keen," she finally whispered, though it looked as though the words were pulled from her.

A smile flashed across his face, though now was not the time for celebrating that declaration. Robert sorted through all he could say and all he wanted to say, uncertain of where to begin. Eleanor hadn't required grand declarations, for she had been confident in his affections; though as he thought about it (and if his memory served him correctly), his first declarations had been more the result of his wife's prodding. Lydia required more. She deserved more.

And now was not the time to think of Eleanor.

"I care for you, Lydia," he said, starting with the foremost truth that was on his mind. "Not as a friend or confidant—though I consider you both."

Taking in a shaky breath, Robert let it out, releasing all the little feelings that had been flitting around his heart of late. "I've been a fool at times, and I know I do not deserve you, but my world is better when you are part of it, and my days are brighter when I've seen you. I know you are not ready to accept such declarations, but I need you to know my feelings. Is there any possibility you might feel the same?"

Lydia's mouth had gone dry, her heartbeat alternating between a rapid pace and stalling altogether. Even sensing where the conversation was headed hadn't given her time enough to prepare for it. The world felt as though it was holding its breath, pausing as the weight of so many conflicting emotions struck at once until her heart felt frozen in place, stuck like one of Ambrose's machines with a broken spring.

"Robert..." Lydia's voice trailed off as she struggled to get her thoughts to coalesce. The shock held her in thrall, keeping her from knowing what to say.

Yet when she distanced herself from that, setting aside all those worries, fears, concerns, and memories that had no place in this beautiful moment, joy flickered within her heart. This man—this incredible man—had all but declared his love for her. Those words, which held little polish but showed all of his heart, wrapped around her, settling into the void her confusion had left.

Robert cared for her.

Then reality snapped back into place, crashing down like a wave, sweeping over her and drawing her out into the deeper waters, far from the safety of the shore. Lydia didn't know what to say, but truths spilled out to match the ones he'd just shared.

"Robert, I do not know if I can ever truly love," she whispered, shaking her head. "I am so very broken, and it is all I can do to care for Isabella and be the mother she needs. You are so very precious to me, but what will come of us if it falls apart and we do not suit? I cannot bear to lose you at this point. I do not know if I can ever even stand to be touched by a man again, and I cannot expect you to wait—"

His hand—the same that held Isabella so gently and protected her from her father's slander—touched her lips, forestalling her babbling words. Robert drew closer, filling her vision until he was all she could see, but he did not touch her any further, keeping his other hand at his side.

"I do not know what the future holds, Lydia, and I am broken, too, in my own way." His voice was as soft as his fingers, and Lydia sighed at the tenderness in his tone. "You needn't say anything more than yes or no—is there a chance we might become something more than merely friends?"

Lydia's breath caught, though it was not fear that held her still. She did not know why or how, but there was something in Robert's eyes that called to her, whispering of peace and safety. And even joy. There was no force in his gaze, only silent patience as he awaited her answer. Hoping, yet not pushing, for the answer he desired.

And it was an easy one to give.

"Yes," she whispered, giving those three little letters all the certainty and strength she felt.

A tremulous smile stretched wide as his hand slid from her face, though he did not step away. And Lydia didn't want him to. His touch lingered for a moment before dropping to take her hand in his. His movements were cautious, watching her with careful consideration as he raised it to his lips. Robert held her there for a moment, as though waiting for any objection she might voice, and Lydia silently urged him on as he pressed a kiss to her palm.

"Then we can sort the rest of it out later and simply enjoy the here and now," he replied, brushing a gentle touch over the kiss before wrapping her hand in his.

He slid her hand through his arm, and the pair meandered along the riverbank. Bathed in the moonlight, they spoke of many things—both great and small—basking in the delight that comes from sharing all those goings-on. With her world at peace for the first time in her life, Lydia knew that what he had said was the truth. They had time enough to decide what their future would be, but at present, she could not think of a better place to be than at Robert's side.

Epilogue

Nine Months Later

Keeping oneself house, clothed, and fed was a time-consuming occupation. Whether it was taking care of those details oneself or earning the funds to pay others to manage them, the majority of one's days were spent in all the repetitive tasks required to maintain one's life. Simply put, one could not be happy all the time, for too much of one's life was occupied with the business of living. Merry moments were welcome but rare things, serving as the punctuation in life and not the whole of it.

Or so Robert had thought.

With growing frequency, those neutral, uninteresting moments were being outnumbered. So much of his day revolved around Lydia and the girls, and if he wasn't passing an hour in their company, merely the thought of them brought a spark of happiness to the dull functions of the day. And Robert thought of them quite often.

There was no doubt in his mind that the past months had brought him more joy and contentment than he'd thought possible. At the oddest of times, the difference between his life now and his life of the last few years struck him, followed by the strongest urge to drop to his knees and thank the Almighty that such a change had occurred. And never was it clearer to him than on such a day.

The sun hung high above them in a sky so perfect that it looked as though someone had painted it in an array of vibrant blues, moving from the lighter hues above to the deep shades of the horizon. Though the sunshine beat down on the world, they'd found themselves a haven beneath a large oak tree; its limbs stretched above, sheltering them from the worst of the heat and leaving them in that ideal state of warm but not hot.

It had taken some time for Robert to find such a prime situation, but it was well worth the effort. Lydia sat next to him, leaning against the trunk as Nell and Isabella ran about the surrounding field. Most of the spring wildflowers had faded, but the grass spread out around them, washing the world in that rich shade of green that begged passersby to stop and roll about in it.

The picnic blanket was laid out, the remnants of their feast scattered across the cotton, though too much of it had been left untouched as the girls had spent the majority of the meal chasing each other about. Even now, they occasionally stopped to take a bite of meat pie or slice of bread, but they remained still for only a moment before rushing off in a flurry of laughter.

Robert smiled (an expression that had become a near-constant fixture on his face) and watched as Nell modified her speed, allowing Isabella to keep pace with her as they chased each other through the grass. Despite Parker's best efforts, the young child's feet would never be altogether healed, but she grew steadier with each passing week, learning to compensate for what could not be undone.

Lydia's voice hovered on the breeze, the words of the novel steadily unfolding, though Robert hardly listened. It was difficult to give more than a small portion of his attention to the story when his heart burned like a fire in his chest. Such a simple afternoon, yet Robert felt overcome by gratitude and contentment. If only he could stave off the march of time and hold them here in this perfection.

In truth, he ought to be at home, turning his attention to some remnant tasks that needed completing before the week's end, but it was growing more difficult to sacrifice such beautiful moments in the name of responsibility. Luckily, his income was healthy enough that it did little damage to ignore his work on occasion, and Robert supposed he was going to need to decide just how much time he wanted to devote to his profession. The time had come to consider a partner.

"It is a gorgeous day." Lydia gave a happy sigh as she closed the book and set it on the picnic blanket.

Her shoulder rested against his, and Robert reveled in the sweet agony that accompanied such tender moments; his gaze turned to her, as it was wont to do without his bidding, and he marveled at the lady beside him. Robert hadn't thought it possible for Lydia to look lovelier, but the pale pink gown she wore brought such roses to her cheeks, complementing her complexion as no other color could. The tree's shadow couldn't dull the brightness of her eyes, and an ache resounded in his chest. Lydia was so very close. Like magnets, her lips drew him in, and Robert wanted nothing more than to surrender to the impulse and lose himself in her touch.

But he'd seen far too many flinches from her. Even innocent brushes of his hand startled her at times, and as much as he yearned to touch her, Robert would not allow desire to dictate to him. Lydia had known too much uncertainty and fear in her life, and he wouldn't give her reason to feel so around him.

And so, he tortured himself with fantasies of what would come. Eventually.

Good heavens, he was so close, and Lydia breathed in his scent, which mixed with the grass and summer breeze. Robert eschewed the colognes so many others cloaked themselves in, and Lydia was grateful for it. Like the rest of him, he did not hide beneath a facade. Robert Bradshaw was a straightforward man. And a frustrating fool! Robert's caution and solicitousness had been welcome at first, but it had become torture over the last few weeks.

Holding his gaze, she infused it with all the desire she felt, her thoughts supplying the image of him closing the distance as her heart conjured the feelings that touch would stir. Yet, Robert appeared unaffected. Lydia had married before she'd been allowed much time to hone her skills, and flirtations were not her forte. Someone had once told her that pouting the lips drew a man's gaze there, giving him a clear invitation, but when she did so, Robert cleared his throat and leaned away. Perhaps she was doing it wrong.

Lydia sighed and chided herself. She was not the only one with demons to battle, and Robert deserved as much consideration as she. Though his were of a different sort, that did not make them any less real or damaging, and if he needed more time, Lydia would give it to him. He was a man well worth waiting for.

With a jerking chuckle, Robert gazed out at the girls and said, "I had an interesting visit with Mr. Peterson yesterday."

Lydia's brows rose, and she looked at him from the corner of her eyes. "Concerning what?"

"Our time together has been noted by him and, thus, the Whitings," he said, relaxing once more against the tree. "Lady Whiting doesn't care for the idea that her son's widow might start courting a tradesman, so she bribed me to break ties with you. Won't they be surprised when they discover you are not merely the owner of your school but the headmistress and sole teacher? I wonder what they will do when they realize you've taken up a trade of your own."

With a frown, Lydia shook off the twinge of disgust that flitted through her at his mention of the Whitings, but that was forgotten as she considered all of what he'd said.

"They offered you a bribe so we won't begin courting?" asked Lydia.

Robert huffed and shook his head. "Ridiculous. But you needn't worry. Mr. Peterson assured me Sir Jude is uninterested in your dealings, and without the baronet behind her, Lady Whiting has little power."

Lydia shook her head. "That is not what surprises me. You said *begin* courting, but I thought we *are* courting. You made it clear that was what you wanted."

His muscles stiffened, and Robert turned his gaze to meet hers again. "It is, but neither do I want you rushed into such formal categorizations, Lydia. I was in earnest when I said we don't need to hurry things along. I can wait as long as necessary."

And this was a perfect example of why she adored him, even when Robert was so very blind. Lydia rubbed at her forehead, a broad smile filling her face as she considered what she ought to say. But it was clear the time for subtlety was long past.

"I assure you I do not feel rushed," she said with a laugh. "If you move any slower, Robert Bradshaw, I might scream."

His dark eyes widened, and he stared at her.

"I cannot promise I am wholly healed, but I am done with waiting, Robert," she said, resting her hand on his. "I would've said something sooner, but you've been hurt as well, and as much as I want to throw myself into your arms, I do not want to rush you—"

Lips pressed to hers, and Lydia squeaked at the sudden touch. Robert shifted to take her in his arms, pulling her flush to him, and whatever shock she felt at first faded beneath the warmth he stirred inside her. Lydia drew him closer and surrendered to the fervor the past months had stirred inside her. The kiss grew frantic, echoing the need of her heart, and Lydia embraced the passion, showing him with every touch how much he meant to her.

Robert Bradshaw was an intoxicating blend of strong and gentle, and his kiss echoed that. It felt as though his fire would consume her, yet the arms around her were tender. Lydia's heart ached as it stretched and expanded, filling with far more love than she'd thought possible for a person to feel.

Good heavens above, Robert's imaginings were nothing like the reality that was kissing Lydia. Her delicate fingers brushed his cheeks as she sank into his embrace, surrendering to it with a love that matched his own. Lydia's trust was hard-won, and knowing that he'd earned it made the kiss all the sweeter. Lydia had the most loving heart he'd ever known, and she was giving it to him without reservation. Robert only hoped he was worthy of such a mighty gift.

Reining in the desperate need that drove him, he slowed the kiss, hoping that with each touch he might show her just how honored and humbled he was to have her in his life. Even if he knew it was impossible to ever show just how deeply those feelings ran.

This was no false construct born of a young heart, unable to see the difference between infatuation and love. Their hearts were perfect complements of each other, suiting the other as no other could. As different as could be in some respects, but surprisingly similar in others, and as the months had passed, Robert had grown more and more surprised at just how right she was for him. And how bright she made his life.

Robert loved Lydia without question or caveat.

"I am sorry, Lydia, for being so blind—"

But her lips brushed his, silencing his words as she caressed his cheek.

He pressed a kiss to her hand with a sly smile. "So, how long have we been courting?"

Lydia arched her brow. "Since the night you declared yourself, of course. We've spent nearly every day in each other's company since then. What would you consider that?"

Robert canted his head as he thought that through. Freeing one hand, he dug into his pocket, though it took some maneuvering to do so without relinquishing his hold on her. "So, if we've been courting for some nine months, it would not be impetuous for me to give you this."

It was not easy to open the box while they were entwined, but Lydia did not shift away and the inconvenience was a small price for remaining so pleasantly situated, so Robert remained as he was with his arm around her.

Lydia freed one hand and lifted the lid of the box that sat in his hand. She gaped, her wide eyes examining the ring that rested inside. A large oval stone was set on a simple band, the iridescent colors swirling as the sunlight caught the various colors in the opal. It was a paltry offering for the widow of a baronet, but when Robert had laid eyes on the gorgeous stone, he knew no other ring suited his Lydia.

Her blue eyes rose to his. "You've been carrying this with you?"

Robert's smile quirked up to one side. "I purchased it a fortnight into our 'courtship,' and I liked the feel of it in my pocket, awaiting this moment."

Leaning forward, he stole her attention away from the ring with another kiss, though it was simple and quick. Then, with her so close to him, he whispered, "Marry me, my love?"

Her head bobbed up and down as joy swept through her, filling her until Lydia felt ready to expire. Dropping the box on the blanket, Robert took the ring and slid it onto her finger, the piece fitting as perfectly as if it had been destined to be hers. Words escaped her, so she leaned forward, allowing her kiss to tell him how full her heart was. But it was an impossible feat. Lydia could not understand or contain it all, so how could she ever express it to this wonderful, dear man?

"I love you, Robert," she whispered, for that was the only thing she could say in such a moment.

His thumb brushed across her jaw, his eyes filled with such feeling that Lydia wondered how she had ever thought him cold and distant.

"And I love you, my Lydia."

With his arms around her, the pair leaned against the oak tree, watching as the girls chased each other about the field, unaware of the promises that had just been made. It felt as though there was too much joy for her body to contain, and quiet tears slid from her eyes to wet his waistcoat as he pressed a kiss to the top of her head.

Lydia had spent so many years feeling out of place that it startled her how comfortable she was in his embrace. And there was no denying it. Robert was her haven. He was her peace. Her joy. He had the power to frustrate her one moment and make her smile the next, and Lydia loved him all the more for it. Added to that pleasure was knowing that Robert needed her as greatly as she did him, for he hadn't only rescued her—they'd rescued each other.

Together, they'd pulled themselves free of the past. Together, they'd built a life filled with love and happiness. Together, they'd found their home at last.

Exclusive Offer

Join the M.A. Nichols VIP Reader Club at

www.ma-nichols.com

to receive up-to-date information about upcoming books, freebies, and VIP content!

About the Author

Born and raised in Anchorage, M.A. Nichols is a lifelong Alaskan with a love of the outdoors. As a child she despised reading but through the love and persistence of her mother was taught the error of her ways and has had a deep, abiding relationship with it ever since.

She graduated with a bachelor's degree in landscape management from Brigham Young University and a master's in landscape architecture from Utah State University, neither of which has anything to do with why she became a writer, but is a fun little tidbit none-the-less. And no, she doesn't have any idea what type of plant you should put in that shady spot out by your deck. She's not that kind of landscape architect. Stop asking.

| Website | Facebook | Instagram | BookBub |

Printed in Great Britain
by Amazon